P9-ARV-866

CRIME

CRIME

IRVINE WELSH

W. W. Norton & Company
New York · *London*

For information about permission to reproduce selections from this book,
write to Permissions, W. W. Norton & Company, Inc., 500 Fifth Avenue,
New York, NY 10110

For information about special discounts for bulk purchases,
please contact W. W. Norton Special Sales at
specialsales@wwnorton.com or 800-233-4830

Manufacturing by RR Donnelley, Harrisonburg, VA
Production manager: Anna Oler

Library of Congress Cataloging-in-Publication Data

Welsh, Irvine.
Crime / Irvine Welsh. — 1st American ed.
p. cm.
ISBN 978-0-393-06819-1 (hardcover)
1. Police—Scotland—Edinburgh—Fiction. 2. Scots—United States—Fiction.
3. Child welfare—Fiction. 4. Florida—Fiction. 5. Pscyhological fiction. I. Title.
PR6073.E47C75   2008
823'.914—dc22   2008026482

W. W. Norton & Company, Inc.
500 Fifth Avenue, New York, N.Y. 10110
www.wwnorton.com

W. W. Norton & Company Ltd.
Castle House, 75/76 Wells Street, London W1T 3QT

1 2 3 4 5 6 7 8 9 0

For Dean Cavanagh and Bob Morris

Prelude

The Storm

She'd wanted to tell Momma that this one was no good. Like the one back home in Mobile. And that bastard in Jacksonville. But her momma was doing her eyes up in front of the mirror, and telling her to hush and make sure that all the shutters was fastened cause they reckoned a storm was going to be blowing in from the north-east tonight.

The girl went to the window and looked out. All was calm. The shining disc of a moon pulsed blue light into the apartment. It was broken only by the limbs of the dead oak tree in the yard outside; spreading keen varicose shadows, creeping across the walls, dark and vital. Snibbing down the springed catch to secure a slatted wooden barrier, mindful of pained fingers past, she strategically pulled her hand back, thinking of it as a smart mouse stealing cheese from a trap. Then she regarded the vacant intensity of her mother in the mirror's reflection. She used to like to watch Momma fix herself up, all pretty, that way she would really concentrate with that little brush and make those big lashes dark.

Not now though. Something sour curdled in her stomach.

— Don't go out tonight, the girl said softly, somewhere between wishing and begging.

Her mother's small pink tongue darted out, wetting her eye pencil. — Don't worry about me, baby, I'll be okay, and then a car horn blared from downstairs and the thermostat clicked on the air con, making it colder in the room. They both knew it was him.

— Lucky this apartment's got them shutters, her momma said, rising and picking her bag up from the table. She kissed the daughter on the head. Pulling away, her big made-up eyes stared at the kid. — Remember, bed before eleven. I'll probably be back around then, but if I get held up I want you asleep, young lady.

I

Then she was gone.

For a while, the girl had the glowing pool from the television screen to make safe the things within its field by bathing them in its soft murky light. But beyond its scope she sensed something lurking. Coming closer.

A balmy eastern wind rapped with firm insistence on the shutter; ominous enough to be the harbinger of a more malign force. The rains started a few stretched heartbeats later, at first slowly pitter-pattering on the windows. Then she could hear the wind twisting and whipping. The distressed black arms of the tree signalled frantically. Suddenly a cannon of thunder roared, and somewhere outside, an object crashed to earth and shattered. Yellow light flared the room in a sulphurous glow for a full three seconds. The girl turned the handset volume up as the tempest raged on, the wind and rain thrashing at the window. After a bit, she retreated timidly to bed, scared of the darkness she tentatively journeyed through, but more afraid to prolong the agony by searching for a light switch.

Unable to sleep, she knew it was late when she heard the door downstairs click open and feet clop on the stone steps outside. The digital clock on her table burned 2:47 in accusation. She prayed it would be one set of footsteps, his were always so soft, he never wore anything but sneakers, but then she heard the voices and the muffled laughter. Her momma would sleep soundly with the pills she was on, right through the storm. But she would have to face it. Pulling her nightdress down and gripping its hem with a handful of bedclothes, the girl braced herself.

Day One

1

Vacation

Ray Lennox is now entering an area of turbulence. Raising a
bandaged right hand to his hooked nose, slightly askew after
being badly set following a break some years back, he looks at his
image reflected in the blank screen of the personal television,
provided for his in-flight entertainment. A thin wisp of air struggles through one grouted nostril, provoking a protesting heave in
his chest. Trying to sidetrack his agitated mind, he scans the body
crushed next to him.

It's Trudi, his fiancée; shoulder-length hair tinted a tasteful honey
blonde indicating the attentions of a proper stylist. She's oblivious
to his discomfort. A manicured, polished nail turns a magazine page.
Beyond her, there's somebody else. Around them, still more bodies.

It's only now registering: now, as he sits crammed into this
economy-class seat on the London to Miami flight. The spiel he'd
gotten from Bob Toal before he took stress leave. It was the altitude announcement that had sparked it.

We are now cruising at thirty-two thousand feet.

You're a high-flyer, Ray, he recalled Toal saying, as he'd stared at
the black hairs sprouting from his boss's nose. A favoured son. It
was a harrowing case. You did well; got the bastard under lock and
key. Result. Take a long holiday. Look forward. A lot of us have
invested heavily in your career, Ray. Don't prove us wrong, son.
Can't have you taking the Robertson route, he'd said, referring to
the suicide of Lennox's old mentor. Don't go down.

And Ray Lennox – gaunt, white-faced, clean-shaven, his trademark floppy fringe shorn at John's in Broughton Street to reveal a
short, sloping forehead – feels his pulse precipitously quicken.

*We are now entering an area of turbulence. Please remain seated with
your seat belts securely fastened.*

Don't go down.

Danger. Threat.

They'd given him the third degree at the airport. He looked nothing like his passport picture. The sallow grey of his Scottish skin, cruelly highlighted by the photo booth's creaky technology, contrasting with his thick, raven hair, eyebrows and moustache, rendering the look joke-shop false. Now all reduced to a post-conscript shadow that spreads across his head before circling round to his jaw.

He'd been vexed by the attentions of airport security, for he was an officer of the law, but they were right to care. His Lothian Police ID helped him negotiate the mini-state the Americans had set up at Heathrow to pre-emptively protect their borders. — Sorry, sir, difficult times, the Homeland Security Officer had declaimed apologetically.

Now Ray Lennox's eyes urgently scan the cabin. Nothing to worry about in front. Nobody looked like an al-Qaeda affiliate. *But that guy looks Indian. Muslim? More likely a Hindu, surely. But might be Pakistani. Stop this.* He himself was white, but not a Christian. Church of Scotland on the census form as recorded for official data, but not religious, until he boarded a plane. The drinks trolley approaching slowly; so slowly, he didn't want to think about it. He turns, craning his neck, looks back at his fellow passengers. Nothing out of the obvious: holidaymakers in search of the sun. A cheap(ish) flight.

Next to him, Trudi, aloof with her hair brushed back and gathered up in a tight black clasp. Those dark, intense hazelnut eyes devouring, almost psychotically, the *Perfect Bride* magazine as her red-painted nail extension flips over the next page.

All lassies dream about the big day, about being the perfect bride: the enactment of the fairy-princess ideal.

Did that wee girl?

Nah, no that wee soul . . .

Turbulence rocks the plane and Lennox's sweat ducts open up under its broadside, as he's abruptly conscious of the fact that he's travelling in a metal tube at six hundred miles an hour, six miles in the air over the sea. A drop in the ocean: just a speck waiting to fall into oblivion. He watches Trudi, unperturbed, small scarlet slash of a mouth, only briefly raising a thinly plucked brow in disdain. As if an aircraft disaster would merely inconvenience the wedding plans.

The shaking in the Boeing 747 stops as the engines thunder through the air. The buzz that permeates the plane constantly in his ears. Thrusting ahead. Into blackness. The pilots seeing nothing in front of them. The instruments in the cockpit would be blinking and twirling on the console.

You can see why terrorists and governments – those with the biggest stake in our fear, Lennox considers – are so focused on aircraft travel. We are scared shitless before we start out. All they need to do is fine-tune this dread through the odd atrocity or its consort, heavy-handed security.

Trudi has a blanket over her legs.

The magnetic dark around him. He can feel it beckoning.

Why should he worry? He's on holiday. He's done his job. What is there to regret? It's self-indulgent. But he can't help it. The metal taste in his mouth. Can't help hurting himself with thoughts. Nerves prickling under his skin. He fears himself again. He wishes he'd taken more pills.

— What if we go down? Lennox whispers, swamped with notions of death as a vast bleak nothingness. — We'd be free from it all.

— I'm still thinking periwinkle for the bridesmaids, Trudi says without looking up from the magazine, — but I don't want Adele upstaging me. Then she turns to him in real fear. — You don't think –

Ray Lennox feels a surge of emotion as he recalls a picture of Trudi as a young girl, on the mantelpiece at her parents' house. An only child: the couple's one shot at immortality. *What if anything were* –

Another jag of trepidation rising in him. — Trudi, I'd never let anybody hurt you, you know that, don't you? he announces in desperate urgency.

Her eyes expand in the stilted horror of the soap-opera heroine. — You think she's pretty, don't you? Don't even try to deny it, Ray, it sticks out a mile.

7

Trudi thrusts her breasts out towards him and he sees the ribbing pattern of her tight brown sweater curve almost implausibly in a way that once aroused him. A few weeks back.

She wants to be the perfect bride. Like wee Britney Hamil might have dreamt of.

He grabs her, hugs her close, breathing in her perfume, the fragrance of the shampoo in her hair. Something in his throat is choking him. As if a foreign object is wedged there. His voice so thin he wonders if she can hear him. — Trudi, I love you . . . I . . .

She squirms in his grasp, wriggles free and pushes him away. For the first time on the flight, her searching eyes engage with him. — What's wrong, Ray? What is it?

— That case I was working on . . . that wee lassie . . .

Her head shakes vigorously and she puts a shushing finger over his lips. — No shop talk, Ray. We agreed. You've to get away from the job. That was the plan. That was what Bob Toal said. If I remember correctly his exact words were: Don't even *think* about the job. Don't *think*. Have a good time. Relax. The purpose of this vacation is to relax and plan the wedding. But you're drinking again, and you know how *I* feel about that, she exhales, protracted and peevish. — But it's what you wanted, and the mug that I am, I reluctantly agreed. So relax. You have your pills for anxiety.

It occurs to Lennox that she's used the American term 'vacation' instead of holiday. The word clatters around in his head. To vacate. To leave.

But to go where?

Where did you go when you left?

The stewardess arrives with the drinks service. Trudi orders a white wine. A Chardonnay. Lennox gets in a couple of Bloody Marys.

Trudi settles back in her seat. Her head tilted to the side. Voice cooing, in sing-song manner. — All jobs are stressful in this day and age. That's why we have vacations.

Again!

— Ver' near two glorious weeks of sun, sand, sea and the other, she nudges him, then sulks, — You *do* still fancy me, Ray? And she does that thing with her breasts again.

— Course ah do. Lennox feels a constricting of the muscles around his chest and throat. His windpipe has become a straw. He is trapped; hemmed in beside the window, far too small to offer escape into the oblivion of sky. He looks at his crippled, bandaged right hand, a bag of broken knuckles, phalanxes and metacarpals. How many more would go, how long would it take for both fists to be pulped trying to punch a hole through this plane? Between him and the aisle sits first Trudi, then a blade-faced older woman, spare-framed, with bony hands. Probably ages with his own mother. He breathes in the dirty, dry recycled air of the plane. The old girl's skin is like melted plastic. Like it has been dried out by the air conditioning. There are orangey blotches. He wonders how many hours an eight-hour flight aged you. He didn't want Trudi to know that he'd only brought a few pills; that he was planning to stop them in Miami.

Trudi drops her voice. — I'll do it if you want, Ray. If it's what you *really* want . . .

He raises the plastic beaker to his mouth and sips at the vodka. His hand trembles. Then his body. How many paltry measures from those little bottles will it take to stop this, to make it go away? — The thing is . . . he manages to cough.

— . . . because I want to please you *in that way*, Ray, I really do, she implores, perhaps a bit too loudly as she'd had a few drinks at the airport bar and with the wine and altitude they are digging in. She turns to the old dear sitting next to her and exchanges saccharine smiles followed by a greeting.

Lennox thinks about the crime. At his desk the morning he heard and −

Trudi's elbow digs his ribs. Her voice now a low whisper. The faintest of downy hair on the top of her glossy pink lips. — It's just that it shocked me at first. It was trying to reconcile the fact that you're a normal, red-blooded, heterosexual male with you wanting to be . . . *penetrated* in that way . . .

Lennox fortifies himself with another swig of the Bloody Mary. It's all but gone. — I never want you to do anything you're uncomfortable with, he says, pulling his features into a shallow smile.

— You're a honey, she kisses him on the side of the face, the kiss of an aunt, he thinks. She holds open *Perfect Bride*, at a page displaying, in several script styles, the same announcement of a fictitious wedding. — What do you reckon about these for the invitations? Her big nail thuds down on a blue script in Charles Rennie Mackintosh style.

Glancing at them, Lennox thinks, with mild parochial resentment, of Glasgow. — Too Weedgie. He then points at the Gothic illustrations. — I like this one better.

— Oh my God, no way! She gasps and laughs, — You are totally bonkers, Raymond Lennox! These are like funeral invitations! I'm not the Bride of Frankenstein. She raises her eyes and fills her wine beaker. — Just as well you've got me organising this wedding. I dread to think what kind of a joke it would be if it was left up to you. She turns to the old girl whose cheery, intrusive smile is beginning to nauseate Lennox. — Men. Honestly! Good for nothing!

— I've always said it, the old girl adds encouragingly.

They cluck enthusiastically over the contents of the magazine and Trudi's ecstatic descriptions of her dress, as Lennox adjusts the seat to its stingy recline, his eyes growing heavy with sleep. Soon his mind is drifting back to the crime. His thoughts are like a landslide; they seem to subside and settle, then before he knows it they're off again, heading for the same downhill destination. The crime. Always plummeting inexorably towards the crime.

You got the call that morning.

At your desk in that small, utilitarian office in Edinburgh's police headquarters at Fettes. A frosty, late-October Wednesday, your sad African violet plant on the window ledge struggling in the meagre light and cold, as the noisy central heating, set to come on late for economy purposes, clattered and cranked into reluctant action. Preparing a case for court. Two youths cabbaged after drinking all day: one had stabbed the other to death in a flat. Something was said and taken the wrong way. A threat made;

a counter, the escalation. One life ended, the other ruined. All in the time it took to buy a pint of milk. You recalled the murderer, stripped of bravado-giving intoxicants, in the interview room under the fluorescent lights; so young, broken and scared. But this case hadn't bugged you. You'd seen so many like it.

What got to you was the phone call, at around eleven fifteen. A uniformed cop, Donald Harrower, telling you about a seven-year-old girl, Britney Hamil, setting off for school at 8.30 a.m. and never arriving. The school had reported the absence to her mother, Angela, just before ten, who, after phoning some friends and relatives, had called the police half an hour later. Harrower and another officer had gone out to speak to the woman, as well as Britney's teacher and some neighbours and schoolmates. Two older girls had seen her walking down the street ahead of them, but when they turned the corner a few minutes later, Britney had vanished and they'd witnessed a white van speeding away.

— The girls, Andrea Jack and Stella Hetherington, were the only witnesses and the white van was the only vehicle they recall seeing in the vicinity, Harrower had explained in his adenoidal tones, — so I thought you'd like to know about it.

The words 'unmarked white van' crackled through your brain in static. That great British archetype: always trouble to a polisman. You'd thanked Harrower, thinking it was unfortunate his dour, taciturn aspect often shielded a thoughtful diligence from his bosses. The van compelled you to go straight to your boss, acting Chief Superintendent Bob Toal, and request to investigate the disappearance and potential abduction of a child.

You worked with Harrower, talking to neighbours, friends, the school staff and children whom Britney might have passed en route. And Angela. You remembered the first time you set eyes on the child's mother, on her way out to the local shopping centre. She'd been due at her cleaning job in the Scottish Office that afternoon, but explained that she'd taken time off to look after her other daughter, Tessa, who had food poisoning. She was the eleven-year-old sister who normally accompanied Britney to school. Instead of asking Angela to hold on, something made you want to walk with her. You followed her around Iceland, as she filled up on cheap burgers, fish fingers, oven chips and cigarettes. Found yourself judging her every purchase, as if they made her not only complicit in Tessa's poisoning but also in Britney's vanishing. — Isn't she a little young to be walking to the school on her own?

— I was gaunny take her, but Tessa started being sick again, really chucking it up. Britney . . . she didnae want to be late. Telt me she was a big girl now. Angela fought back the tears as she pushed her shopping trolley down the yellow neon-lit gangways. — It's only five minutes' walk, she pleaded. — You will find her, won't ye?

— We're doing everything we can. So Tessa was ill this morning?

— Aye. I took them oot tae that burger bar last night, the yin at the centre. For a wee treat, then tae the pictures, at the multiplex tae see the new Harry Potter. Tess came doon wi it in there. Ah mind ay Britney bein that sad that we had tae go hame . . .

— Right, you had said, feeling then that missing a film might be the least of the girl's worries.

Leaving Angela back at her flat, you walked the walk to the school and found that it actually took fourteen minutes. Out the housing scheme, past the Loganburn roundabout, round the corner into Carr Road (where Britney vanished), and alongside a long, stark brick wall, behind which sat a disused factory. Then, round another corner, a block of tenements and the Gothic black-railed gates of the Victorian school.

Everyone at Police Headquarters knew that the next few hours were crucial, the something-or-nothing time. An alert call was made to all cars to be on the lookout for the girl and the driver of an unmarked white van. But as morning rolled into afternoon there was no news, and outside of Andrea and Stella, the girls walking behind Britney, only a couple of neighbours — a Mrs Doig on her way to her work, and a Mr Loughlan out walking his dog — could specifically recall seeing the girl that morning.

You went back to Bob Toal and asked if you could put a proper investigation team together. In the era of sex-crime awareness a missing child was big news and the media-savvy Toal quickly concurred. — Take Amanda Drummond, he'd said, — and Ally Notman.

You expressed gratitude. Drummond was thorough and had good people skills, while Notman had an engine on him and knew his way around data management. Like you, he had an Information Technology degree from Heriot-Watt University, but you were envious of the more efficient way your younger charge put these skills to use.

Then Toal had added, — And Dougie Gillman.

You felt the air inside you ebbing away. There had been a serious personal fallout with Gillman a few years back. But you said nothing, because it was personal. You'd keep it off the job.

You got Harrower and another reliable copper, Kenny McCaig, out of uniform. You commandeered an office at Police HQ and started your formal investigation. McCaig and Harrower continued knocking on doors. Notman examined speed camera and CCTV footage to identify any white vans tracked in or around the vicinity of Carr Road at the time, pulling out possible registration numbers, checking the list of owners against the Vehicle Licensing Agency's database in Swansea. Drummond and Gillman took a forensics team out to give the bend on Carr Road, where Britney had vanished, a good dusting down. Neither forensics nor IT were the forte of Gillman, an old-school street cop, but he'd coldly followed your order.

As for you, you busied yourself with the 'register': the database of sex offenders. Seeing who was out, who was on parole and who was under surveillance; who was considered to be high-risk and low-risk. You'd clicked through the mugshots that Wednesday in your office, as the light declined in the drizzle over the Castle Hill, calling Trudi and telling her that you'd be late meeting her at the Filmhouse. When you got there, you'd coughed out an apology. — Sorry, babe, shit day at work. This weather doesnae help.

She didn't seem to mind. — Thank God we've got Miami to look forward to!

But you weren't looking forward to anything. You'd felt a building tug of unease from Harrower's call; through your job you'd learned to define evil not just as the presence of something malign, but the absence of something good. Experience had taught you that the only misfortune worse than a having loved one murdered was for them to vanish without their fate ever coming to light. The torment of uncertainty, where the heart pounded each time the doorbell or phone rang, and desperate, hungry eyes devoured every face in every crowd. The inevitability of the cherished person's death could be mentally reasoned, but it was harder to stifle the soul's defiant scream that they lived on. But were they coming home or had they gone for ever? After time spent in this hellish limbo, any news, no matter how searing, was welcomed beyond the endless waiting and searching. In Britney's mother, lone parent Angela Hamil, you saw a woman slowly drowning in this terrible madness.

By that evening you all knew that somebody had snatched Britney. The next day Toal decided to go public and give it to the newspapers. If the situation couldn't be managed, then the news had to be. The later editions of the *Evening News* in Edinburgh carried a smiling, wholesome-looking picture of the girl that would become iconic. Adults would gaze at their children with a tender ache, giving strangers a suspicious glare. The term 'like an angel' was used a lot in the press. You recalled her grandad saying that.

The police switchboards became jammed with the usual litany of busybodies and sickos, as well as the genuine but largely misguided members of the public. And that creeping unease, how it had spread like a virus through your investigative team. Whatever you all said on the PR front, or to the family, you knew as professional law enforcement officers that after twenty-four hours you were probably dealing with a child sex murder.

The team quickly swung into action. Gillman had been the first to find something, a single page of yellow notepaper wet in the gutter on the other side of the road to where Britney had vanished. Angela confirmed it was from her school notepad. Its very presence indicated some sort of struggle between child and kidnapper.

The villain needed some degree of tangibility in the minds of his pursuers, and was dubbed the usual nicknames, 'The Stoat',

'The Nonce' or 'The Beast'. But another moniker in the police canteen was Mr Confectioner. It came from the Toblerone chocolate advert from television: *Oh, Mr Confectioner, please . . . give me Toblerone.* The boys in Bert's Bar thought the cartoon confectioner looked like a stereotype sex beast, bribing kids with sweets.

Stop this.

No crime . . .

Vacation . . .

His actions strangled the empathy from us like they had the life from . . .

Because . . .

Because he was born like that, he had to be, the fuckin beast. That dirty bastard was put on this earth to prey on us . . .

We had to be strong and vigilant and alert to stop them; stop them from destroying our flesh . . .

He jars back into something like full consciousness as the beaker crushes in his fist. A gloopy vodka and tomato mix slops over his undamaged left hand. He puts it down and catlicks himself, mopping up with a napkin. Trudi hasn't noticed; she's engrossed in the magazine with the old girl. He tries to think about some of the games he's seen over the years at Tynecastle Park. His dad taking him along to watch Hearts beat Leipzig five–one. Curtis Park, one of his mates from school, and a Hibs fan, seeing it on television and telling him that the Englishman, Alan Weeks, was commentating. Iain Ferguson scoring the winning goal against Bayern Munich. That three–two Scottish Cup victory over Rangers. Lifting the cup at Parkhead. John Robertson's numerous derby winners. Shaking the wee man's hand in the carpet department at John Lewis's. John Colquhoun, teetering on the brink of world class for a season. That fateful afternoon in May 1986, when they threw it all away. The charity dinner a couple of years back, when he'd sat next to Wallace Mercer, the former chairman, who told him some great stories about games past and that terrible day up in Dundee. Now who was in charge?

A Russian millionaire as chairman. A convicted sex offender as manager.

Heart of Midlothian FC.

Tradition.

It all means nothing now alongside our vile decadence. How long before we have paedophile reality TV shows? Michael Jackson, Gary Glitter and that whole BBC crowd, like the former football pro working as a pundit. Those who were on the right side of the divide and got their noncing in before we cared.

He shuts his eyes. With the sound of the engines it's like going through a long, dark, tunnel. Hopes they stay closed until he steps into the light with the blood of other men on his hands. Even if it takes for ever.

2

Miami Beach

As they come to the glorious salvation of land, Lennox can see how quickly the powerful 747 jet plane devours the toytown miles beneath them. America is not a big country, he remembers. He's jumped across it before in aircraft; New York–Chicago–New Orleans–Vegas–San Francisco–LA. It was like going round Scotland in a bus, only at ground level you could see the vastness of the country in the changing landscape. One function of wealth is to shrink the world. And, like poverty, it has at least the potential to breed dissatisfaction. Florida, he knows, he will encounter as Scotland, immense and irreducible by the plane. A tremor of excitement passes through him as he awaits its grandeur. For beyond the plexiglas he sees Miami, gleaming silvery-white constructions straddling the edge of a milky turquoise sea and its harbours. The water is rashed with emerald-purple shadows cast up from below by submerged islands. Tiny sailboats surge along like yellow dots against a radar display backdrop, leaving a fading trail behind them.

People clap as the plane lands – so smoothly he's barely aware of the touchdown he had braced himself for hours ago, since surviving take-off and turbulence. Despite this sense of anticlimax, Lennox's wrapped and damaged hand gently squeezes Trudi's.

Their room is in a boutique hotel in the art deco district of Miami Beach. The historic art deco district, as it seems to say everywhere. *Historic? Art deco? Where's the history in that?* He goes into the shower, and realising that he badly needs to urinate, lets himself pee as he washes. The heavy, gold streams of his piss weave down the drain-hole. The bathroom is mirrored on opposite walls. He watches his cloned naked body purging into infinity.

Then, without warning, he's hit by an acute desperation to get outside. The bathroom, the bedroom, they seem too small. He drips over to the sink. Rubs at himself with a towel. Fills a glass with water and downs two antidepressants he has left out. The Seroxat. Consumed like M&Ms. At least one hundred milligrams more than the maximum recommended daily dose. The anxiety isn't as bad when you're on them. Yes, it's always there, you can still feel it, it just doesn't bother you as much. But he hasn't brought many; he wants to stop them. Thinks the sun will help. Light is good for depression. A natural cure. *A good dose of winter sun will do you more good than all the pills in the world.* Somebody had said that. Trudi? Toal? He can't think. But they were right. It was a relief to leave the cold and dark of winter Edinburgh. There had been the horror of the funeral. Then Christmas was a washout. Hogmanay too. Lennox had no head for it. The chanting crowds: people seeming boorish and hateful as they tried to enjoy themselves. Beneath the surface bonhomie there was desperation, a barely submerged fear that the next year would be just as miserable as the last. He steps out of the bathroom, towel round his waist. The tumbler of water is still in his hand. He sets it down on the glass table by the phone.

Trudi is lying on the bed in her black underwear still reading *Perfect Bride*. Cooling off under the overhead fan that augments the air con. Lennox admires her feet, with the red-painted toes.

He gets hold of the nail clippers on his key ring. Then he switches on the television. It's what you do in America. That big holiday, years ago: with Caitlin Pringle, an old girlfriend, pre-Trudi. Her father worked for British Airways; a big noise. Alasdair Pringle. Cheap travel. Caitlin; Alasdair-Big-Noise-from-the-Airline's daughter. A sexual relationship, a baseball pennant procured from every city they'd fucked in. Then, the second time, New York, with some of the boys on the force. A piss-up. Las Vegas for a wedding: this time with Trudi. Whose wedding? He can't think. But every time he'd watched loads of telly. You just went to the TV automatically here, like you did in no other foreign country. That one clicking gesture with the handset and you were into America. The breaking news. The infomercial. The daytime soap with the moving mannequins. The courtroom show.

18

The fat poor people who screamed at each other while Jerry or Ricki or Montel kept order. Tried to help, even. Attempted to understand the problems faced by the poor and the fat. Empathise with their need to shout and point their blobby fingers at each other in public. The evening dating shows. The thick, complacent studs, wearily referring to themselves as 'players' as they slowly suffocated in their own ennui. Bored, manicured girls, faces immobilised, unmoved by anything other than the boys' salaries. How those crazed inanities were rendered understandable, even palpable, by the context.

As he chops at nails already close to the quick, voices fill the room. They drown out the slow rattle and hum of the air conditioning. There's one channel that appears to be devoted to culture in the Miami area. To Lennox, this seems to mean mainly real estate and shopping. A series of impeccably groomed yet tacky presenters, reading in clipped tones from autocues, expound various opportunities in different high-rise apartment developments. Clearly something exciting is happening. Missing out isn't an option. The failed actors and Botox-faced models stress the high-concept, *architectural* qualities of what to Lennox appear to be Scottish scheme tower blocks in the sun.

— You can't keep clipping your nails, Ray, Trudi says, — your thumb's bleeding! Compulsive behaviour!

He turns to observe her lying on the bed, reading her magazine.

— I have tae or I pick at them. I need to keep them short.

But she's no longer concerned; her mouth has gone round and her eyes stare at the magazine as if seeing something she can't comprehend or quite believe she's reading. Before, he might have found that look sexy. Caressed the inside of her bronzed thigh. Up to where several pubic hairs curled enticingly outside her panties. Put his hand between her legs. Or maybe on her breast. His lips pressing on hers. His cock's belligerent push against her thigh.

But now she looks other-worldly.

— An alien wedding, Lennox says softly, rummaging through his case, which lies at the bottom of the bed, on a fold-out stand with straps. Did these things have a special name? Whatever, there is a Motörhead T-shirt in there somewhere. *Ace of Spades.* He picks it out. It lies on top of a white one with BELIEVE in big maroon letters.

Lennox looks out into the street and sees a white van, brilliant magnesium sunlight reflecting from it as it pauses at traffic lights.

Trudi lowers her magazine, watches him go through his suitcase. His movements have the attractiveness of the awkward man who has learned to circumvent this condition by slowing everything down. Catlike in his languid movements, with his slightly hunched shoulders, hands a little too big for his body, like he's never quite known what to do with them. Legs perhaps a tad short for the frame; in tandem with the slouching tendency and his hairiness, they could occasionally hint at something simian. But he's always carried the air of a large wounded mammal; how the potentials of vulnerability and violence never seem far from him.

It is easy for her to relate to grace as a destination rather than a state. A few years back she'd decided to shed the sugar and carbohydrates in her diet, do a regular gym programme, spend more money on decent clothes and make-up and *invest time* in her appearance. It came as a shock to her that new cheekbones and a slim, athletic body quickly began to emerge. The blonde tints followed, and the biggest surprise was that the world could so lazily reclassify her as conventionally beautiful. It was a disappointment to learn just how much perceived female beauty was about diet, exercise and grooming.

Nonetheless, Trudi had become entranced by the shallowness of it all; the easy power it conferred. The exalting attentions of others; how men in groups at bars would graciously part for her like the Red Sea for Moses. How spite would sting the eyes and tongues of other women who saw only the make-up, clothes, diet and exercise; the effort they couldn't or wouldn't make. How men and women at the public utility where she was employed gave up chairs for her at crowded meetings. She'd be the first to be asked by the new start in the office what she wanted brought back for her lunch. Handsome Mark McKendrick, a young senior executive, challenging her to lunchtime games of squash. Then the several workplace promotions came easily, fast-tracking her all the way up to the glass ceiling. That relentless evolution of Trudi Lowe: from office junior to corporate female managerial icon.

And now back with Ray Lennox. A broken boy soldier. She watches his muscular but lithe body negotiate his clothing, a pair of long canvas trousers and the Motörhead T-shirt. Notes a slight thickening around his waistline; no, she isn't imagining it. The gym would sort that out.

The TV programme changes emphasis, discussing Miami's museums and monuments. Lennox can't believe it when they get to a Holocaust memorial, which is situated here in Miami Beach. — So that we never forget, the presenter says sincerely, patently more downbeat than when he talks about condominium prices. — A place of healing.

— Why the fuck do they have that in Miami Beach? he asks incredulously, pointing at the screen. — It's like having something tae commemorate the Rwandan atrocities in Las Vegas!

— I think it's great. Trudi puts down the magazine. — There should be one in every city in the world.

— What's Miami got tae dae with the Holocaust? Lennox raises his eyebrows. Sunlight suddenly rips through the blinds, casting tight, gold bars across the room. He can see the dust particles floating in them. He wants to be outside: away from the air conditioning.

— It's like the guy said; a place of healing, Trudi contends. — Besides, I think the *Rough Guide* mentioned that there were a lot of Jewish people in Miami. She reclines back on the bed. That is what she does. He knows that recline. Used to love it. But, please God, not now.

— I need to get some air, Lennox says, avoiding contact with her hopeful eyes. Instead, his wrapped hand depresses some slats on the blind and he looks across to the sun-reflected, smiling facades of the vanilla apartments opposite. They seem to be beckoning him to come out and play. He picks up the phone on the dark glass table. — I said I'd call Ginger Rogers. He's a good mate. He hears the plea in his voice. — No seen the old bastard in yonks.

— Does it *have* to be right now? An internal tautness distorts

Trudi's sexy purr into something quite high and fey. She turns her head and glimpses at the empty side of the bed. Perhaps sees the phantom climax that could chill her out. — I don't want to sit nattering with old people. I've nothing to say to them.

— Me neither. But let's get the boring shit oot ay the way while we're jet-lagged, Lennox says, shaking the phone.

— Okay, Trudi concedes, — I suppose we've got plenty time.

— Attagirl, he responds, instantly aware of the strange inappropriateness of the term. Lennox can't look at her, as he calls his friend Ginger. Trudi can hear the voice of the old retired cop through the receiver: grating and loud, charged with the dangerous enthusiasm of Scotsmen bonding.

Lennox puts the phone down. Informs Trudi that Ginger will pick them up later on, and that they'll get a drink and a bite to eat. Watches something sink inside her. Defensively, he looks across to the table. The glass of water seems to have shifted a few inches to the right.

Then, Trudi's elevated sigh of resignation: — I'll only come if you promise not to talk about police stuff.

— Deal. Lennox feels his face muscles relax in relief. — But we should go down for that cocktail first. It's complimentary, he picks up the voucher they had given him at the desk during check-in. Displays it to her.

A South Beach welcome:
Complimentary afternoon cocktail: 2–4 p.m.

— You have to watch the drinking, Ray. It's so silly. You put in so much work at NA . . .

He moves over to the table. The glass from this angle seems normal. — I just want to drink socially. I don't want to be *in recovery* all the time. It's not as if I'm going to get cocaine here, he shakes his head, realising where he is, adding tamely, — even if I wanted to, which I most certainly don't.

Her eyes roll. She changes tack. — Why don't you phone your mum? Just to tell her that we got here safely. She'll be worried.

— No way, Lennox says emphatically. — Let's grab that cocktail, he urges, trying to keep the need out of his voice.

During the check-in Lennox had already decided that the boutique hotel was not to his taste. The slick metal-and-chrome surfaces, exuberant artwork on the walls, draped mirrors and lean chandeliers didn't bug him; he has nothing against luxury and decadence. It just felt too public, and when they get down to have their cocktail it's become very busy at the bar. Lennox kills his vodka Martini quickly. Then he's struck by an inkling that, with her marginally deeper breathing, and control over her glass so that it makes no sound every time she sets it back down on the marble table, Trudi is as tense as he is. Her behaviour frays his nerves more effectively than any violent outburst, and makes him want to go outside. The people, both staff and customers, strut and preen like catwalk models, everybody sneakily checking out everyone else while all the time cultivating an air of studied aloofness. He looks to the door. — Let's explore a bit before Ginger comes tae pick us up.

Outside it is hot. He recalls the TV forecaster saying it was unseasonably warm for winter. It was usually only around seventy-five degrees in January, but it has soared into the mid-nineties. Lennox is baking. That is how he feels. Like he is baking in a big oven. His brains a stew in the casserole dish of his skull. It's too hot to walk far. They sit down on the patio of a bar-restaurant. A flashbulb-smiling girl flourishingly hands them a menu card.

— It's roastin, he says lazily, from behind his shades as he and Trudi sit al fresco sipping another cocktail, this time a Sea Breeze. They have only gone one block. Collins Avenue on to Ocean Drive. Strutting holidaying youths pass by, enjoying the bounty of their years and wealth; waxed macho boys pumped up with muscle, giggling and pouting girls in bikinis and sarongs, older women trying to emulate them with some help from pills, scalpels and chemicals. Tropically smart Latin men in white suits smoke Cuban cigars the same colour as their girlfriends. Salsa and mambo music fills the air, and a programmed bass pulses out from somewhere. The sea is close, across the busy two-way street. Behind a couple of Bermuda-grass verges, some tarmac and a few palm trees is a strip of sand and then the ocean. You can't see it, but you know it's there.

— Ray! Trudi's hand scalds his forehead. He winces. Like she'd branded him with a heated iron. — You're burning up!

Rising and skipping off towards the shop next door, Trudi returns with a New York Yankees baseball cap. She pulls it over his head. It feels better. — Sitting frying your brains out! With that haircut you've no protection in this sun!

She delves into her straw bag, producing a tube of sunblock and swathing it on his neck and arms, disdainfully regarding his *Ace of Spades* T-shirt. — A black T-shirt! In this heat! And I don't know why you won't wear shorts!

— For wee laddies, he mumbles.

Lennox remembers his mother making similar administrations to him as a boy, at home in the small utilitarian garden with its cut-grass lawn and its paved path meandering down to a ramshackle tool shed. Or in the summer at Dingwall: a rare Highland heatwave when they were staying at his aunt's. Again at Lloret De Mar, on their first family holiday abroad, with his father's pal and workmate, Jock Allardyce, and his wife, soon to be ex-wife, Liz. It was also their last, as Avril Lennox's stomach was swollen with his kid brother, and his older sister Jackie was on the cusp of being too cool for such excursions. He'd met a mangy old dog on the beach and they'd become friends. He'd introduced the animal to his dad, horrified when his father chased it off. — Keep away from that filthy bugger. Rabies, John Lennox had explained in alarm. — Standards of hygiene in Spain are different from Scotland.

He takes the cap off and regards the ubiquitous NY symbol. He reluctantly puts it back on his head, pulling a sour face. Something about it depresses him. It was the sort of hat that might by worn by someone who had been to neither a baseball match nor New York City. The sort of hat Mr Confectioner might have had in his wardrobe.

— What's wrong with it? Trudi asks.

— I don't like the Yankees. No Boston Red Sox hats?

— There's loads in there, I didn't know what you wanted. I just got it to keep the sun from burning out your brains! It's New York, she urges.

— This is Florida, Lennox shrugs. He tried to think of a Florida baseball team. The name Merlins seems to ring a bell. *The Magical Merlins.*

— Yes, but it's all American and that's where we are, she says, then sips her Sea Breeze and returns to her notes. — Go and see if they'll change it if you want . . . I think Mandy Devlin and her boyfriend should be at the evening do, rather than the church and the meal . . . what do you think?

— I agree, Lennox says. He gets up, stretches, and steps next door. Some football shirts: Real Madrid, Manchester United, Barcelona, AC Milan. The baseball caps. He chooses a Boston Red Sox number and puts it on. Returning to the patio, he sticks the Yankees one on Trudi's head. Her hand goes to it, as if he's messed up her hair, then stops.

She simpers at him, squeezes his good hand. Something rises in him, a surge of optimism, which is crushed when she speaks.
— I'm really happy, Ray, she says, but it sounds like a threat. — Are you winding down?

— I need to get the Hearts score. We're at home to Kilmarnock in the Cup. Shall we find an Internet café soon?

Trudi's expression is briefly acerbic, then her face lights up. — There's some stuff I want to show you on this website, some really good ceilidh bands.

She is reading in another magazine about the television actress Jennifer Aniston; her recovery after her divorce from the actor Brad Pitt, now with a different actress, Angelina Jolie. Lennox glances at each magazine on the table. Both were about relation-ships: one focusing on a day of happiness, the other dealing with a lifetime of misery and uncertainty. He'd glimpsed at it on the plane. Jennifer Aniston was supposed to be with another actor now, whose name he couldn't recall. Trudi points at her picture on the cover. — It must be so difficult for her. It just goes to show: money can't buy happiness. She looks at Lennox, who has caught the waitress's eye and ordered another two Sea Breezes. — We're okay though, aren't we, Ray?

— Hmm, he muses to himself, trying to think of the last decent film Brad Pitt was in. Decides that the remake of *Ocean's Eleven* wasn't too bad.

— Well, thank you for that vote of confidence! We're only going to be spending the rest of our lives together! She looks at him, harsh, shrew-like. He can see the old woman in her. It's like she's fast-forwarded forty years. She throws the notepad on the table. — At least *pretend* to be interested!

Jennifer Aniston and Angelina Jolie. Different women, faces, bodies.

The body had seemed to shrink in death, washed up on the rocks at the bottom of that cliff. It was strange, but it hadn't bothered him at the time. Well, it *had* bothered him, but not obsessively. He thinks of his old mate, Les Brodie. How they used to shoot seagulls with their air rifles. How, when you shot a gull, it was different from shooting a pigeon. Les and his pigeons. The gull, though, it just reduced, went into nothing, like it was a balloon, all air. The difference between a dead adult body and a dead child's (and Britney was the first dead child he had seen) was that sense of reduction. Maybe you were just seeing for the first time how small they really were.

Lennox feels his heartbeat rising again, as sweat coats his palms. He forces down a deep breath. That cyanic corpse and its mysterious, unyielding opacity; it was just a body though, Britney had gone; what counted was bringing the bastard who had done her to justice. But now he can see it as vividly as ever; the eyes popping out of the head, the blood vessels on the lids haemorrhaged where he'd throttled her, while penetrating her, wringing the life from her for his own fleeting gratification.

A human life bartered for an orgasm.

He wondered if it was really like that. It was when he tried to imagine the little girl's fear, her last moments, that those corporeal images came racing back. But did she really look like that? Was it not his imagination filling in the gaps?

No. The video. It was all there. He shouldn't have watched the video. But Gillman was present, staring coldly at the images Mr Confectioner had filmed. His act demanding that Lennox, as superior officer, had to sit as implacably as his charge, even though every second of it was crippling him inside.

He thought about the moment before he squeezed the trigger, the gull in his sights. That timeless pause before release: the hollow shabbiness inside him afterwards, as it lay small and lifeless on the tarmac or the rocks at the Forth estuary at Seafield.

Les Brodie. The pigeons.

Suddenly he is tuning into a voice.

— . . . you won't talk to me Ray, you won't touch me . . . in bed. You're not interested. Trudi shakes her head. Turns in profile. Her eyes and lips are tight. — Sometimes I think that we should just call the whole thing off. Is that what you want? Is it?

An ember of anger glows in his chest. It seems to be coming from so far away, cutting through a maze of paralysis. Ray Lennox looks evenly at her, wants to say, 'I'm drowning, please, please help me . . .' but it comes out as, — We just need to get some sun. A bit of light, likes.

Trudi hauls in a huge intake of breath. — It *is* a stressful time, Ray. And we *really* need to make our minds up about the venue. I think that's the big one hanging over us, and then she gasps, — September is only eight and a bit months away!

— Let's take it easy tonight, his tones are soothing, — go and meet Ginger back at the hotel.

— What about your Hearts score?

— It can wait till I see the papers. We're on holiday, after all.

Trudi twinkles, her face opening up further as a carnival float crammed with children in fancy dress chugs along in the traffic of Ocean Drive.

3

Fort Lauderdale

The mottled late-afternoon clouds head in from the Atlantic and the palm trees move loosely in the gentle breeze. Trudi and Lennox have settled back at a table on the hotel's front patio to wait for Ginger. They people-watch on Collins Avenue, Lennox drinking a mineral water to try and prove some point, when he's craving alcohol so badly he could commit any number of crimes for a vodka.

He's changed into a short-sleeved blue shirt and tan-blond canvas trousers. Trudi wears a yellow dress and white shoes. The cloud cover has thickened, and although the sun still pulses out occasionally, she can feel the coolness on her limbs. Then a familiar accent shouts out the surname Trudi has guiltily practised signing, but all she can see is a 4x4 Dodge, which has pulled up outside the hotel. Though its tinted-glass window is wound down, the driver remains concealed. The door opens and a fat man wearing a garish yellow and green shirt emerges, squinting in the sun, before staring at her. — Hey! Princess! he sings. She can tell he's forgotten her name, as they'd only met once before: back in Edinburgh at his retirement do.

— Ginger! Lennox smiles. He gets up and hugs his old friend. Feels the increased girth. Ginger is a big brown leather suitcase wrapped in a Hawaiian shirt. He gets a thin smile back. — Look, Ray, I'd appreciate it if you didnae call me that here. I've never liked it, makes me sound like a fuckin nancy boy.

Lennox nods in taut acquiescence as Trudi reviews her elementary knowledge of Eddie 'Ginger' Rogers. A retired Edinburgh cop with nearly forty years' service on the force. His first wife had died a year before his retirement. He had married Dolores Hodge, an American whom he'd met in a ballroom-dancing chat room. After some Internet romancing and a few transatlantic visits, they had tied the knot, Ginger moving over to his new bride's home in Fort Lauderdale.

— What's this? He notes Lennox's bandaged hand. — Wanking injury? Then, aware of Trudi, he gives a contrite smile. They climb into the 4x4, Trudi in the back, and drive on to Washington Avenue, and down 5th Street. Soon they cross over a long bridge heading towards what Ginger tells them is Miami proper. Trudi watches a rusting, low-built sludge tanker as it creeps past some dazzling white cruise ships berthed at the docks, like a jakey sneaking into a society wedding, and then they're on a five-lane freeway. It's a mess: tagliatelle rather than spaghetti junction.

Ginger drives in the aggressive manner of the TV cop, perpetually jumping lanes. Trudi believed that Americans were generally decent drivers compared to the British, being used to travelling on roads actually designed for that purpose. Ginger seems intent on confirming his reputation for cavalier performances behind the wheel. He pulls out in front of some college kids in an unhooded convertible. Despite being in the wrong, his response to their blaring horn is to give them the finger, US style. — Spoiled little cunts, he chuckles, before snorting, — Think they're entitled. Then he recklessly weaves in front of another car and is tooted again. — No hesitation: reservations are for yuppies and Indians, he grins broadly, glancing back at Trudi. — Awright, princess?

Her tight-stretched, tooth-bearing smile at the back of his head. One hand checks the seat belt; the other, white-knuckled, grasps the exit strap above the door.

Ginger's section of Fort Lauderdale is situated right by the beach. The apartment is in the Carlton Tower Condominiums, a twenty-storey building behind a Holiday Inn, just one block from the Atlantic Ocean. Lennox has noted the relative proximity of the thin strip of beach to the road in comparison with the art deco district. Externally and from afar, the tower might have given the initial impression of British council flats, but closer examination makes Lennox revise his opinion. The ground level is opened up with floor-to-ceiling plate-glass windows. They step inside to a large lobby and reception area, the marbled floor and walls impressing him, and Trudi too, he can tell by the arch her biro-thin brows make. It is furnished with couches and coffee tables full of glossy magazines, and decorated with exotic and lavish floral arrangements, which it takes Lennox a couple of glances to ascertain are actually plastic. The concierge, a large black woman, sits behind the reception desk. She smiles at Ginger who waves cheerfully at her. — Nice woman, he says humbly, as if apologising to Lennox for his previous police-canteen racism, and underlining that it's a thing of the past.

Lennox stifles a chuckle. Scots have schizophrenic views on the issue of ethnicity. As most of them never see a black face from one day to the next in that whitest of countries, they feel free to be either as racist or as right-on as they like, enjoying the extravagance of unearned certainty.

In the elevator, Ginger hits the button for the fourteenth floor. In a playful gesture, he gently and in slow motion punches Lennox's shoulder, then winks at them both. Trudi grimaces in a nervous smile. They emerge into a tight corridor, seeming to herald a depressing uniformity of brown-doored rabbit hutches, before having their expectations again confounded as they enter an apartment both spacious and luxurious. It has an open-plan living room and kitchen, which leads through sliding glass doors out on to a balcony. There are two bedrooms, both with en suite facilities, in addition to another, larger bathroom.

Lennox can't believe that a home with two bedrooms can have *three* bathrooms. He is about to say something when the door opens behind them and an elegant, well-dressed woman who looks to be in her late fifties walks in with a West Highland terrier on a leash. On its release it bounds up to Trudi and Lennox, tail wagging, sniffing proffered, patting hands.

— This is Dolores. Ginger makes the introductions to Lennox and Trudi, both of whom are greeted with great enthusiasm. — And this wee rogue here is Braveheart.

The beast evidently does not like Lennox; a shared 'Skarrish' heritage means nothing. It hatefully bares its small front teeth below the rubberlike gums. It's a narky wee bastard, liable to attack, he reckons.

— Braaay-ve-*heart*! Dolores warns.

Then the dog seems to collapse a couple of inches and skulks slowly towards Lennox as he sits down on the couch. It briefly looks up as if to bark, but then drops at his feet, coiling around them. — See! Dolores sings in triumph. — He likes you!

— Aye, Braveheart, Lennox says warily, tentatively leaning forward and stroking the animal's neck, becoming more bullish as his hand sinks into fur and he ascertains how thin it really is. Well chokable, he thinks, relaxing back into the sumptuous settee with cheery malice.

Dolores seems fascinated by Trudi. — Well, aren't you a pretty one? she luxuriantly observes, looking her up and down appreciatively. Trudi's coy embarrassment is evident, as her hand involuntarily moves to her hair. Then her face stiffens in anticipation of the wedding guest list rising further.

Dolores takes the bag she is carrying and waltzes gracefully across to the kitchen area. Ginger had said she used to teach dance. Lennox can see she's light on her feet and in excellent condition apart from a bit of a distended stomach. Like Ginger, she has a sparkle in her eyes under that lacquered hair, which Lennox and some of the other boys on the force would habitually refer to as 'shagger's glint'. They wouldn't be going quietly into old age.

Dolores and Ginger give Trudi and Lennox separate tours. Everything in the apartment is new: pristine, gleaming and dust-free. Lennox notices the smell; that slightly burnt aroma that many places in America seemed to have. It's probably the cleaning agents they use. He wonders if the UK has a distinctive scent for American visitors and what it's like. In the master bedroom, Ginger shows off his electronic coin distributor. — You put all the coins in and it sorts them out, up to twenty at a time. Automatically stacked and bound intae paper wrappers. Amazing, eh?

— If you accumulate that many coins, then why no just take them tae the bank?

— Fuck the banks. Ginger drops his voice, taps his skull and winks. — These cunts take the fuckin pish as it is.

In the other room, in spite of herself, Trudi is warming to the earthy candour of this American woman, who is older than her own mother. — My mom married a cop, and she told me not to make the same mistake, Dolores laments. — I did, twice. Two words of advice: short leash.

— I'll bear that in mind.

Hearing talk of weddings, dresses and venues filtering through the walls, Ginger whispers to Lennox, — The girls seem to have hit it off. What say we slip our markers and I take ye somewhere special?

— Okay, Lennox cagily agrees, wondering how he can sell this to Trudi. The problem in acquiescing to the idea that he's depressed, or even its more benign bedfellow, 'under stress', is that it intrinisically means the ceding of his moral assurances. The potential at least existed for every comment he made to be viewed as a symptom of the disease. And he senses that Trudi's management of his supposed condition is about control (hers) and disenfranchisement (his). Her logic is that his thoughts will take him back to the trauma of his work, therefore all independent deliberation by him is inherently bad. She will replace this with *her* projects, with nice things to think about, like the wedding, the new place to live, the furniture, the future children, the next house, that limiting narrative unto death that so terrifies him.

Just then Dolores reappears and announces, — I'm gonna take this beautiful lady of yours away for a little while, Ray, show her some of the bridal stores in town. I guess you boys will have a bit of catchin up to do.

— Aye, sound. Lennox registers Trudi's sly smile, then Ginger's raffish wink.

They wait for a few minutes after the women's departure, then leave and get back into the Dodge. Driving west on Broward Boulevard, they pass a large police station before stopping at the Torpedo men's club on 24th Ave. They park in the lot behind the one-storey concrete building, which, from the outside, looks like a pillbox. At the front entrance it advertises 'Friction Dancing'.
— This place rules, Ginger informs him.

A huge Hispanic guy in a black T-shirt, pumped up on iron and steroids, stands in the doorway. His threatening scowl dissolves into a broad smile as he sees Ginger. — Hey, Buck, how ya doin, man?

— Awright, Manny, Ginger says, slapping the man's big, broad back. — This is my buddy Ray, from Scotland.

— Hey! Al-right! Manny sings, as Lennox's mouth creases in a grin and they are ushered into a dark, cavernous space. Lennox evaluates it as one of the type that cops, villains, daft young lads and sad old men all over the Western world frequent. Then he wonders exactly which category he himself now fell into. An elongated catwalk stage, with several pole-dance podiums branching off it, twists towards the Mecca of a large, glittering island bar. Although it is still early, the place is reasonably busy and quite a few of the tables that line either side of the stage are in full tenure. Lennox knows instantly by the alienation from their clothing, that sense of being dressed by somebody else that all uniformed men give off, that the occupants of one space are off-duty cops.

The waitresses wear tight, white T-shirts that buzz electric blue under neon lights and they work hard keeping the drinks flowing as the dancing girls perform. It's tame at first, but as the beers go down, they get more raunchy and explicit. Ginger and Lennox order some ribs and fries. — Tell Dolores I was having a tuna salad plate, he says earnestly, — no mayo. She wants me watching my weight. It's this ballroom-dancing finale we're in next week.

Lennox nods slowly. Rubs his shorn skull. — The guy on the door called you Buck. What's all that about?

— Buck Rogers; that's what they call me here, Ginger mouths in proud, emphatic defiance.

Lennox considers this. Raises his glass to clink it with his friend's. — Here's to the twenty-fifth century, he toasts.

The beers are going down nicely, as are the shots of tequila. Lennox rises to go to the restroom. With the drink and his anti-depressants, he feels a bit shaky. He steadies himself with one hand as he pishes, heavy, thick and steamy, into the latrine.

Life isn't so bad. We got the bastard that did Britney. He's gone.

— Gone like the nonce cunt ye are, Lennox spits at the full-length mirror indented into the tiled wall. He holds his right hand up as if to swear an oath and makes a fist through the slackening bandages and the pain that the drink has dulled.

Going back outside, he heads towards his seat as Tina Turner's

33

'What's Love Got To Do With It' blasts from the sound system. But a dancing girl intercepts his journey, rubbing up against him, her pelvic thrusts full on his groin. The girl's face is garish and almost clown-like under her warpaint, and layers of foundation can't conceal brutal pockmarks from the harsh overhead spotlights. Wild eyes and a twisted, cruel mouth throw down a gauntlet.

Lennox freezes; stiff everywhere but where she wants him. This is friction dancing. She isn't going to cease her gyrations till she's brought him off. He feels a blaze of anger rise in him. *This is for old men and losers, for nerds and retards.* Clocking the bitter desperation in her eyes, he sees how he's now a challenge and he *will* get aroused and come. To force him to take part in the circus and become as desperate and degraded by it as her – it's the one way for this crackhead stripper to keep face. He understands this as he's participated in versions of it so many times back home in Edinburgh on police stag nights. He discerns the uptightness on the men's faces. Knows he's implicating them all by not playing the game, by being better than them, and humiliating this woman by rejecting the only thing she has to sell, her sexuality, or this cartoon version of it. It was less a self-esteem issue than a professional pride one; this was what she did for a living.

But he can't do anything other than win this terrible stand-off.

Eventually she gives up and her face contorts as she whispers, — Faggot, spitefully in his ear, then twists with a gleeful smile to rub up against the next sweaty crotch. The men in the bar cheer as one in palpable relief.

He sits beside Ginger, whose head throbs psychedelic purple from an overhead light. His old friend looks at him, first in hostility then in greasy admiration. — Fuck sakes, Lennox, that dance cost me twenty bucks and ye didnae even blaw yir muck! That Trudi lassie, she's fair got you sorted oot, eh! The beast has been tamed!

Lennox bristles at the use of Ginger's terminology. — Sorry to waste the dosh. Then he thinks: let him believe what he wants. But now his own mental river is diverting again, away from the stripper, Trudi and Ginger. The drink that had distanced the crime now bubbles it up in his head, like percolating coffee.

Britney Hamil. Now the beast *had* been tamed. How will Mr Confectioner be serving his sentence? What would he be doing right now? Isolated from all the other prisoners for his own safety – even the other nonces – would his arrogance have evaporated? Lennox suddenly needs to know.

— Do you ever think aboot these cunts we bang up in Serious Crimes? he asks Ginger. — How they can live with what they've done?

— They live with what they've done cause they're scum. They couldnae care less. Fuck them, let them rot, his reddening face snarls, as he signals to a waitress for more beer.

It seems to Lennox that this reprimand is as much directed at him as any criminals Ginger can recall. They have another drink, but he senses that things have soured a little.

When Ginger does speak it's to call a halt to proceedings. — Better no have any more, I'm way over the limit as it is, he gasps. A girl showily licks the fingers that she had previously used to breach herself as she swivels on the catwalk stage in front of him. — Let's head back over my side and dump the motor, he says, looking at the girl and raising his glass in appreciation, — after this wee cutey-pie has done her thing, but. Christ, Ray, if I was twenty years younger . . .

— You'd still be auld enough tae be her faither.

— Cheeky cunt.

Ginger's driving is better with a drink in him; he takes greater care and actually watches the road, as they get down on to the beach area neighbourhood. It looks run-down in the murky twilight. It seems that many local businesses have gone bust or are hanging on by the skin of their teeth. On the block behind the Holiday Inn, drunk, young vacationers and the transient workers and beach bums who survive on their patronage and carelessness, inhabit the bars and cheap eateries. And all around are old people, solitary and depressed. Lennox comments on this as he and Ginger go into an open patio bar, well removed in its grime and sleaze from the sterile glitz of the Miami Beach establishments.

— A lot of poor bastards have retired down here with a partner, who's since kicked the bucket, and now they cannae afford to move elsewhere. I know tons of codgers in that situation. Ginger swirls back a mouthful of beer and signals for some shots of tequila. — The retirement dream becomes a nightmare, he muses. Two men walk in, hand in hand, and sit in a corner of the bar. — This place was meant for retirees. Now look at it, Poof Central.

They down another few drinks and briefly walk along a strip of beach before heading back up to meet their wives present and future.

Trudi and Dolores have evidently enjoyed their early-evening shopping. — The best time to do it in this heat, Dolores explains, as Trudi defiantly holds up some purchases at Lennox. — It's stuff I *need*, Ray. I know that we're meant to be saving up . . . but I never ask what you spend your money on.

Resentment bubbles in Lennox. *As if I care what she spends her money on.* — Who's asking questions? Ah've no said a fuckin word.

— I know that look, Raymond Lennox.

— What look? Lennox protests through his semi-drunken fug. — You're makin something oot ay nothing. This is ridic, he appeals to Ginger.

But it's Dolores who pitches in. — Shopping's what we do best, son. Get used to it, she playfully chides, shifting her gaze to Ginger, — right, lover boy?

— Aye. Ginger flushes through his drink. Lennox thinks it could have been with pride or embarrassment or perhaps a little bit of both.

Ginger Rogers then presents his guests with two alternatives. Either Dolores can run them back to Miami Beach, as he concedes that he's drunk way too much, or they can go out for a meal at his favourite restaurant and spend the night in the spare room.

— We can get a cab, Trudi suggests.

— Won't hear of it. Fifty bucks? Robbery! Dolores or me'll whisk you doon there in the morning.

— Okay, Lennox agrees, heading out on to the balcony and looking over the rail. The Holiday Inn can't totally obscure the view of the ocean. The darkness has thickened but some heat is still in the air, despite a thin breeze whistling coolly on his arms. Down below, the soft thump of beats from a disco bar. He can

36

tell Trudi isn't happy. As she would say herself: he knows that face.

Ginger comes out to join him, closing the patio door behind them. He has two cans of Miller in his hand; issues one to Lennox.
— Paradise, eh? he says, scrutinising his pal's reaction.

— Nice, says Lennox, and they bang beer cans together. He knows that he would go crazy here, but each to their own.

— So why the long face, Raymondo?

— The long face is on her through there. Lennox twists round and looks in, fuddled and aggressive in drink. — I don't give a suffering fuck what she buys. And that makes her worse. What I was meant to say was: 'C'mon, baby, we're supposed to be saving up for the wedding,' so she could go, 'Don't spend all your money on drink then.' Ah didnae gie her thet satisfaction, so she got nippy and had the argument anyway: with herself. Only it's worse now because I supposedly don't care aboot the poxy wedding.

Ginger's eyes take on a manic gleam as they dance in his head. Lennox has the sense that he is watching something moving behind him. — This is your first night here?

— Aye. He briefly glimpses round, but there's nothing.

— And you're on holiday?

— Aye.

— And you're on med leave after stress breakdown?
Lennox can see where this is heading. — Aye.

— And you're seeing an old buddy you havnae seen in five years?

— Aye, Lennox hesitantly replies, — but aw the same, I –

Ginger cuts him off. — And she's been hassling ye wi wedding plans?

— Well, aye, I suppose –

— Tell her those three magical little words every woman needs tae hear now and again, he smiles in defiant cheer, — Get tae fuck!

The door slides open and Braveheart charges out on to the balcony, barking skittishly in circles as Dolores shouts, — Buck! Get that Caledonian ass of yours in here. You too, Ray! Bill and Jessica have arrived!

Bill Riordan is a retired New York City police officer. Thin, but looks granite-hewn hard, his whole body like one big bone. The sort of man age had chiselled rather than bloated. His wife, Jessica, is a slender woman with meandering eyes and a lazy smile. Time had given her a light sack of fat under her chin but little anywhere else. They are part of the ballroom-dancing competition, and Lennox is already writing off Ginger's chances. They move into the kitchen, where Ginger steers Lennox to the hot-dog cooker. — Put the buns and the dogs into vertical slots and they all pop up at once, he announces proudly. — Dolores disnae like me going too crazy with it, he whispers, glancing at Bill, who chats to the women, — likes me to keep the weight doon, wi the competition finals up in Palm Beach next week.

More drinks follow as the evening dissolves around them. They decide they won't make the restaurant and phone for a pizza delivery. As the party finds its way back out on to the balcony and the plastic chairs, Ginger's voice rises in a rasping catcall. Lennox dimly remembers drinking sessions past and an obnoxiousness that could come out in him when he was pissed. — You fuckin Paddies, he turns to Riordan, — all you supplied the New World wi was the numbers, the expendable brawn. Fucking worker ants. The Scots, we provided the know-how. He thumps at his chest. — Right, Ray?

Lennox pulls a tight smile.

— That's a very misty Caledonian perspective, Buck, Bill Riordan cheerfully offers.

— What about Yeats, Joyce, Beckett, Wilde? Trudi intervenes. — The Irish have given so much to Western culture.

Ginger is now drunk enough to openly scoff at her. — Couldnae write their names on a giro compared to the bard. Rabbie Burns, right, Ray?

— I'm keepin ootay this one.

— You stop it, Dolores shouts, leaning forward in her chair and punching Ginger in the chest. — I'm Irish. And Danish. And Skats. My paternal grandfather came from Kilmarnock.

She pronounces it Kil-mir-nok.

— A wise choice to get on that boat, Ginger teases, mellowing under her intervention.

Lennox turns to Riordan. — Must have been some tough beats in New York, Bill.

Riordan nods in cautious affirmation. — The city's a lot different now, Ray. But I loved my time on the force. Wouldn't have changed a thing.

— It must be so dangerous compared to the UK, all these guns, Trudi shudders, glancing briefly at Lennox.

This time Riordan gestures in the negative. — I certainly wouldn't like to work in Britain and not have a pistol in my holster.

Trudi clicks her teeth together. She often does that when she's nervous or excited, Lennox considers. — But isn't it dangerous? Doesn't it make you more likely to use the gun? You must have shot a few people, right?

Smiling genially at her Bill Riordan lowers his glass. — Honey, in all my years on the force I shot nobody. I worked some of the toughest precincts in Brooklyn, the Bronx, Queens. You name it. I've never personally known a New York City cop who shot anybody. I unholstered my gun twice in thirty-five years.

Lennox watches her almost purring under his kindly gentleman-uncle patter. Sees the wedding guest list grow by two.

— Uh-oh, cop talk, Dolores gripes, — time to evacuate, girls. She stands, sending her plastic chair hurtling back along the tiled balcony floor. Jessica follows suit. Trudi hesitates for a while, preferring the company of one youngish and two old men, to that of two old women, but realises that Scottish sexist protocol will set the social agenda tonight, and follows back through to the lounge.

Ginger cranes his neck to watch the sliding glass door slurp along its runner, before thudding closed. — Course it's aw fucked now, he slurs, as he pours some shots from a tequila bottle he's opened, — the job. It's the same everywhere. The high-flyers come in, tell all us old pros how it's done, eh, Bill?

— I guess, Riordan smiles warily. Like Lennox, he seems keen on avoiding the fight that the host is spoiling for.

— Ray? Ginger challenges, his eyes narrowing on his ex-colleague.

Lennox feels himself swallow his beer in a hard gulp. That

promotion was eight years ago. His career has stagnated since, but some cunts wouldnae let it go. He shrugs again in a non-committal manner.

— I reckon that's the way of the world, Buck, Bill Riordan chuckles.

— Aye, but it shouldnae be. Ginger closes one eye, focusing the other in accusation on Lennox. — Polis, they call them. That job you got, that should have gone tae somebody like Robbo. Now there wis a polisman!

Lennox takes in a long breath through his nose, pleasantly surprised to hear his sinuses pop. — Robbo was a fuckin washed-up nutjob, he spits. And he wants to add: *And now I'm just like him. Just like the lot of youse.*

— A fuckin good cop, Ginger mumbles, seeming to run out of steam. Then he asks, — How's Dougie Gillman? Some boy him, eh, Ray . . . His voice tails off.

— The same, Lennox says through tight lips.

— Course . . . ah forgot that you and Gilly had that wee fawoot. Kissed and made up yet?

— No.

A silence falls. Rather than let it hang, Lennox rises and heads through to the open-plan lounge where Jessica is playing with the dog and Dolores is teaching Trudi some dance steps. — I'm heading for my scratcher, he announces. — Jet lag kicking in.

— Ah . . . lightweight, Trudi teases, now lost in the drink and the dance.

In the en suite bathroom he washes down his last two anti-depressants and prepares for another night, hoping he's ingested enough to obliterate its horrors. Sliding into the bed, he listens to the chatter and laughter from the front room dissolve into the madness inside his head. Though exhausted, a harsh, regressive calculus seems to dictate that sleep will be denied him again. Instead, he has thought.

What was it Toal said in his briefing about Angela Hamil? – A wanton slut, he'd ventured, putting his pipe back in his mouth and sucking on it. Since the ban he wasn't allowed to smoke it in the office now, but he still brought it out as a prop, chewing on the stem when he was nervous.

Then he'd added, — I reckon that it's some scumbag she's had in her orbit. You know the kind of rubbish the likes of that woman's bound to attract.

Lennox blinks, tugging on the duvet. Images of Angela, her straw hair and haggard face, form into clarity around him, not like in a dream because he is painfully conscious that he's in this bed.

Then he can see him, Mr Confectioner: his cold, fishlike eyes, his monstrous, rubbery, scandalised lips, and Britney, helpless, at his feet.

And Ray Lennox thinks of that balcony outside, beyond the cackling party. Just to step over that railing and let go. To be away from it all: the Nonce, Britney. Just how hard could it be?

4

Edinburgh (1)

It was the morning following the disappearance. You'd broken off a long session sifting through data, stealing a few hours of sleep at your Leith flat. Awakening with a start in disorientating blackness, your missed calls list told you that Keith Goodwin had phoned. You'd forgotten about last night's NA meeting. It was still shy of 6 a.m. when you were back at Police HQ's IT lab, re-absorbed in the CCTV footage.

Not that there was much of it. The mind-boggling network of cameras that recorded every Briton's movements on an average of between ten and forty times a day, depending on your source, had thinned out when it left the city centre and was threadbare by the time it got to Britney's housing scheme. There was some coverage of her yesterday morning: a grainy shot on security film that lasted just under a minute as she left her block of flats, school-bound, then a few beats more, courtesy of a speed camera, as she traipsed towards the roundabout. You deployed every program and procedure that might enhance these shabby images. You stretched them out, slowed them down, closed in and pulled out to scan the peripheries and all the nooks and crannies where somebody might be lurking. From the back of Britney's head and the side of her face, you'd try to trace her line of vision, to see the world through her gaze. Like a fevered prospector, you sifted through the data swarm hoping to find a pixel of gold that might provide a clue to the kidnapper's identity. Nobody in Lothian and Borders Police knew more about sex offenders. And nobody was more inclined to cast the net wider.

Through the repeat black-and-white viewings of the pensive child, the name Robert Ellis kept resonating in your skull. A man who'd been under lock and key for three years now for the murder of two young girls, one in Welwyn Garden City, Hertfordshire, the other in Manchester. Britney's case seemed to have many of the same characteristics as the murders of Nula Andrews and Stacey Earnshaw. Predictably, Ellis had protested his innocence to those heinous crimes.

The other name that came back to you was George Marsden, part of the Hertfordshire team who had put Robert Ellis away for the kidnap and murder of twelve-year-old Nula. The prosecution had established that Ellis was prone to hanging around the local park where the girl had last been seen, by a tree-lined path that she was traversing en route to her aunt's.

Only George believed that they'd got the wrong man. There were similarities with the case of Stacey Earnshaw, whose body had been found dumped in woods in the Lake District two years previously. When Hertfordshire Police hauled in Ellis, they discovered he'd had a girlfriend in Preston whom he'd visited regularly around the time of Stacey's murder. The girl, Maria Rossiter, disclosed some fairly mundane details of their relationship to a tabloid, which were luridly recast and spiced with innuendo. Alongside a disturbing tape Ellis involuntarily made, this helped establish his guilt. George Marsden was sure it was same person who snatched Nula Andrews who had got Stacey Earnshaw in Manchester. Only he was absolutely convinced that it wasn't Ellis. In Welwyn Garden City, a white van had been reported leaving the side street adjacent to the wooded parkland near the time of Nula's disappearance. Now Ellis was inside and White Van Man was back.

You'd felt a disturbing weight settle around your limbs as you'd looked up at the wall clock at around 9 a.m. It was now over twenty-four hours since Britney had gone. You opted to give those stinging eyes a rest, head to the Stockbridge Deli and get another black coffee and call up George Marsden. You were on friendly terms, having got drunk together after a DNA-testing training course in Harrogate several years back.

—White van, was it? George casually asked after you'd explained the crime in broad brushstrokes. Refusing to confirm or deny this detail as a smile pulled at your features, you hoped your silence didn't speak too many volumes.

You seemed to get immediate pay-off from the break when you returned to the footage. Once again Britney stepped out of her stair, turned, but this time you noticed that she seemed to give a half-wave; a furtive acknowledgement to someone approaching from her right. An enhancement of the image confirmed this impression. The person was out of shot but would be heading into the stair. You looked at the list of names of the neighbours. Then you loaded up the sex offenders register and the image of Tommy Loughran leapt out at you.

When you got down to the Hamil family's house with Notman, it was discovered that Loughran was the man just beyond camera range. He'd been walking his dog yesterday morning. And he was the people's choice, with votes cast in brick through his shattered window, and campaign graffiti dubbed on his wall:

NONCES DIE

The security guard, an old flasher, was an ex-alco turned Christian teetotaller. He carried the air of the sinner who had repented with gusto but still expected more retribution before the slate could hope to be wiped clean. Such was Loughran's masochistic self-loathing, you figured that he could easily have been induced to admit that he'd committed the crime. The only problem was that after taking his dog home and seeing Britney leave for school, he boarded a crowded bus to a cinema, where local students had started a morning movie club. The transaction on his Bank of Scotland card and the film theatre's records indicated that Loughran was watching the Werner Herzog documentary *Grizzly Man*. You recalled how the movie – about a self-righteous, liberal environ-mentalist, eaten by the creature he was trying protect – was a hit in the police canteen. Remembered Herzog dismissing the subject's claims of the spiritual superiority of the bear. In the face of the beast, the German film-maker saw only 'the cruel indifference of nature'. — What do you think the message of that film was, you'd asked the bemused Loughran.

Billy Lumsden, a janitor at Britney's school who regularly talked to the girl (although he talked to most of the kids), was late for work on the day of the disappearance and was taken in to assist the inquiry. You learned that his marriage had broken up the previous year, when he'd left his wife and their three kids. Lumsden had already been suspended for being intoxicated on duty, and he confessed to you his feelings of loneliness and despair. The compassion you experienced for this man shocked you in its intensity. What if Lumsden was the beast? But he seemed so broken, so quietly desperate. Then it was established that his mother had suffered a bad fall at her home. Neighbours and a local shopkeeper verified his presence four miles away at the time of Britney's vanishing.

The case continued to seep under your skin. The clock was ticking. The disappearance of a child was harrowing enough. But it was also showing you how the vulnerable were lining up to be devoured by the criminal justice system. The potential for miscarriage was so strong everywhere. It sowed a sickening moral relativism into your psyche, spreading a rash of doubt and uncertainty. You steeled yourself with the thought that *somebody* had taken Britney. She couldn't have just vaporised into the misty air in those three minutes she turned the corner into Carr Road out of sight of Stella and Andrea. Somebody was evil. And you vowed that you were going to get them.

The starting point had been checking out the men who came into contact with the girl, at school, home and work, and slowly eliminating them from the investigation. Britney's biological father was off the list; long estranged from the family, he was on an oil platform in the North Sea. One man remained unaccounted for and, chillingly, he'd vanished around the same time as the child. They couldn't find her grandfather, Ronnie Hamil, at his flat in Dalry. Neighbours informed you that this was nothing new; Ronnie could vanish for days at a time when his giro arrived. It had been Gillman who had cottoned on to the grandfather connection first. — That cunt's up tae something, he'd sneered over a photograph of Ronnie with Angela and the girls. — Auld Gary Glitter.

You put everyone in the team on a full-time search for Ronnie Hamil. All squad cars were instructed to be on the lookout for him. His tenement flat was staked out around the clock. The team spent hours visiting his haunts: the bookies, the off-licences and the bars of Dalry and Gorgie Roads. But you declined to join the hunt. Try as you might, you couldn't stop yourself pursuing another avenue. — I'm heading off to do some snooping around, you'd informed Bob Toal.

Toal had given you his trademark lemon-sucking look. He knew you were up to something. Somehow you'd suspected this wasn't going to be a typical child sex case; a bubbling in your innards told you that the trail wouldn't lead to a traditional British nonce. You'd studied the mugshots of every paedophile on the register: the priests, schoolteachers and scoutmasters; the pervert uncles, opportunistic stepfathers and twisted blood-fathers with their arrogant and chilling rationalisations. Nobody fitted the bill. It seemed an American-style crime, or rather the kind of crime of US fiction, as you supposed that real American crimes were like British ones. But it was culturally American: a lone drifter, a predator, not driving across long and lonely interstate freeways over a vast continent, but shuffling along in a white van through crowded, nosy Britain.

What you did was drive to the airport, surreptitiously boarding a lunchtime flight to Gatwick, then jumping on a train down to Eastbourne, where George Marsden now lived. He'd resigned after the Nula Andrews case and now installed security systems and offered advice to nervous retirees. George had never struck you as a maverick. Ex-forces, Royal Marines; had fought in the first Gulf War. A straight-backed divorcee with a rugby player's build, a floppy head of thick grey hair and sportive smile that suggested he wouldn't spend too many lonely nights. With his pressed trousers and freshly laundered shirts, everything about him suggested steadfast adherence to procedure. Except that when he'd seen the evidence and it didn't add up, he'd lost faith.

Over espresso in a café, you and George watched his prospective clients amble along the seafront as he explained that Ellis had been the town bad boy back in Welwyn. A charismatic and sly young man, he wasn't a hard case, but was somehow able to get tougher souls to do his bidding. Ellis had several offences, mainly burglary, but there had been one charge of rape, dropped through lack of evidence. While there was nothing to link him to minors,

46

he was easy to detest; the sort of shitbag that every community manages to produce. Nobody, police or public, would lament him being banged up for a long time. Nula Andrews was the opposite: small, frail, elfin-faced, an innocent looking much younger than her twelve years. You recalled the picture of her they'd circulated, and those blazing doe eyes that blitzed into the psyche of the British public. Nula was on her way to help her aunt with some decorating. She was easy to cast as Little Red Riding Hood to Ellis's Big Bad Wolf. So Robert Ellis became the most hated man in Britain: a Huntley, a Brady. And, in a sickening fashion, he did make an unsolicited confession of sorts.

But whatever Ellis was, he was not guilty of this crime. George Marsden was having none of it and honour compelled him to resign, ending his police career on a sour note. He had a troubling belief in right and wrong. If it was religion, it wasn't the insurance policy stuff most people took out by nipping to church on Sunday. So George talked through the Nula Andrews case with you: the similarities and differences to Britney. Then you'd discussed Stacey Earnshaw, snatched near Salford Shopping Centre. — It wasn't Ellis, he said emphatically.

Every city produced its share of Ellises. Bob Toal was anxious to see if any in Edinburgh could be linked in some manner to Britney. He himself had cried wolf about retiring for years and now that his compulsory date loomed, he wanted to do so on a high. Some sections of the press, which had originally crucified Ellis, now, in light of Britney's case, had started to hint at a grave miscarriage of justice. The public, meantime, were doing what the public will do in such instances: clamouring for a body.

You hadn't told a soul about the Eastbourne visit and feared the phone call that might force the truth, but received nothing other than routine messages informing you Grandad Ronnie's whereabouts still hadn't been uncovered. Guilt was beginning to strike hard; you felt you should have been knocking on doors and sitting in cramped vans on stake-outs with the others. You'd fallen asleep on the plane back to Edinburgh, not fully waking up till you picked up the local newspaper at an airport stand to see Britney's face, with a vibrant, insolent grin, staring at you. Tomorrow

47

it would go national. You took a taxi back to your Leith flat, in a new development by the docks. You were planning on speaking to Toal about the Ellis case. Then you realised that in your tiredness you'd neglected to switch on your mobile after coming off the flight. There was a message from Trudi and two from your boss. — Think we've got our man, Ray, he'd chirped in the last of them.

You were sure you knew who this was, but when you headed down to HQ you were surprised to find Ronnie Hamil still missing and a youth called Gary Forbes in custody. Forbes had confessed that he had taken Britney, killing her and burying her body in woodlands in Perthshire. Then you looked at Bob Toal, now utterly despondent; between leaving that message and you joining him, Toal's confidence in this arrest had completely evaporated. It wasn't surprising; Forbes was an idiot, desperate for attention. A gangling, introverted young man, he was obsessed with murders and serial killers and kept scrapbooks documenting their deeds. You'd watched this sad, socially neglected teenager revel in his faux bad-boy status. He was already clearly fantasising about the crazy women who would write and visit him in prison. Worst of all, though, was the way your investigative team were desperately stretching him to fit the template. Seizing on pathetic anecdotes; the neighbour who claimed he'd tortured a budgie, the young cousin who'd sustained a bad wrist-burn at his hands.

— Is this the best we can do? you'd asked. You looked around at the faces in the office; Harrower, Notman, Gillman, Drummond, McCaig.

Toal, meanwhile, sat in an ulcerous silence.

— We can comb the Highlands at this halfwit's instigation and we'll just be wasting manpower, Bob, you'd said. — Let's get him to show a couple of cops where he's supposedly hidden the body, then charge him with wasting police time.

— Yes, Toal snapped grimly, scarcely moving. — Get on to it, he'd said to Gillman, nodding curtly. The others took their cue to leave. Toal shut the door behind them, his expression and body language warning you to brace yourself. — Where in hell's name have you been? Why did you have your phone switched off?

— You're not going to like this.

Toal hadn't moved a muscle.

— I flew down to Gatwick and met George Marsden. He was investigating officer on the Nula And –

— I know who the fuck he is, Ray, Toal had spat. — He's trouble! Then your boss shook his head in disbelief, — You took off down south to meet a bitter ex-copper, a civvy, when your team are looking for a missing girl and a prime suspect? I'm disappointed in your judgement, Ray. Very, very disappointed.

You'd wanted to discuss Welwyn and Manchester, but it wasn't the time. Anybody who had made a serious study of the latter case would have seen that there was no way Robert Ellis could have kidnapped Stacey Earnshaw. And the evidence tying him to Nula Andrews was highly contentious. But it meant taking on senior police officials and judges. It wasn't a war you felt you could even start at this point, let alone hope to win.

Toal was incredulous. — Do you know that Ronnie Hamil's still missing?

— We're doing everything we can to find him, you'd said, shabbily.

— No. Your team are doing everything they can to find him. Toal's voice was getting high and excited. — You won't solve this case dicking around in Welwyn Garden City or Manchester. It's the family that's the key, mark my words! Find Ronnie Hamil, Ray!

You nodded meekly at your boss and looked forward to another long night.

Day Two

5

Two Ladies

The lunchtime traffic is light on the freeway, as Lennox sits next to Ginger, who has been uncharacteristically cowed and silent. This suits him; he feels good that somebody else is feeling bad. He's exhausted, but he'd been glad to see the dawn fill the room, delivering him from his sweating torment. He shakily recalls one of last night's tortuous dreams. He was on Ginger's balcony. Inside the apartment, through the glass, the grinning Mr Confectioner with a frightened Britney, who then became a terrified Trudi. Lennox's own mother Avril sat in a chair watching, like she was almost encouraging the Nonce. Lennox had pulled at the door but it wouldn't slide open. He pounded the glass till both his hands bled. When he looked behind him there was no balustrade on the balcony. And the veranda area had shrunk to become a small ledge.

A horn blares, tearing him from his thoughts.

— Spastic! Ginger roars, as he zooms in front of a big truck that dazzles Lennox with a magnificent chromium blast of reflective sunlight. He turns to Trudi in the back. — Was I out of order last night?

— No, not at all, she says, a little too emphatically. — You were great hosts and it was a good night out, I'm just suffering a wee bit now, with the jet lag and everything.

At the hotel's rear courtyard – a small jungle of cypress, oak, pine and the ubiquitous palm trees, designed to allow revellers to sneak in discreetly – they say their goodbyes. Lennox and Trudi look obviously wrecked as the concierge dispenses an obsequious and collusive *this is South Beach* grin.

— I have to lie down, Trudi moans, flipping the plastic key into the room's lock, delighted when the green light appears first time.

She is bad with hangovers, Lennox considers, as he heads to the bathroom. The sleep he'd gotten at Ginger's had been non-existent, and the antidepressants are now gone. He can't tell her. Something is going to happen. He can feel it as he sits on the toilet. But not from his bowels. Nothing will happen in his bowels.

When he comes back into the room, Trudi is lying on the bed. Her arm is draped across her face, covering her eyes from the sun. She wears only a sky-blue thong. It contrasts nicely with her sunbed-tanned skin. Why had she not gone under the covers? The light ribs her body. He can see the hardness in it. Gym and diet. Now he feels something in his gut. Saliva ducts working in his mouth.

He gets on to the bed and grabs at her breast; an awkward and adolescent lunge that surprises him as much as it does her. Trudi pulls away, wincing. — My nipples are sore, she grumbles in protest. — It's my period coming on.

Lennox feels his body relax in relief. Sex has been avoided again. He can't believe it; he is actually happy. He is doing every-thing in his power to avoid shagging her. Usually it's all he wants. How long has it been? A cold sweat breaks out on his forehead, across his back. He knows that if it doesn't happen soon, they'll be finished.

They get under the duvet. She turns away and Lennox wraps himself around her. Spoons her. She used to like that. Made her feel safe and loved, she said. Soon she's writhing and sweating, pushing him away. — Don't touch me, Ray. It's too hot.

Now she's feeling trapped by him. Confined. He rolls flat. She soon falls asleep. Lennox lies awake, shivering in a private hell. He remembers that boy in Jeanie Deans pub on the South Side of Edinburgh. Just another daft cunt telling sick jokes to his mates: still too young to have learned about hurt, loss and taste. A game of pool in the boozer. Forgot where he was.

A young boy named Martin McFarlane had recently died after a bone-marrow transplant. He was a brave, sweet-faced wee kid and his sad story had been widely reported in the local media. The community rallied round with fund-raising activities for life-saving operations at American and Dutch clinics. But they hadn't worked; Martin had succumbed to his disease. The young guy in the pub loudly asked a mate, — What's the difference between Martin McFarlane and Britney Hamil? When his friend shook his head, the boy emphatically contended, — Martin McFarlane died a virgin!

The extreme bad taste and the local, contemporary aspect caused most of his friends to gag or shudder. Lennox, who was sitting in the corner with some Serious Crimes boys based at the South Side station, stood up and walked across to the young man. The youth saw that he'd crossed the line and immediately stammered out an apology.

They knew that Ray Lennox had lost it when he didn't attempt to strike or even verbally abuse the joker. When he tried to speak, he started to choke. — Ah did ma best . . . he pleaded to the terrified bar comedian, — ah did ma best for that wee lassie . . .

It was only when he felt the pull on his shoulder, heard the repetition of his name and focused on a crack in the hardwood and gauged its proximity, that Lennox realised he'd fallen to his knees. His friends picked him up off the pub floor. One took him to Trudi's flat. She called the doctor and the police personnel department's welfare people.

Now he's lying in bed, at their boutique hotel in Miami Beach, thinking about Britney. Trying not to think of the moment when her virginity was taken from her. Compelled to do so, as if turning his back on the magnitude of her terror was in itself a form of disrespect and cowardice.

Maybe that was the lunacy . . . maybe that was the problem, getting too involved like that . . .

He trembles from his very core. It only stops when he attempts, instead, to think of her mother. He can see Angela Hamil, a cigarette in hand. The start of the investigation: her daughter missing. The urge to violently shake her and say: Britney's gone. And you're just sitting there smoking cigarettes. That's right. You just sit there and *smoke cigarettes* and leave us to find your daughter.

The sweat seeps from him, soaking the bed. His heart punches a steady beat in his chest, like a boxer's jab on a heavy gym bag. His throat is constricted with tension as he tries to fill his dry lungs with the sterile air of the room. His body is in revolt against him and he can hear Trudi snoring; loud, truculent snarls that could be coming from a drunken labourer. Dream demons are forming as his eyes shut, pulling his exhausted soul into their realm. He doesn't want to go there but his fatigued mind is surrendering.

It's mid-afternoon when they wake up. They're both ravenous. Lennox feels like his brain is expanding and contracting in his skull, fraying its outer edges against rough, unyielding bone.

They get ready to head outside, into the heat. Lennox wears his Ramones *End of the Century* T-shirt. He'd chosen it in preference to a Hearts football top; the material's too much for this heat. Cotton is a better bet. There was the maroon-and-white BELIEVE shirt. But he decides that he doesn't want to explain anything to anybody, to talk to Scots abroad and lie about his job, like all cops have to around real people. He puts on another pair of light canvas trousers, dressy enough if they want to go and eat somewhere a bit upscale. The Red Sox cap is pulled back on to his head. Trudi wears a short, white pleated skirt. Her legs are long and brown. A pink vesty top. Her arms also tan, her hair tied back. Shades. Outside, his arm goes to her waist as they walk in silence. It's the first time she's worn this skirt without him getting an erection. Unforeseen fear grips him again.

They are hungry but can't agree on what to eat. The hangovers and the strange location conspire against decision-making; neither self nor significant other is to be trusted with that choice. A wrong call would mean recrimination: brooding silence followed by a row. Both of them know it. But they need to eat. Their brains and guts fizz from last night's tequila slammers.

They pass a Senior Frog's Mexican Cantina. Lennox recalled that some of the boys had been to a Senior Frog's on a polis beano in Cancún. There was a long-running canteen joke about it. He'd wanted to go with them, but it was when he and Trudi had just got back together, and things were in flux. They were always in flux. Besides, Gillman had gone on the Cancún trip, which effectively ruled it out for him. He shows her the restaurant. By now she just wants to sit down somewhere – anywhere

— out of the heat. A pretty but severe-looking Latina girl escorts them to seats at wooden tables and issues them laminated menus. The place is half full, some groups and couples dining. At the bar a bunch of white guys wearing red-and-white-striped soccer shirts are drinking. Trudi has a free local newspaper, and mutters something about a show on at the Jackie Gleason theatre.

— Minnesota Fats, Lennox says, recalling Gleason's turn in *The Hustler*.

The tables are big. Like the ones in the polis interview rooms. The distance between him and Trudi is about right. He needs a drink. He wants to question her. Instead he questions himself, again.

The rising. The breakfast. The walk. The turning. The snatching. The footage. The pictures.

Now he's desperate for a drink. He *needs* one. The waitresses seem busy. — I need a beer, he informs Trudi, pointing at the bar, — my throat's gaunny close up in a minute. Want one?

— That's the *last* thing I want, Ray Lennox. You're supposed to be in recovery! *We're* supposed to be planning our wedding! What if the waitress comes?

— Get me a margarita.

Trudi looks contemptuously at him, then tuts and goes to her white shoulder bag. She produces the copy of *Perfect Bride* and her small notebook.

Lennox hits the bar and orders a pint of Stella. He is astonished and relieved that they have it on draught. That red background with the white font: it's like meeting an old friend. Just a sip first, in order to feel that dry, alcoholic taste in his mouth. Then he downs half in a gulp. One of the guys in the football tops catches his eye. They have English accents. West Country. A little bit drunk. The strips are Exeter City Football Club. He asks them if they've gotten any scores. They tell him Exeter have won. They hadn't heard any Scottish results. They chat, the Exeter lads expressing goodwill towards his team, Hearts. Lennox is surprised to hear that Exeter are no longer in the Football League. It's the Conference now. A crazy chairman. A financial crisis. These things happened.

He traverses back to the table where they are served corn chips and salsa. Then, to his astonishment, two frosted margaritas appear. — Well, we're on holiday, Trudi informs him, a terse, defeated smile coming as close as she would surely get to levity. The main courses arrive: seafood fajita for her, a steak burrito for him.

Lennox watches her construct the fajita with care. The cheese and refried beans omitted, pushed to the side. The rest wrapped in a low-carb South Beach tortilla. Trudi eats in small, economical bites. He, conversely, bolts down huge chunks of his burrito. At one stage it burns his throat so intensely that he almost blacks out.

At the bar the group from Devon have obviously hit drunken critical mass. They burst out in chant: — OOH, AAR, EX-I-TAHR! AH ZED OOH-AAR, EX-I-TAHR!

A waitress and barman dispense indulgent smiles, before a flustered manager approaches the group, diplomatically pointing out the other customers. The West Country lads gracefully drink up and take their party elsewhere. One gives Lennox a wave, which he returns. — Nice guys, he tells Trudi. — Exeter boys.

— Bet you wish you were with them, she scowls, reading his mind as the Devon crowd depart, — football lads getting pished and acting the goat.

— Don't be silly, Lennox says, squeezing her hand with his good one.

The meal sits rock-heavy in his belly as they turn on to Ocean Drive. Trudi wants to see the beach but Lennox objects: — Let's spend a full day at the beach the morn, he proposes, as they pass a jungle-themed dance-bar. The girls outside are clad in leopard-skin bras and pants, dancing on the pavement, trying to entice people in. Lennox doesn't need much encouragement. He needs another drink.

He wanders in, Trudi reluctantly following him. They find a table and two stools and Lennox orders a couple of Sea Breezes.

— I don't want to sit around drinking all the time, Ray, I —

— You don't come to a place like this for culture.

— You don't come anywhere for *anything*, other than drinking. You could have stayed in the BMC club!

Lennox's excited head fills with the notion that our bodies and souls desire the poison, crave the superhuman promise and temporary madness it offers; the chance to throw off all the shackles of decency, surely the prerequisite to real intelligence and love. — At least I'm trying to enjoy myself.

— Is that what you call it?

And it hits him, in her look and tone, just how desperate he really is. He wants to say, 'I'm dying, help me, please,' but it comes out in a monotone shrug as, — I'm just doing what I want to do on holiday. If you don't like it, fuck off.

She looks at him in wide-eyed horror. As he watches her features shrink in tight malevolence, he wishes he could suck the words back into him. — Naw, *you* fuck off, ya prick! She springs up and, grabbing her bag, charges away.

Lennox sits stuck to his chair, his limbs heavy, watching her incensed departure. He looks at the table, noticing that she's left her notepad and *Perfect Bride* be'iind. A gentle gust of wind flips its pages over in a measured manner, one at a time; it's as if her spirit remains at the table. But he thinks: *she's not fucking about.* One puny consolation pulses in his brain: *at least I didn't criticise her job at Scottish Power. She hates it when I do that.*

The embarrassed waitress, who's observed the scene, arrives with the drinks, sets them down, and hastily departs. Picking up the cocktail designated for Trudi, Lennox quickly kills it. Then he slowly sips at his own. Contemplating its azure, murky beauty, he almost doesn't want to touch it. A couple at an adjacent table briefly gape at him before turning away. *I'm the nutter everybody wants to avoid*, he thinks in desperate cheer. Then he summons the waitress and pays the bill. Lennox feels his shoulders shake in a nervous, mirthful laughter, but when he gets up from the table the tears – terrible, thick, salty tears – are running down his face from under the shades, drying on his cheeks in the heat, stinging him.

Scarcely realising he is carrying the magazine and the notepad, he walks down the street. All he can think of is the drink he needs. Not just the drink, the *place* to drink it. The sun has fallen behind the skyscrapers that line the Biscayne Bay, and murky particles of darkness accumulate in the warm air around him.

He walks on, without any real sense of what he's doing or where he's going. It feels good to walk. Look at things. People. Buildings. Cars. Billboards. Shops. Apartment blocks. He walks until he realises that fatigue is setting in with the heat, his leg muscles becoming knotted and cramped. It's still a holiday and beach area, but he's passed the colonial low-rise hotels of the art deco district, moved into a zone of uglier, more mainstream tourist accommodation. Big high-rise hotels and apartment blocks have sprouted up around golf clubs and beach complexes.

Lennox wonders how long it would take to walk to Ginger's place up in Fort Lauderdale. A long time, if, indeed, it was even possible to do so. The whole place seems to be built around the car. Then it twigs that the numerous green-and-white posts he's walked past are actually bus stops. Most people sitting on the bench by this particular one look non-white and non-rich; different to the occupants of the convertibles that stream by. They seem to regard him uneasily. It doesn't bother him. A bus comes and he gets on, imitating the stick-thin black man in front of him by putting what he thinks is a dollar bill into a rolling slot.

— That's a five, buddy . . . it's gone thru, the driver purses in disdain, — and we don't give change. You jus wasted three and a half bucks, man.

Lennox nods and takes a seat. He looks at the blacks on the bus with the same furtive, curious glances they steal at him. The few black people he'd known growing up in Scotland had hitherto seemed exotic, but he now sees just how Scots they are. The blacks here fascinate him, the way their bodies move to a different rhythm. Their voices so different from the whites and Latinos, it's as if they're from Mars. He feels something deep in his bones and prays it's curiosity rather than racism.

Feelings in the bones. Gut feelings. Instinct.

Procedure. Designed to scientifically eliminate bias. Follow the force of probability. Seventy per cent of murderers know their victim. Thirty-three per cent come from the same family.

The bus jolts over a rough piece of road. Lennox shudders.

He needs to be safe. He needs to be dangerous. They are every-where, the nonces. On this bus there's bound to be one. He looks around at the suspicious eyes. He can smell them, the stink of them.

The vehicle is going nowhere; after a bit it turns round heading back the way he's just come. He keeps his gaze hawklike. There is pain to be fought. To be drunk through. Then he sees it, on 14th between Collins and Washington. Where he knows he wants to be. It's a bar. The Club Deuce.

He gets to the front of the bus, panic rising in him as it accel-erates for a stretch, and seems to go a long way past the bar, before it slows down and pulls over at a stop. Lennox alights and walks back towards the cream bunker that is Club Deuce. Outside it, a shopping trolley full of a homeless person's possessions. The bar blacked out with blinds he guesses are permanently shut. He passes through a wooden-and-glass door and enters the club. It's so dark that it takes him a few moments to order the objects in his vision.

Club Deuce is dominated by a long bar which meanders like a Formica river with two island lips, snaking in a double horse-shoe at the front and running right round the back of the room. In the corner hangs a big plasma screen. Near the pool table at the rear, a homeless woman sits, occasionally peering out from behind the blind, checking on her trolley. It's a real drinkers' bar of social design; the bends mean that it would have to be almost empty to enable patrons to sit too far from each other. A mirror runs the length of the pub, making it doubly difficult to avoid eye contact with anyone. He checks the time on the clock framed by green light above the jukebox.

Two neon female forms, both lying prone, boobs and buttocks outlined in the glaring red, impress Lennox. They might have been mermaids, but a leg held up seductively announces both as terrestrials.

The effect is of a slightly seedy but classy joint, with an old clandestine atmosphere of speakeasy sex that its present-day incar-nation as a drinkers' den can't quite dispel. Lennox sits at the bottom 'U' of the horseshoe, close to the door, behind a couple of portraits of Humphrey Bogart and one of Clark Gable. He looks at two old mirrors and their ornate carvings. He realises then that Club Deuce has to be one of the greatest and most beautiful bars of its type, indeed of any type, in the world.

The bartender is a large, tattooed guy, with long hair and a beard and moustache. An ex-biker type, long gone into civvy life, Lennox reckons. He has a big, but slightly shy smile.

— What'll it be? he asks, arching his brows.

— A Stoli vodka and soda. Lennox rubs at his top lip for the moustache no longer there. He had it for years, and now, like an amputee with a missing limb, he feels it itch in its absence.

The barman looks approvingly at Lennox's T-shirt as he pours the drinks. — English? he asks.

— Scottish.

— Burns, right?

— It certainly does. Lennox looks at the redness on his wrist that the bar lights have shown up, and takes a swig on the vodka.

The barman studies him, thinks about explaining; changes his mind.

The vodka is a good measure; Lennox liked that about the States, freepour. They didn't fuck about with all that petty, penny-pinching weights-and-measures shite. That sort of stuff alone made the American Revolution worthwhile. He supplements this with a bottle of drinkable European imported beer.

He eases himself round on the bar stool and looks up at the television screen. American Football; the Bears versus the Packers. Lennox can't tell if it's live or recorded. He feels like asking, but reasons that if it's highlights he'll find out soon enough. He puts the copy of *Perfect Bride* down on the bar, and stuffs the notebook and pen into the back pocket of his trousers. The first drink fails to banish the non-specific anxieties that shiver through his mind and body; merely crystallising them into a solid, tumorous lump inside him, which slips down through some psychic highway running in a rough tandem with his intestinal tract, coming to a leaden rest in his lower gut.

The bar is almost empty. Two skinny young white guys, who he reckons are drinking on fake IDs due to the nervous looks they shoot every time the door opens, play eight ball in the corner. Further down from him two women sit at the bar; probably only late twenties, but with life's pummellings visible. A homeless lady sits in a corner, a hawk-like eye checking her possessions through the window. On the other side of Lennox, a fat guy talks to the bartender in a dissenting squeak about some tax that he reckons is unconstitutional.

Lennox orders another vodka. Then another. His decent tips ensure that the barman fills them up. This man evidently understands that some people, just because they come into a bar alone, and with their drinking heads on, don't necessarily want company. They want to see if the shit they've been trying to think through straight plays any better drunk.

He is contemplating that he'd probably been wrong to walk out on the counselling. But he'd clammed up. He'd tell the sneaky, intrusive bastards nothing about himself, nothing that would go on his personal file, despite their claim that everything was confidential. Lennox had gone twice after they picked him off the floor of the Jeanie Deans pub. The woman, Melissa Collingwood, had only been trying to help, to make a point, but she'd angered him. It was when they had got talking about death. Britney's death. — I can't stand the thought of her dying alone, being frightened, he told her. — It's that that does my nut in.

— But isn't that how we all die, ultimately? Alone? Frightened? Collingwood had said, her eyes widening in a sincerity that seemed too pained to be anything other than contrived. And he'd reacted to that.

— She was a fuckin bairn, ya spastic, Lennox had shouted at her, and charged out the door, not stopping till he hit Bert's Bar in Stockbridge. Where he had gone since the case started. Ignoring the messages on the voicemail from his NA sponsor, a cheerful fireman named Keith Goodwin, whose mounting pleas were a voice-over to his descent into oblivion.

Now he has no antidepressants and he wants cocaine.

A country and western song sparks up from the jukebox: a witty number about alcohol. Imperceptibly, the bar has gotten busier. Maybe fifteen people in the room. The homeless lady has gone. Lennox takes a swig of beer. First the talk is louder then the music takes over. It goes back and forth. A few people come and go, but most remain, their elbows on the bar.

From his peripheral vision, he sees one of the women looking at him, being egged on by her friend. He instantly discounts it: his senses are not his to trust. But she slides off her bar stool and approaches him. Slightly built, she wears a short denim skirt and a lime-green top, tied in the middle, supporting her breasts. Her white midriff is bare, and a lip of flab hangs over the waistband of her skirt, a piercing on her belly button drawing attention to it. — Got a light? She pronounces it 'laht'. Her accent is distinctly Southern rather than the mainstream American that seems to dominate Miami.

— Aye. Lennox pulls out a lighter he picked up in the hotel. It has FLORIDA emblazoned on it, with some palm trees. He clicks on the flame that will draw her closer.

A bottle blonde with skin an almost translucent white, her lipstick-red slash of a mouth is like a gaping wound. Her eyes are sunken, with dark bags under them, which Lennox thinks is bruising until her proximity to the light reveals it as fatigue. Her face is hollowed out. A bit more flesh might have heightened a good bone structure. Its almost total absence makes her look skeletal. Lennox sees a woman chiselled by drugs, though he supposes that bad diet – one based on coffee and cigarettes – could produce the same effect.

— Where's that accent from? she asks in those smoky, honeyed tones.

— Scotland.

— That's cool! she exclaims, with an excited verve that animates her to the extent that Lennox immediately feels like reframing his assessment. — Y'all on vacation?

— Vacation . . . aye . . . Lennox says, thinking about Trudi. Would she be back at the hotel? Perhaps already on a flight home? Surely not. He can't tell. His perspective has gone. He looks at the bandaged hand that grips his beer glass. It's like a foreign body.

— I'm Robyn, she proclaims. — With a y.

— Ray-with-a-y, he retorts. — Funny, it's only guys that get called your name back home, he tells her. He feels like explaining that it was usually just posh guys, but decides against it. — Are you from Miami?

Robyn-with-a-y shakes her head. — Nobody's *from* Miami,

everybody jus ends up here. My home town is Mobile, Alabama. She turns to her companion, compelling Lennox to do the same. — That's my friend, Starry.

He faces a woman about five seven, with an elongated face and long, raven hair that curls down on to her shoulders. She has the classic Latin features he's quietly appreciated in many of the women here since he's gotten off the plane; brows sculpted into thinly plucked lines to highlight huge, striking dark orbs that could vaporise the unguarded. Her nose is long and straight, of the kind you rarely see in Scotland.

Age, lifestyle and possibly circumstance has almost driven out a classical beauty, but in its remnants a vivacious power has been retained. She wears her tight blue jeans well and Lennox notices the Converse All Star footwear only because it looks the same as the design worn by people in Oxgangs when he was growing up. His gaze goes back and forth from her eyes to a grey-silvery effect top that just about manages to master the formidable cleavage behind it.

Starry gives him a smile of slow, evaluating grace. It's obviously manufactured but displays a calculating intelligence that in spite of himself elicits his respect. The woman is as tough as nails but something tells him her power is as much hard won as God-given.

A survivor, Lennox thinks. *How cheap and bebased that term has become. I'm a Christmas shopping survivor. I'm a Holocaust survivor. I'm a holiday with the in-laws survivor. I'm a child sexual abuse survivor.* He makes his own list: sex crimes, drug addiction, relationship breakdown, career frustration, mental breakdown, life.

It was too much. He's tired of surviving. It's time to live. Lennox sees that Robyn is standing waiting in open anticipation.

— Would either of you ladies care for a drink?

They nod in the affirmative and state their choice. As the barman pours, Lennox feels he's been hustled but his only mild resentment comes from the girls' apparent belief that he doesn't realise this. — This here's Ray-with-a-y from Skatlin, Robyn grins.

— What kind of work you in, Ray? Starry asks.

— Sales, Lennox lies. He never says he's a cop when he's in company. Not unless he wants rid of it.

Starry flashes a shit-eating grin as she accepts his drink. She steers Robyn, almost pushing her forward into Lennox. The women smile at each other. There is no doubt as to who's in charge here, he thinks. The petty victories. He's seen it so many times before, in so many of the women he's encountered through his work.

Angela Hamil asked for so little. She was destroyed that her daughter had been abducted, raped, murdered. But there seemed no real anger. Life had long since defeated her; she acted like she expected and even deserved this horror that had been visited upon her, that it was her due. It was just another misery piled on top of the ones she'd already had to endure.

Serious Crimes.

Lennox thinks about the name of the department and the actual activities that gave it its title. Murder. Rape. Serious assault. Kidnapping. Armed robbery. Obviously, most people who committed serious crimes were in a bad way. But so many of the victims shared that characteristic. Too often it was the same set of circumstances that threw the victim and perpetrator together.

— Scotland must be a damn fine country, Starry is saying to him in her more generic American voice.

Lennox pulls a taut smile. — It's okay.

— Cause it looks like your head's still over there. Tell ya what I think, there's usually only one thing makes a strange man come into a strange bar alone and throw back those drinks like you been doin. And that's a strange woman.

Angela Hamil. Trudi Lowe.

— Strange women. Aye, there's a few of them around, Lennox retorts.

— So, how are sales these days? Starry asks, imbuing the innocuous statement with cryptic sleaze.

— Oh, not so bad. You know how it is, Lennox enigmatically rejoins, getting into her game.

She looks at him as if prompting him to say more. Then she asks, — So what do you sell?

— I never talk about work when I'm socialising, he says.

All I will say is that it's not the commodity that's important, it's the customer.

Starry seems to glow at his bland response. She pulls her friend forward again, and Lennox tries to figure out what the game is as the girls shuffle around him with the nervous energy of punch-drunk, traumatised old contenders in a seedy gym, evidently ready to sing for their supper. — You're cute, Robyn giggles. Lennox knows that she's drunk, they probably both are, but Starry is holding it better.

As they chat, his ears quickly become desensitised to the super-ficial glamour of the American accent, and he can now see these women in any scuzzy backstreet Edinburgh pub. A lifetime of cigarette consumption seems to induce all the bar's smoke to congregate around Robyn's grey skin and cheap, flashy clothing like iron filings to a magnet.

— So you know a few strange women, Starry says, her eyes going to his bandaged hand. — Does that make you a strange man? Who am I kidding, is there any other kind?

Lennox has sparred in too many Edinburgh meat markets to be wrong-footed by some apolitical feminist jibes. — We do stupid very well, he says, then adds, — but you girls beat us hands down when it comes to crazy. That's just the way we are.

Starry laughs, opening her jaws so wide it seems she could swallow up the bar and everybody in it. Lennox stares into the ribbed, pink cavern of that mouth, the protruding red tongue a welcome mat, quickly coiling into a threatening snake. — And don't you forget it!

— Excuse me a second, ladies, while I answer the call of nature. Lennox slides from his stool and makes for the restrooms in the corner of the bar.

Why did they call it a restroom?

Lennox feels like he really wants to rest. To lie down on the tiled floor covered in men's pish, shoe leather, dirt, cigarette ash, and sleep like a baby. Instead, he stretches out his bad hand and starts to unwrap the elasticised bandage with his good one. The dressing is discoloured and a stink rises from it. A spasm of fear seizes him, and he almost expects to be confronted by a withered,

67

black and green gangrenous object. In the event his hand is stiff, red and a little swollen and angry-looking around the knuckles, and his eyes water when he tries to make a fist of it. But it's still visibly his hand, and is probably on the mend. He entrusts it with the holding and pointing of his penis and can't bear to watch his dark and stagnant urine splash against the metal of the latrine.

Lennox washes his hands with care, welcoming the other back into the family.

It took him thirty-five seconds to grab her, bundle her into the van, gag and secure her with electrical tape and drive off.

Puts his hands under a dryer. Enjoys the heat sensation against the numbed, sore paw.

The two women face Lennox as he emerges back into the pub. Starry has picked up the copy of *Perfect Bride* and is leafing through it. But now there is someone else on the scene, another man who has emerged from the shadows at the back of the bar and who approaches the women at the same time as the returning Lennox. He looks at Starry in confusion.

Lennox realises that the guy is about the same height as him, around six two, and also in his mid-thirties. — I'm in sales, he beams at Starry and Robyn, ignoring Lennox, who gently seethes. *This cunt has been listening in to me talking, and now he's taking the piss.*

Pulling on his shoulder, Lennox pivots him round. — I'll tell what you're in if you don't fuck off right now. Trouble. Big fucking trouble. Is that clear?

The guy blinks, taken aback.

— Hey . . . Starry begins, laying down the magazine on the bar, — no need for that!

— Listen, buddy . . . the guy starts, but Lennox can see that any certainties he has are evaporating.

He feels himself smouldering with violence. This guy has rubbed him up the wrong way. — I'm no your buddy. Got that?

— Have it your way —

— I intend tae. Now fuck off.

The man shrugs, raises his palms in appeal and skulks back into the corner of the bar.

— What was that about? Starry says, evidently upset.

— I didn't like him, Lennox tells her, as he keeps his eyes on the man, who promptly finishes his drink and leaves.

— He seemed a nice guy, she says, looking to Robyn.

— I dunno, I thought he was kinda creepy.

— I guess you would know all about that, honey.

Robyn screws up her face a little and shrugs, turning to Lennox with a tight smile.

Starry seems to relinquish her anger. — Look, let's move on somewhere else.

They discuss where to go. Lennox thinks that he should head back to the hotel. Make his peace with Trudi. Tiredness is kicking in. But he can't face her. Better to wait till she's asleep.

— What's this? Starry asks Lennox. She holds up the copy of *Perfect Bride*. — You planning a wedding?

— Aye. Not my own though, he says, surprised how effortlessly falsehoods pirouette from his mouth. The difference between a cop and a villain is that we get paid a salary and make better liars, his mentor Robbo once told him. — That's what I sell, he qualifies. — Weddings; the whole package.

— You're a wedding planner? Like the Adam Sandler movie? Robyn squeals in delight.

— Well, yeah. He looks at Starry who is forcing a grim smile, before her cellphone ringtone starts to play 'Won't Get Fooled Again'. She apologises, moving to the door of the bar to answer it.

— I guess that must be a happy job. A lot of fun, Robyn says.

— It's stressful, but it has its uplifting moments.

Starry returns and is keen to go on to a place called Club Myopia, but Robyn is reluctant. — I gotta get back soon for Tia.

— She'll be okay, Starry says. — Just one drink. I got us a little something.

Robyn's eyes light up. — You mean you been – She stops herself.

Lennox knows that the little something is coke. It's what he wants. Needs. One line of white powder. Something to make him strong. To make him not think about dead children. To make him not care.

Robyn tells him that Club Myopia is just a few blocks south. It would be on the way back to the hotel. — I'll keep this safe for you, she smiles, putting the copy of *Perfect Bride* into her shoulder bag, — it's getting pretty messed up lying on that bar.

— Ta. Lennox winks in gratitude, and they head out and walk down Washington Avenue to the club.

For ID, Starry and Robyn flash driver's licences at the doorman. Lennox offers his Lothian and Borders Police Authority pass, replete with an old mustachioed picture of him. The bouncer, a big black man, meets his eye with a downward head motion, minimal, stern. Lennox slips the card back into his pocket, taking care to conceal it from the girls. He badly wants them to get the coke out. Can envision it, sweating in the wrapper, inside Starry's handbag. So, too, from the focus in her eyes, can Robyn.

Myopia is a dance-music club, and cast adrift amid a sea of toned, fit, beautiful youths, they are the oldest people there. Starry and Robyn waste no time in heading to the restrooms. They are gone for so long, Lennox fears that they might have slipped away. He grows restless then anxious standing at the bar alone, drenched in the pumping music and the strobe lights, with the well-dressed youngsters seeming to scan him in disapproval. The girls wear short, slinky dresses of largely one colour, which cling to their bodies as if by static electricity. The predominantly dressy shirts of the boys highlight the grubbiness of his Ramones tee. He thinks: Michael Douglas in the *Basic Instinct* nightclub scene, salving himself with the knowledge that he could never be quite that ludicrous.

His edginess heightens. Over by the bar, he is aware that he's being watched. It's the guy from Club Deuce, the smart-arse salesman. Letting anger energise him, Lennox hits the floor, snaking through the frolicking crowd to the back of the room, then sharply double-backing so he's standing behind the guy who's craning his neck, scanning the floor for him. — Looking for somebody? he shouts above the sound system's quake, causing the man to jump. — You want tae fuckin dance, or something?

— Look, I – he begins, halted by Lennox's hand, the one with the power in its fingers, which fastens on to his thin throat, choking him to silence.

— Naw. You look. I don't know what your fuckin game is, but you turn round and you get your arse out of that fuckin door right now, he demands, his grip tightening further. — You know what I'm sayin?

In the man's fearful eyes he can gauge the extent of his own murderous rancour. Aware that some people are observing the scene, he releases his grip. The heaving-chested man backs away, rubbing at his neck. A bouncer has partly observed proceedings, but, like Lennox, he's content to merely track the salesman all the way to the Exit signs.

Ordering another drink to vainly compensate for his leaking adrenalin, he fretfully waits for the girls. He commands himself to stand still and do nothing, telling himself that real composure will boomerang back if he fronts it long enough. When they finally return, Robyn particularly looking flushed and animated, they discreetly present Lennox with the gear, in a small, resealable bag. — Thought you'd run out on me, he smiles.

— No chance of that, Robyn says. He sees the confidence the cocaine gives her. One sniff and she can be the person she's always wanted to be. He understands. Starry doesn't really need it. She tosses back her curly mane and grins at him. He heads to the men's restrooms. The cubicles are flimsy with small doors. Not as private as the UK. You could see right in through the crack of them, or even look over, if you had a mind to. *Not to worry.* He racks up a big line on the top of the cistern. It looks good gear. Chops it finer with his Lothian and Borders Police ID card. He thinks for a second about Trudi, probably back in the hotel room, then Keith Goodwin at the NA and all the good work he'd done. Was it good work? Now he'll flush it all away. Britney's face: cold, blue and bruised. Mr Confectioner's sickening gloat. He'll flush it all away.

The line obliterates them and Lennox emerges striding on to the dance floor like a colossus, jaw protruding. Starry and Robyn are dancing, and he moves easily with them, sleazy and invincible. The other dancers, they can feel his power, his radiant contempt for them. They shrink away like the pygmies they are. He painlessly recalls his infidelities of the past, which wrecked things for

71

him and Trudi the first time around; each conquest a trinket on a charm bracelet of fool's gold, every single one of them executed when he felt *exactly* like this.

Why is he doing this, he asks, apart from the drive of the cocaine? His fiancée is back at the hotel, or so he assumes. Lennox is always beset with the notion that the big event, the real party, is happening somewhere else. His radar – that distressed feeling under his skin – tells him that this is the case. Then he realises that he is a cop and that the big party is *always* happening somewhere else, namely in civvy street. And if he finds it, his role is not to join in, but to break it up. Now, though, for these two weeks, he is a civilian. And it's good here. *The world's crumbling around us and thank fuck there's people just too new or plain stupid to climb on that dance floor, and act as if the party's just begun.*

Starry sweeps her hair back and meets his predator's glance with hard, flinty eyes of her own. — We're gonna go back to Robyn's. She looks to her friend.

— You're invited, Robyn says. — Come over and have some more blow?

By blow he assumes that she means coke, rather than marijuana, which he hates. — Okay. Whereabouts? he shouts above the beat.

— I live over in Miami.

— I thought this *was* Miami.

— No, this is Miami *Beach*, silly, Robyn playfully scolds. — Miami is across the causeway.

— Right. He recalls how both Trudi and then Ginger had explained it all to him.

They head outside, buzzing from the coke. Lennox goes to flag down a cab, but Starry stops him. — Here's a bus, she says, nodding to the approaching vehicle. — Cheaper.

This time he pays the proper money. The bus is full of drunks: the ubiquitous mobile theatre of late-night public transport. They find seats at the back, Lennox at the window with Robyn by his side, Starry in front of them. She's conversing in Spanish with somebody on her cell. Robyn looks agitated, this soon starting to infect Lennox. The bus has no windows at the back, which adds to his unease. It's unnatural; not to be able to see where you've come from.

— Who were you talking to? Robyn asks suspiciously as her friend finishes the call.

— Just some friends from the diner, Starry cossets Robyn, rubbing her friend's neck, while she expatiates about her work-place hassles. — That Mano, he's such an asshole . . .

After courting the coastline, the vehicle suddenly veers, crossing a stretch of water on a long bridge and comes into what Lennox thinks must be Miami proper. Starry's nail scrapes at some glitter that's stuck to the bus windows, before she realises it's outside. The docks come into view with the towering cranes, then the freight tankers. But most impressive are the cruise ships, about a dozen of them, like floating apartment blocks, grandiose yet still dwarfed by the big towers of downtown Miami, massive sentinels guarding the harbour. Lennox is impressed, as the coke pounds his head, making him strong. His teeth grind harshly. He wants those mysterious yellow lights that glisten on the water across that filthy, slithering, black bay. Wants to become part of it all: away from the sunlight and the spotless, white, perfect brides.

6

Party

Through a murky shroud of near darkness illuminated only by a peppering of lights from the overhanging skyscrapers of the commerce district, downtown Miami appears to Lennox not only scabrous and bedraggled, but also sinisterly deserted. This impression is confirmed as they step on to the concourse of the bus station at the Government Centre. Many of the tower blocks ahead are under construction. They stand like a silent army of zombies, emerging from the earth in varying degrees of composition but unsure of what to do next. Giant skeletal cranes seem to be feeding off them like monstrous birds of prey.

— Cheaper to get a cab from over here, Starry explains as they swagger with the purpose of the intoxicated across to a taxi rank, adjacent to the bus disembarkation point. The earlier stops at the Port of Miami, Omni Station, the American Airways Arena and the down-at-heel district of small jewellery stores, have been the points of egress for most passengers. Now only one lone drunk staggers ahead of them, his look of open-mouthed bemusement as the bus pulls away indicating that he's alighted here by accident. Lennox looks up at the support pillars and overhead tracks of the Metromover as it snakes around and through the city buildings; Miami reminds him more of Bangkok than of any American or European city he's previously encountered. The only older building he's seen has been the grand, multi-tiered Dade County courtroom, impressive and beautiful with its steps and pillars, a stately home surrounded by tasteless imitations.

They get into one of the three waiting taxis and Robyn coughs on her cigarette, rasping out an address to a suspicious-looking driver, an address which seems all numbers to Lennox sitting in the front passenger seat. A pendant flag hangs from the cabbie's

74

mirror, which Lennox takes to be Puerto Rico. The cop in him has quickly deduced that Miami's most dangerous profession wouldn't be police work or firefighting. Murder would be an occupational hazard for taxi drivers, most of them poor immigrants. The all-night gas stations would now be mainly self-service while convenience-store clerks would invariably be locked in bulletproof booths, the stores probably fitted with drop safes. But working these deserted streets with cold-callers, in cash transactions, seems a particularly risky enterprise.

They continue through what is a barren section of the town; there are no homes down here, everything seems to be cheap and tacky retail. Grubby steel-shuttered shops are in abundance, but Lennox has yet to see a bar or anywhere indicating the possibility of social life. Growing concerned, as he feels he's come far enough, he senses the taxi driver's edginess from behind the Perspex screen. By the shrillness in their voices, he's aware that Robyn and Starry are arguing in the back seat. There is a mention of a dead child. Starry's son. It burns him. He tunes it out in favour of the city surrounding him. Miami proper seems a very different beast to Miami Beach; the city comprising flyovers like the one they sweep on to, and for a while it appears as if they are going to the airport. Then they suddenly veer from the concrete artery, down a steep slip road and into a neighbourhood off 17th Street. It's like falling from the edge of one world and landing in another. — Welcome to Little Havana, Starry says, raising a single curved brow, recovering the effervescence Lennox feels has deserted her since the incident with the strange guy earlier.

— This ain't really far enough south for Little Havana, Robyn says, a little stridently. — It's more like Riverside.

— Bullshit; you jus don want people to know you live in a Cuban neighbourhood, Starry challenges her, only half joking, her accent changing into Rosie Perez Latina.

— Newsflash, Robyn says. — This is Miami. Every neighbourhood here is Cuban.

Lennox cringes at Robyn's bland epithet 'Riverside'. The planners back home had attempted to redesignate Leith and the other river communites as 'Edinburgh's Waterfront'. As Leith

75

was associated with Hibernian Football Club and he was a Hearts fan, he'd enjoyed referring to his new flat as being 'in the Waterfront district'.

— See that, Starry says, looking to Lennox, — you gringos can't see the difference between the Latino neighbourhoods!

Lennox has to concede that his eyes detect little divergence in the dimly lit streets they drive through, all of which are cut into uniform blocks. This area doesn't seem hugely affluent, but it isn't a ghetto either. Most of the homes on these blocks are low-rise dwellings of one storey. When they drive through the backstreets, interior and porch lights illuminate some houses showing him, on closer examination, that no two domiciles are alike. Some fronts and gardens are well kept, to the point of obsession. Others are dumping grounds. Lennox guesses a mix of owner occupancy and rented accommodation. Robyn's place is different; it's in a gated apartment block, the stucco-fronted building painted a pastel orange illuminated by uplit wall lamps with a driveway for parking. An aluminium panel of intercom buzzers announces twelve dwellings, confirmed by the number of mailboxes in a chaste, functional hallway navigated by low-level night lights.

He's used to mounting steep Edinburgh tenement stairs, but chemical impatience and the slight gradient on these tiled plat-forms compel him to take two at once in long, loping strides. Robyn's place is on the top floor, two up from ground level. Prospecting a key from the chaos in her bag, she whispers, — Shhh, as she opens the door. Lennox feels Starry's hand nestling on his arse. He lets it hang for a bit, then moves off down the hallway, passing a table with a phone on it, above which sits a large whiteboard full of numbers and messages. Stung, Lennox quickly turns away, moving into a front room whose chattels suggest a furnished tenancy; the black leather sofa, with fawn-coloured throw and matching chairs belong to some ubiquitous 1980s warehouse that seems to supply rentals in every city he's visited. These sit on oak hardwood floors, with a rug in the middle that looks more expensive than it probably is. A smoked-glass coffee table is stacked with magazines; the garish glint from the light above reflecting on to that cocaine accessory seems to be issuing a challenge to him. An alcove, fringed by Christmas fairy lights, leads through to a small terracotta-tiled kitchen.

— Nice place, Lennox observes.

Robyn tells him that she's been here for a year. She'd come from south Alabama and moved over to Jacksonville with her daughter (it sounds like 'daw-rah' to his ears) in search of work. After that dried up she'd headed further south, first to Surfside where she'd briefly worked in a residential home, and then down here. She explains that the rent's cheap and it was convenient for her job in a daycare centre. — But I had to stop working there, she says guiltily, — to spend more time with my daughter.

— How old is she?

— Ten. She flushes with pride, then departs to check on the kid.

Lennox catches Starry regarding her exiting friend with a primal malevolence so poisonous she's briefly flustered that he's noticed. Defensively, she tips back her head, pushing out her mouth with its lipstick gleam.

Robyn returns, closing the lounge door behind her. — Fast asleep, she announces with relief. She tells him there have been problems at the school with the daughter. Most of the kids talked Spanish at home and in the schoolyard, so Tianna, that's the girl's name, feels isolated. — She's gotten so withdrawn lately, Robyn says sadly, then catches Starry's disapproving scowl and quickly switches into breezy mode, — but hey, this is a party. Right?

— Right, Lennox acknowledges, slumping on to the couch, his eye falling on a dark stain on the hardwood floor spilling out from under the rug. About to comment, he hastily corrects himself. It *was* a party, and he was on holiday. Murder investigating, no. Wedding planning, no. Holiday, yes.

Starry shoots another contemptuous glance towards Robyn, who turns from Lennox to the CD player. He tracks her to avoid Starry's rapacious gaze, but the thin, distressed back of Robyn's neck perversely reminds him of his father's on their last meeting. She inserts a disc and as cheesy pop sounds fill the air, stands up and pulls him to his feet. The music is bland, drenching the room in spineless reworkings of rock 'n' roll classics, forcing Lennox to think of his old mate Robbo, a soft-rock aficionado, supermarkets, and what Americans call elevators.

Robyn steps into him, and as they dance close, he feels the sewer ebbing from her mind; him suffocating under the confining cloak of sleaze she's draped around them. In an automated manner he responds to her tight mouth as it bites on his numb lips, the cocaine rendering the tobacco smoke from her breath just about bearable. Her eyes are as glassy and dead as Marjorie's, his big sister Jackie's favourite doll. Lennox recalls 'loving' and 'wanting to marry' Marjorie as a small child, coveting the toy at least as much as his bossy sibling did.

He'd told Trudi this story once. — You like women to be passive toys, she'd snorted uncharitably, before climbing on top of him and riding him raw.

Trudi. He can't allow himself to be stupefied by Robyn's kisses. Catching Starry's eye and a nod to the coffee table, he breaks away and moves over to where some lines are racked up. She has set down the copy of *Perfect Bride*; it has melded into a pageant of women's, television and celebrity magazines. Lennox picks up a thick glossy called *Ocean Drive*, which he suspects is a boutique-hotel freebie. A blonde woman who seemed to be famous for being an heiress and also for not really appearing to enjoy it much as her boyfriend fucked her on camera, was discussing her music, and how it was the thing she did best. Lennox recalls watching the commercially available video at a police stag do. It wasn't up to much; he hoped the singing was better.

He rolls a note and fills his nostrils, using the generous cavity. The surf comes up inside his head. It's good gear. He looks up at Robyn, who's smiling at him. — How's your voice? Can you carry a tune? he asks.

— Ah guess. She coyly cocks her head, provoking both attraction and nausea in him.

He heads to the bathroom, this time watching his urine, so thick you could stand a spoon in it, stain the water a deep orangey gold. Alone, his critical faculties replace his social ones. Now good intentions and weak wills are signalled everywhere: a dust-covered empty bottle of mouthwash has obviously lain there for months.

An unopened tube of sealant sits next to a leaking shower trickling into a puddle of water on the terracotta floor tiles. A rusted gold-top battery hangs out the back of a broken electric ladyshave.

When he returns he sees Robyn seated and his eyes go up her thighs and between her legs. She catches his line of vision and settles back on the couch, smoothing short skirt to thigh in a parody of demure.

She's a damage case: little-girl voice and vacuous flirtiness. A pathetic victim. Her kid will probably turn out the same way. But I have to watch myself on the gear: I'd fuck the hole in a dolphin's heid.

Starry has set up the drinks; Millers all round with vodkas and Pepsi, and she's racking out more lines of cocaine on the coffee table. More is good: first law of consumer capitalism. Second law: immediate is all. Lennox feels a binge coming on. Starry catches the hunger in his eyes. — Go on, Scattie, her manner is coquettish. He thinks of Braveheart the dog, and is about to test the more constricted vent, when a young girl wearing a nightdress appears in the doorway of the room.

Her skin is a tawny contrast to the paleness of her mother, yet the girl still cuts an almost spectral figure. Brown hair hangs down the sides of a longish face on to her shoulders. She rubs sleep from her eyes in a very obvious, theatrical manner. Shamed, Lennox immediately ceases his activity, and stands up. — Hi. I'm Ray, he says, getting between the kid and the stuff on the table.

— Tianna Marie Hinton . . . you get back to bed, young lady, this is grown-up time, Robyn declares in a panicky voice he can envisage one of the women on the South Beach real-estate commercials privately deploying, perhaps after hearing of a market slump. All the time she looks at Lennox with a stupidity teetering between sheepish and bovine. The kid briefly glances at him for the first time. It's a cold look. Appraising rather than judging, but referencing that he's something she's seen before. Something not good.

It dawns on Lennox that she's been alone while they were cavorting at the Club Deuce and Myopia over in Miami Beach. It wasn't right. *Kids shouldn't be left alone like that. Britney Hamil should never have walked to school alone.* He feels anger rise in him and fights to swallow it down with a gulp of his beer. All the time he keeps his frame between the girl and the table. As she's distracted by her mother's ministrations, Lennox places the copy of *Perfect Bride* over the white stripes. Catches Starry sneering at Robyn again.

— I couldn't sleep, the girl says, — I heard you guys comin in. She looks at Lennox again and nudges her mother, seeking confirmation.

— This here's Ray, honey. Ray's a friend from Skatlin.

— Where men wear skirts, Starry laughs, — right, Ray?

— Right. Lennox practically ignores her, focusing again on the young girl. Her arms and legs are too long for her body. Her hair is a scraggy mop and she seems all angles. A kind of ungainly ugly duckling. But her eyes . . . he catches the brief glimpse of a terrible knowledge in her eyes. For a second Lennox has a sinking sense that they are asking the world for help. Then it's gone, and she's another tired kid, short-changed on affection, security and sleep.

—Y'all get yourself off to bed now, y'hear, honey, Robyn says.

The girl lopes away mumbling and waving a cursory goodbye without turning round. As she leaves the room, Starry changes the CD and turns up the volume as Cuban music fills the air. Lennox's knowledge of this genre starts and stops at the *Buena Vista Social Club*, which he'd seen with Trudi, who had bought him the CD. He'd liked it, though he had been embarrassed when Ally Notman, the energetic young cop on his team with a penchant for womanising, had spied it and slagged him off for being a *Guardian*-reading liberal. Some of the boys had come back to his place for a late drink. He recollects the cold-eyed presence of Dougie Gillman, his sour and troubling nemesis, who'd tagged along all night. But this music is nothing like that. With its poignant beats, sweeping strings and muted brass, it's the saddest he's ever heard. Although with Spanish vocals and purporting to be Cuban, it somehow feels as if it's been made locally, in this Miami neighbourhood. He stifles the temptation to enquire about the artist; he would be relieved never to hear its terrible beauty again.

Fitfully he wonders about Trudi. What will she be doing now? In the hotel room. Indulging in one of her two bathetic responses:

'worried sick' or 'not giving a fuck'. Perhaps occupying both states simultaneously.

— This is fucked, Lennox whispers, bouncing down on the couch in melancholy laughter before Starry shimmies over and drags him back to his feet. They dance together a little, before Robyn moves in. The women are being sexy. Lennox thinks speculatively about threesomes. Isn't that what he needs to feel his masculinity again: *extremis*? It worked last time job and drug had combined to cauterise his body and soul. But a nasty current now hangs between Starry and Robyn. They are harshly and nakedly competing for him. Grinding closer, suggestive eyes expanding with need, their mouths tight with aggression. He thinks about yesterday at the Torpedo. He feels Robyn move into him, her arms reaching up around his neck. Hanging from him like a charity-shop suit in a reckless bid to shut Starry out.

Then the doorbell buzzes and while he's aware that more people have appeared, Lennox feels his nostrils, even as they bubble with snot, filling up with the scent of Robyn's hair. The buzz of the coke works in a square throb with the beat, booze and jet lag. A wave of exhaustion, almost breathtaking, hits the back of his eyes. Letting them close for either seconds or minutes, he watches the exploding purple blotches swirl around the universe inside his head.

Then he feels Robyn pull away from him. He opens his eyes to be confronted by a lined ashen face, with short grey hair plastered back over the scalp; gelled and spiked enough to see comb lines. It belongs to a thin white man, yet who looks wiry and strong, and his ophidian eyes burn Lennox, and, he notes, Robyn too. The proximity moves him to take a backward step. Then he sees a denim shirt *tucked into* jeans of the same material. Looks down at brilliant white trainers, or, on this side of the loch, sneakers. Curtly nodding at Lennox with a smile so slight it would have needed a moving camera to record it, the newcomer then says to Robyn in a low-fi country accent, — You been out shoppin again?

— This here's Ray, Robyn replies apologetically. Already Lennox scents not only history, but unfinished business.

81

— Name's Lance, Lance Dearing. Pleasure to meet ya, Ray, he grins, extending his hand. Lennox strategically takes it in his good left, despite the awkwardness, relieved he's presented that one due to the power he feels in the grip enclosing it. — Busted a mitt there? Dearing asks, nodding to his dangling right.

— Industrial accident, Lennox boldly retorts.

But Lance Dearing can evidently read the trepidation on his face, as he calmly says, — Don' you worry none, Ray; you ain't stepping on no toes here. We all been round the block enough times to know to take our pleasures where we find em. No questions asked. Ain't that right, gals?

Starry's pearly teeth flash, her brows arching like a corporate fast-food executive who has sold face as well as soul to the company store. Robyn smiles weakly, dutifully pouring some drinks for Lance and another man present. He's squat and stocky, Latino, with collar-length, oily hair and a sandpaper chin. His gaze at Lennox is one of undisguised hostility. — This here's Johnnie, Lance smiles.

— You gotta be the guy from outta town, Johnnie says in a scratchy voice, looking Lennox up and down. His head seems way too big for the features squashed ungenerously into the middle of it. Age, Lennox senses, will enhance this effect, like a ratchet inside his brain will screw the top and sides of his skull and his jawbone outwards to the compass points. The big slaughterman's hands look formidable; along with the dense body and shifty eyes, they suggest a man prepared to take what he wants without expecting much in the way of debate. This notion is countered by a flabby gut straining at a T-shirt bearing the slogan: WILL FUCK FOR COKE.

— I don't think he's the same guy you're thinking of, Johnnie. Lance grins at Lennox. — But I do hear you're in sales.

Fucking sales, Lennox thinks. What is this? — Yeah.

— Me too, Lance smiles, eliciting a giggle from Starry.

— But I guess that this fella ain't the same type of salesman as you, Johnnie laughs.

— I guess he probably ain't, Lance Dearing says in mock sorrow. — But then again, I reckon that there might just be two types of salesmen: good and bad. Ain't that right, Ray?

Lennox remains silent, Starry's capricious g.
was them she had talked with on the phone ea
ence is certainly a surprise to Robyn, and not, it se
one. Lennox moves away, sits down on the settee. Sile
the best way, he has found, in such situations.

His eyes scan around the room, seeming always to
back at Robyn's legs, hips or arse. He's aware that he wa   to
fuck her, but considers, shamefully, this is probably just because
the opportunity has receded with Lance and Johnnie's presence.
But now anyone will do. Something has gone off behind his cock.

Instead, he chops out another line from the big rock in a larger
packet Starry has placed on the table, all the time on edge against
the kid reappearing, and he takes it down. He looks at the print
of a semi-nude woman on the wall. Then he considers Johnnie
and Lance again. The concern he felt at their intrusion has gone.
His fear evaporating, he fancies it kicking off. Now all that's inside
him is a black anger, still and even. He's not thinking of Britney
Hamil any more but he knows that when he does, he can kill
anyone for her demise.

And he feels like killing. Just hurting would be insufficient. His
dark mood creeps through his veins like a poison. He knows those
faces: Dearing's mocking reptilian smile, Johnnie's pudgy, vacant
stare. If only those men knew the danger they were in. He grinds
his teeth till he imagines he hears the enamel crack. But he is a
cop. Abroad. *Calm the fuck down.*

So he goes to the kitchen and gets another beer from the fridge.
Dull those coke rushes. Robyn follows him. He wants to fuck her
and kill the rest of them. Even Starry. Especially Starry. Something
about her has disturbed him. That protean presence: one minute
sexy, the next malign and controlling. She changed when those guys
came in. He could feel it. See it in her eyes. Maybe it was just the
coke. It was good stuff. Not too chemical. Maybe it was because
he was doing all her gear. He wonders about offering her some
cash. Feels a wad of twenties in his pocket.

He can't think laterally. His thought pattern is linear, like a
high-speed locomotive, careering towards one destination.

All he can do to stop this is to take some more coke. It helps.

You can outrun your thoughts. He heads back into the living room, Robyn still pursuing him, ranting something about star signs, and he lifts up the copy of *Perfect Bride*. The lines he'd hidden from the kid are intact. Starry moves over and augments them for Lance and Johnnie. They are nothing now, the other three, no threat, just a source of drugs. A defiant sense of entitlement fuses him. *On holiday. Prudey Trudi.* Starry has another big bag of the stuff. A big rock. It might be a long night. A long, long night that lasts half an hour. They take another line each. Lennox needs the drug now more than ever. He recalls how they would sit near the toilet in the Grapes, the young coppers' bar, or up in somebody's flat, often his, snorting and boasting of how they had put away this cunt and threatened that cunt and done this cunt and would get that bastard. The real vitriol was not reserved for the criminals though, but the bosses: senior police officials, local and national politicians. It was these spastics that fucked everything up, that *fucked up the job.*

Lennox has done what he refers to as 'the rehab thing', and still goes to regular NA meetings. He knows how the drug presses you like a wild flower into something resembling yourself but a one-dimensional representation of it. Jagged and volatile, all sneers and jeers pushing back your boundaries of verbal and physical and sexual violence.

That lassie in Thailand; she was just a fucking kid.

The lads' holiday in Bangkok. The girls were very young, but you could never tell with Asian lassies — so slender and petite. And, after all, we were on holiday. Drunk in that Patpong bar, the Thai girl with the dyed blonde hair who'd sat on my lap. Notman drunkenly whispering, — *If you want tae ken the colour ay a bird's minge, look at her eyebrows, no her hair.*

Would upright George Marsden with the pressed blazer have behaved like us? Or would he have behaved like cops were supposed to behave? And how were law enforcement officers meant to behave off duty? Work together. Play together.

Then I saw the one with Gillman: she was just a kid. I told him to leave her. — *She's fuckin peyed fir, so she's gittin it, he said. I was drunk. We argued. I pushed the blonde away. Pulled the other one, the kid, off*

Gillman's lap. He got to his feet. Then his head was in my face and I was on the deck, before being helped into a taxi by Notman. Waited ages at the Bangkok hospital to get my nose badly reset. Later on I heard that he'd taken my half-arsed intervention out on the girl. She was just a kid. Once a girl, then made like Britney was, reduced . . .

You have to stop thought.

The line goes up his nose. Britney's face dissolves, becomes the attractively sluttish woman opposite him.

Robyn. The cloying, irritating girlish voice somehow grows sexy. A Southern belle: Scarlett O'Hara to his Rhett Butler. *Way down in Alabama.* Milky tones enquiring, — Y'all wanna go lie down for a while, honey?

And Lennox knows that even feeling like fucking the world, it will take extremity, violent, perverse extremity, to make his floppy penis anything like hard enough to do the job. — In a bit, he says, charging his glass with the bottle of vodka. He feels trapped, in a skanky vortex of his own making.

Lance Dearing has swooped down to rant at him. Ostensibly telling him about fishing, but Lennox knows the charged power of words on cocaine and that Dearing is trying to establish presence, power and dominance. — Pulled a big ol bastard out of the sea yesterday. Took a while and I thought he'd bust the line at one point, but I stayed on his ass. That was the thing: I stayed on his ass. Sucker was goin nowhere once he bit on my hook.

So Ray Lennox kicks back with a skinny smile on his lips and gives monosyllabic answers. As he looks into this man's leathery face, watches the spittle shoot from the corner of his mouth, he feels nothing now; he neither likes nor dislikes Lance. How can he? They are strangers, on cocaine. Grinding their teeth. Obstacles for each other to navigate: Formula One drivers trying to go round traffic cones at high speed. They rant in short bursts at each other in an ugly intimacy, each exposing the same raw nerve of ego to the other. Then Lance gets up to dance with Robyn, who obviously fears him, and a smiling Starry, as Lennox considers his lot.

He can't marry Trudi. If they were ever going to get married then they would have been by now. He met her when she was eighteen and he was twenty-seven. Eight years ago. He'd just got his second big promotion. Detective Inspector Lennox. He'd be the youngest Chief Constable in Scotland, they'd only half joked. But after that, nothing. Treading water. Snorting more cocaine. Then Trudi and him had split up.

Three years later, though, they started going together again. He had come back from Thailand and was cleaning up, going to NA, and was back at the kick-boxing. They met at a new gym he was trying out. Unbeknown to him, she was a member. A coffee. Catching up. Both free agents. The spark. Still there. Catching up. Dinner. A film. Coffee. Bed. Catching up. The sex; it was better than before. Trudi: now a sleek, confident mid-twenties gym rat rather than a slightly pudgy teenager. Him: a sober shagging machine; the carnal obsession dominating everything. Shrugging aside the words of several guys on the force: reheated cabbage. Beware. Bad move.

But she loved him. She loved him because he was a lost cause and her own vanity was strong enough to convince her that with her brand of tough love, Ray Lennox, *Project Lennox*, could be successfully realised. He could become a superannuated superman, a breeder of good Scottish Protestant children who would excel not just academically but at the BBs and school sports, and be model citizens of the world as the Scots always were. Or at least the ones designated for export.

Trudi saw how he'd changed. Matured, was the term she frequently used. The first time she'd touched him again was to run her finger down his nose. — It's bent a little, she'd said.

— Accident in Thailand. Broke it, he'd explained, looking into her eyes. — That was what made me give up the gear. I realised what it was doing. What I'd lost.

She liked what she saw.

But she'd seen what she'd wanted to see. He was a mess. Affecting a seen-it-all blasé front, when his insides were like chopped liver. Cool Lennox with the shredded nerves. His old associate Robbo always saw through him.

Sometimes punching and kicking the bags helped. Sparring with the gloves. Building up the strength, speed and confidence that came with it. Earning the swagger, knowing other men sensed that it wasn't empty, that there was something behind it. Sometimes, though, when something really bad happened, only talk helped. But in Edinburgh you only talked in drink and cocaine helped you drink and talk longer. The Britney Hamil case was that something bad. Soon he was struggling at NA, scrambling and sweating half-heartedly at the gym. Every time he flipped through the register with all those nonce faces to deal with he wanted coke more than ever.

— C'mon, honey, Robyn says, cutting to the chase in frustration, — I wanna fuck, her savage desperation reminding him of the stripper in Fort Lauderdale, or Trudi, even. — Does that sound so bad? So selfish?

Lennox thinks: *aye it does, ya fuckin hing-oot, your wee lassie's in the next room.* — No. But I don't want to shag you. I mean, he stalls, grimly savouring the power of rejection for a beat, — I can't, I've had too much coke.

Robyn steals a fearful glance at Lance and Starry, locked in a flirtatious Latin dance. With their swampy grimaces and scornful whispers, they seem to be conspiring to destroy them both. Meanwhile, Johnnie sits in the armchair, broody and splenetic, his eyes bulleting out bad vibes. Lennox looks at Robyn's shrunken, haunted face. — Let's just go next door and lie down a little, she whispers in an undisguised plea. — I need to be with someone, Ray. I'm fucked, my life's going to shit. I don't know what I'm going to do. If it wasn't for Tianna . . . she's the only good thing I've done in my goddamn miserable fucked-up life . . .

She hasn't realised that her voice has picked up and that the others have been listening to the exchange. — That sounds like real fun, Starry mocks, — A professional victim and a guy who can't fuck her!

— You lil' sweet-talker, you, Lance rolls his eyes and Johnnie laughs heartily. It's now officially a house divided.

— Why, Robyn squeals as she tugs Lennox on his bad hand, compelling him to follow her to the door, — do people have to be mean like that? Why?! It's *fuck*ing cruel!

— Oh spare us, Starry snaps in disdain. Lennox hears her laugh, — She'll be back when she needs more blow.

— I reckon 'bout twenty minutes from now, Lance adds, in sagely mocking tones.

Lennox finds himself being led away from the bag of coke, the source of his power. How we love what kills us. He is still everywhere but where it matters as Robyn drags him on to the bed, her skirt ridden up, revealing a flesh-coloured thong emblazoned with the slogan: I HAVE THE PUSSY, I MAKE THE RULES.

She tears this garment to the side, exposing a thick tuft of pubic hair like a punk mohawk, and kisses him on the mouth. He catches the dirty, foul stale tobacco on her breath, feels his own jaw clamping. Robyn pulls away from his tight, unyielding lips, and lies back on the bed. By the light he sees her jawbone sink into her face, melting into the obscene bloated flesh of her neck that seems to have appeared from nowhere, making him think of that exotic frog with its shocking instantaneous expanse of throat. Lennox is frozen, an insect in the proximity of those hypnotic, bulging eyes. So she springs back up and she's on him, unzipping him, her hand inside his trousers and pants, her urgent fingers asking the same question repeatedly, without getting the reply they crave.

A yawn of exhaustion bubbles up through the cocaine rushes. Lennox tries to stifle it but it tears free from his face, almost sending his jaw into a spasm. He can hear Robyn panting desperately, — Sexy . . . sexy boy . . .

It's probably not that long after midnight, yet he can sense the next morning's dawn spinning relentlessly over him from space.

A glance at Robyn reveals her eyes still protruding like a mad scientist's. — I can get you going, Ray. I know what you guys like!

She lurches over to the bedside locker and produces a pair of fur-lined handcuffs from a drawer. — We can do anything you want. You wanna fasten me to the bed? You can do anything you wa—

Robyn is cut short as a terrified shriek fills the air. It doesn't stop. Lennox's first thought is that it sounds like a child. Then both he and Robyn realise it's her daughter. She's screaming. Lennox zips up and runs towards the noise, with Robyn following.

He pushes the door of the kid's bedroom open. Johnnie is in there, on top of the struggling child, trying to get his hand over her mouth. The covers are pulled back and his other hand is inside her nightdress.

Lennox bounds over and grabs his lank hair in both hands, his weakened grip first struggling to fasten with the grease in Johnnie's hair, then feeling the sting of pain in his bad hand, as he yanks him off both the girl and the bed. Johnnie screams out, his cries joining Tianna's regular car-alarm shrieks, as Lennox pulls him along the floor, laying into him with his feet.

Then Lennox feels his left arm being twisted up his back, followed by a blinding, searing pain that spreads out from his shoulder to bruise his soul with sickness. His heel swings back and cracks into a kneecap and the grip weakens. Lennox tears free and is face to face with a grimacing, limping Lance Dearing. — Enough now! he warns, pushing Lennox's chest, jostling him back into the lounge as Lennox shakes his arm, trying to get some feeling back into it. He turns side-on, putting his weight behind his shoulder, to lock in and stand his ground, his arm, still useless, dangling in front of him. — Get that cunt out of her fucking bedroom! he shouts, and he can hear the girl crying and her mother and Starry arguing hysterically as he springs forward, pushing past Lance Dearing. Dearing grabs him, attempting the armlock again, but Lennox knows what's coming and the feeling is surging back into his left arm. He slips Lance's grip and they wrestle, staggering forward, crashing through the glass coffee table.

— My fuckin stash . . . Starry shouts as the coke and broken glass spill into the rug and on to the wooden floor.

Both men, miraculously uncut, stumble to their feet. Lennox is up first, running back into the bedroom. He smacks Johnnie in the side of the jaw with a right hook, which burns his damaged knuckle. Robyn is pursuing Starry, shouting, and catching a plea on the face of the screaming girl, Lennox takes her by the hand, running into the bathroom and locking the door behind them.

— Keep them away from me! the girl, Tianna, howls at him, sitting cowed on the toilet seat, gripping her hair in balled fists.

— It's okay, doll, it's okay, Lennox coos as his right hand throbs

89

and his left arm stings, — everybody's just had too much to drink. Nobody's gaunny hurt you.

— He tried to . . . I told him to lemme alone! Why won't they lemme alone!?

— S'okay . . . Lennox tries to deploy soothing tones as he can hear the arguments raging outside; Robyn's shrill hysteria, Starry's bullying sneer. Then Lance Dearing's voice from behind the door, cool and authoritative: — We all gotta calm down. You come outta there now.

— No! Tianna screams.

— Tia, honey, Robyn bleats.

Lennox puts his face up to the door and shouts through: — Listen, youse, get that fat fucker out of here. I'm telling youse, now!

Perhaps the odds with the both of them and that psycho Starry are a little too steep. And he doesn't want the kid to see any more of this. He's keeping the door locked.

Tianna looks at this man who is protecting her. Perhaps, though, he's just like the rest. Wants to do something bad with her. He was full of that crazy powder they all took. She turns away, and looks at the plastic parrot sitting on the tiled window ledge. The one she got from Parrot World, with Chet and Amy. If only they were on the boat now, away from this terrible place.

From the snakepit outside Lennox hears Johnnie dumbly protest something that sounds like, — I just like the taste of young pussy.

— GET HIM THE FUCK OOT! he roars against the door, briefly looking back at the girl sat on the toilet.

Then Dearing's voice again: calm, conciliatory, in control. — Okay, okay. We do it your way, Ray. We do it your way. We all got a lil' carried way on the silly stuff. Don't wanna make things worse. Johnnie's on his way out. I'm taking him away and I'm gonna get the girls some coffee round at the twenty-four-hour diner. Jus takin a lil' bitty time out to let us all simmer down. Y'all hear?

— Aye. Get him out.

Some negotiations and the front door slams. Outside: sounds of multiple feet on the steps of the tiled staircase.

Lennox is aware that his heart is thrashing in his chest. He sits on the edge of the bath. The girl, trembling on the toilet, weeps soft and wretched. *A kid shouldn't have to put up with all this shit.* — You okay?

She nods miserably, pinched features just visible through strands of hair.

— Did he hurt you?

Tianna tersely shakes her head, obviously in shock, he reckons.

She lets her hair fall in front of her face, watches him from behind its shield. He has those crazy eyes that they all have. It might be the liquor and drugs. But he looks strong: maybe even as strong as the likes of Johnnie or Tiger.

They wait for a while. He is almost convinced that everyone has gone, but he suddenly hears a cupboard door slam, then a solitary set of steps followed by the front door closing.

Lennox cagily opens the bathroom door. As he goes out he hears it snib shut behind him. He looks around the apartment. — Nobody's here. They've all gone, he tells her. After a couple of minutes, she warily emerges from the bathroom. — Your mum'll be back soon, go to bed. Go on, he urges, — I won't let anybody else back in the house. Only your mum.

— You promise? Only Momma?

— Yes, Lennox insists. — Please, go to bed.

As she heads tentatively for her bedroom, Lennox goes through to the front room and tries to tidy up the broken glass. *Perfect Bride* lies amid the wreckage, the saccharine smile on the white bride of the cover picture now spectacularly incongruent in the surroundings. Starry has obviously undertaken a salvage job on the coke but there is still evidence of some on the rug. For a second he considers trying to hoover it up through a dollar bill, but then he kicks and stomps it into the tread with his boot.

Lennox goes to the hall, bolting the front door shut. Anybody who wants in, they'll have to get past him first. Back in the lounge, he sees the couch and, drained, gratefully slumps on to it.

7

Edinburgh (2)

Despite your exhaustion, you tiptoed out of your Leith flat that Friday morning like a novice burglar, guilt-laden at having expropriated a few hours' sleep. Outside it was taut and crisp with the October leaves turning brown, and you stopped off for a double espresso at the Stockbridge Deli, knocking it back before crossing the road and heading for Police HQ. The police personnel called it Fettes, but for the general populace, it never really wrested that mantle from the old private school across the road. As birds chirped in the growing light that spread thinly across the grey pavements, you thought how that little section of Edinburgh defined not just the city, but the UK in general. The grand educational institution for the wealthy, standing over Police HQ, as if supervising its own elevated observation of Broughton, the state comprehensive for the masses.

Britney Hamil had been missing for two days, but it took the staff at Forbidden Planet bookstore on the South Bridge just five minutes to shatter Gary Forbes's Britain's Most Evil Man fantasies. They testified to Amanda Drummond that he was browsing in there, as he did almost every day, when Britney vanished. He was, as you predicted, charged with wasting police time after dragging two uniformed officers around some woods in Perthshire for half the evening.

Ronnie Hamil was a different matter. Still nothing was reported from the observation of his Dalry flat. Locals testified to his erratic wanderings, and a consensus emerged that he was a gruff, dirty-looking character who lived a marginal life and habitually stank of baccy and booze. You knew he'd surface soon, was probably holed up drunk somewhere, and you hoped beyond your expectation that it would be with his granddaughter: alive and well.

Britney's disappearance hit the national media. In the small, claustrophobic room the investigation team shared, a siege mentality was kicking in as tight faces gaped at Angela Hamil on Sky News, making a tranquillised but emotional plea for her daughter's safe return. Gary Forbes was always a non-starter but your team's disappointment was still evident. With the possible exception of Amanda Drummond, they looked at you like a bunch of heavy drinkers are wont to when one of their posse orders an orange juice. They had blood around their mouths. They weren't going to stop feeding. You couldn't tell a pride of hungry lions that they had just brought down the wrong zebra. You'd never been in such close proximity to Gillman since the Thailand holiday. Found your fingers tapping your nose nervously on a few occasions.

But the man everyone wanted remained undetected. Accompanied by Amanda Drummond, you'd gone to visit Angela Hamil. Desperation, and your guilt at being less than enthusiastic about the obvious candidate, compelled you to play hardball. You sat on Angela's worn couch, a cracked mug of milky tea in your hand. — Your dad's unemployed and you work all day. But he never helps you out with the kids?

In response to your promptings, Angela had lowered her tired, shadowed eyes. — He's no good with kids, she mumbled, taking another comforting pull on her cigarette, then stubbing it out.

Her passive resignation irritated you, and you really had to fight not to show it. — Why don't you trust your father to help out with the girls?

Angela's breaths were short and tight as she lit up another cigarette; it was as if she feared that taking air into her lungs unaccompanied by tobacco smoke might just prove fatal. You could see her one day forgetting to have cigarettes on her and dropping dead through a seizure in the street, on her way to the corner shop. — He's nae good at that sort of thing, she croaked.

— You'd think he'd be able to take them for a few hours, you'd pushed, briefly glancing at Drummond, her eyes saucer-like. — To help you out.

— Ma sister Cathy helps . . . he sometimes comes round . . .

Angela Hamil fretted. She was not a good liar. Amanda Drummond looked sympathetically at her.

Your demands grew harsher. — Aye? When was the last time?

— I don't know. I cannae remember!

You sucked down hard, trying to find some oxygen amid the fumes around you. — I'm going to be blunt with you, Angela. I'm doing this because your daughter is missing, and your father hasn't been seen for a few days. Do you understand me?

The woman cooked in the silence that hung in the air. The hand holding her slow-burning cigarette went into a spasm.

— Do you understand me?

Angela Hamil nodded slowly at you, then Drummond.

— Has your father ever given you cause to believe that he'd behave inappropriately towards the girls? A brief pause. — Did he behave like that towards you when you were growing up, you'd added evenly, scrutinising the terrible stillness of the woman. Felt her crumbling slowly inside. — Please answer me, you pursued in a low voice, like a dog almost ready to break into a growl, — your daughter's life could be at stake.

— Aye . . . she gasped breathlessly. — Aye, aye, aye, he did. I've never telt anybody before . . . Her cheeks buckled inwards under a massive inhalation of the cigarette. You could scarcely believe the speed at which it had burned down. She crushed the butt into a blue pub ashtray and lit another. Panic fastened to the surface of her sallow skin. You watched her wilt under its onslaught. —You dinnae think – and she broke down, — him and Britney . . . no Britney . . . no . . . and Drummond slid across on to the couch and put her arm round the woman's thin shoulders. — If he's touched her, her creased face threatened, — when ah git ma hands on him . . .

Those empty, impotent threats, you'd scornfully thought. — I know this is distressing. Amanda, will you stay with Angela? You nodded, but your sly wink at Drummond added: find out what you can.

You had no inclination whatsoever for the details. You headed outside, calling Bob Toal. The boss was right, you were wrong. Ronnie Hamil was a nonce, and your hunt was now solely for him, forsaking all others. You dug out as much CCTV footage as you could find covering the Dalry area for the last few days, working forwards and backwards from the time of Britney's disappearance. This time the difficulty lay in the abundance of material; Ronnie's home was close to Tynecastle Stadium and there were cameras galore in the vicinity. Trying to identify an image of the grandfather from the crowds of football supporters, shoppers and drinkers was like looking for a polystyrene bead on a glacier.

What about the rest of your life? There was Trudi. Back in the office, you opened a locked drawer and pulled out the sparkly engagement ring that had lain there for around four months. There had never seemed to be a right time. Perhaps, you'd thought, it was best to do it at the wrong time, give you a lift you so badly needed. As you sat looking at the diamond, allowing it to mesmerise you, Dougie Gillman poked his head around your office door. — Nae sign ay Gary Glitter yet?

— Nope. Slowly shutting the ring box and placing it on the desk, lowering your head to your paperwork, you could feel Gillman's eyes still on you for a few cold pulses before you heard him withdraw. The African violet seemed to have withered further. You put the box in your pocket, furious at Gillman's intervention.

After a brain-bruising but fruitless shift, you went to the pub and had your first drink in a long time. The second compelled you to leave your car at Fettes and take a taxi to Trudi's. On the way up, a radio station was broadcasting a tepid debate on what should be done to commemorate the tricentennial anniversary of the 1707 union of Scotland and England, some eighteen months away. Nobody seemed to know nor care. Your attention was diverted as you caught sight of Jock Allardyce walking up Lothian Road, and for a second you thought he'd seen your wave, but you were obviously mistaken as he gave no acknowledgement.

When you got to Trudi's you found her busy with a work report, about a restructuring in her section. She was telling you about it and you weren't listening. — What is it, Ray? she'd asked. — What are you thinking about? She looked at you in sharper focus. — Have you been drinking?

— Yes, you'd said, with a smile on your face.

— But the NA . . . Keith Goodwin . . .

— I've had something on my mind.

— The job? This case with the wee girl?

Emotion drowned you as you looked at her. — I was thinking that we should get married.

And then you'd crawled across the floor on your knees and buried your head in her lap, taken out the ring and looked up and asked her. She had said yes and later you'd gone to bed and made love most of the night. It's bizarre for you to think that that was the last time.

Because when you woke up on Saturday morning Britney had been gone, without trace, for three whole days. The realisation deflated you. It got worse as Trudi paced the living room, talking into her mobile phone, shrieking with excitement as she broke the news to her friends. You could have done without her saying, — I've booked Obelisk for Sunday. Just me, you, our mums and dads, Jackie and Angus and Stuart and whoever . . .

She caught your frozen expression.

— I couldn't get anywhere decent on a Saturday night at such short notice!

— It's no that . . . could we maybe no just keep it a bit low-key for a while . . . ?

— We have to let them know, Ray. It's family, Trudi insisted as she silenced you with a kiss, — this is meant to be a happy occasion! I've called everybody, and I think they know what's up! Then she declared, — All you need to do is show up at eight o'clock tomorrow, and be nice!

— Okay.

Then a call from Notman came in on your mobile. — Ronnie Hamil's just shown up at his flat. He looks fucked. Will I bring him in?

— No. I'm just up in Bruntsfield, I'll meet you there in ten minutes. I want to check out his doss.

Trudi's pleading gaze, trying to paint in your cold, white spaces.

— Sorry, babe, but I think we've just got the fucker, you said, and recalling you'd left the car at Fettes, had to ask her for the keys to her Escort.

Notman was waiting for you in a blue van outside the block of flats. Ronnie Hamil's place was a top-floor dwelling in a tenement building that had miraculously escaped the renovations of the area that had been ongoing for the best part of thirty years. Rubbish-strewn and with its poor lighting and worn stairs, it seemed, like the grandad, to be a remnant of the seventies.

Two firm knocks brought Ronnie Hamil to the door. He was a shabby, furtive, accordion-faced wee man, his black and yellow teeth exposed in a knowing leer. With his attendant bronchitic wheeze, he seemed central casting's identikit Minging Old Pervert. You thought of Angela, how his nicotine-stained fingers had violated her as a child. But was he now, you wondered, responsible for the fact that her own similarly marked hands only tucked in one of her kids at night?

— Police, you said, almost gagging on the word; when you stepped into the apartment, you and Notman physically recoiled under the impact of a vile stench, your eyes burning. Amazingly, Ronnie Hamil apparently didn't notice as he invited you in to take a seat in the lounge.

You found a battered armchair, pushing aside some old newspapers to make room for yourself. You'd never seen so many: in neat stacks and unruly piles, strewn over the floor and furniture, some yellow with what you hoped was age. All seemed to be copies of the *Daily Record* and the *Edinburgh Evening News*. It was a fire trap, you considered, but you had more crucial matters to concern yourself with. — Where have you been, Mr Hamil?

— That's ma business.

— No, it's ours. Don't you read the papers? you said without thinking, then looked around the room and raised your eyebrows. Could tell it was only the pungent aroma that was stopping Notman breaking out in laughter.

— An angel, that wee lassie, Ronnie Hamil said sadly. Then enmity filled his eyes. — If ah got muh hands on the bastard –

— Where have you been since Wednesday?

— Went oan a wee tear. The incestuous paedophile allowed a smile to crease his lips. — Dinnae mind much aboot it.

— You're close to the kids? you said, coughing as the smell grew deeper, acquiring greater density, ripening in your nostrils.

— Aye, I'm ey roond for a cup ay tea n a blether.

— But they never come to you?

His face subsided so violently, it was as if an invisible object had struck his jaw. His voice dropped an octave. — No very often.

—What is that? Once a week? Once a year? You'd think you'd want to see more of them, you challenged, looking around in distaste at the old wallpaper, the mess of takeaway cartons and wrappers, but mostly those newspapers. Worst of all, however, that rank, violent odour! You coughed, then found yourself almost retching again. You noted Notman had opened the top buttons on his shirt and his left eye shivered uncontrollably. The aroma was beyond anything that old rubbish, burned food, stale bread and baccy could produce. Something evil was stinking the place out. It was killing you. A terrible thought grabbed you.

—What's aw this aboot? Ronnie Hamil growled, still somehow oblivious to your discomfort and its source.

— You're coming down to the station to help us with our inquiries, Mr Hamil, you said, struggling to effect nonchalance as the pungent odour continued its remorseless, overwhelming assault, filling your mouth. You saw Notman's eyebrows and hackles raise and you were going nowhere until you found out the answer to another question: the origin of a stink that could burn skin. — There's a very strong smell in here, and you rose and started looking around. Your first thoughts were the roof space.

— Aye, ah thought it was comin fae next door . . .

Notman located the source: a dead black kitten, which had electrocuted itself by chewing through a cable running to a
and lay under a pile of newspapers behind the settee. It was c
in what appeared to be rice. At first you thought it h
poisoned by an old carton of Chinese food left out, bu
that the grains were moving. You bent closer: the d
crawling with maggots.

— Emlyn, Ronnie Hamil gushed in genuine heart
that's where ye went, ya daft wee bugger . . . He sank
in front of the animal's decomposing corpse.

98

You beat a hasty exit, making a note to call both the Environmental Health Office and the RSPCA. On the way out crowds were milling around, heading for the stadium. Bundling Ronnie into the back of the van, Notman turned to you and moaned, — Top of the League and we're missing the game thanks tae a fuckin paedo.

You climbed into the van – you would pick up Trudi's car later – letting Notman drive past the asbestos-ridden stand designed by Archibald Leith, the last surviving part of the old stadium. On the field, foreign mercenaries in maroon sandwich boards had replaced local lads. Instead of steep terraces where men roared, drank, fought, hugged and urinated on each other, there were the pink grandstands. The adjacent brewery had shut down, removing the pervasive smell of hops from the area.

Ronnie Hamil provided his own distinctive aroma on the drive down to Fettes HQ, where you carried on the interrogation. On Wednesday morning when Britney vanished, he said he was out for a drink, then took a walk by the canal. No witnesses. All he claimed to remember was waking up this morning on the floor of a drinking acquaintance at Caplaw Court, a tower block of flats in Oxgangs, scheduled for demolition. Again the wagons were forming in a circle. But you had your doubts. The old boy was feeble. Even with the element of surprise, would he be robust enough to overpower Britney so quickly? There was nothing to link the grandfather to what Toal saw as your damaging obsession, the white van. Ronnie Hamil could drive, but he didn't own a vehicle and no record of him recently having rented or borrowed one could be unearthed.

As well as questioning Angela Hamil, you'd got Amanda Drummond to quiz Britney's older sister Tessa. The girl, recovered from her food poisoning, confirmed that they'd been told to avoid their grandad. — Mum says we shouldnae go near him. Says he's no right in the heid.

You and Notman, buoyed by the news Hearts had won two–nil, extending their unbeaten run to eleven games, intensified your interrogation of Ronnie Hamil. As the booze-tainted rivulets streamed down from his face, you had a sense of him dissolving under the overhead strip lights. His vanishing and Angela's confessing to his abuse of her would almost have been enough for Bob Toal, but there was no body. So no charges were brought against the alcoholic rapist of his own child, but he was put under twenty-four-hour surveillance. You wanted him outside, in the hope that he would take you to Britney, or her remains.

Escorting Ronnie Hamil to the front desk, you watched him shamble off into the early-evening darkness, then went back up to your office. Notman poked his head round the door. — Other news, he said glumly, and for a second you had expected to hear of the child's body, — Romanov's just sacked Burley.

You swivelled round in your seat. — You're fucking jokin!

— Naw, it's on Sky.

— But we're top of the League and unbeaten! What the fuck is he playin at?

— Fuck knows.

You were suddenly seething. Your anger wasn't really directed at Hearts although you were moved to gasp, — The fuckin derby next week as well.

Your football club had shot themselves in the foot again, but you felt they could now appoint anybody and it wouldn't matter; the glory days of the late fifties and early sixties weren't coming back. The Glaswegian sides had positioned themselves better, using bigotry to forward their interests, then getting on the right side of consumerism. But they and their fellow-travellers were welcome to it, the hollow glory by proxy. All you craved was to find a child unharmed.

The following day, two Sunday hikers, braving a cold, slashing wind and pinpricking rain, had seen something washed up on the rocks down by a stony inlet in cliffs near Coldingham. They looked down at the naked blue-grey body of a young girl. — It was like a doll, one had said. I couldn't believe it was a child at first.

You'd been at Trudi's Bruntsfield flat when you received the news. On the drive down the A1 you'd felt oddly calm. Then you'd looked at the dead child, the water lapping against her cold skin. — Sorry, sweetheart, you whispered under your breath as you felt your own hands freeze and numb. Part of the job you hated most was talking to the victims of sex offenders. Usually they were female, so departmental procedure and protocol often spared you this ordeal. But this child would never be able to tell you who had done this to her. Cupping your hands in front of your face, you expelled your hot breath into them. Some yards away, Britney's school bag, with its books, had been discarded. As there was no sign of her clothes, it seemed a deliberate rather than careless act, but out of kilter with the rest of the crime.

A helicopter team retrieved the body and they took it back to the morgue. Britney hadn't been dead for more than fourteen hours, but had been gone for over three days. The murderer had strangled her before he'd thrown her off the cliff, hoping the tides would take her out to sea. Divers combed the coast, but nothing else was recovered. Three hours later, around lunchtime on Sunday, Ronnie Hamil was formally charged with the murder of his granddaughter.

It wasn't enough for you. The grandad reeked of old drink, he'd obviously been inebriated for days. Would he have been together enough to do all this? Other than the incongruous discarding of the books, it seemed like the work of a meticulous planner. Some traces of lubricant were present on the body, but no sperm. The murderer had used a condom. There was no blood or anything else to evidence foreign DNA, only some tape marks on her wrists and ankles. Nothing on the girl's body could tie Britney to Ronnie. Some of his prints were found on one of the school books, but so were many others. It was plausible she'd shown it to him when he'd visited last week, as he'd claimed. Instead, it all seemed so much like the Ellis cases.

So you made a call to someone you'd met last year at a training course on the psychological profiling of sex offenders. You recalled him as a tubercular-looking man, with a slouch that indicated a terrible burden, but whose nervous eyes hinted that the invisible escape hatch of impending retirement was in his peripheral vision. Will Thornley was investigating officer on the Stacey Earnshaw case in Manchester. Unlike George Marsden, Will was decidedly a company man. He was off duty and didn't like being interrupted at his gardening. He was so unhelpful that by the end of the call he'd completely convinced you that Ellis had absolutely nothing to do with Stacey's murder.

The celebratory mood at Police HQ left you cold. Thankfully, Gillman wasn't around in Fettes small lounge bar, when Notman had heartily slapped you on the back. — Well, we nailed the bastard, Ray.

— Aye, you'd agreed, — he's certainly that, glad for the first time to be booked in for this family meal with Trudi tonight.

So you left the team to it, first biting the bullet and heading for Bob Toal's office. Your boss offered you a Cuban cigar, which you declined. — I don't like that look, Ray, Toal warned you. — It's happy-camper time.

— Bob, I know this isn't what you want to hear, but I'm duty-bound to tell you about the Hertfordshire and Manchester stuff, as it was part of my investigation.

— Pish on our parade, Ray, go on.

There was a frozen moment of dread between you as your eyes locked. He wanted you to stay silent. So did you. But you spoke. — I'm worried about this Ellis business. It's not safe. It'll blow up.

— So you want to undermine convictions that involve two police forces?

— If they've done the job right then they've nothing to worry about, you said, and even as it left your lips it sounded ridiculous to your ears.

Toal was in no mood to spare you. — I wonder what planet you've been on, Ray. Cause it ain't fucking Earth.

— Ellis's connection to the Earnshaw case is nonsense. It's a total dustbin job. And there's no substantial forensic evidence to tie him to Welwyn.

Toal shook his head so violently his jowls flapped, reminding you briefly of a bloodhound emerging from a river. — Did you hear him on that tape, by that wee lassie's grave? Did ye listen? His eyes bulged. — The things he said he'd done with her?

You squirmed in recollection. — He's a sick bastard, but he didn't kill her. There's nothing to link him to the white van –

— FUCK THE WHITE VAN! Toal bellowed. — Every cowboy in Britain whae's daein a job on the side, or knocking off some tart he shouldnae be, or having a wank at passing schoolies, they've all got white vans! Forget it, Ray! We have our man!

You felt the paranoid tingle of humiliation after this chewing-out. Then, the first person you saw in the corridor was the grinning Gillman.

The Obelisk restaurant was an upscale two-star Michelin joint, dimly lit with copper lamps fixtured on its terracotta walls and placed on the big wooden tables. You weren't in the best of moods when you arrived. Your mother Avril and sister Jackie had just beaten you to it, the maitre d' fussing over their coats. Your mother greeting you in bug-eyed trepidation. — What is it? Everything okay?

— Aye, you'd dismissed her agitation. — All will be revealed.

— This is nice, she offered in relieved concession, swivelling and scanning before presenting her face for a kiss, which you dutifully delivered, with another for your tight-featured sister, who was less easily impressed by the surroundings.

— Angus can't make it, he's at a conference down in London, Jackie informed you. You'd nodded sombrely, just about managing to keep the smile of your face.

Donald and Joanne Lowe were already seated beside their daughter. Trudi was wearing a blue dress you hadn't seen before, and she'd had her hair done. You kissed her, complimented her and winked, then greeted her parents. You liked them both. They were a youthful couple of around fifty, but seeming closer to your age than your folks. Donald was a handsome, fine-featured man with slightly thinning, greying hair. He worked as a transport manager for a bus company, and had once been a professional footballer, keeping goal for Morton and East Fife. Joanne was a trim, beacon-eyed woman with a smile like a lottery win, who ran a cards and gift shop in Newington.

The Lowes greeted Avril and Jackie enthusiastically, compelling both women to apologise for the absence of their husbands, Avril stressing that in her case it was temporary. — He's been down at the office, she rolled her eyes. — Sunday! she added, too loudly for your raw nerve endings.

Your father always worked on a Sunday, he said it was the busiest day for rail freight. John Lennox supervised local operations from a small office in Haymarket, transitioning there after a long-ago heart attack had stopped him driving trains. You liked the hoary, Gothic feel of his dark office and occasionally met him there to take him for a pub lunch in one of the local bars. Even though the operations had long been computerised, your father maintained neat files of hard copies of dispatch orders, delivery notes and route plans, taking pleasure that he could carry on working when the systems went down.

Arriving a few minutes later, he nodded to you, kissed Trudi and shook hands with Donald and Joanne, giving his wife and daughter cursory acknowledgement before sitting down.

— No Stuart? John asked.

Fuck Stuart, you thought, the spoiled wee bastard would make the evening all about him soon enough. — He'll come when he comes, you said, ordering some champagne for the table. It amused you to watch everyone pretend they didn't know what was happening. They stole glances at Trudi's hands, both of which she kept covered with cream gloves. — We've got something to announce, you said, determined to get this part out of the way with as little bullshit as possible, — we're getting married next year, probably September.

Trudi whipped off the gloves, unveiling the ring to delighted gasps and comments. You tried to gauge the reactions: nobody was overtly pissed off. The least enthusiastic responses seemed to come from your own parents, and as Trudi was hugged and kissed by hers, you felt the smack of envy. Your father merely nodded with the same look of quiet vindication he deployed when the Hearts dugout finally obliged with the substitution he'd been calling for all after-noon. You could almost hear the 'aboot time n aw' coming from the old man's lips. You watched something in your mother's sinewy neck sliding up and down like a pump-action shotgun. She held that motion for a moment before finding her voice: — El Mondo . . . my wee El Mondo, bleating out your childhood nickname, the one that had graced the bullfighting posters on your bedroom wall, procured from old Spanish holidays.

The meal was well under way by the time your semi-drunk brother arrived. John Lennox moved away from his wife so that their younger son might sit in between them, as if he was a child they had to take turns watching. — Had an audition yesterday in Glasgow, he explained, — Stayed over in the land of the Weedge and my train got held up. Engineering works.

You set your face in a scungy smile, turning to your father. — The decline of the railways, eh, Dad?

John Lennox was a man prone to splenetic discourse on where Britain had gone wrong, invariably tracing it back to the railways. The words 'Beeching' and 'privatisation' he would pronounce as others might sexually transmitted diseases, but tonight your father was keeping his counsel.

— Your big brother's getting married, Stuart, Jackie said. Her appeasement of Stuart grated; as a ball-crunching criminal lawyer she never behaved like this with anyone else.

— Well, no shit, Sherlock, Stuart laughed. — I *had* sort of gathered that was what this wee shindig was about, and he poured himself a glass of champagne. — To Ray and Trudi, he toasted, — may the force by with you!

— Stuart, Jackie warned.

Your brother ignored your sister, looking over at the bride-to-be. — Well, Trudi, I can't help being the brother of a polisman, he said, — but marrying one? That's a very brave choice, I shiteth thee not.

You would if you could find one that fancied you, you'd thought, but bitten your tongue. Instead, you contented himself with, — I'm sorry I've been such a big trial to you.

— I bear it with dignity, Stuart laughed loudly. He looked over at Donald, who had an eyebrow raised, and Joanne, who seemed to be enjoying his performance. Her eyes fizzed like aspirin in a glass. — You know, years back, a bunch of us from the drama college went every morning up to Dundee to join the Timex factory picket line. I said to my brother, 'How can you do that job: protect the rich, shit on the poor?'

— I'm sure you're going to tell everybody what I said. You acted bored, drumming your fingers on the table and looking to the ceiling.

— Aye. You said you asked yourself that every day. Stuart paused, looking around the silent table. — Every day, he repeated.

— Yeah, you tried to affect weariness.

But Stuart had now clicked into actor mode, enjoying his audience. — Naw, I shiteth thee not; you said something like: 'I do it to get the bad bastards out there. Ask any of the most vulnerable people in Muirhouse or Niddrie who they really fear and they'll all tell you that it's the bad bastards in their own midst.' So I said something to the effect of: 'Fine, Raymond, but what about the rich bad bastards?' Then he looked pointedly at you, encouraging everybody else to do the same.

You made an exasperated farting noise by expelling air through your lips. — They get away, unless they're really careless, you conceded. — That's Jackie's department, the criminal justice system. I'm only a gofer.

— Leave me out of this, Jackie said.

You recalled how Stuart was never satisfied with this response. And he was right to not be. While it was the truth, there was another factor, a personal element, that you could never bring yourself to include in your stock speech. Now Stuart, with his open, imploringly sincere eyes, manifestly sensed the omission, and not for the first time, but disclosure wouldn't be prised from your lips.

— Help me out, Ray, he pleaded, — I'm trying to understand you.

The Lowes were now, sensibly, you thought, engrossed in their own conversation with your dad at the other end of the table. As the food and drink went down your mother was trapped, with her children arguing across her.

Then you said, — Remember that doll, what was its name? though you remembered Marjorie very well.

Jackie looked poisonously at you.

— Raymond, Avril pleaded.

— It's okay, Mum, Jackie said. — This is what happens when we get together as a family. Stuart resents Ray for who he is and Ray resents me for who I am.

You were taken aback by this. All the more so because you realised it was true. You'd been trying to hit back at Stuart in a roundabout way. Preparing to develop the theme that you'd loved that doll so much your dad worried you were queer. By the time Stuart came along (who actually was gay), John Lennox had grown more laissez-faire in his parenting and had forgotten about the Marjorie-and-biro incident, which had so shamed you and your sister.

— He was such a lovely wee laddie, your mother announced in desperation to the gathering. — My sweet wee El Mondo.

You know fuck all about me, you thought bitterly, looking round the table at your family.

Donald Lowe had put an arm around Trudi. — Well, I have to say that this one never gave us a day's trouble, did she, Joanne? The perfect daughter, he announced with pride.

— I wouldnae go so far as to say that! Joanne laughed, bringing up a trivial childhood anecdote, and you were delighted that it was now Trudi's turn to squirm. Then, for a second or two, the table vanished and all you could see was a slab with a small blue body on it.

Hyperventilation shook you and you fought it down, staring at a wedge-shaped lamp bolted to the wall. — You okay, son? your mother asked, noting your discomfort.

You switched your stare on to Stuart. The angel-faced wee crawler who'd turned into the opinionated obnoxious wanker, and everyone still made a fuss of him. — I'm lucky having you to tell me how Scotland would've been a free socialist utopian republic by now if I hadnae joined the polis.

Stuart raised his hands in mock surrender. — Okay, Ray, I apologise. I was out of order. I'm just a wee bit pissed off that I didn't get this *Taggart* part I was up for.

— But you've been in *Taggart* before, son, Avril consoled.

— Aye, Mum, but that was a different role.

But you weren't going to let him take over this time. — And I'm glad you know my job well enough to tell me that I oppress the poor. Here was me hallucinating, thinking about the dead body of a sexually abused and tortured seven-year-old girl I'd pulled out of the sea. And it was all my fault. She came from a housing scheme: maybe I was oppressing her.

— Enough! John Lennox snapped. — A bit of respect from you two. C'mon!

A worn glance of truce flashed between you and Stuart as the waiter moved to the table to announce the desserts. As you recharged your glass, you heard the conversation drift to Hearts and the sacking of George Burley. You were about to chip in with some gusto when your mobile rang. It was Keith Goodwin. — Hey, Ray. What's up? Where ye been?

— I'm sitting drinking champagne with my family, you said. — I've just got engaged.

— Congratulations, but, eh, the alcohol, is it wise? I mean to say —

— Call ye later, Keith, you said, snapping your mobile shut. A pub bore was a pub bore, with or without alcohol or drugs. You vowed that night to have a decent drink. It was what people did when they got engaged and put child killers behind bars.

It hit everybody in the face that Monday morning. The team were hung-over after their celebration and you were also feeling fuzzy after your engagement meal.

Ronnie Hamil couldn't provide an alibi but the hospital records of the Western General's Accident and Emergency Department could. A man had fished him out of the Union Canal after he'd stumbled in drunk following a session on heavily fortified wines the Tuesday night before Britney's disappearance. They'd kept him in hospital till ten o'clock the next day, when he'd resumed his binge at a friend's flat, drinking himself comatose, oblivious to being Scotland's most wanted man. He'd been too inebriated to remember this incident but his rescuer, a passing jogger, very clearly could.

Following the grandad's release, the first thing you did was phone George Marsden and tell him the situation. — Quite, George had crisply retorted.

Perhaps some of this smugness had transmitted to you. The scent of failure hung in the air that evening, as your Serious Crimes team trooped wearily into Bert's Bar. You weren't aware of an

I-told-you-so look coming off your face, but couldn't absolutely swear it wasn't there. In the bar tension built like a bonfire all night until Ally Notman slurred, — He's a fuckin nonce. He would've done.

— He's a bag of shite but he's no a child killer and it would have meant impunity for the real one, you'd sniped back. One or two heads around the table nodded. Most refused to make eye contact with you. You were isolated, and not for the first or the last time, for the crime of not taking part.

The following evening, as you were leaving Police HQ following another lonely night of searching through records, statements and video recordings, a silver-haired figure in a coat shuffled through the automatic doors and approached you. — You okay? your boss asked.

— I'm sorry, Bob. We've nothing. Zilch, you said. It was the first time you'd seen Bob Toal since the Ronnie Hamil connection had proved a dead end. Now your boss looked as worn out as you felt.

— Keep at it, Toal nodded, and his shoulder punch, the paternal blow of the football coach, was enough to relaunch you back into the thin darkness of a chilly Edinburgh night.

You felt utterly useless. The cop as Popperian philosopher: disproving every hypothesis your department came out with. As the next few days rolled by, you empathised with the boss. The pension was so close, and Toal wanted to get to the finishing line unscathed. A blaming culture always came to the fore in any police department in which a big case seemed to be going nowhere. Those were the rules. They were operating in a tight financial environment. Cost-cutting measures were already planned. There would be a disciplinary hearing. Charges of gross negligence made. Summary dismissal. The only issue was how far down the line the buck would be passed.

Dissenting voices were starting to be heard. A comprehensive investigation appeared on the *Independent*'s front page. It raised doubts about the strength of the case against Robert Ellis, affirming your belief that a multiple murderer was on the loose. But pressure from Toal compelled you to keep on at Angela Hamil and the men in her life.

— There's fuckin shite gaun oan here, she's covering for some cunt, Toal had said, his Morningside accent thickening to Tollcross, showing you a different set of possibilities for your gaffer. Somebody who, perhaps in other circumstances, could have been a villain. — Ride her hard, Ray, he had said. — I've seen it before with weak women like that. They become mesmerised, dominated by some bad bastard. Find out who he is!

So like the rest of Serious Crimes, you became obsessed with Angela's sex life. Openly scoffing at her in an incredulous manner when she said she 'never brought men back to the house because of the bairns'. Knowing the woman would be too broken to challenge you. You hated her passivity, saw yourself – felt yourself – becoming a bully, perhaps like many of the other men in her life, but unable to stop. You wormed one name out of her, a Graham Cornell, who worked at the Scottish Office. He was described as 'just a friend'.

A couple of days later you'd gone back to the office at Serious Crimes and studied the dreaded whiteboard again. After a while Ally Notman invited you for a drink. When you stepped into Bert's Bar, they were all there. It was a set-up. Relaxed at first, then Gillman and Notman started the ball rolling. — It's him. Cornell, they harmonised.

It was the cue for Harrower and McCaig to join the chorus. You're our boy. Our leader. The boss. Don't let us down. He's making cunts of us all.

And part of it chimed with you. Because there was something about this man. But then you spoke to Cornell on Halloween evening. You caught him about to leave his flat, dressed in a red costume with horns and a forked tail. Even discounting this attire, Graham Cornell's bearing announced him as transparently gay. To your mind it was ludicrous to think he'd snatch a female child. But for some of the boys, like Gillman, gay equalled pervert, equalled nonce. You could stick them on as many equal-ops training courses as you liked, but the algebra, long formed, couldn't be totally encrypted, and was always waiting to return. It came back with a vengeance in the fatigued, desperate group, sweating under the strip lights in that small office, burning their eyes on computer screens, knocking on doors asking the same questions over and over again. You feared that you were the only one privy to the collective psychosis that had them all in its clenched fist. They would fall silent whenever Drummond, the lone female officer on the team, entered the room. Even Notman, who was living with her.

Your response to the voices jabbering at you was to engage with your own increasingly urgent naggings. One bleak early-November afternoon, a train took you over the border to Newcastle. Then, a short taxi ride and you were in a dilapidated tavern in that city's West End, where, as a Scottish cop, you felt safe enough to score your first grams of cocaine in over four years.

And you needed it like the rest seemed to need Cornell. It couldn't be admitted that a multiple child murderer was on the loose. The myriad legal and police careers that had been built on Robert Ellis's arrest and prosecution would be for ever tarnished. And a hated figure would be living the rest of his life in the Bahamas at the taxpayer's expense. The groupthink of the bureaucratic organisation went into destructive overdrive: Cornell was the man. And in your own way, you did the same.

Day Three

8

Everything But the Girl

Trudi Lowe sits in the hotel room, ostensibly watching the television, but immersed in the recounting of incidents, from their 'last life', as she habitually refers to it. Years ago, when he'd shown up the self-hating drunk, using crass, fabricated outrage as a crude shield against his own guilt. She knew where he'd been. They'd argued about his behaviour and he'd shouted, — You haven't got a clue what the fuck guys are like, have you?

Now the last life has come back. *And I thought he'd changed.* That putrid cliché slithers south into her chest, as a voice sneers back from inside her head: *you fuckin mug.*

But the rage that brims somehow refuses to overflow. She's got up to pace around, looks outside. Her anger is stronger seated. So she's fallen into the chair again and feels the poison flow through her.

Clean when they'd got back together, he'd blamed it all on the cocaine. And NA seemed to work for him. Their new life together felt like a genuine renaissance. They went to the gym, attended French classes, watched movies, enjoyed vigorous sex, engaged in camping and hillwalking expeditions. His job was always there, but he seemed to be treating it as just that: a job, albeit a particularly intrusive and demanding one. But then the drinking started again. He blamed the horrible case of the murdered little girl, and there was obviously his father and the subsequent estrangement from his family. But whatever the causes, the drink was there and would lead to cocaine, and that would lead to other women. And then they'd be finished.

You haven't got a clue what the fuck guys are like. In the empty hotel room, that hurtful proclamation from the past resonates more acutely than ever. But her dad isn't like that, and she recalls her child's gloved hand in his, waiting in the queue for the cinema on Tollcross's blue-grey streets. Can envision it so clearly, his younger self, his scent, that when she stops she feels a dissonance like she's reincarnated into the body of a future descendant. And his own father was a kind and decent man. Trying to stop herself picking nervously at the skin around her manicured nails, all Trudi can think is: they are supposed to be here to *make love*. To get their sex life back on track. She is hormonal and premenstrual, and she needs him. And he's gone.

She knows his contempt for her career and, thinking of that bundle of services that gives the country its pulse, suddenly finds a way of converting all the anger that has paralysed her into energy. It propels her down to the bar, but it's empty and she doesn't stay, stepping out on to the street. Walking for a bit, she entertains the vague notion that she can do anything he can, but isn't inclined to patronise the local hostelries, raucous with beery, obnoxious males; there seems no acceptable category between boorish youth and sleazy middle age. On Lincoln Road, she is becoming more acutely conscious of her solitary status, when the vivid colours of the artwork on display in a gallery window beckon her inside. The place is almost empty. The originals are expensive but she can see a mounted print that's reasonable. She lingers at it, wonders if Ray would like it. Probably not. Thinks that might be a reason to buy it. Then he approaches her.

Noises in his head, as a white ceiling comes into focus through one eye. The other is held shut by gummy secretions. He rubs at it; feels the springs of an old couch prong his back. A throw pulled over him. He had unravelled in the night and achieved a kind of exhausted peace. The events of last night gatecrash into his head. *You've fucked up again*, keens in self-flogging mantra. The sunshine bursts through the old yellow lace of the curtains as the neuralgia stabs the inside of his skull.

Trudi.

The noises. The television. Pulls himself up into a sitting position. Sees the kid, Tianna, lying on the floor, watching the box and drinking from a can of Pepsi. Tries to stand. Manages it. Stretches and yawns. Looks down at the girl.

She is locked on the telly, but had been watching him in his sleep. His face contorted, like he was still fighting, but in his dreams. His snoring so loud, she'd needed to turn up the volume. But she'd also wanted to waken him. To figure him out.

— Where is everybody? Lennox asks as he registers the glass from the broken coffee table. He recalls trying to tidy it up, but there are still plenty of shards around.

Fuck sake, the kid's barefoot.

Lying prone on the rug, watching the television, the girl wears a pair of blue shorts and a yellow tank top. Some kind of rash: red, angry burns on one shin. She doesn't even turn round as her right leg beats out a rhythm on her left. It's like he scarcely exists. Doesn't exist or is always there, Lennox wonders. — Where's Robyn?

— Dunno. Tianna sits up. Swivels round. Her top has BITCH emblazoned on it in gold glittering letters. She regards him briefly, before pivoting back to recumbency by the box.

She isn't a kid you can take to, Lennox thinks. He wanders around the apartment. It's empty. He shrugs to an invisible audience and makes for the door. Stops. He can't leave her alone like that, not without finding out when Robyn will be back. That creepy shitbag might come along again.

He considers Trudi. Will she be worried about him? Possibly. Probably. Once she'd calmed down, would she not think: 'Where's Ray?' Lennox finds it nigh on impossible to conceive of anybody missing him.

But of course she would. She's his fiancée. He's been ill. Is ill.

I've stayed out all night. What the fuck have I done?

I have the pussy, I make the rules. Jesus fuck Almighty.

No. Trudi would be hurt. She may even have gone home, got a flight back to Edinburgh, perhaps telling his family – what's left of it – that he's had another breakdown. Maybe the police are looking for him! Or she might possibly be with Ginger and Dolores.

But he can't leave the girl here alone.

It isn't right. Her mother is . . .

— Do you get left on your own often? Lennox asks the supine figure as he starts to pick up the rest of the glass. The table as fragmented as last night in his mind. His head pulses like a wasp's nest. Nasal cavities and throat stung raw.

— Dunno, she shrugs.

— When's your mum due back?

— Like *you* care? she says, and he almost reacts, but as well as reprimand her tones carry a smidgen of enquiry.

So he gives up with the glass and sits back on the couch. He feels like leaving. But what if they'd gone on to another party and forgotten about her? You take enough coke, you can forget about anybody and anything. And Robyn looked like she took enough coke. An empty cigarette packet on the floor: it makes him miserable.

He rises and goes into the kitchen. There's some beers left in the fridge, cans of Miller. How he wants one. Just one. But it isn't right to drink it in front of the kid. It isn't right because that's what they all did. They lumbered to the fridge, every guy that had ever come into her mother's apartment, at all hours. He could see them. Trace that path from the couch like a biologist would a bear's salmon-fishing route. He wants to show her that it isn't normal. Not taken as given that a kid would see guy after guy come into her home, into her life, with beer on his breath. Cause if she thinks it is normal then she will grow up and be with guys who have beer on their breath all day, every day. And guys who have beery breath all day, every day, they're bad news to women. What else can they ever be?

What else?

So Ray Lennox makes himself a cup of coffee and he waits.

And waits.

Minutes stretch into quarter-hour blocks, pulling piano-wire nerves to their tensile limit then swiftly contracting, letting a sharp fatigue leak in pulses from his brain into his sinuses and eyes. Each of these temporal blocks resembles a stretch of ocean and he feels like a manacled, oar-pulling slave in the bowels of a coffin ship trying to cross its choppy expanse. Penance for the drink and drugs, their playful uncoupling of time and space last night. Thoughts of strategy come slowly and tentatively.

He should call Trudi. Feels the plastic room key in his pocket. She has a duplicate. A separate card with the address. She'll be fast asleep. It's still early: the digital clock says 8:33. Maybe she won't thank him. What can he do? There is no excuse. That's what she'll tell him. *No excuse for that kind of behaviour.* What excuses can you make? He has reasons, but at what point do they stop becoming excuses?

When you should be old enough to know better. He was thirty-five on his birthday. Officially middle-aged – if you accept the old three-score-years-and-ten dictum. He sits back, looks at the cartoons on the telly. The Roadrunner humiliates the Coyote for the millionth time.

Tianna occasionally glances back at him. She gets up once, to replenish her cola. The pulsing glow of the narrative – the circumstances that have delivered him to this room – are intermittent in his head, but in someone else's voice-over. Continued sanity compels action, and Lennox inventories the kitchen. There is no food in the house.

Plenty fuckin beer: but nothing for the kid's breakfast.

He sits back down and watches Tianna channel-hop. She's growing restless, Lennox can tell. It isn't just the chemicals from the cola.

Stretching and bending to test his racked muscles, he picks up *Perfect Bride* from the floor. Reads about wedding etiquette. Thinks about who his best man might be. His old pal, Les Brodie, how they'd made a pact as kids. Playing on the old Tarzan swing down Colinton Dell. Agreed that they'd be each other's best man if they ever got married. But then came the incident at the tunnel and they'd stopped going down the Dell. And he hadn't seen Les in years, not until a few weeks ago: at his father's funeral. When he'd made such an exhibition of himself. *But I was right to, because the bastards in this life: they fucking tore your heart out. They had to be told.* But here he was. Marriage. The best man. Inevitable that he'd ask one of the boys from the force, if only because there was nobody else. No Les, no Stuart. It would be Ally Notman probably, on the grounds that he was the least likely to cause offence. That was if getting married remained on the agenda.

He is aware of the mass of Trudi's notebook in his back pocket. Gripping his arse cheek like her hand used to. He pulls it out and examines it: all one- or two-word entries. Lists. Websites. Her handwriting: slender, curvy and expressive. The vivaciousness of it makes him pine. Then even more as he flips a page and sees Trudi Lennox written several times; the same 'L', 'o' and 'e' in her current surname. Perhaps it's time to call, to try and explain.

Nothing happened.

But that isn't true. Plenty has happened. Is still happening.

Tianna glances from the TV set to him, as if steadying herself to say something. Before she can, the splintering ring of the phone lying on the floor skewers them both. They regard each other urgently. Both want the other to pick it up. — It might be your mum, you'd better answer it, Lennox says, shocked at the fearful child in his own voice.

Tianna lifts the receiver. There is a gap in her front teeth; he hasn't noticed it before. It makes her look like a proper kid.

Rather than a —

It makes her look like a proper American kid. *The Waltons.* A white picket fence. She is the sort of kid who if she had a different American — what? — ma, mum, mother, mom, she would have braces in her choppers. Suffering the pre- and early-teen years of Hannibal Lecter teasing in order to get that winning infomercial-presenter smile.

— Hi, honey . . . Tianna is relieved to hear her mother's voice, but she knows that paltry tone, the one which will deliver a million apologies before she screws up again. *And Momma'll be in big trouble cause that table got broke good.*

— Hi . . . Tianna says. From Lennox's point of view she seems to visibly relax. Her shoulders, which were tensed forward, now slump back. The voice on the other end, though, is panicky and jittery. He can hear it from where he sits. Knows to whom it belongs. Then Tianna looks over at him, — That guy who talks

120

funny, yeah. Yeah . . . and she holds out the receiver in one hand and phone in the other in appeal.

As he takes them, Tianna, in sudden, disturbing fleetness, bounds out the door. — Hello?

— Ray . . . is that you?

It's Robyn. He hasn't been mistaken.

— Yeah. Where are you? I should –

— Listen, is Tia okay?

— Aye, she's been watching cartoons. What time will you be –

She cuts him off again. — Is she listening?

He checks. She's gone. — Naw, I think she's in her room –

When she talks over him for the third time he knows her assertiveness is fuelled by desperation rather than cocaine. — Ray, please listen to me, her voice, pleading and urgent, pushes down on him like a dark, ominous cloud, — I ain't got long to talk. You gotta pen and paper to hand?

— Are you okay?

— No, I'm not okay, Ray, I am *not* okay. I cain't come back to the apartment yet, but I need you to get Tia out of there right now! *Right now*, y'all hear me?

— What is it? Where are ye? Lennox snaps, angry at the further imposition, — If you're in some kind of trouble we should phone the police. These guys last night –

— No! Promise, Ray, *promise me* that you won't phone no po-leece. They'll take her away from me, they'll put her into care! Please, Ray, please, she begs in rasping, almost strangulated tones, — don't you be phonin no po-leece. Just promise me!

— Okay.

— I need ya to do me a favour, please! Do you have a pen and paper?

— What? Lennox says, with a scribbling mime to Tianna, who is entering the front room, but the girl flinches and steps back behind the door. Of course – Trudi's small notebook, with the pen clipped into the ringed spine. — I've got yin. What's going on here?

— I need you to take Tia somewhere. Right away.

— I – you can't leave your daughter with me, he protests. — You don't know a thing about me!

— I trust you, Ray, Robyn whispers urgently, and coughs out the address.

He's seen the kind of men she's trusted – incarcerated many of them, those men who have somehow managed to win the confidence of a woman. Until you've seen the women in question, and then it all makes perfect sense. Lennox reluctantly scribbles it down. Prepares to read it back to her, when a guttural squawk flares down the line then fades into silence.

A shivery spasm seizes him, along with the notion to dial 999, before he remembers it's 911 here. — Robyn? A failing gasp as his throat scorches.

From behind the door, Tianna squirms. She can see him through the crack, his face hard, his eyes dancing, as he holds the phone. *Maybe he could tell em all, creepy Lance, that Johnnie pig and that mean Starry bitch to just go away and leave Momma and me alone. Tell em all!*

Lennox is aware that she's watching him, but then another voice is on the line. — Hello. Who's there?

— Who's this?

The caller coolly answers in kind, by announcing him. — Our Skarrish friend. Ray.

That guy Lance, Lennox recalls in icy tremor, Lance Dearing. They'd broken Robyn's table. Her landlord's table. — Aye. Where's Robyn?

— We got ourselves a lil' problem, Dearing says calmly. — She's gone kinda crazy on that stuff. That ain't right around a kid, you know that.

— Yeah, Lennox says, as his mind does cartwheels. He looks at Tianna, partially lurking behind the door. Half her face and one arm and leg visible to him. Her bottom lip quivering: the goose-bumped skin on her limbs.

— I dunno what you guys were up to in that toilet last night, Lance laughs, and Lennox feels bile rise in his gut, — but you sure as hell wouldn't open up. Ol Robyn, she was losin the plot real bad. Got herself into a whole heap of trouble.

— It didn't seem like it was Robyn that was losin it tae me.

— Well, I guess we all kinda lost it. That table sure got broke good, Lance Dearing says, forcing Lennox to regard the cold metal frame and legs. — No hard feelins though, huh, buddy?

Lennox lets the silence hang.

Dearing seems in no hurry to fill it and Lennox almost wonders if the line has gone dead before the American eventually speaks. — I'm gonna come on by real soon. Right now I'm gonna send Johnnie round to wait.

— Are you fuckin crazy? No. No way! Lennox barks. He looks at Tianna, who's come back and sat down on the couch. She brings her knees up to her chest, resting her head on them. Her hair tumbles down, concealing her face.

— Ol Johnnie was only messin last night. A lil' too much of the funny stuff.

— I saw his messing, Lennox says evenly, — and if he comes near that kid again, his voice pauses, slow and deliberate, — I'll cut his fuckin balls off and feed them to the cunt. They'll be his last meal on this earth, he hisses, then starts, realising that Tianna is present and not wanting to look at her.

— Whoah . . . hold on, Ray, buddy, what kind of fool talk is that?

— I'm no your buddy, Lennox spits.

Dearing raises his voice slightly, but remains composed. — I think you got it all wrong here. I'm sorry about our lil' mis-understanding last night, but you must know that Robyn is a mighty troubled lady, and Lennox feels himself being wooed by the rational, reasonable tone. — She attracts trouble and I guess I'm jus a little overprotective, is all. But I can see you got her best interests at heart.

Then he thinks of Johnnie. — It's *whom* you're protective of, that's the issue here. Now put her back on.

— She's hysterical, Ray. You saw her last night.

— It's her daughter, Lennox insists as Tianna pushes her hair back, — put her on.

— I'll be round there in a short while, compadre. Why don't y'all just simmer down a little –

123

— I'm telling you this *right now*: if you don't put her on, I'm going to the police.

— Al-righty! Lance chuckles, then Lennox's mind's eye sees him turn away from the phone, his voice switching volume and direction, addressing another party, recasting him as eavesdropper. — Hear that, you crazy bitch? Ray's got himself of a mind to do the same as me and go round to the po-leece with that lil' gal!

— NOO! Robyn's vivid scream, crushed to his ear to shield it from Tianna. It dies, and his arm has gone rigid. The receiver held tight in his bad fist. Pulling it away, with a silence at the other end, he settles it down on the cradle with a click.

The girl's eyes blaze at him. — What's happened? Where's Momma?

What can he tell her? — Your mother's sick. Just not feeling so good.

His words deflate the kid. Her eyes glaze over as she crumples back into the chair. — Is it the drugs? Her voice is weary in resignation. — She cain't be takin that powder none.

— What do you know about that?

Tianna looks at him in a measured way and asks, — Dunno. What bout you?

— Nothing, his voice weak and faltering.

— The way you're sniffin and snufflin seems like you know plenty, Tianna says, and he hates the worldly scorn in her tone.

He tries for levity: — I've got a cold. I'm from Scotland. It's not like Florida.

She tugs her hair back from her face again, as her hawklike eyes scrutinise him. — Yeah, sure.

Lennox feels low and nasty. — Has your mum . . . gotten sick before? You know . . . He can't bring himself to say 'on drugs'.

— She jus got out of rehab.

— Who looked after you when she was in rehab?

— Starry, I guess.

— Don't you have a gran or grandpa, like your mum's mother and father?

She shakes her head in the negative and lowers her eyes.

Recalling Ronnie Hamil, Lennox leaves it; the last thing some children wanted was to contact grandparents. — You don't like Starry, Johnnie and Lance much, do you?

Tianna looks fiercely at him. — They say they're Momma's friends but they ain't no friends of hers.

This convinces him of the urgency of getting away from this place. He doesn't want to see Lance Dearing or Johnnie again. — What do you want to do? Are you hungry? he asks. Robyn has given him an address. If it's local, he could make good her request and leave the kid there. Then get back to the hotel. Make his peace with Trudi. Go to bed. Lie out on the beach, even.

Trudi. Jesus fuck Almighty.

— I don't wanna be here. Tianna evidently feels the same as he does. — I wanna go stay with Chet.

— Who's Chet?

— Uncle Chet. He's kinda cool, she says, her smile suggesting that power children have to purify jaundice.

Lennox looks at the scribbled note on the pad. He can barely recognise it as his own writing. CHET LEWIS, OCEAN DAWN, GROVE MARINA, BOLOGNA.

Robyn hadn't provided a phone number, but at least Tianna knew who her mother wanted to look after her and it was fine by the kid. — Do you have Uncle Chet's phone number?

— I guess it's over by the other phone, she points to the hall, — on the big board.

Lennox goes across to where the whiteboard is mounted on the wall. He freezes in panic as it gleams back at him, stark in its nakedness. Before it had been teeming with numbers and messages. — Who wiped this?

Tianna has followed him and looks from Lennox to the board and back. — Dunno.

He recalls Ally Notman, cleaning the whiteboard at work, sweeping a sponge across it in long, loping strokes. Erasing everything. End of investigation. The big, bold name BRITNEY eradicated for good.

He'd shivered as he'd watched that board being wiped clean. Now, in the hall of this Miami apartment, he feels a familiar chill.

In cop mode, he systematically searches the place for letters, notes, bills, bank statements, anything. All gone. Lennox knows that nobody as chaotic as Robyn could be so fastidious. This was a proper clean-up job, even though it had been done in haste while he was locked away with the kid in the toilet. *Dearing. The last person to leave had to be him. It would have taken him seconds to wipe down the board and minutes to load her personal stuff into a bin liner if he knew where to look.*

Tianna is standing a little bit away from him. Waiting. Her arms folded. — We gonna go to Chet's?

— How far is it?

— Dunno.

— Can we walk there?

Her withering look indicates there's little chance of that.

— Let's go and get some breakfast and work out how far it is. I'm hungry. What about you?

— I guess so.

He looks at her bare arms. Her tank top and its salacious proclamation. — Better stick on a jacket. I think it's colder than it looks, he says, heading to the lounge and picking up the copy of *Perfect Bride.*

9

Police

The sun radiates through a thin mesh of cloud, but a cool, persistent wind steals the heat from the air. Lennox is right; it isn't as warm as advertised. Tianna, carrying a backpack designed as a flattened sheep, and wearing a light blue denim jacket, kindles some jealousy in him; he could do with something to cover his arms. He's lost the Red Sox hat and his shades, probably left behind in one of the bars or on the bus. His good hand clutches the bridal magazine. He doesn't have a clue where he's going, or why. A white van sets his hackles rising as it pulls up outside the apartment block. A boiler-suited man emerges with a metal canister on his back, and is cursorily greeted by Tianna.

— Who's that? Lennox asks.

— The exterminator, she explains, his glaikit expression compelling her to add, — They spray all the apartments for bugs.

They walk through the streets of square blocks over huge cracked concrete sidewalks, past houses and yards, coming on to a main road and a strip mall. There's nothing of interest: a real-estate agent, a security firm and a hairdresser's. It isn't a bad neighbourhood, though. He's seen a lot worse. The girl keeps step alongside him, deep in thought. Her hair blows a little in the breeze, and he imagines her walking to school, like Britney used to.

For Tianna walking to school was always Alabama. Sucking in the medley of forms, sounds and movements along the Tallapoosa River route, the swampy aromas taking the urgency out of the day's excited voices. It was different in Miami, that mirthless ride in the school bus rambling down the palm-treed avenues. Teased from the start for her rudimentary Spanglish. Her bag seized on her first day by two boys who tossed it back and forth to each other. She knew they'd wanted her to exasperate and humiliate herself by trying to retrieve it. But she'd been suddenly stung by the dire recall of what he'd said to her about being a woman, not a little girl, and she'd simply waited disdainfully till they'd become bored. They'd cursed her in Spanish as they dropped the bag at her feet, but it was half-hearted as they were quickly off in search of a more responsive victim. Pappy Vince, she remembered, had shown her good things too.

The apartment, a palace of functional understated luxury, is a short cab ride from the cocktail bar. A pool and hot tub built into a glass-enclosed patio look out on to the ocean beyond, the inky blue of each almost imperceptibly blending in the night. He'd suggested the nightcap at his place, and when she thought of Ray, out carousing full of cocaine, and probably in the arms of some slut, she was happy to agree.

Aaron Resinger seems as designed as his home. Hair dark and wavy. Body heavy with muscle built and honed in the gym since college years. An admitted workaholic, he tells her that he is one of few native South Floridians. He'd studied Real Estate Finance and Urban Planning at the University of Miami and made his money in the condominium boom of the early nineties. Success has come at a cost, as a few months ago, he'd split up with a long-term partner. — I guess I've been licking my wounds since, he sings with a hint of melancholy through a grill of perfect white teeth.

After pouring Trudi a drink, and showing her his art collection, they stand on the patio, looking out to where the Biscayne Bay meets the Atlantic Ocean. — When I built this place I decided that I simply couldn't find anywhere better to live, he purrs. Trudi feels like a film star, ennobled and exalted by the attentions of this man. When he kisses her, she responds. At first tentatively, then, as she thinks of how Ray Lennox has treated her, with ferocious abandon. When they break off, he sweeps the hair from her face, looks into her eyes, and says with a sincerity she finds crippling, — I would really like to make love to you.

Trudi smiles and allows herself to be led by the hand into a master bedroom. She knows at that moment that when she tells this story to the girls in some wine bar back home, they will all be letting out volleys of uncontrollable laughter. But right now, in this luxury, under the moonlight, with the crashing waves outside and her burned by alcohol and thoughts of a treacherous, uncaring fiancé, it is by far the best show in town.

He beats out an edgy rhythm on his thigh with *Perfect Bride* as they walk. Lennox had tried to chat but the kid wasn't forthcoming. It was easier getting information out of hardened cons. He didn't push it because he sensed she carried the sort of hurt that engendered introspection.

His mouth feels bad, and he thinks about getting some gum. It's a strain with the American kid, and he's relieved when they come across a local police station. He doesn't want to alarm her. Luckily, there is a diner across the street. — I been there before, Tianna says uneasily, pointing at it. — Starry works there.

Perhaps Starry would be able to help sort out this mess. She was a total bitch last night but then she was coked up. And she is Robyn's friend. Or is she? He'll soon find out.

Mano's Grill might have been considered a good place to waitress. A very narrow L-shaped space, there are no tables as such, just a counter that runs along the length of one wall, alongside which chairs are positioned. The customers can almost reach over and touch the short-order cooks: one of whom he believes to be Mano himself. Another counter with more stools underneath runs round the periphery, along some big plate-glass windows. Lennox can envision Starry stretching across to pass the plates to these customers over the heads of the poor stiffs at the counter.

But he'll bet that she never does that when Mano's around. An aggressive caricature posted above the counter depicts a younger, hairier, slimmer version, but still instantly recognisable as him. It warns underneath: THIS AIN'T BURGER KING — HERE WE DO THINGS MY WAY.

With Tianna reluctantly alongside him, Lennox watches Mano in action. As he shouts at a waitress, bitterness seeps from him, strong enough to taint every bite of the food he cooks. Then Lennox sees that there is an alcoved passage leading to restrooms, then a bigger dining space. Mano's empire extends to a busy area of tables, chairs and another counter with a register. Even a separate kitchen seems to be in operation.

Lennox hazily recalls Starry telling him last night that she'd been working there for four years. It was probably a lifetime in a place like this, he considers. In caustic semi-drunkenness, she'd told him somewhere between a boast and a lament that it was the longest she'd ever held down a job in her life. No matter how crazy her own lifestyle got, Starry contended she'd never missed a shift. This had seemed doubtful to him at the time. It's exposed as nonsense as he asks the waitress – the one Mano chewed out – if she's due in. The woman glares confrontationally at him. — You know that beetch? Where ees she?

— I was hoping you could tell me.

— Ha! How should I know? I have to cover her sheeft, she spits in uncontrived anger.

Lennox sits down with Tianna who seems relieved at Starry's absence. He fancies a milkshake. He remembers the ones in the Howard Johnson's on Times Square in New York with the boys. They were good. But they'd soon turned into Bloody Marys.

They order a chocolate shake for him, with toast and eggs. Tianna gets a Coke, burger and fries. Lennox's appetite is shot. He dabs at the eggs with toast, dropping an accidental bomb of yolk on *Perfect Bride*, and sucks on the shake that cools his raw throat. The kid is hungry. There is a quick, methodical single-mindedness about the way she attacks her food. He wonders when she last ate. — You stay here, he tells her, standing up. — I'm just going to get some cigarettes next door, he raps out the easy lie of the infidel cop.

— Uh-huh, she replies and now her eyes seem so big, — That would be way cool.

— For me, he snaps in exasperation. — Wait here, he reiterates.

Striding out of the diner, Lennox marches across to the smart new building bearing the sign indicating Miami–Dade County Police Department. It takes up a good part of a city block. Inside there would be men and women, like his colleagues back home, earning a living through law enforcement. It's crazy. He's an experienced cop, but he doesn't know what he's going to say. Without authority or status he's pared down to his essence: a doubter, operating in a world where such luxuries were frowned upon. Lennox stops outside the glass doors. *Now is not the time to doubt. Now is the time to act.*

The likes of Dougie Gillman would stride in and report the kidnapping, abandonment, molestation and attempted rape of a minor to the desk officer. Not only that, he'd do it with a sneering contempt that said: 'Where the fuck were youse?' And that's what he is steeling himself to do, thinking of his actor brother, Stuart, telling him how he got himself into role.

As he opens the door, he sees a very large woman leaning across the desk. Her outsized rump, encased in pink stretched leggings, sticks in the air and partially blocks his view of the officer behind the reception counter who attends to her. Then the man shimmies to one side and lifts his head and Lennox and the desk cop gaze at each other in mutual shock.

It is Lance Dearing who speaks first, as the flight urge explodes like a starter's pistol in Ray Lennox, who twists away from the desk.

— Why, you jus hold on a minute there, Ray – Lance begins, but the barrel of a woman is shouting at him: — You gotta get him outta my house! He ain't got no business to be in my house!

— Ma'am, if you don't mind . . . Dearing says, stepping out from behind the counter.

Ray Lennox walks quickly through the glass doors and out of the police station. His jarring staccato descent down the steps evokes a pianist playing chopsticks. At the bottom he breaks into a trot and then a sprint. The lay-off from his sporting endeavours is painfully evident: his weight hangs around his heart and lungs and his leg muscles ache. Under his soles the slabs on the sidewalks are cracked and uneven, and he self-consciously fears for his footing. Then the bilious mass seems to lift, his chest holding the air, lightening him, and Lennox is flying.

Tianna is sitting where he left her, finishing off her food, looking at the wedding magazine. The urgency signalled by Lennox's entrance makes her pack a few ketchup-laden fries into her mouth before he reaches the table.

— We have to go, he gasps, counting out some bills.

— What about Momma? Tianna asks, making Lennox briefly think of his own mother.

— Your mum's not well, but she's gonna be okay. He rests his hands on the counter, shoulders heaving. He is rewarded by a suspicious glance from Mano that reminds him of a scene from some movie. — We have to go now, go and see Chet, he emphasises, picking up the magazine and heading to the register. He pays the clerk and ushers Tianna towards the door. — You have to tell me about those two guys who came by last night. Johnnie and Lance.

— I don't wanna talk about them. She turns her head in rapid, emphatic movements. — I don't like them!

— Who are they? he persists. — Have they tried to hurt you before?

The girl's line of vision shoots past him, her eyes wide with the expectation of impending trauma. She's gone somewhere and he needs her here. Gently but firmly, he grips her shoulders and she meets his gaze. — I know you've heard this bullshit line before in your life and I absolutely guarantee that you'll hear it again. But now it's time to believe: trust me.

A spark ignites in her as she glances over his shoulder again. — Quick. She takes him by the arm and leads him through the doors to the restrooms. Following her, he steals a look across the crowded diner. At the other door Lance Dearing has walked in and is scanning the joint. Their eyes meet and Dearing's brows knot, his bottom lip curling. Guessing that the man would have the balls or the desperation to shoot him dead in a packed diner, then claim he abducted a Florida minor, Lennox lets the sprung door snap shut behind them.

Tianna evidently knew that the restrooms also led to the restaurant extension, the back of which empties out on to a parking lot. They move swiftly across the space, which contains only a few cars and a skip. The terror of a marksman's bullet in his back pulls him inwards in expectation of impact. His head swivels to Tianna but she's keeping an even, measured stride with him as they run on to another road. Again, he glances back for signs of Dearing, but there's nothing. Rather than give chase by foot, he'd be back in his car, trying to track them down. The main road opens back on to one more set of neighbourhood side streets cut into blocks, and they steal down one. To Lennox they seem featureless in their uniformity, as they move swiftly, looking back for pursuing vehicles. It's hotter now and heavier after the effort he's expended in this flight from Dearing. The sun spreads across the back of his head and neck, his brain numb and oxygen-deprived as they slow to a trot and then a walk, mute with fear and breathlessness, just waiting to be apprehended.

Yet nothing happens as they continue to trek in zoned-out quiescence, glad of the meagre cover of the trees sprouting from street and garden, affording at least some shelter from both sunlight and passing eyes.

Tianna is thinking about the boys on the school bus. She didn't mind them calling her a slut. They said the same to the white-socked Catholic Latinas in the plaid school dresses, even when they came out of church. That old stucco one with the crude stained glass, colour weakened by constant sun spitting through the palm leaves. Tianna had even thought about going in there, wondering if other girls had shared her fate, and if they'd found peace inside. But her momma had no time for it, for the dirty old pious-faced men in frocks and bad shoes. *The only men she didn't have time for.* Now she's looking at the tall Scotsman – Bobby, she'll call him, after Baseball Bobby from Scotland – but he's talking to himself like a real crazy asshole, his eyes bulging: a loony man for sure. She hears him saying something weird under his breath, about needing to keep walkin, about kids, about how he always has to look after kids, and just who in hell's name does he think he is, this Scottish creep who knows jack about her. *Walkin was always Mobile. Doesn't he know that?!*

One thought in Lennox's head: I am the uncomfortable silence. Yet he must have been mumbling, delirious in the heat, effort and drugs comedown, maybe said something about needing to walk.

133

Because now Tianna is shouting at him. At first he can't hear her, only a noise as uniform as silence. He has to stop, to consciously tune in.

— . . . and I like to walk and I ain't no kid, she declares violently, her face creasing in anger, — so don't you be treatin me like one!

— Right, he says, humbled. They walk silently on for what seems an age, distrustful of each other and 7th Street they've emerged back on to, blinking like chain-gang fugitives in the desert. Every cruising police car makes Lennox's heart pound. The magazine beats in stronger cadence against his thigh.

Gamekeeper turned poacher.

He feels that people are watching him. Dress, bearing, skin tone, he doesn't fit in here. Perhaps it's the girl; her slow angel eyes tracking him in his grim mission of mercy. The air thickens in the heat and the glossy magazine sweats in his hand. They seem to be the lone pedestrians: this white man and this young girl. It strikes him then that he can't even tell from Tianna's features and colouring anything about her father's ethnicity. He could conceivably have been black, Asian, white or Latin. He thinks of the golfer Tiger Woods: a new model American. Tries to mentally Photoshop Robyn out of her daughter and see what's left, but still no compelling image presents itself. The only thing that comes distastefully to his mind is Robyn's pubic hair.

In Britney's neighbourhood nobody would have noticed us. Their wars in that scheme were against the Bosnian refugee who was rehoused by the council, or the quiet model-railway enthusiast who lived alone. Or the moonlighting house painter. Maybe the nippy cow who got the last packet of beefburgers from the corner store and the slimy Paki bastard who sold them to her. Or the burly thug who kicked in the door and grabbed the telly and stereo while the scrawny, cadaverous sheriff officer waved the warrant in their bemused faces. Or the guilt-ridden pisshead of a husband who blew another month's rent on drink and horses. Their wars were with each other and were all-consuming; born out of underemployment, poverty and frustration. Meanwhile, a real monster had slipped undetected through their midst.

Mr Confectioner would never have been casing an affluent middle-class

134

district, with its busybodies and its neighbourhood watches quick to call the police about the white van parked in their street.

Then a sports stadium – a jubilant sight for a Scotsman – bears imposingly in front of them. Tianna tells him it's the Orange Bowl. Heading towards it, they come upon another short and shabby strip mall. But at this one sits a taxi, and its sign indicates that it's ready for hire.

In the stifling cab, paranoia has taken a couple of layers of skin from him. Lennox is now determined to keep the girl away from Dearing, Johnnie and Starry; she's in danger from these people and Robyn can't protect her. But maybe this Chet guy could. The problem is that she's gone into a strop. So he shows the cab driver the address. The man speaks poor English and doesn't know where it is. He explains that he is from Nicaragua. — No from here, he keeps saying.

I'm stuck with retarded people who don't know this country, Tianna is thinking, but Bobby Scotsman's trying to help her, to get her to Chet's, so she relents. — It's pretty far away.

Lennox first sinks at her words, then feels a spike of elation. It's the first time she's volunteered anything. — How far? Out of the state?

— No, it's in Florida. By the sea, but kinda right across the big freeway.

Lennox considers the airport: the car-hire concessions. It isn't too far. They head out there, as he tries to gather his thoughts. His head spins. He has no antidepressants. He is scared. Think like a cop, he tells himself, trying to put his scrambled brain back into order. His eyes are full of the phantom grit of sleeplessness and his head throbs.

Lance Dearing. Think like a cop. How did he think? What was his game?

It makes sense that Dearing's a cop. The armlock is a standard polis move the world over. The voice: full of easy authority.

Lennox knows that he ought to have suspected straight away. Even if it was the first time he'd been the recipient of the lock, the fact he didn't twig tells him just how ill-equipped he is for this.

Tianna's lips quiver. — Are we runnin away from the po-leece, or jus Lance?

A good question. — Just Lance, he ventures. — Your mum wanted me to take you to Chet's, not leave you with anybody else. So I don't care if he's a cop; that's what I'm going to do.

That seems to placate her, so Lennox converses in broken English with the driver who confirms what he's suspected about the lot of the Miami cabbie. — No way I work nights. I have family. My boss he too goddamn mean to get bulletproof glass fitted!

Lennox hears a roar and looks up, sees a plane coming in to land. Wonders how many men Lance Dearing, with or without his badge, has shot.

10

The Best Shake in Florida

All those times she'd sat practising denunciations, honing them to intensify their devastating impact. *The number of times you've let me down, Ray. Change? You'll never change. You can't. You've said it yourself: you are what you are. I've been taken for a mug again.* And now, in the bed of this stranger, all that rehearsal has been laid to waste.

The sleeping man next to her. Breathing lightly, not quite a snore; harmonised with the almost silent air con. He'd gotten up in the night to dispose of the condom. Like he had the first two. As if it would be unseemly for her to set eyes on it. But she had noticed the blood on the last one, when he'd discreetly pulled it off his exhausted dick. Trudi had taken that as her cue to get up, use the bidet and insert the spare tampon she kept in her bag. A corrosive-looking patch of her blood on his sheets; she'd felt its wetness as she'd climbed back in, perceiving herself as soiled. *What have I done?* Because it dawns on Trudi Lowe, in a violent, uncompromising shock of clarity, that Ray Lennox, her fiancé, is ill.

Mentally ill. In a way that transcends the habitual stupidity, selfishness and weakness of men. Submitting to a rising panic, she slips from this stranger's bed, struggles silently into her abandoned clothes, and sneaks from the apartment. Emerges into a sumptuously furnished and planted common area of the housing development. An understanding concierge, a small, nimble man, who looks and moves like an ex-flyweight boxer, calls her a cab to take her back to the hotel. They chat for a while, and when the taxi arrives he links arms and escorts her – like a father with his daughter on her wedding day, she fancies – up a staircase to a split-level exit that emerges into a palm-tree-lined street on the other side from the bay. Strangely, it doesn't feel weird or intrusive, the man moving with a controlled grace and no sense of sleaze. The cab is waiting and she climbs in with gratitude.

Her guilt fades as she thinks of Lennox. Anxious but determined, she will trade him night for night, event for event. *Oh, you met some people and went to a party? Funny, so did I. How was yours? Good. Mine? Oh, not so bad.*

She needs to be there, to suck down some more pain if that's what it takes. The wild infidelity she'd enjoyed much of the night excites and repels her. Reaching the hotel room she feels a relief mingled with a horrible sadness and anger that he's still not in, *what the fuck*, but she gratefully heads straight for the shower, to wash her real-estate man away. There is no message indicator light on the phone. No note. *The bastard hasn't even called.* Hasn't been back. Good, she thinks as she lies back on the bed and feels a pulse between her legs. A big man, hard and strong. *Fuck you, Lennox.*

You haven't got a fucking clue what guys are like.

But what if – if Ray Lennox is in a hospital, or dead in an alley?

Trudi sits up. The room still Rayless. *My Ray of sunshine.* Even in hushed and sullen depression, his presence makes everything haphazard and chaotic, like an electrical storm without the sound of thunder. His tendency to overcomplicate life makes her sad; that arbitrary switching from sullen alienation to passionate engagement. What is the point?

A lurid sun whites out a section of the pallid blue sky. One eye closed for the glow that hits his profile, his unaligned nose points the other across the street to a row of brightly painted homes with their broken, uneven yards. A fuzzy-haired man, wearing a filthy yellow shirt, pushes a shopping cart at a slow, uniform pace, his head bowed into its contents, only occasionally looking up as traffic zips, roars and grinds along to the intersection. A series of concrete planters filled with eucalyptus trees have been positioned in front of a cinder-block office building, to prevent people parking there. Tianna sits on one of them, legs crossed, reading the magazine on her lap. Lennox tracks the bum with the cart, following the man's line of vision to a sign:

BARCLAY AND WEISMAN
WE WILL GET YOU COMPENSATION
FOR YOUR INJURIES

Close by the office entrance, a discarded old tyre with a dead pigeon inside its black circle makes Lennox feel somehow cheered, as if it shows local wildlife's determination to resist the incursion of the ubiquitous temperate bird. He stretches and yawns, pulls his shirt from his skin. Feels his upper body draw breath.

Inside the office: T.W. Pye feels the padded chair creak under his corpulent frame as he collapses into it. He sucks on the super-sized Coke and chomps into the Big Mac as grease runs through his sweaty fingers, down three wobbling liver-spotted chins that sprout like truffles from under his mouth to the top of his chest. Now forty years old, Pye has been chronically overweight since his teens, due largely to an addiction to franchised fast food and cola. He has recently come to see that this has robbed him of health, vigour and sexuality. He's never enjoyed congress with a woman he hasn't paid for.

Now his sassy defiance is crumbling in the face of this compulsion, the resulting breathlessness, chest and arm pains, and the soul-crushing depression and anxiety attacks that plague him in the night. Most of all, it is undermined by the relentless flood of information. Coming at him from all angles, telling him in unequivocal voices: the stuff he was reared on is killing him. He can't switch on a TV without some smug liberal nutritionist notifying him that he's the draughtsman of his own ruination.

The world, or the part of it that comes into contact with him, will pay for this. The Qwik Car Rental franchise's reputation as a less stringent operator than the bigger players ensures that Pye's customers are often desperate people in a hurry. He gets at least one police inquiry per week. But T.W. Pye loves to ask questions; enjoys his sense of power over his more hapless patrons. The phone on his desk rings out shrilly just as Ray Lennox walks into his empty office. An incongruous nightclub-red velvet rope herds the non-existent customers into a utilitarian line. Pye sets down his burger, picks up the phone, cursorily regarding Lennox in petulant disapproval. — Hey! Gus! How's it hanging? *Who in God's name is this skinny-assed faggot . . . ?* — Yeah . . . sure do, Gus . . .

Lennox regards the obese man, shifting his stare to the image of a busty girl, obviously silicone-enhanced, who bursts out of the yellow two-piece swimsuit from the calendar on the wall behind him.

— Strange, Gustave, mighty strange. Sure thing, buddy. Bring em by tonight. I'll be home.

Impatience blazes in Lennox as he meets Pye's gaze. In the instant that follows a reciprocal abhorrence is conceived.

— Till tonight. See ya, Gus. Pye lets the receiver slide from his hand on to its cradle. Thickset eyes regard Lennox in cheery malice. — Now, he says, breaking into an obsequious grin.

— Need a car. Going to Bologna.

— Nice, smiles Pye, as Lennox hands over his licence. He regards it for a few seconds, holding it up to the light like it was a high-denomination banknote. — Ain't plannin on crossin the state line, are you?

— No. Bologna, Florida. Just need it for two days.

T.W. Pye dips his head, feels his smile slowly extending out towards the limits of its treachery. — Only we can't give you no car if you're planning on crossin the state line, not with you bein a foreigner n'all. New rules: war gainst terror. The big boys, Hertz, Avis, they'll be able to help you out there.

— No state line. Bologna, Florida, Lennox repeats, uneasy in the role of supplicant. — Two days max.

— Well, I got me this Volkswagen Polo. Pye's smile holds up, even as a trickle of sweat rolls from temple across cheek, like the slow slash of the psychopath's razor. — European. Economical. Ought to appeal. Where you from?

— How much? Lennox pulls out his platinum Visa.

Pye sits back, scowls, coughing out rates, terms and conditions. Lennox motions in stony accord, as the door swings open. Tianna breezes in, her jacket hooked round her finger and draped casually behind her. She beats the magazine on her leg in imitation of him. Pye takes in the indigo shorts and mustard tank top with its sparkling slogan. Sees the rangy, bony limbs coming out from them. He responds with a predator's leer; eyes narrowing, face tightening and draining of blood. Lennox catches that stink of torpid lust, causing his teeth to grind together again.

Pye senses this reaction and turns to him, feigning polite nonchalance as Tianna rocks against the desk. — Your daughter? he enquires.

Lennox glares at him in mute menace. His hands grip the edge of the counter. The bad one beset with an urgent, broken pain, which he fights down.

— He's my Uncle Ray, Tianna intervenes sweetly, turning to Lennox in a disturbing air of conspiracy, — Uncle Ray from Skatlin.

— Thought you had an accent, Pye unctuously declares, smiling at Lennox, then Tianna.

— Everybody's got an accent, Lennox says evenly, easing off the grip, enjoying the incremental receding of the pain. — You got the keys?

— C'mere. The obese clerk rises and wheezes round the other side of the counter. Lennox and Tianna follow him across the harsh brown carpet tiles, some bone-breakingly loose, that cover the concrete floor. The frosted-glass door, set in a fake-walnut partition, is grimy and caked with scum at the handle. Lennox is loath to touch it; he senses that doing so would be like removing Pye's dick from his trousers and pointing it at porcelain half a dozen times a day.

They go down a corridor, through two sets of wedged-open fire doors, out to the lot. On their way, Lennox sees it on the wall, listing returned cars: another whiteboard institutionalising idiocy, pornographically displaying the predictable meanderings of thought. He wants to rip it down.

From a distance, the board snaking round the walls of the Serious Crimes Unit office resembled a nursery-school representation of the Mardi Gras. It had become festooned with data to the point that it almost assumed sovereign sentience. The fluorescent highlighter pens and markers, the photos and Post-it notes, produced a garish effect inconsonant with the grim tale: the death of Britney Hamil. There was a manifold, slightly offensive quality in the way Drummond and Notman kept it so meticulously attractive.

Then the whiteboard at Robyn's; wiped clean. Despite all the coke, they'd been together enough to remove everything, every contact name and number. *Only Dearing, only a cop, could have been so meticulous and premeditated. Only a cop, or a villain.*

And now here he is, driving away from a weirdo at the car hire, with a young girl, a kid he doesn't even know. *But I'm fleeing from the nonces and they're in pursuit. That stoat at the car hire, could he know Dearing? Perhaps it's a network. Nonces everywhere: a free-masonry of paedophiles. Nonce-craft.*

It's ridiculous. His judgement is shot to pieces. He is in over his head.

But kids need protection. Sex offenders: they have to be stopped. It's why he's a cop, the unambiguous, unerring certainty of that particular crusade. Nonces made being a cop real: a workable and justifiable life. This time it isn't about enforcing ruinous, antiquated laws, or protecting the property of the rich. It really does become the straight-forward battle between good and evil, as opposed to that mundane norm of trying to stem the consequences of poverty, boredom, stupidity and greed.

Now they are in the hired Volkswagen, Lennox cagily driving along a wide boulevard in steady traffic. The girl silent next to him, smouldering, chewing on her bottom lip. Stuck in a side lane, they are siphoned on to a freeway. Realising he doesn't know where he's going, Lennox comes off at the next exit. — So how far is this Bologna place?

Tianna's head is in the copy of *Perfect Bride*, the bride's dress rendered grubby by his prints. — It's a long drive.

— How many hours?

— I dunno, maybe two or three. Maybe longer.

Fuck. He had to find a garage. A gas station. Buy a map.

Eminem's 'Like Toy Soldiers' plays on the radio. The chorus sets a shuddering wave of emotion coursing through Lennox. His hands whiten on the wheel. The right one stings again. That cunt is a fucking genius, he thinks, almost choking with emotion. Tears well in his eyes. *We all fall down.*

142

Britney's body, cold and lifeless. Bruises all over it; especially the throat. Bulging eyes, frozen in her last moment of pain and terror. To wrench the soul from a child in that gruesome manner was the most foul, evil transgression he could think of. *Mr Confectioner. So cold.*

He thinks about Britney in the morgue, looks at Tianna in the car seat. Wonders what Johnnie – and, for all he knows, Lance and Starry – had planned for her. Not the same as Mr Confectioner with Britney, surely. But he's a foreigner in a hired car with a child who was all but a stranger to him. Shedding light on his actions to a cop if he's pulled over will be as hard as explaining them to Trudi.

Tianna evaluates the man driving her. Both of them outlaws, on the run from Dearing. Chet would never let Lance put her away though, that was for sure. Neither would Scots Bobby, she thinks. She wonders what would happen if he tried to touch her. Recalls Vince, his doughy-faced kindness, the slowness of his caresses, those reassuring words as she stifled the urge to cry, endlessly welling and dying in his soft, ladylike hands. That's the sort of monster this one would be, transformed by a black venom seeping through his veins to make his eyes glassy and deafen his ears; not like Clemson, always an inimical force, with that crinkled smile suggesting a swarm of torment, and whose stare could bring a pack of wild dogs to heel. She closes her eyes to see Scots Bobby clearer. *Heard around the world.* She flicks them open and asks, — So we really gonna go to Chet's?

— At Bologna? Yeah, I suppose we are.

— Awesome, she says, surprised at her unexpected sparky enthusiasm.

— I'm gaunny find a petrol station, a *gas* station, get a map of the area.

Tianna chews her bottom lip thoughtfully. — A petrol station, she parrots, finding this amusing.

— Do you know his house number? Your mum gave me this address, but there was no number, he places Trudi's notebook, with his scribblings, on her lap.

She studies it and shakes her head. — He kinda stays on a boat. It's pretty awesome.

Lennox looks at the address again. A low clunk of belated recognition in his upper body; there was no house number because it was a boat. It's there in his own accusing scrawl: *marina*. For some reason, he'd imagined that term would signify nothing here: just real-estate jargon for a housing development that was at least a few miles from water. Despondency settles on his shoulders; he's a bad cop, still ignoring the obvious, prone to daft flights of fancy. The 'getting results' myth was exactly that, and his distant promotions had been gained through playing organisational politics, choosing the right master to serve at the right time. The sides of his face start to colour. — I also need to find an Internet café, soas I can get the Jambos result for the Scottish Cup, he explains, meeting her blank look. — Hearts. It's a football team: what you call soccer. Do you like soccer?

— I guess. I used to play.

— Why did you stop?

— I dunno. It's kinda lame. I don't get it, all that offside stuff.

— It never fails to amaze me how lassies never get the offside rule. It's so straightforward; the principal attacking player has to be at least level with the last defender when the ball is played through, otherwise you're offside. However, if the most forward attacker is deemed by the official not to be interfering with play, as in the case of, say —

— Whoah! My brain's kinda crumbling!

Lennox laughs and considers American sports. Baseball is the big one. He's never been to a game. He recalls a drunken conversation in Vegas with an earnest American frat boy and an old Irishman, a GAA stalwart. The Yank kid had proclaimed that the hardest thing in sport was to hit a fast-moving ball with that bat. The old GAA boy had gurgled like a choked drain in dismissal, telling them that in Irish hurling, they had to catch the ball with a stick, control it and run at speed with it while a bunch of nutters tried to chop them down. Lennox thought of the version of the game they played in Scotland, with bigger sticks. Kingussie and Newtonmore battling it out for the Shinty World Series. — What about baseball? The Merlins. Called so because they're magical, no doubt.

— It's the Marlins.

— Like Marilyn Monroe?

— M-A-R-L-I-N-S, she spells out, screwing up her face, but she's smiling a little. — They're fish, you know, like . . . swordfish, I guess.

Lennox nods, suddenly aware of his need to concentrate on the strange roads, the traffic and caffeine jangling his nerves. He's far from comfy changing lanes; trucks clank along, convertibles dart past with an arrogant flourish and SUVs rumble by with slow menace, the unstable nightclub bouncers of the automobile world.

Tianna is thinking of when she played T-ball in the park. Those polyester tops and pants they wore always smelling so good. How she was going to make the softball team. Momma sat in the bleachers, hair pulled through the back of the baseball cap, shirt and jeans tighter than the other moms, busy eyes flirting under the visor. Then one day another face appeared beside her; Vince, with his big easy smile. Then they were in Jacksonville, then Surfside, then down here, heading south all the time, like they'd be driven into the ocean. Pushed into soccer with the enthusiastic Latina girls, the game taking place around her. Momma watching on, hair shorter, face puffier, as she tried to control the ball while looking out for the next other by her lone parent's side.

On the radio Lennox listens to a recording of Elvis saying how much he loved army life. He recalls hearing this entire speech at a Graceland exhibit; in its respectful antipathy it sounded nothing like this crudely edited propaganda broadcast to motivate today's impoverished young Americans into joining up for military service. But for the current crop of GIs, there would be no private apartment in Germany or a fourteen-year-old Priscilla. Like the army, her parents cast a blind eye at the King's noncing of their daughter. He was a gentleman, they said.

Lennox pulls into a gas station. The stench of petrol fumes blends with the deep-fried chemicals from the adjacent McDonald's. In this heat they are probably more intoxicating than the weak beer a blue neon sign makes him dream of sucking on. The attached shop is a scruffy enduring variety store that sells fridge magnets of several states, various newspapers, convenience food like chips, which mean crisps to him and scary-looking stuff called 'beef jerky'. Packaged like a bastard child of meat and cheap confectionery, it could never be health food. Pigeon-sized chickens roast on a spit inside a glass case. A bank of cigarettes in vending drawers stack up on the wall behind the counter and smutty mags on high shelving are indicated by uniform, blacked-out covers.

Tianna looks at the magnets of the different states. Her momma collected them in a half-assed way; two of Illinois graced their fridge. *It was crazy to collect stuff like that, shit always got lost, you never got no full set.*

Lennox buys a map book, covering the Miami–Dade County area, and a fold-out showing the main roads and towns across the state of Florida. — Any Internet cafés around here? he asks the clerk.

— No, I know of nothing like that. Where are you from?

— Scotland.

— Sean Connery!

— Aye. I just wanted to get a football result.

The clerk looks around to ensure the place is empty, then beckons Lennox through into a small room marked STAFF ONLY. He fires up a computer and goes online. — I am from Mexico. Scotland will not be in the World Cup, no? He shakes his head in sad acknowledgement and logs on to the official Hearts website. It was two–one against Kilmarnock. *That'll do nicely, safely into the draw for the next round.* He quickly glances over at Kickback, the fans forum. Maroon Mayhem has posted again.

That cunt is criticising, nay, abusing Craig Gordon for one fucking mistake. He won't let it go.

Lennox posts as Ray of Light.

What is it with some radges? The best goalie Scotland's produced in decades and he's somehow not good enough for Hearts, he's only here to be slagged off by bams like Maroon Mayhem?

He thanks the garage attendant, wishing Mexico all the best in the World Cup, before remembering that they play in Hibernian

green. Outside, squinting in the sun, Lennox studies the Miami–Dade County street plan, finding nothing to approximate this Chet guy's living or mooring location of Bologna. Then he searches the Florida map. Bologna is on the state's other coast, on the Gulf of Mexico. The table at the back of the book tells him the kid was right. The drive is likely to take at least three hours.
— You go back to the car. I've a phone call to make.
— You callin Momma?
— You know her cell number?
Tianna shakes her head.
— Why not?
— Just don't, she frowns. — Look, she ain't got no credit on it, and she changes it too much for me to be rememberin it.
— Okay, we can call her when we get to Chet's. He'll probably know it and she might have things sorted out by then.
— Maybe, the kid says wearily. — I gotta use the restroom.
As Tianna departs to the toilets that adjoin the shop, Lennox heads across the gas station concourse to the mounted phone. A deep breath prepares him to call the room at the Colonial Hotel.
— Hello! comes the sharp cry.
— Trudi, it's me.
— Ray! Where the hell have you been? I've been worried sick! I was going to call the local police, go round the hospitals; I was even going to phone your mother and Bob Toal, she wails. Guilt hits her like a train and she's glad that he can't see her face. — Are you okay?
— Aye, I'm fine. Lennox has to mentally punch back another wave of fatigue. — Don't get in touch with the police.
— Have you taken anything? she interrogates in sharp, urgent panic. — Any cocaine?
He hesitates. Decides to come as clean as he feels he can. — I had a couple of small lines at this party. He pauses, wanting to spit out all the deceit. The pop psychology, the self-analytical tones that chime with her. He's glad she can't see his face. — But I was okay. I suppose that I just wanted to know I could walk away. It was a one-off, his tones are grave, — and I know it sounds strange,

147

but I felt I just had to be sure it wisnae for me any more. Be sure I could walk away.

— And that was you *walking away*, Ray? Staying out all night? Where *were* you, Ray?

— I know . . . I'm sorry . . . I just needed time to think . . . It was a mistake.

— Time to think? You've had time to think, Ray. It's *time to think* that's caused all these fucking problems! Then she desists for a moment. — What's going on, Ray? Are you in trouble? Where *were* you, Ray? Where *are* you? Are you in trouble? *Are you?*

— No, not me. Somebody else. I got a bit drunk last night. Met some people . . . this couple, and I went to a party at their apartment. These guys came by, one of them tried to mess with this kid. Her mother's in some kind of trouble. Her boyfriend left, they fell out, and she wants me to take the kid to her uncle's place. It's about a two- to three-hour drive, and we're on our way now. I hired a car.

— What?!

— I hired a car. I couldn't leave the kid. She was all alone.

— But where's the mother? And why are you involved? Listen, they have their own police across here, Ray. It's nothing to do with you!

— I can't leave the kid, Lennox protests. — I'm only dropping her off at her uncle's.

The line was a trail of gunpowder, the receiver at his ear the explosive and her rising voice the approaching flame. — Who do you think you are? This has nothing to do with you. *I'm* something to do with you. I'm your fiancée! This is our holiday!

— There's some dodgy shit going on here. I need tae make sure that this kid's safe. He gazes in sudden urgency across the forecourt. Tianna is talking to a couple of young guys. *She looks like a wee lassie. She looks like a truck-stop hooker.*

— *You* need! *You* need! You're havering shite! What the fuck! Don't you hear yourself, Ray? Don't you ever just stop for a few seconds and actually listen; listen to the crap that comes out of your mouth? Is this to be the pattern of our married life? Trudi moans miserably. — You can't stop playing the policeman. What kind of an idiot are you?

Those fucking weasels. One kid at the age of realising he's not somebody's property, a mutinous twist to his features. With him, an older boy, charged with the hormones of youth, looking for a hole to fill with his nagging self. — I have to go. Everything's okay, he snaps. The two young guys. Talking to Tianna. They can't see him watching them.

— Okay!? With you playing *Miami Vice?* Who the fuck do you think you are? Trudi hisses in loathing. — You stay out all night, getting up to fuck knows what –

— People are in trouble. That might not mean anything to you, but I don't work for the fuckin lecky board, he roars, keeping his eyes on the girl. *Was she going to get in the car with those guys? Surely not!*

— That's right! Demean me and what I do! You self-important, pompous prick! All I wanted was to kick back and plan our wedding. I apologise for that, Ray. Sarcasm whips down the phone line. — I'm genuinely sorry. *Sorry* that I wanted a holiday with *my* fiancé. Sorry to be upset that he stayed out partying all night with some woman I don't know and now has her *child* in tow. Sorry to be such a big fucking weirdo!

Tianna flirting, provocatively leaning back on the car bonnet like a model, as she flicks her hair. The older boy, stiff-faced: feet slow-dancing on the spot. The younger one: staring at her in open-mouthed awe. — Look Trudi, I –

In the hotel room, Trudi slams the phone down. Then she panics and wants to call him right back. Dials the desk to ask for the ring-back number.

Lennox smashes the receiver on to its hook and walks quickly across the forecourt. The youths take note, alarmed at the speed at which he advances towards them. — Guess what, Tianna? A dry rasp distorts his voice into a growl. — It was two–one for Hearts. At Tynecastle. Didnae get the scorers. But ah tell you that. Did I tell youse? Dinnae think so, he says, now right in the boys' faces. — Ah didnae tell yis cause ah dinnae ken who the fuck youse are. Gaunny tell me?

149

— We was just talking, sir, the younger boy says, now just a nice kid. The senior one is harder; flinty eyes look sullenly at Lennox, gaining a sly confidence as an older couple approach. The man, he assumes it's the boys' father, is a brawny guy in a short-sleeved shirt and green khaki shorts. A growth on his face hints at a rough night. The mother is clad in a tight dress that shows a pregnant stomach. Her arms are big and flabby. — What's goin on here? the man asks.

— Ask your boys, Lennox says. He sees dirt under the man's fingernails. Feels something ring inside his brain.

— We was just talking, the nice kid repeats.

— Is that right?

— Don't know what you're getting all high and mighty about, mister. The man looks at Tianna. — You let your daughter dress like that? What age is she? Know what I think? I think you'd better haul your ass outta here before I call a cop. They put sons of bitches like you behind bars, ya know that?

— What –

Tianna blushes in embarrassment. — They were, I mean, we was all jus talking, like he said, and she nods to the young boy.

Lennox looks at the man, then at Tianna. He notices for the first time that she's wearing make-up: eye stuff and lipstick. She doesn't look like a ten-year-old. She must have put it on in the restroom. Outrage punctured, he takes a mental step back. — No harm in talking, eh? C'mon, honey, he looks to Tianna, — we can't keep Uncle Chet waiting.

The couple regard him suspiciously as they walk back to the car. Lennox trembles inside every step of the way. *They'll probably call the police and I'll get done. I can't be so stupid. Not with Dearing connected.* He thinks about the Edinburgh man, Kenny Richey, kept now for twenty years on death row in an Ohio prison, for a crime even the state acknowledge he couldn't possibly have committed. *The legal system is as medieval here as anywhere, if you didn't have money and connections and you fell foul of the power brokers. It had a colour, and that colour was green. There was Rodney King justice and O.J. Simpson justice.*

Oblivious to the sad, lonely ringing of the payphone, they get back into the car and Lennox hits the gas pedal, watching the outraged family recede in the rear-view mirror. They drive through residential blocks, broken up by parking lots and strip malls with low-yielding enterprises like cheap insurance brokerage, electrical repairs and pet supplies stores.

Taking a wrong turn north on 27th Avenue, they pass through a district full of black youths glowering in brooding menace from street corners, or the porches of fading homes. By instinct he understands their terrible anger; under economic and social quarantine in the ghetto, beset by this need to kick holes in a world so confining and unyielding.

— Try not to stop at no lights, Tianna urges, — I think this is Liberty City.

Complying as far as is possible, Lennox drives west, then south, then west again, as he asks Tianna, — Do you always dress like that?

Sour defiance tints her expression. — I suppose.

— Do the other girls at your school dress like that?

— Sure they do.

Lennox feels himself make a doubtful *moue* as the network of slip roads begins to fall away, the city thinning out. Tianna pulls something from her bag. They are cards: baseball cards. As she looks through them, he turns the radio back on.

A tinny, wiffling disco groove hisses out from the car speakers. He deft-tunes it, till the sound comes in stronger. The music infiltrates him, sparking his nerve-jangled body like the useless excitement of the cocaine rush. The beat sticking him between his ribs like a blade. Lennox feels like he is doing something illegal, and wonders whether or not he is. He struggles to control a sudden spasm on one side of his face. Craves the blunting edge of his pills. Wants to fast-forward to when the hangover will be gone and he'll open up like a flower to suck in the world's goodness.

Tianna knows she's annoyed him, talking to those kids. The older one, she knew what he wanted. *But no way he could've made me, or tricked me or nothin. He was just a kid. And the Scotsman, this Bobby Ray, it was like he was jealous of him. Maybe if a girl could be a woman, then a man could be a boy.* She winds down the window, tossing back her hair in the breeze, resting the crook of her arm on its edge, wishing she had a cool pair of shades.

After a bit they pull into the parking lot of a large mall. — Why are we stopping here? Tianna asks.

— We get some new clothes for you.

— Awesome!

— I get to pick them, Lennox says, opening the door car, — or at least veto. You're travelling with me, he says firmly, in response to her disgruntled pout.

Tianna gets out and slams the door shut. She looks at him from across the vehicle, squinting in the sun. The model pose again. — What do I get?

Her pitch is teasing in a way that makes him feel queasy as she moves towards him. — You get a milkshake. He points over at one of the franchises, an ice-cream parlour. — It says they do the best shake in Florida.

Tianna gyrates, sticking out and shaking her backside, proclaiming, — *I* do the best shake in Florida!

Lennox wants to laugh because the kid is funny. But she isn't a pole dancer and it's wrong for her to behave that way. He converts the nervous impulse to giggle into a frown.

She catches his evident distress. — Jeez, lighten up.

He goes to speak but can think of nothing to say. He is just a Scottish cop with a mental health problem and an uptight, controlling fiancée who needs his weakness so that she can play Mother Teresa once in a while. It doesn't equip him for this. — I'd just like it if you covered yourself up a bit, that's all.

— Why?

— Well, when people see lots of skin exposed, they react to that. You're a bright girl, but people don't see that. They just see skin. They don't take you seriously, they don't see you as a person . . . He hears the most extreme feminisms meet with the Taliban in his tone.

Tianna feels something punch her hard inside her chest. *Skin. That was it with Vince and Clemson, all of them. Skin.* She contemplates this simple mystery, eyes adroit and pained. — But you see me as a person?

152

The kid got it. The kid fucking knew. For the first time Lennox senses that deep down inside, she has the stuff. Maybe he's just seeing what he wants to see. — Aye, of course I do, he smiles, patting her lightly on the back, and quickly withdrawing his hand as if it's touched hot coals. *How many grooming nonces start that way, with normal human contact, before shifting gear?*

The mall is bland and sterile from the outside but, as its automatic doors swish open, its air-conditioned superiority to almost any equivalent in the UK is evident. The grime of Salford Shopping Centre, near where Stacey Earnshaw went missing, was a million miles from this brightly coloured mall of pastel oranges, lemons and salmon pinks. There was a record store, across from a rack of phones. Lennox gives Tianna two twenty-dollar bills. — I've got a call to make. You go over to that record store and get us some sounds for the drive.

— Awesome, Tianna says again, takes the bills and skips across the mall.

Lennox gets a hold of a phone book from the attendant at the information desk. There are numerous entries for the local offices of the police department under the City of Miami. He is going to see if he can get a reaction from Dearing, the cop who seems to be calling all the shots. He looks first at Allapattah 1888 NW 21st. *No.* He is so tired now, feeling the jet lag, the coke withdrawal. He wants his antidepressants as waves of panic hit him in irregular pulses. They have to be faced down, but sting his psyche like a bad curry would his gullet. He worries about driving in this condition with the kid. The receptionist tells him that no Lance Dearing works here. So he tries West Little Havana just because Flagler Steet, where the office is listed, sounds familiar. A female, Hispanic voice comes on the phone. — You try North Leel Havana. You find Lance there, she cheerfully informs him. He sees the entry and the address for North Little Havana. *Starry's right about Robyn and her Riverside pretensions.* He calls the number and asks for Lance.

— Officer Lance Dearing, North Lil' Havana Station. How can I help you?

Dearing's voice creeps him out. But Lennox draws power from

his revulsion, and braces himself. It's time to turn up the heat. —
You can pray for somebody to help *you*, Dearing. That's all you
can fuckin well do at this stage.

— Who the hell is . . . ?

Lennox hears the realisation seep down the phone line. He's
comforted by the fact that Dearing is just a police officer, not a
sergeant. *An expendable uniformed spastic. But he might be getting his
arse covered by some dirty nonce further up the line.* Lennox recalls the
swaggering typeface of Maroon Mayhem, and his threatening
remarks to other posters on Kickback. Although he was obviously
a retard who lived with his mother, Lennox finds himself aping
his style. — I know you now, prick-face. I know who you are,
where you live and where you work. Most importantly, I know
exactly what you're up to and who you're up to it with. I'm going
to take you right down, sunshine.

If Lance Dearing is fazed, his concealment skills are consum-
mate. — Our Skarrish friend. Listen to me, Ray: you are in serious
trouble. Let me tell you this: if you do not return that girl to the
custody of her mother, a long-standing personal friend of mine,
I'm going to issue an APB on you, charging you with the kidnap
of a Florida minor. You do *not* want that, Raymond: trust me on
this.

Nice, Lennox thinks. Professional tones. Letting me know the
gravity of the situation, but at the same time the use of the
Christian name to indicate friendship and acceptance. Attempting
to isolate you while simultaneously presenting himself as your only
ally. — I take it that means you'll issue my description to all squad
cars, he says. *Dearing might not be bluffing.*

— That is *exactly* what I'll do. I've only refrained from taking
this action so far as it would jus get Robyn and Tianna into more
trouble with social services. Also, and I may be a damn fool, I
believe that you got their best interests at heart. But let me tell
you one thing, Ray: you are misguided and you will bring big
trouble on yourself, and Robyn and that child, should you continue
to keep her from her home.

— Home? A place full of fucking paedophiles, he hears himself
say, — that's no home for a kid!

It strikes Lennox that every atom of his body is pulsing with the same sense: that he's stumbled on to something bigger than a drunken pervert and some coked-up, low-life mother who'd left her kid again. He just doesn't know what, nor can he elucidate Dearing's role.

— I think you got it all wrong, Ray. You are way, way out of line.

He has to think, to find out from the kid. And this Chet guy. — I'll call you back in a while. It can either be here or on your cell. You decide.

— Where are you, Ray? Lance Dearing calmly asks.

Lennox has had enough of telephone interrogations. — Give me your cellphone number. Now. Or I hang up.

After a pause, Lance Dearing seems a little cagier when he speaks again. — Okay, Ray, but jus you take good care of that lil' girl, y'all hear? Then he deliberately enunciates the number and Lennox scribbles it down in Trudi's notepad, feeling the flush of his small victory.

— Do the right thing, Ray, Dearing says, — by that lil' girl, and her momma.

He's too quick to cede control. Is he bluffing, or holding all the aces? Lennox can't trust himself to judge.

Then, in savage flashback, his brain sears with an image of Johnnie on top of Tianna, trying to rape her. *Guess I jus like the taste of young pussy.* Lance's easy, unperturbed carriage: *We all been round the block enough times to know to take our pleasures where we can get em. No questions asked.*

—You haul that child across the state line and you are in big trouble – . . . Lance begins.

— Shut yir fuckin hole, cunty baws, Lennox sneers. — And the trouble will be all yours, that I guarantee, and he slams the phone down. Sees Tianna eagerly making her way towards him. Tries to stop shaking.

— They ain't got much of a choice. It's a pretty crummy mall, but I got some good stuff, and she pulls a plastic bag from her sheep's head backpack.

— Humph. Lennox looks through the CDs. It was going to

be a long ride. He shifts his gaze to Tianna. — Let's get you something to wear. Cover up some skin.

— I guess.

It's Monday morning and many of the shops are shut, including the Macy's, which, as a notice informs them, has closed for inventory purposes. — Sears is open, Lennox says, pointing at the big store.

Tianna's features pinch. — Even Momma's grandma wouldn't go in there. It's true; inside everybody is old. *If my ma was American, this is where she'd shop*, Lennox mulls. In trying to dress Tianna appropriately, he feels as if he's been transformed from pimp into fussy old maiden aunt. *But she's just a kid, she cannae be allowed to dress like a tart.*

Lennox buys some loose-fitting clothes for her, replaces his lost Red Sox baseball cap and picks up a new pair of shades. Then Tianna heads for the mall restroom, emerging in jeans and a T-shirt. It's better, but he begs her to wash the make-up from her face and she reluctantly heads back in to comply.

— That's great, Lennox says, encouraged by the result on her return. She looks like a ten-year-old.

— I look like a geek, she says, but it's a token protest.

They go to the ice-cream parlour and order. Lennox gets the best shake in Florida, chocolate. Tianna has a strawberry-ice-cream float. He looks at her again, both delighting in the crackle as the bubbled remnants of the dessert rattle up her straw. She's just a kid. Why is he with her?

I'm a cop.

I'm not a good cop. I've gone as far as I can go.

No. Not true.

He'd gone as far as he needed to go. Far enough to hunt the bad fuckers, and lead the investigation from the front. Another promotion and he'd be a Toal: deskbound. His grim lot was that he was drawn to the dark side of policework – anything else would be a waste of his time – but he let it get to him. To do that sort of job, sleep soundly and get up and repeat the process the next day, you had to be like Dougie Gillman. Gillman would never get promotion. He would go before any board of suits and cough back monosyllabic answers to their bullshit questions and quietly judge them. They would feel his contemptuous wrath and scorn. Wouldn't be able to meet those loathsome gelid eyes. Because Gillman spoke a truth – a particularly dark and brutal truth, but one that still had the power to shame and damn the liars around him.

And like Robbo before he cracked, Gillman was a good cop. The fear he inspired made you happy he was on your team. Lennox would never be like that. In a square go he could kickbox Gillman into a pulp. But he'd never end his life. So Gillman would pick himself up and come for him and snuff him out like a candle. Unlike Lennox, he set no limits. As the superior cop in the hierarchy Lennox was as powerless as a liberal parent who didn't believe in corporal punishment dealing with a calculating, psychotic offspring.

Strange then, to be thinking of Gillman, while gazing idly at the pretty Hispanic waitress, light and graceful as she hops like a small bird between tables, dispensing coffee.

— Do you think she's good-looking? Tianna asks.

— I suppose so, he says, musing that the kid missed nothing. It strengthens his resolve never to have children, especially a daughter. *Fuck that.*

Tianna's voice goes musical. — I want my hair cut so I get bangs.

Lennox decodes the glint in her eye as sly and the blood ices in his veins. Tianna quickly picks up on his reaction. She pulls strands of hair across her forehead. — Like here, she explains.

— Oh . . . a fringe. Lennox is relieved, as his heartbeat normalises.

She glances up at him with an unexpected coldness, laying something inside of him to waste. The fond, paternal vibe that was settling in evaporates as he sees himself through her eyes; from the knowing, contemptuous ferocity in her glance, he might as well be a jug-eared rookie cop telling a snooty, rich woman that she can't park here.

Uncle Chet will be the man, he thinks, his head buzzing. *Chet will sort it out.* He signals for the bill. The ice-cream parlour is filling up with mothers and children, cops and sales clerks. Tianna tells him about Chet's big boat on the Gulf coast. Then her conversation abruptly changes. — The men Momma brings home are bastards, she says in a low, quavering voice, like she half expects Lennox to punish her for the profanity.

— Chet's not like that, though?

Her head twists vigorously.

— Is he your mum's brother or your father's brother?

— Just Chet, and she clams up into silence again. The waitress skips over with the bill, looking to the line that has formed at the door. Lennox takes the hint and settles up, they rise and make their way outside.

Another surrogate uncle. But did that have to be a bad thing? He himself was now attempting to fulfil that very same role, and knew practically nothing about young girls. He tries to remember what his sister Jackie was like at Tianna's age. It was different evaluating someone when looking up at them from a kid's perspective. Five years his senior, Jackie was the one they thought would do well. Her horse-riding lessons were a big deal in the family, making a powerful statement about them. And she had prospered. Became a lawyer; then married a top one, a man whom Lennox, burdened with an unshakeable belief that anyone who talked for a living was a bullshitter, had to fight every impulse not to openly detest.

He'd sensed Jackie's contempt for the rest of them growing with every riding lesson she completed. Hated his mother's perverse pride in his sister's disdain of them, regarding it as a victory that they'd brought up a child who had learned to patronise and loathe them, simply for their working-class status.

Jackie had her Georgian New Town home and her country place up in Deeside, her successful husband and her polite, Merchant School kids. It was her life and as far as he was concerned, she was welcome to it. But he sensed that Trudi was covetous of this status, like she believed Lennox was essentially made of the same stuff, and with her scalpel-like love she could scrape off the bad bits and put this career policeman back on the right track.

The horse-riding lessons. Horsey, horsey.

While Jackie was on horseback, Lennox and his mate Les Brodie would cycle everywhere. Told to stay off the main roads, they'd take their bikes to Colinton Dell, along the path through the woods by the river, into the darkened mouth of that old stone tunnel.

Lennox suddenly blenches as something spins past his face. His heartbeat normalises: three kids are throwing a Frisbee around in the parking lot, as their mother loads up the car with groceries.

— Sorry, sir, says one fresh-faced, skinny wee boy. With his eager but sad puppy eyes, he's the sort of kid, Lennox considers, who will always invoke a slight sense of pity, even outside of his melancholy thought stream. He picks up the disc and spins it at the boy, who catches it and throws it back to him with a light in his eye that indicates a bona fide game has started up. Lennox chucks it in Tianna's direction, but she doesn't move to intercept as it flies past her.

She wants to join in, but they're just bone-headed kids. That's what he told her: *Don't be a stupid kid, you're a woman, a beautiful young woman.* He'd explained to Tianna how numerical age meant nothing; it was all to do with maturity. Some ten-year-olds were ten. Some were like five. Some twenty-year-olds were like four-year-olds. Not Tianna, she was always a woman; strong, proud and sexy – it was nothing to be ashamed of. Vince, Pappy Vince, told her that she should never be ashamed of not being a silly little girl.

And her childhood glided past her like the Frisbee, destined for the hands of another.

11

Road Trip

As the map shakes in his trembling, swollen hand, Lennox is simultaneously squeezed by the sense that he's fucking up big time. Trying to drive while reading a Miami street plan and a Florida road map is inviting trouble. To his weary eyes the urban cartography is just badly printed lines of different colour: grid-like black, some reds, a few blues and the odd green. The print is so small he can barely decipher it. What did it all mean? He's discomforted to find himself driving west on Highway 41, away from his intended route, the 75 Interstate they called Alligator Alley. Worse, it seems to take him back through the district they were fleeing from, where Robyn and Tianna lived. She's stiff in the passenger seat, back into that silent world to which he's denied access.

All he can do is keep going west. The two to three hours to get to Bologna on the interstate will be longer on Highway 41, the Tamiami Trail. It comes upon them bearing its frustrating announcement of a fifty-five miles-per-hour speed limit, as a median barrier of aluminium, dispassionately bearing the scars of accidents past, splits the concrete lanes of the highway.

Lennox is surprised how quickly and resoundingly the outskirts of Miami become the swamps of the Everglades. Birds of prey he has never seen before, like giant crows cross-bred with hawks, hover above. Many are splattered beneath the wheels, scavenging for roadkill and ending up victims themselves, smearing the highway in varying degrees of pulverisation. Some forested areas are decimated by what Lennox assumes to be hurricane damage. Trees are bent, buckled and wilted as if warped under intense heat rather than wind, and areas of perimeter fence are ripped aside. In the swamp big white cranes hang unfeasibly in threadbare trees, making him think again of Les and the seagulls.

Tianna has redeemed her old set of baseball cards and is counting them.

— You like these cards, eh. Do ye collect them?

— Uh-uh. I jus keep these ones. They were my daddy's. She regards him through the shield of her hair, waiting to see his reaction. — They ain't worth nothin but he did have some valuable ones. Do y'all like baseball?

— Not really. To be honest, I'm not mad keen on American sports. I mean, baseball's just rounders, a bairn's game, he scoffs, before realising her age. — I mean tae say, there was never a Scotsman who played baseball!

— Oh yeah? Tianna challenges, handing him a card.

BOBBY THOMSON
(b: October 23, 1923, Glasgow, Scotland)
264 home runs in 14 seasons. Famous for the winning 'shot heard around the world', which won the National League pennant for the New York Giants against the Brooklyn Dodgers in 1951.

The 'Staten Island Scot' was the youngest in a family of six who immigrated to the USA in his childhood. He played for the Giants, Braves, Cubs, Red Sox and Orioles. Now retired, he lives in Savannah, Georgia.

Lennox steals glances as he holds it tight to the wheel. — That's me telt!

Tianna laughs, taking the card back, and is suddenly distracted by a passing motor with two racing competition bicycles fastened on to its roof rack. — Awesome, she says, pointing at them. — Did you ride a bike as a kid?

— Aye. Lennox is cut to the quick as he recalls the prized blue-and-white Raleigh he got for his eleventh birthday. How his parents stressed he was to look after it, not give anyone in the scheme a shot of it.

— What was it like?

— Just a bike. His reply curt, as the memory stings home; his

161

gullet acrid with last night's liquor, his brain razing open old overgrown neural paths. He swallows hard and his sphincter muscle tightens. — What else do you like? he says, changing the subject. — I mean, do you like animals?

Tianna considers this question for a bit. Her grace in giving it the gravity it doesn't merit paradoxically makes him feel even more of a simpleton for asking it. — I guess I like dolphins. We saw some when we were out on Chet's boat. And I kind of like seals, alligators, fish and manatees; all the marine stuff.

— You must have seen a lot of that, living here.

— Mostly jus read about em.

— Aye, but you must have seen an alligator.

— Nope, not a real one, she says. — We drove through the Glades a whole buncha times but they always said that we ain't got time to stop and look at no reptiles. Guess they was jus in a hurry to get to their parties. Momma and Starry and . . . She turns to the window, unable to finish the sentence.

He could see Robyn and Starry coked up, heading for some soirée, Tianna all drowsy in the back of the car. — Who? he asks. — Who would be driving you? Your mother?

— Momma and some other people.

Lennox watches her chewing her hair and looking towards the floor of the vehicle. — Like Lance and Johnnie?

— I don't wanna talk about them, Ray. Her face crumples and her voice rises. — Can we *please* not talk about them?

— Okay, sweetheart, no worries, Lennox clumsily pats the distressed girl's shoulder. He decides not to push it. It's a long trip; let her tell him when she's ready. It's the first time, he realises, that she's addressed him directly by his name. *Fuck sakes. They won't even let the kid stop, in the fuckin Everglades, to watch the alligators. Who are these people?*

Lennox lets some avant-garde jazz soothe him, but it soon morphs into pan-piped rest-home gloop that saps his mojo and really galls Tianna, whose arm lashes to the dial, killing the sound.

— This is grossing me out!

— What about the stuff you bought at the mall?

162

She digs into the sheep bag on her knee, eagerly producing a Kelly Clarkson CD which she slides into the player. Lennox is relieved as the car stereo keeps expelling it. The others get the same treatment. — This is so lame!

— That's one to report to the car-hire place, he says, struggling to keep the smile off his face. He fails, and she catches him and play-hits his arm.

— You!

They switch over to 101.5 Lite FM, which announces itself as 'South FLA's number-one radio station'. Chicago's 'So Hard to Say I'm Sorry' comes on and he thinks of Robbo.

There follow numerous talk adverts from sincere but excited voices proffering personal loans and credit facilities on just about everything, but mainly real estate and cars. Then a plethora of agencies earnestly offering packages of debt consolidation and reduction services. Probably the same people, Lennox considers, raising a bottle of Evian to his lips, another broadside in the battle against his broiling thirst.

An eerie voice interrupts proceedings hissing: 'If you're sitting in a dark room holding your shotgun, thinking bout killing your boss, turn on the light. Turn on Lite FM.'

At Tianna's urging, he changes channels. The Beatles sing 'Love Me Do'. Lennox is thinking of Trudi, as they pass a truck with a 'Support Our Boys' sticker, and begins singing along in an exaggerated Scouse accent. Tianna joins in, at first under her breath, then with increasing gusto. Long before the end they are cheesily serenading each other.

When the song stops, both are embarrassed by the new-found, gaudy intimacy that has crept up on them. They retreat self-consciously like a couple in a Hollywood musical who have just enjoyed a spectacular dance. Tianna pulls her hair from her face and shyly asks him, — Back at the gas station, I guess that was your girlfriend you was callin, right?

— Aye. Eh, yeah.

— Back in Skatlin?

— Naw, eh, she's here in Miami. He nods to the magazine on her lap. — We're getting married later this year.

Tianna falls silent and seems to think about this for a while. Then after a bit she asks, — What's she like?

— She's nice, Lennox says, instantly feeling the tameness of his response. He's put her through so much, and here he is, speeding away from her with a kid he hardly knows.

Tianna stares at him in vigilance. — You ain't, like, one of Momma's boyfriends?

— No, he says emphatically, as a vision of Robyn's caterpillar bush and her hand in his trousers, jerking him, almost makes him squirm, — we're just friends.

That seems to cheer the kid up. — I kinda like you, Ray, she says with a toothy grin.

— I like you, Lennox smiles, looking ahead, suddenly aware that he does. Then his body stiffens as he feels the girl's arms wrapping round his torso in a reckless hug. Registering his agitation, she immediately retreats, finding his hand simultaneously pushing her back into her seat. — Don't do that, Lennox snaps, adding, — I'm driving!

He grips the wheel tightly with his right hand, feeling the small fractured bones dig into his tendons as Tianna sits back in her seat, eyes glowing. She gets the baseball cards back out from her bag.

Lennox realises that he fears this child; fears her physical proximity, the damage she could inflict upon him now that she senses her power. He's frequently observed the calculating tyrant emerge from those who've undergone unfair victimisation; all he can do is try and keep her intelligence and humanity to the fore.

The radio plays 'Angel of the Morning' and Lennox snatches at the dial. It settles on a hip-hop urban rhythms channel, where the presenter squeals: 'This is Beyoncé with the big titties.'

Tianna laughs as Lennox cringes and hits the dial again. As he drives he can feel her evaluating gaze on him. The silence continues, but as they approach a commercialised Indian village, Lennox pulls up. He needs to get out and stretch. Stiffness and languor have been nibbling at him. He puts on the new Red Sox hat, fiddling with the strap, unable to get it as comfortable as the last one. Sees a sign advertising swamp tours. They had been talking about alligators and he's never seen one, nor has Tianna. It was crazy, a kid living in Florida. Another hour's stop would do no harm. Tianna leans forward to put the magazine above the dashboard, and Lennox sees his hot breath bending the thin hairs on her wrist. He gets out the car, aware as he rises that his shirt is stuck to his back like a second skin. He gives a shrug and tries to free it, then accepts the futility of it all. He extends his gnarled limbs, letting the lavish sun spray him. — Let's have a look at those alligators, he smiles, clocking her widening eyes, waiting for her to say 'awesome' again, and she doesn't disappoint him.

They book a ride on a swamp cruiser: an outboard-motored launch with a wire-mesh cage around the seated passenger area that's both foreboding and reassuring. Apart from the skinny, wild-eyed guide, whom they sit opposite, so close Lennox can feel their knees touch, there are two elderly women and two young couples, one with a toddler. The engine splutters into action and the boat pulls away as the guide, who has introduced himself as Four Rivers, warns: — Keep them fingers inside the cage if you want em back!

As they splutter on to the mangrove swamps, Tianna is impressed by the ubiquity of alligators of all sizes. Some cruise by like drifting logs with only their eyes above the waterline, others lie partially submerged in the shallows. Most bask on the banked mudflats under the mangrove trees, looking quietly sinister. — This is sooo neat! she squeals in delight.

Lennox isn't too sure about the alligators. Especially when they pass a group of larger ones. These fat, grinning creatures look as contented and conspiring as veteran football hooligans relaxing under the parasols of continental cafés. They aren't going dart around in search of prey. They'll wait patiently for the opportunity to arise, before ruthlessly striking. No wonder Lacoste is such a popular thug brand, he considers.

Then a long, throaty, trumpeting sound accosts their ears. Picking up on their disquiet, Four Rivers smiles. — That's a gator.

— I didn't know they made noises like that, Tianna says, surprised at the mammal-like resonance.

— I gotta say it's pretty rare durin the day. But when it gets dark out here on the swamp, you can hear em good enough, callin to each other in the night. I wouldn't recommend anybody comin out here then, the guide says, and starts telling outlandishly scary stories about the reptiles. His close proximity and spooky eyes have been unnerving Lennox, who feels there's something not quite right about him. It's his voice; it seems a fusion of different accents he can't place, that and the fact that he's taking a particular interest in Tianna. — What about you, young lady, never seen a live gator before today? And I don't mean in no zoo, I'm talking bout the wild.

— Well, I didn't see it cause I was sleepin in the back, but my momma was drivin out along the highway and we almost hit one. Momma said he crawled back on to the verge along the banks into the swamp. We stopped the car, but didn't get out.

Four Rivers' laugh exposes a mouthful of rotten teeth and Lennox can smell alcohol on his breath. It makes him think of Scotland and work. — Well, that was mighty wise. Cause gators can grow up to seventeen feet long and over short distances they move as fast as a lion and –

— Seventeen feet, eh? Lennox cuts in. — Have you ever seen one that big here?

— Close on it. Saw one critter, must've have been about fifteen feet long, the guileful Four Rivers beams. — So where you from, sir?

That familiar paralysis come over Lennox; what to say when abroad. Scottish? British? European? — I'm from Scotland, in the United Kingdom of Great Britain and Northern Ireland, in the European Community, he says, taken aback at his own pomposity.

— Well, Brin or Skatlin, or whatever you call it, now that's jus a tiny little island, and you sure won't see no wild animals of any size over there, Four Rivers mockingly dismisses him, encouraging some tourists to join in.

— Yeah. It's not so big in land mass compared to the USA, Lennox concedes. — Mind you, when I was in Egypt along the banks of the Nile, we saw crocodiles that made your alligators look like fish bait.

Some chuckles emanate from the group. They are evidently enjoying the joust, especially Tianna. — Crocodiles are bigger than alligators then, huh, Ray?

— An alligator, as our friend here has stated, Lennox luxuriantly stretches out in the sun as he nods to Four Rivers, who now regards him in brooding silence, — can grow up to seventeen feet. But a crocodile can grow over thirty foot long, twice the size of this boat.

Lennox realises he's feeling good now, still so tired, but nice tired, as the hangover is receding. He hasn't vibed with Four Rivers, but has no qualms about this; reasoning that if he liked everybody from a race of once-proud warriors who stank of drink, he'd never have made a single arrest back home. But he can't believe that he's pathetically competing with him for Tianna's attention.

As the launch pulls up to the small jetty, Lennox freezes. A police car is waiting, with two cops and three sharp-suited Native Americans in attendance. One of the men points at him, and he feels Tianna grabbing his arm in panic. They share a missed heart-beat till both twig that it's the guide they're after. Four Rivers bows his head, and is led away by the two officers, who deposit him in the back of the squad car.

Relief dripping from him as he watches it depart, Lennox quizzes one of the suited men, who informs him that Four Rivers had no permit to operate that launch, and was trespassing on the reservation.

— He's not from the Miccosukee tribe, then?

The man snorts dismissively. — He's not even Native American, he's just some crazy Irishman who won the boat in a poker game.

Lennox and Tianna's eyes meet; they settle their nerves with a shared chuckle.

They get lunch at the restaurant adjoining the Indian village. Lennox loves the fried catfish, clarty bottom-feeders like prawns, but there was something about that taste. They'd do a fair turn in Scotland, and he imagines it served at the chippy, with plantain and sweet potato: a good cultural exchange for the mince-pie supper. They follow this with some ice cream and Lennox knocks down a double espresso before the road beckons.

Tianna seems happier. Tells him about Mobile, Alabama. How it's a miniature New Orleans. As she speaks, her voice grows more Southern. She admits that she misses her old school and her friends. After a spell she becomes contemplative and reads more *Perfect Bride*.

On one page, a well-dressed groom has his arm around his betrothed. In his joyous expression she can see Vince, and feel that phantom recharge of desperation to prolong his supreme bursts of tenderness, but the transformation to the puppet face lodges in her mind's eye and she's thinking about what she had to do to bring the nice Vince back. She'd always pleaded with him that she didn't like it. That it didn't feel good. Well, someday it will, honey, he'd reassured her. It's all new to you, baby, you just need to get used to it, to get used to being a woman. *Then later he'd have his arm round Momma, and she'd be starin up at him all lovin and he'd be grinnin at us both like nothin else had happened.*

— Look, a voice in her ear, and Ray, Scottish Bobby-Ray, is pointing to a large white crane and then many more in the swamp by the side of the road. Then he stops the car to see some alligators in the waterway behind the highway fence, a whole bunch of them, even more than they'd seen from the boat. Again they are all different sizes, and basking or lying on the banks under the mangroves. Tianna watches him take off his shades and squint at the sun. She'd really wanted a pair, but he'd been good to her with the clothes n all, and she didn't want to take advantage.

The vegetation, thinned out and browned off since Miami's outskirts, has grown denser and lusher by the time they get to Big Cypress National Preserve. — This was where *Tarzan* was filmed, Tianna says.

— Aye?

— Yup. The first *Tarzan*, the guy from Europe who got the job cause he could yodel.

— Johnny Weissmuller? Lennox says in surprise. He and Trudi are both film buffs and Friends of the Filmhouse Cinema in Edinburgh. Cinemas are sacred temples to him: places of cultural worship. A picture house is the one place that he can just sit in, totally relaxed and engrossed, no matter how bad the film, and not feel the pull of the pub. Sometimes he'll go to three screenings in one evening, often drifting off into a light slumber, where the soundtrack merges with his thoughts and dreams, occasionally creating a potent, transcendental remix of narrative, sound and image that's more satisfying than the movie in question.

— I guess so.

It's bizarre, a kid her age knowing this sort of stuff. — How do you know all this? About Johnny Weissmuller?

— Uncle Chet told me. He knows everything about Florida.

Lennox mulls this over. He wonders how much this Chet guy knows about Robyn. About her drug problems and her disappearance. Or about Starry. Or Lance Dearing and Johnnie. It helps him to think of Chet as a benign force, and he sees an image of his own father. Recalls watching the old man joking with his grandsons when he brought them back home from some museum visit. He'd imagined that being the recipient of that easy, loving kindness was the preserve of him, his sister Jackie and his brother Stuart. For an instant or two he hated Jackie's young usurpers.

— There, look! Tianna shouts, as the first city road signs appear before them:

Bologna 32
Punta Gorda 76

Lennox feels the kiss of solace. They'd done it, crossed the state: the Atlantic Ocean to the Gulf of Mexico. Florida always looks as if it's about the same size as the UK on the maps, but it feels smaller. He starts to relax. Lets the exhaustion ease out of his shoulders. Driving in America's a piece of piss, when you get used to it. The roads are bigger, better and, best of all, straight. He'll check that this Chet guy is on the level. Then he'll call Trudi, apologise for his behaviour and head right back.

The need to know what has happened to Robyn nags at him. But that's Chet's department; he's more than fulfilled his obligation. Thanks to him, this wee Tianna was now safe from scum like Johnnie and that Lance character. And he'll find a way to get at those bastards. There are international contacts in the law enforcement world and he'll put the word out. There are always ways and means.

That song has come on again: Brad Paisley's 'Alcohol'. Now they're crooning along to it together. He's a little disturbed by that knowing way she chants the lyrics. *It isn't right for a young*

169

*girl. But she isnae a bad kid. She's funny and clever and she's got spirit
and you can take to her. She deserves better.*

Tianna is fascinated with Trudi's magazine. — Will you get
married in a castle? How neat how that be!

— It's awfay dear.

— It is *so* dear, she says, picking him up wrong. — Madonna,
she got married in a castle in Skatlin.

— Aye. Somewhere in the Highlands, Lennox confirms. It was
to an English guy who made crime films. Lennox had gone to see
one. He'd liked it. It was nonsense of course, like most crime in
fiction and on television, but it kept the action moving along. It
entertained.

Is crime essential, he ponders, in order to provide such diverting
extravaganza? Where would we be without human frailties?
Hollywood would be fucked. Perhaps we owe the gangster and
the criminal a lot. By supplying the crime they created demand.
For security guards, cops, screws, lawyers, builders, administrators,
technicians, politicians, writers, actors, directors. Where would we
be without them?

He can't think of the castle's name though. — It's a big castle.
Up by Perth or somewhere. They have loads of dos there.

— Is it near where you live?

He wonders about that. A three-hour drive? Yes and no. Is
Muirhouse near Barnton? Yes and no. — Kind of.

Now Tianna is explaining baseball to him. Takes a notebook
from her bag and draws the diamond, elucidating it all with care
and patience. Innings: the top and bottom of. Pitchers, hitters and
fielders. Four balls. Three strikes. Loading the bases. Home runs.
The bullpen. She likes the Braves from Atlanta, Georgia, because
they are the nearest Major League team to Alabama.

She shows him the cards. Lennox sees that they are not valuable, all modern reissues with their 1992 Kitemark. Scots Bobby.
Mickey Mantle. Joe DiMaggio. Babe Ruth. Reggie Jackson. Willie
Mays. Most of them probably dead before she was even thought
of. But the names mean little to Lennox outside of the movies. He
seems to remember that Marilyn Monroe fucked one of them.
DiMaggio. *That's it, the Simon and Garfunkel song. She also shagged*

the likes of JFK and Arthur Miller. Was she a gold-digger, attracted to
powerful men, or a trophy shag for rich sleazebags? Or was it, as the feature
writers might gush, the devastating mutual attraction of the charismatic,
which both parties were powerless to resist?

— Yeah, I reckon you oughta get married in a castle, Tianna is persisting. — That would be awesome.

Lennox plays with the thought: him in full Highland dress, Trudi in what else but bridal white. Brides all seem the same to him though, especially when they have their hair scraped back; that stern, graven-imaged look. He doesn't want Trudi like that. She could say something with her hair pinned back that would cut him ten times more deeply than the exact same words would with it down and flowing. He'd read an article in *Perfect Bride* stating that the average British bride weighs nine pounds *above* her normal weight at the wedding. The conventional wisdom of the boozer; they starve themselves to look great in the wedding pictures, then pig out on the honeymoon and engage in a lifelong battle against obesity. Not so, apparently. Pre-wedding nerves encourage overeating so they go into the ring overweight. This sounds true: it explains the number of bloaters in the *Evening News* pictures. — I dunno. It's a funny thing, Lennox considers, pursing his lips, — Trudi, my girl-friend . . . my fiancée, he corrects himself, — she wants a big wedding. I'd rather spend the money on a good holiday, you know, a honeymoon.

— Will you try and make a baby on your honeymoon? Tianna's searching knowingness stings then nauseates him. *She's just a wee lassie, teasing you.* Skin tingling, he looks back to the road. A silver car overtakes them, slows down. It was the second or third time. — That's the sort of thing that the two people involved talk about. It's not for public discussion. His tone is haughty and he can hear his sister in it.

Tianna is puzzled by his response. — But people do talk about it. Brad Pitt told everybody that Angelina Jolie is having their baby.

— That's Hollywood stars, but. They want to tell everybody everything because the publicity is like a drug . . . like candy to them. They need it. A lot of people are into it now, but then they find that it's too much like candy: it makes them sick afterwards, he reflects, looking at the silver car ahead. *Fucking prick. Where was the cunt going?*

Tianna turns away and runs a brush through her mane. Scraping it back she secures it with an elasticated band. It feels soft in her fingers, so different from Clemson's; that hair that grew like spines on his moist skin. Her flesh crawls in recollection of the touch of his putrid lips. Then trembling up in the roof space, ladder pulled to her, and him shouting: *Where the fuck you gone, you lil' whore,* her momma asleep downstairs, with the sedatives he'd given her. Thinking that it was better to go down and get it over with than live with that fear.

12

Bologna

Trudi sips at her bitter coffee as she watches a grinning couple on the television, in workout gear, slowly cat-flexing with two large docile domestic felines. The idea is that this practice gives busy professionals the chance to combine fitness maintenance with quality pet time. The woman has the ginger cat's chest supported on one outstretched palm, her other hand under its belly. She raises the animal in slow, rhythmic, repetitive motions. — Twenty on this side, twenty on the other, she says.

— Great, Melanie, the man grins, and Phoebe seems to be enjoying it too, as we cut to a close-up of the sleepy cat's face. As we switch back to the man, he sits down on a bed and lifts the big tabby on to his shins. — This is a tricky one, but remember, if your cat gets uncomfortable and leaves, you're going too fast, and he slowly raises the animal with a leg extension. — Slooowww . . . that's the way, almost imperceptible. Luckily, Heidegger's a little tired right now. One . . . two . . . three . . . I can't emphasise enough the importance of keeping it slow and controlled . . . Melanie?

Trudi Lowe packs her gym gear into a small bag and heads round to the Crunch fitness studio on Washington Avenue. She has remembered Aaron Resinger saying, — I use Crunch. It's functional and friendly. All shapes, all sizes, but everybody seriously working out. I don't like gyms where people just go to pose.

The effeminate young man on the desk has attempted lofty indifference, but in response to what he clearly perceives as the exoticism of her tones, decides that gushing theatrics now suit his mood better. — My God, I love that accent, where are you from?

Trudi dutifully explains as she procures the day pass for twenty-four dollars. A self-respecting daughter of Caledonia, she switches back to sterling to assess relative value. Thinks of possible sweet add-ons, but it's unlikely that Aaron will be around. He'll be at work, selling high-end real estate. Surely. *Fancy meeting you here. Sorry I had to leave without saying goodbye. Forgive me? Coffee? Great.*

She has to think of him because when Trudi thinks of her fiancé all she experiences are waves of rage, frustration and despair. He had the nerve – *the fucking gall* – to ask her about the men she'd seen during their relationship hiatus, which *his* cheating had precipitated. Now Ray is taking a strange child – *a young girl* – from here to God knows where.

As she climbs the narrow stair from the reception area to the gym, a cold chill creeps up on her. She recalls Ray sitting on the ground, head in hands, moaning disturbing stuff about young girls in Thailand. The emotion twangs into a reverberating thought, igniting in a dark section of her brain, only gaining potency when she grasps that her fear isn't for him.

Highway 41 slashes across the Everglades to Bologna, where it becomes a coastal road all the way up to Tampa. Despite the air conditioning in the car, Lennox's hand greases the wheel's leather covering. Trudi is getting further away and the kid next to him has fallen mute again, studying her cards. It seems a pattern: she cautiously raises her head above the parapet, then something in the present recalls the spoiled fruit of her own past, and the retreat into herself is unequivocal. No matter: he can play the long-ball game.

The Tamiami Trail, in its south-west Florida section, is a blemished conduit of shopping malls, fast-food outlets and used-car dealerships that alloy into the city of Bologna. Some rudimentary guide notes on the Florida atlas explain that while it was named after one Italian city it was modelled on another: the miracle that was Venice. The similarity was to the degree that both relied on an extensive canal system for transit. This carriage, though, is pretty much of the leisure variety in Bologna,

FLA. Retirees and second-home recreational sailors enjoy the watery network, which surges out from back gardens with docked boats into the ten thousand islands and beyond to the Gulf of Mexico.

Lennox contemplates the well-marked roads that lead to planned communities with their guarded security gates, Bermuda-grass vistas and dredged lakes. The advertising agencies have invented pastoral and tropical names like Spring Meadow, Ocean Falls and Coral Reef, unconnected to any geographical reality. But to the retirees of the northern states with their unforgiving winters, the notion of a sanctuary in the sun would have Arcadian appeal on the glossy brochures and websites. So the developers razed bare the lush terrain and threw up their prefabricated house frames, attached the panels and the cinder block, the PVC and plasterboard. Then they wrapped the residences in high boundary walls, despite selling them on the promise that crime in the region was negligible. They'd invariably finish the job by sticking an Old Glory up a flagpole, to flutter in lax entitlement.

Lennox and Tianna drive towards the hub of the community, which is more established than most that have sprung up in south-west Florida. The houses vary in scale of wealth and grandeur, many surrounded by mature palm trees, mangroves and less tropical vegetation. The small downtown area has superior retail outlets clustered under wrought-iron balconies in two-storey buildings, modelled on older Southern towns like Savannah, Charleston and New Orleans. Further down towards the marina it again grows blander; armies of condominiums line the coarse grass verges and lawns. Lennox rolls down the window as they cruise the narrow streets in the sun, the green Volkswagen miscast among the big 4x4s and the swank convertibles that proliferate. The glitzy wealth on parade should preclude crime. Everyone seems to have money here, but people with money often want other things. The most seductive of all being the illusion that it isn't just their money that sets them apart from the rest of humanity.

The road ends at a wall, with a gated entrance and sign above it: GROVE BEACH CLUB AND PRIVATE MARINA.

175

— This is it, Tianna says excitedly.

Lennox pulls into the parking lot outside a row of offices and shops. The marina is busy; most of the moored boats are gargantuan, with several pristine ones in adjacent broker's yards. Tall new constructions of condo blocks tower over the harbour. One is a work-in-progress, scaffolded, with Hispanic workers in hard hats bouncing along the gangways.

The lot is busy. Just as they've secured a parking space and left the car, a black Porsche, driven by a red-shirted white man with blond hair and shades, attempts to pull out and instead reverses into a stationary pickup truck. His convertible suffers minor damage at the rear. Furious at his own carelessness, he gets out the car and starts shouting at the man in the truck. — You goddamn idiot! What in hell's name . . . my car!

The reluctant recipient of his attentions is a small, stocky Latino man in a hard hat and construction-worker clothes, who makes a flabbergasted appeal. — But . . . but . . . you backed right into me!

— I did not – don't you – what the hell – where do you work? That site over there? The thyroid cartilage in the white man's larynx bubbles as he points across the inlet to the development under construction.

The builder looks to the rising apartment block and falls silent.

The white man casts his glance towards Lennox and Tianna, who have been watching the exchange. Lennox turns away. — Did you see that? Excuse me, sir? The man's insistence grates and Lennox stops and faces him. — Did you witness that? His mouth open: a snide air of belligerence invoking someone else.

— I did. Lennox slowly scans the complainant, then glances at the construction worker. He removes his shades and hooks them into the neck of the Ramones shirt and stares harshly at the white guy. — And I'd strongly advise that you apologise to this gentleman. He nods towards the Hispanic builder.

The authority in Lennox's voice takes the man aback. The dark patches in the armpits of his shirt ebb a millimetre outwards. The skin on his face, around his sunglasses, flushes a deeper shade of red. — But I –

— You're out of order. I suggest you apologise or I'll be compelled to take this further.

— Who the hell are you —

Lennox steps closer to the man, so that he can see his eyes wavering and watering, behind the tinted glass of his sunspecs. Ascertains the anger and the dogmatism are leaking from him. Now several onlookers are taking an interest. — I'm off duty. If you put me on duty, then it gets personal between you and me. A simple 'I'm sorry' to the gentleman and we walk away and get on with our lives. Or you can see where I'll take it. What's it to be?

The blond man looks at Lennox, then to the construction worker, who seems as embarrassed as he is. — I'm sorry . . . I guess I reversed . . . I just got this car the other week . . . this damn lot is always so busy . . .

— It's okay, the construction guy says, palm upturning at Lennox in a discomforted gesture of acknowledgement, before he climbs back into his truck.

The white guy skulks into the convertible and drives off.

Lennox looks up at the sun, screws his eyes against the hazy heat and replaces his shades. Looks across the lot to Cunningham's Lobster Bar; the social hub of the marina.

— You sure told that asshole, Tianna remarks appreciatively.

— That's exactly what he was, Lennox says, a complicit grin on his face.

— Are you a cop? Back in Skatlin? Tianna interrogates him in some concern. — Was that what you meant by not being on duty?

— Worse than that, Lennox says, slipping back into lying detective mode, — I'm in insurance. That guy in the smart car was lucky. He could have been paying through the nose for years.

— Do you like your job?

A derailed pause. Back in Scotland working-class kids were generally encouraged – often with good reason – to say nothing to the police. It probably wouldn't be that different in America, and Tianna knows what Dearing does for a living. — Aye, it's

177

okay, but I *am* on holiday and it's good to get a break from it. He cuts himself off to avoid compounding his fabrications. — I'm thirsty. Want to get a drink? He thumbs at the bar-restaurant.

— But . . . Tianna turns and points to the harbour, — Chet's boat'll be jus round that corner there.

— My throat's gaunny close up, he pleads.

— Sure thing, she smiles. — You got a sore throat, huh?

— Aye.

— Aye, Tianna sings, tossing back her hair. — Aye! I like it when you say 'aye'. Say it again!

— Aye, Lennox shrugs and she giggles as they make their way across the lot.

His throat *is* sore and dry – it always is – but he wants to find out what she knows before he turns her over to Chet.

Inside the bar, the wealth hits them like ozone. Humanity had been brushed out of the equation, sucked like a fart into the extractor fan of an expensive hotel toilet. They take a seat. Tianna asks the waitress for a Diet Pepsi and Lennox follows suit, although he really wants a beer. *We're never having kids. I'll go through the ceremony. I'll build a nice home. But no kids.*

He wonders how Trudi is doing back in Miami Beach. It already seems like days since he's walked into this. But a terrible elation buzzes inside him, intensified by the encounter with the guy in the lot. Getting better: he'd handled it more satisfactorily than the conflict with the family at the gas station. *Fuck it. It's needed. It's therapy.* He's starting to feel alive, like he did on the job back home, with that familiar taint of vengeful wrath in his mouth. Fuelling the sense that somebody is going to pay for the crime.

And there *was* a crime: Johnnie's assault on the kid. Could they convict him? Would Robyn testify? What would Lance and Starry say if they were called as witnesses? It would be a difficult one. His judgement is shot to pieces, but his gut tells him that it would be hard to get an arrest and conviction with Dearing evidently hell-bent on protecting Johnnie. *But why?*

Lennox studies the menu. Alcohol withdrawal has produced in

him that insatiable demand for bad food. He tries to talk himself out of it. He waves the card around in disdain. — For such a swanky joint the grub seems quite run of the mill. Surf and turf, burgers . . .

Tianna shrugs off his quizzical stare. — This is an ol-boys-with-money place. They ain't gonna go for nuthin too fancy.

He looks around and reassesses. The stressed-out, second-home arseholes like the yuppie in the parking lot were actually in the minority. It *was* mainly older people who had worked all their lives and had a bit put by and had staked their place in the sun. *The kid isn't a dummy. She's a fuckin bright wee lassie. In the right circumstances she could develop the resources to get rid of her neediness, like most kids did when they became adults. Get an education. Develop confidence, and real social skills. Not just that faux hard-assed sass that would only end her up in the arms of some wife beater. This kid could, given the encouragement, break the cycle of abuse that had possibly gone on for generations in her family.* Or possibly not, maybe Robyn had just fucked up because she was the weak link. — Your mother's not had it easy, eh?

Tianna's eyes and lips tighten as she rubs a lock of hair between forefinger and thumb. — Momma's okay . . . she been real good to me. I guess cause she's still young she kinda wants to party n all. But she always jus seems to meet the wrong guys. I mean, they start off good at first but they soon change. You're the only one who's been okay.

Lennox feels his pharynx shift. He'd left Trudi, gone out and taken lots of coke with two strange women. A shiver crawls up his vertebrae. *What the fuck was I thinking of?*

— What's your momma like, Ray? she asks, then adds in raven humour, — Is she as crazy as Robyn?

— She's a mother. He hears the brusqueness of his retort, thinking about how odd it would be to call her by her first name. *Avril. Avril Lennox, née Jeffreys. A mother. What the fuck is that?*

— I'll bet she's nice, Tianna is saying, pulling Lennox from his thoughts, forcing him to look at her briefly in loose-jawed incomprehension. — Your mom. I can tell, cause you're nice . . . not like

179

the other guys Momma brings around . . . That Vince; he was nice at first.

— Was he a boyfriend of your mum's?

She nods slowly and falls silent, lowering her head.

Lennox pulls back, he wants to keep her talking, not induce her to clam up. — What about your dad, do you ever see him?

— He died in a car crash when I was a baby, she says, looking up for his reaction.

— I'm sorry, he says. He knows the kid is lying.

— I don't remember him much.

That is the truth. It was the *extremis* of her father's absence that made his presence loom so large. Lennox contemplates the baseball cards as he fights a fatigued yawn. Looks to her squashed-sheep backpack. — That's why you like the cards.

— The cards . . . yeah, she says, averting her gaze again.

She deserves more, but first she has to survive. The likes of Dearing and Johnnie have to be avoided. Scumbags, but not lone wolves, like Mr Confectioner. There's something wrong here. It seems as if nonces are every-where: it's like some half-arsed pack of paedos are snapping around Robyn and the kid. It isn't just my paranoia. This Vince guy; does he know Dearing? Johnnie?

They finish the drinks and venture outside. The sun has retreated across the horizon but is still strong in the cloudless sky. Lennox rubs more grit from his heavy eyes and puts the baseball cap on, adjusting its band, moulding it to the contours of his skull. Tianna can't recognise *Ocean Dawn*, but he realises that those gleaming, white, opulent vessels might all look the same to her. Gazing across the inlet to the building under construction, he sees the workers taking a break on a gangway. One of them waves slowly at him: the guy from the incident in the parking lot. He returns the gesture.

The harbour master's office is in a strip of broker and yacht insurance storefronts. The manager of the marina is a man in his sixties, clad in jeans, boots and a green guayabera shirt, who intro-duces himself as Donald Wynter. A man of unbridled enthusiasm, with white hair in a side parting, he bears a striking resemblance to the actor-comedian Steve Martin. It's so strong that Lennox

feels like cracking jokes. Instead he asks, — Do you know Chet
Lewis?

— Everybody knows ol Chet, Wynter says, taking them outside
and showing Lennox and Tianna where *Ocean Dawn* is usually
moored.

Only it's gone.

Don Wynter reads Ray Lennox's crestfallen face. — Chet's
gone down the coast, put out a few creels to catch some fresh
uns. The good stuff is overfished, gotta cast the net a little wider
these days. I dare say that he'll be back early tomorrow. In fact,
I know he will, cause he gotta pick up some stuff he ordered
here at the office. Usually goes to see ol Mo over at his place
on one of the islands. They'll be in a card game and drinkin
beer. Wynter talks like a man frightened of keeling over before
he's spoken his allotted words.

— How do you get over there?

— You don't, not less you got a boat and know them waters.
Wynter shakes his head. — Yep, probably hooked up down the
coast right now.

His help is appreciated by Lennox, but he's so weary and the
man's verbosity grates as he launches into a spiel about tides and
the weather. And a glance at Tianna's pained face tells him her
boredom threshold has been breached. As Wynter rambles on,
Lennox finds himself thinking back to the elderly witnesses he'd
interviewed in connection with the Britney case. They gabbed
twenty to the dozen, talking up their roles as central in the drama
of her short life. Of course they were just lonely and initially you
couldn't help but be sympathetic, but they soon contrived to
exhaust that well of goodwill. Eventually he would want to crack
a brittle old head open and scream: *This is not about you, ya selfish
cunt. This is a murder investigation.*

*Ronnie Hamil, Britney's chimney-stinking grandfather, he was the
worst of them all.*

*Then Angela, and now Robyn. You couldn't even trust your fucking
mother.*

Stop this.

The appearance of a well-dressed, middle-aged woman gives

Lennox and Tianna the alibi to sneak away from the distracted harbour master. They leave the marina and drive into town, then out on to the highway. Lennox feels at a loss as to what to do. He curses himself. *If I hadnae fannied about with alligator boat trips and milkshakes!*

— I don't wanna go back, Tianna's hushed tones, her eyes big orbs of fear, — I wanna stay with Chet.

It would soon be getting dark and they wouldn't see Chet till tomorrow. Lennox ponders the options. Her apartment in Miami was out. They'd come here to get away from that place and the people in it. He could take her back to the hotel in Miami Beach for the night, or to Ginger's place in Fort Lauderdale, then drive her out to Chet's. Suddenly a truck horn blares and Lennox's body seems to lose five layers of skin as he slams on the brakes, thanking a higher power nothing is behind him. He was almost into the back of it. This, and Tianna's fearful response, makes the decision for him. He's too tired; he needs sleep. In his current state of fatigue, he's more of a danger to her than anybody. He pulls into the next gas station and calls Trudi again.

— Ray, where the hell are you? You said you'd be back —

— I'm with the wee girl I telt you aboot. She's ten. Her mother and her are in big trouble. I can't let them down, Trude, not like I did with Angela and Britney. I just can't.

— Don't they have police here?

— Aye. I've met one of them. It's him that's harassing them. So I can't risk going to them right now, I don't know the score with this cop. I've got to find somebody that's definitely kosher. I'm gaunny have tae stay here tonight. The morn I can leave the lassie with her uncle; that's when his boat's due back. You know what I'm saying?

— You're with this young girl now?

— Aye, Tianna.

— You're going to spend the night, *spend the night*, with this young girl in a *hotel*?

— A motel, Lennox says, thinking about the ones they'd passed earlier, stuck alongside the strip malls of Highway 41.

182

— I mean . . . we'll be in different rooms, obviously! Fuck sakes, gie's a break.

— You give *me* a break, Ray! Trudi says. — Tell me where you are and I'll come and get you! Ginger'll come and pick me up.

— It isn't safe.

—You're mad. You're mad and deluded, you – She gasps, suddenly visualising helping him into her apartment, his hand shattered, him gibbering nonsense about the Britney Hamil case, Thailand and God knows what else, and sees her own fingers with his engagement ring, around a real-estate dealer's circumcised, veiny cock. Her tone softens. — Ray, please listen to me. You . . . you've had a terrible time. I know you haven't got your pills, Ray. You need them. If you don't want to come back, let me come to you . . .

Lennox is blown away by her about-face. When the anger dissipates, she is genuinely worried about him. He'd missed everything she'd done for him. Failed to see that the hiding in the wedding plans was a manifestation of her own personal stress. His voice croaks, pregnant with emotion. — No, baby. Honest, I'll be back tomorrow afternoon. We'll go round the dress shops and sit down and finalise the guest list . . .

— I don't care about the wedding! I care about you! Trudi says miserably, thinking of that stupid tryst with the smarmy real-estate guy. Ray loves her. He needs her. — I couldn't see it, honey, couldn't see you were still breaking apart inside. I thought you were on the mend. Please come back to me, baby, please!

Lennox shrinks and sucks in his breath. — I need you to trust me. I'm begging you to trust me.

You don't know what the fuck men are like.

— I need *you* to trust *me*, Ray. At least tell me where you are, Trudi sobs.

— I'm about three hours' drive west of where you are, across the Everglades, on the other coast, the Gulf of Mexico. That's as much as I can tell you. I'll call soon, I promise.

An excruciatingly long pause follows. Eventually, Trudi's voice: — Promise?

— Yes.

— Okay. Be careful, she says. — Bye for now. Her voice is flat, and when she adds, — I love you, it almost seems to be coming from beyond the crypt in its tired resignation.

Then the line dies. Lennox stands looking at the receiver, the guts ripped out of him.

She lies back on the bed, her body aching in that satisfied way it does after a good session at the gym when the adrenalin has been spent and a delicious fatigue sets in. There had been no Aaron which was good and bad news for her, but one guy had hit on her; also good and bad news. There is life without Ray; potentially a very good life. She is young. This is her time. Can she afford to waste it on a guy who might never shape up?

This obsession with sex offenders. This obsession about sex. The weirdness about sex.

That stuff he'd said, in the tunnel, when he had his breakdown. About Thailand. About young girls in Thailand.

Ray has secrets. Not silly little secrets. Big ones. Possibly bad ones. Trudi Lowe shivers and sits up. Takes a sip of water. Moves over and lowers the air con.

Earlier on they had passed the American Inn, with its one-storey H-blocks, tatty Stars and Stripes flag, and dull, red neon sign which buzzed the word VACANCIES. Its walls looked like they'd housed all kinds of desperation and broken dreams. Now Lennox fancies he can smell the stale sperm of a thousand beasts impregnated into the building's fabric. It compels him, challenges him to confront it. Tianna looks blankly at it, betrays no emotion as he says in fake breeziness, — Looks as good a spot as any.

They stop off at a Walgreens to get some bars of soap, toothpaste and toothbrushes. In his weary irritation, Lennox is aggrieved at the discrepancy between the marked and actual price – he still hasn't gotten his head round sales tax – then they're back at the motel, ready to check in.

The desk clerk is a cadaverous old white man. His skin is

translucent and his face so weary and pained he gives a sense that you'd be able to see the tumours inside him if he removed his shirt. He asks Lennox for some ID. This time he produces his passport. The clerk's body stiffens like a hangman's rope under its consignment as he swivels to produce a simple register, which he requests Lennox sign. As he complies, the old man looks at Tianna, who is going through the garish brochures that sit in an ancient plastic mounting on the wall, below a map of the area that looks like it dates back to pre-white settler times. He turns pointedly to Lennox. — Daughter?

Lennox meets his stare. — No, I'm a family friend, he states, adding, — We'll need two rooms.

The clerk briefly raises his brows, evaluates Lennox for a second, and then lowers a sulky head as he checks them in. Lennox shudders, now feeling that this is not a good idea. But he's clapped out and desperately needs to rest. He catches a long yawn from Tianna. Wonders how much sleep she's had over the last few days or weeks or months.

As they head back outside to check out their rooms, an ochre brass-plaque sun like a logo to life lost is falling before Lennox's stinging eyes. Underneath it, he notes, through the thin fading light, the welcoming glow of a neon sign of a Roadhouse by the strip mall across the highway. It isn't that late. A couple of beers – no more – would be great, ensuring that he slept soundly. But he can't leave her, even if she falls fast asleep. Instead, they go to a drinks vending machine back in the reception, getting a Pepsi for her and mineral water for him.

Stressing his exhaustion, Lennox tells Tianna he is retiring for the night and advises that she does the same. She hesitates for a second before heading to her lodgings, two doors down from his.

Lennox's room is shabby and functional: bed, nightstand with lamp, table and chair, bathroom with toilet, sink and shower. Two battered green easy chairs with yellow cushions containing more tales than anyone would want to hear sit close to a big but venerable television set. Walking across an anaemic carpet scarred with cigarette burns, his parting of the rear window curtains unveils a vista as uninspiring as the freeway to the front. Rows of high-fenced, prefabricated buildings of a storage and distribution estate glisten defiantly in the fading sun, limelight-hogging starlets enjoying their bit-part roles.

He finds the implausibly tatty handset and clicks the TV on. Turning up the volume to drown out the industrial thrashing of the antiquated air-con unit – a big metal box dug into the wall – he picks a glass from the table and holds it up to the light. It looks clean so he fills it with some water from the bottle and puts it down on the nightstand. He sips at the remains in the plastic container, slumping into one of the easy chairs, leg draped over the armrest, as he regards the telly. Surfing the channels he feels his tight mind unwind and empty, thought spooling into nothingness. Trudi had been okay, better than okay. *She was loyal, one in a million.*

A knock on the door tears him back into the shabby room. He opens it to see Tianna standing before him. Her eyes are big and hopeful. — I ain't tired. Can I sit here a lil' while and watch TV with you?

— Sure, Lennox says, — but just for half an hour, cause I'm really beat.

She sits down in the other chair. He can really do without the company, but he reasons that the kid has been left on her own so much, he should try and make the effort. Besides, she might feel relaxed enough to volunteer some more information about the Miami crowd, and this Vince in Mobile. Picking up the handset, Tianna settles on MTV. Queasiness rises in Lennox as he's confronted with the old Britney Spears school-girl video. She was telling the world she was a virgin when they were shooting that one. He was scornful at the time, but it now made some kind of sense. Tianna is transfixed by it. Eventually she turns to him and says: — Do you think Britney's still hot? I saw her in my mum's magazine and she looked so fat and gross. Ugh!

And he thinks of Britney Hamil's throttled body, lying dead on that table in the mortuary. A child named after a pop star who would outlive her.

— She's just had a baby, Lennox says, — give her a chance.

He's not comfortable watching it with her, and urges her to change channels on the remote. — It's a bit old hat, he lamely explains. Tianna moves through the programmes, excitedly stopping at one show. — *Beauty and the Geek*! she shrieks.

Lennox finds himself secretly enjoying the dating programme, although he'd've preferred to watch it alone. The premise was that these supposed 'beauties', most of whom were actually pretty ordinary young, poorly educated lassies, would pair off with the specky, obsessive-compulsive, repressed but intelligent nerds, who usually excelled at business, science or computing.

At first Lennox's sympathies are with the awkward, tongue-tied boys, who seem easy meat for the vivacious but crass gold-diggers. Then it becomes apparent that all these guys want to do is to refine their social skills so that they can get laid. The women, underneath the superficiality, often appear to be looking for genuine romance. While keen to find a partner with money and prospects, and wanting to make these geeks dress, look and act cool enough to take good wedding pictures, they can generally conceive at least the possibility of something beyond a shag. Eventually, however, the banal predictability of it all begins to depress him. That Tianna is riveted disturbs him. It soon becomes a struggle to keep his eyes open.

— Did you like *Beauty and the Geek*? she asks, as the closing credits roll up.

— Aye, it was okay.

— Momma and me love that show.

He can see Robyn now, a feckless icon of cool motherhood, luminous with broken promises. Casting herself as Tianna's surrogate, big-wee sister, subjecting the girl to a litany of such reality TV shows, particularly the ones with a dating element. Battering her neurons with the shit that would, in tandem with Robyn's own behaviour, forge the template of the kid's world view. As they channel-hop through similar shows, it seems that the television oozes more ennui than the streets and bars, the presenters struggling to deliver sufficiently high emotions to let their subject matters fly. It is as if the TV companies can't find people quite thick enough not to be a little embarrassed by the fact that they are managing extreme banality, while the real momentous things are out there, in view, but not up for discussion, as if ringed off by an invisible electric fence. A despondent anger settles in his chest. — You should be watching stuff that other girls your age watch.

— Like what?

— I don't know. There must be some stuff. Cartoons?

— *The Simpsons* is funny. *South Park* is neat. I like *Family Guy*.

— Yeah, Lennox says. Appeals again: — I'm knackered. I'm going to get my head down. He gestures to the door.

Tianna is reluctant to leave. Lennox has to get up and open the door, then escort her back to her room. But about ten minutes later, there's a knock. He knows who it is. She is chewing on her hair and smiling strangely at him. — Cain't sleep, she simpers.

Her grin and her body language have a quality that is making him nauseous. He isn't going to let her step over this threshold. — Look, just go tae your room and watch the telly.

— Cain't I get into bed with you? she pleads.

His heart bangs in his chest, in concert with the rhythm of the air-con unit. He holds the door tight, like a bouncer confronted by potentially aggressive clientele. — No. Why would you want to do that?

— I guess cause I like you. Don't you like me? She widens her eyes in appeal.

— Yeah, but we're friends. I don't –

— It's because of Trudi. You love her! I finally want to *really* be with somebody and they love somebody else! she moans, stamping her foot in exasperation.

What the fuck –

— No, Lennox says sharply, glancing around outside in panic. The place is deserted. He takes a deep breath. — Look, she's my girl, but even if she wasnae, you're a young lassie. Guys my age . . . he begins, then her years resonate with him, — . . . guys *any* age, don't get into bed with girls your age!

She looks piercingly at him. — Some do.

— Aye, Lennox says, — they call them paedophiles. I've met a lot of them. Some are evil, others are just weak and pathetic. But they're wrong: every last one of them. Because they don't have the right to do that. Now please, he says with force, — go to your room!

He watches her dejectedly depart and vanish into her billet, then shuts his own door and switches off the air conditioning. The machine winds down in weary, fading clicks of protestation as he climbs into bed. Disturbingly, his thoughts run to Robyn's lush bush. His brain is at war with itself as part of it, in renegade obscenity, wonders about the daughter, then the hairless genitals of the doomed child in Edinburgh. Although this thankfully offers him no arousal, he curses those thoughts outside of his control. He's sullied by this baseness and the notion that he's no better than *them*.

A couple of doors down, Tianna goes to bed. Her soul is in distress, brow wet on the sticky, discoloured pillow. She discards the torturous, suffocating sheet to let cool air blow over her stomach, chest and legs, but the room is full of shadows from walls that teem with a million nightmares. Her jacket hung over the bathroom door has assumed the shape of a malevolent hunchback. She hears a squeak rise from within her and pulls the covers back to her chin, hoping she'll fall into a quicksand of sleep. And this happens, but minutes later she's drowning and battles back into a gasping consciousness.

A few walls away, Ray Lennox is distracted by a fluttering in his ear. *Some fucking insect.* A flurrying sound. Again. Then it seems to settle. He takes a drink of water from the glass by his bed. Then Lennox sits bolt upright in mordant panic, unable to draw breath. Something is jammed in his throat. He starts to gag. It's alive, moving and whirring inside him. He staggers to the spore-laden bathroom, eyes burning and streaming like he's crying blood. He tries to gag up this invader, but can't. Then his guts erupt in violence, but the burning blast of vomit seems to hit something in his throat and the acid in his bile burns him as it cascades back down into his belly.

One thought in his head: *this is how it ends.*

Desperate now, dizzying and fearful, throbbing head about to explode, he retches again and it all comes up in a racking, forceful cough. He looks into the toilet pan and sees it, more flying hamster than moth; the tiny coal-beaded eyes in the furry golden body, struggling in his milkshake vomit, one rattling wing aloft.

— Get tae fuck, he half gasps, half wheezes at the huge moth, and yanks the flush, watching the creature spin and whirl like a dervish before vanishing.

For a few minutes he stays on his knees and pushes his hot face against the cool vitreous surface of the sink.

Rising shakily and climbing back into bed, the whirring noise still going off in his head, like the ghost of the moth would be for ever part of him, Lennox collapses into an exhausted, fuddled sleep where dark, conscious thoughts meld with deranged dreams. Time passes, how much he doesn't know. After a broken, fevered narrative, he can vividly see Trudi in front of him, by the side of the bed. She is removing her clothes. — I want you, Ray, any way you want, she is saying. He can almost touch her.

He can almost touch her because she is here.

The door of his room has opened. He can see her figure backlit by the moon for a second or two till a breeze slams it shut, plunging him back into darkness. He glances at the display on the clock: 2:46. She is – *somebody* is – getting into bed with him. — You know I love you, her breathless voice whimpers. — You can do anything you want. I know you won't hurt me.

Lennox's body freezes. He jumps up out of the bed and switches on the light. Tianna is there, sitting up, in T-shirt and yellow knickers with a white butterfly stitched on to them. He reaches for his trousers draped across the chair, pulling them on over his underpants. — What the hell are ye playing at!

She looks up at him with a sad pout. — I cain't sleep.

—You'll have to try cause you cannae stay here! Lennox shouts. She starts to sob. He lowers his voice. An ugly, desperate fear grips him: *if the clerk hears her.* He can see Lance Dearing, hear him,

'Why, I jus took her momma out to calm her down, left ol Ray here with the kid. Didn't figure he'd grab her and take her clean across the state. Guess I kinda blame myself . . .' Terror eats at his gut. — Look, just go back and watch the telly. Please, he begs. — You'll soon drop off.

She grimaces and shakes her head. She isn't moving. — I don't wanna. Please let me stay here, I ain't gonna try n touch you –

— No! Go to your room. Now!

Tianna pulls her legs and the blanket to herself and looks up at him. In an instant the twisted little predator is gone and she's a gap-toothed kid again. — But I . . . I guess . . . I guess I kinda messed things up. In my room.

Lennox takes a deep breath. — Okay, okay. You stay here. He heads to the door. — I'll crash at yours and I'll see you in the morning, he gasps, his throat still raw and burning. — Please. Just try to sleep!

His bare feet step outside on to the cool porch, as he smells the diesel and gasoline. It's still warm and nobody's around, the only limited sign of life was the night light that glowed softly from the office. In the distance, the faint hubbub of a convoy of big trucks rattling down the highway, and the lights of the Roadhouse clicking off. A lick of wind chills his naked torso. He yawns, stretches and gets himself another bottle of water from the machine before moving back towards Tianna's room, this time bolting the door shut behind him. Inside, the blankets look in disarray but everything else seems fine. Removing his trousers, he dives under the covers, quickly pulling his leg back as it plunges into wetness. — Fuck . . . he growls, as he hastily gets out the bed. — Fuck sakes!

He tugs off the blankets and climbs on to a small settee, cramped and uncomfortable. He gets up again and pulls the mattress from the bed, feeling the other side. Fortunately, her pee hadn't gone right through. After turning it over, he balls up the soaked bottom sheet, then pulls the blankets back over him. Though exhausted, his nerves are now like piano wire and

191

he can't sleep. He finds himself rising again, taking refuge once more in the television, channel-hopping till he finds a nature programme on Discovery.

The documentary concerns itself with the growing extinction of the panda in China and the attempts to save it. These mostly seem to involve scientists molesting pandas and their cubs. Separating the young creatures from their mothers, tagging their ears with transmitters, tattooing them inside their mouths. An American woman, who is accompanied by her son, narrates the programme, described as a 'personal journey'. They assist the Chinese zoologists in interfering with the pandas to the animals' obvious distress. Lennox thinks that if those creatures could communicate, they'd just say: — Fuck off and let us eat our bamboo and grow extinct in peace.

But it wasn't the human way. Our greed is killing you, so our vanity demands that we must save you.

Tianna. Is she his own personal panda cub? Is he doing this for her, or because his own ego refuses to allow him to be bested by nonces? The likes of Mr Confectioner or Dearing? Ultimately, he supposes, it doesn't matter about the motive. What's important is the action. Doing the right thing.

Lennox clicks off the television and tries to settle down again in the bed. He still can't sleep. Tianna's bag sits on the table. The sheep's stupid face mocks him. He reaches over and picks it up. He doesn't want to go through her things, but he's a cop, and she's in some kind of jeopardy. He needs to know stuff about her. Opening the various pouches and compartments of her bag, he feels the shameful power and acute agony of this newer violation of the girl. The cop and the nonce: brothers in atrocity. Apart from the baseball cards, a hairbrush and some cosmetics, there is the black-bound notebook. On the next page to her illustrative diamond is a scribbled entry:

Hi Nooshka,
  I'm sorry that I ain't had a chance to write you in a while. I guess I'm getting lazy. You'll never guess what's happened to me. I met this guy. His name is Ray. He lives in a castle,

over in Scotland, way across the sea. I call him Bobby Ray.
The big news is that we're very much in love and we're
going to get married! I want you to be my bridesmaid! In
a castle over in Scotland where we both shall live. You can
come and visit, come to stay. You and Momma. We're going
to let her live in the cottage in the grounds where we can
take care of her. She can come watch TV with us and eat
with us in the grand hall.

Ray ain't like the others, like you-know-who. Ray's more
like Uncle Chet but kind of younger and better-looking.
He's got sort of brown hair, cut real short, like he's a US
Marine or something.

I guess I'm worried about Momma. I pray for her. But
I know that Ray will help her. I know that my Bobby
Ray and Chet will make everything good. I wish we had
stayed in Mobile. But the liar Vince was there and any
case I would never have gotten to meet my sweet Bobby
Ray.

Your dearest friend,
Tianna Marie Hinton

He lets the notebook fall on to the desk. Gets up once more
to try and squeeze the last of the urine from his bladder. Nooshka
sounded like an imaginary friend. Part of him, though, is flattered
by the way the kid sees him, the trust she has in him. It's just a
silly crush. Like the one he had on his primary-school teacher,
Miss Milne, simply because she was nice to him. But then he was
a sexless child; she's been fucked up by nonces, which gives the
fantasy a dangerous edge. But even if it comes out messed up, the
fact is the kid believes in him, wants to believe in him, so much.
He can't let her down. Yet he's still sullied by the episode, crawling
furtively back into bed on all fours.

Lennox puts the book back in the bag and looks at the cards
again. Babe Ruth. Reggie Jackson. Mickey Mantle. Joe DiMaggio.
Scots Bobby. He reads the career details on the back. Bobby
Thomson wasn't in the same league as the others, who were obviously giants of the game. His legendary status was based on that

one shot, rather than his career record. Yet she'd kept him. He doesn't get baseball. Maybe you have to be American. A yawn rips open his jaw; sleep is gnawing at him again.

Happy to succumb, he sinks like rainwater into a drain.

13

Edinburgh (3)

You thought about Britney's last days as you sat in the Stockbridge Deli, the uncertain silvery sky outside offering you no reassurance. It seemed her body was dumped from the grassy clifftop to the pebbled inlet on that treacherous Saturday night, before the hardy walkers had found it the next morning. The murder though, the coroner had estimated, had been done earlier on Saturday afternoon, through strangulation. Mr Confectioner had kept her prisoner for three and a half days of a hell meticulously pieced together by pathologists and forensic scientists.

An old woman was staring at you in the café; you were rattling the cup of black coffee against the saucer. You stopped, scoured the occupants: a sea of blonde, ginger and black domes fading to a ubiquitous pinky grey. Everyone looked both archetypally North European and slightly shabby, perhaps a trick only the Scots could properly master.

For the Nula Andrews investigation, the Welwyn Garden City police had set up a false grave complete with headstone and attendant publicity in the local newspapers. It was a tactic police forces often deployed. They knew that the confessional urge was strong and that the killer often felt the irresistible compulsion to visit the resting place and talk to the victim. CCTV camera and microphone equipment was concealed in the overhanging trees, filming and recording the disclosures of Nula's posthumous visitors.

George Marsden had been an advocate of this approach, but now he had reservations, as you found out when you'd gone back to the office to make another lengthy phone call to Eastbourne. — It got the wrong man banged up, Ray.

But you were starting to think that it was the last chance; bar the Graham Cornell dead end, the trail had gone cold. Robert Ellis was just one of the misfits who cheaply 'confessed' to the victim at the Hertfordshire grave. Ellis's tape made sickening listening. Innocent Nula was cruelly derided as a rabid slut who craved all kinds of sexual practices. Though his back was to the camera, it appeared that Ellis was masturbating over her resting place as he gasped out his demented spiel. It confirmed him as a disturbed individual who'd gone badly wrong somewhere along the line, but, the cool heads asked, was he the murderer? Logistically, in the time frame, it would have meant that he possessed superhuman organisational skills and extraordinary focus. But the investigating officers knew that the public scented blood and the bosses would have retired long before the press, who had cheerled the lynch mob, had the inclination or courage to investigate fully. It quickly became unfashionable to be a cool head.

You studied the Welwyn files again, taking particular interest in the one person who hadn't checked out. He'd made just one appearance, wearing a snorkel-hooded parka, and had stood silently at the grave till he was disturbed – ironically by the appearance of Robert Ellis. He'd crouched down before the headstone, looked at it for a bit, then, as Ellis came into the picture, got up and walked away. They'd briefly exchanged words. Ellis's comments were picked up, but his back and his elongated hood ensured that nothing was heard from the other party.

You jumped in your car and drove down to Manchester. Ellis was in Strangeways Prison. He'd made a couple of visits to that city, en route from his Preston girlfriend's place, and now he had got to know a little corner of it very well. You wanted to see if time had improved his memory.

Robert Ellis had fitness's sheen and his eyes glinted with purpose. You never smoked but always took along a pack of cigarettes when visiting prisoners. Ellis politely declined the offer. You hated that this impressed you, but it was clear that some sort of a journey had been undertaken. Ellis was well aware of the irony of his condition: the prison in which he was wrongly incarcerated, and had spent the last few years trying to get out of, was perversely the making of him. — Even though I shouldn't be here, this place has saved me, he admitted. — I was a fucked-up idiot. But a child killer? He laughed in derision. — Do me a favour.

— Parka man.

— Didn't see much of him. He wore a scarf over his mouth. All I got was crazy eyes pointing at me from inside that big hood. I'm normally dead good at staring people out, but I felt the chill in his look, I'll tell you that for nothing.

— What did he say?

— After I said, 'It's a sad thing,' he goes: 'Kids die all the time. Malnutrition. Disease.'

— Has anything about his voice come back to you: pitch, accent?

— I couldn't place no accent. It wasn't, like, Jock, Ellis smiled at you, then nodded to the silent screw in attendance, — or Northern, or even like mine. It was sort of posh, but not like a toff, just pretty nondescript.

— Why did you say those things about Nula? At her grave?

Ellis's jaw clenched and something dulled in his eyes. You thought it might have been shame. — Cause I was a saddo. Fucked up, full of anger and desperate for attention. And guess what? He looked around his spartan surroundings and smiled broadly. — It worked! Then his grin receded a little. — But I don't plan on getting too comfortable here.

— Oh aye?

— Cause you're gonna get me out, ain'tcha?

Perhaps the journey wasn't as pronounced as you'd given Ellis credit for. Under the polished facade, you smelt the old incarnation rising to the surface. — I'm gaunny find the bastard that killed Britney Hamil.

— Same thing, mate, Ellis said.

But for an excruciating few days the heat continued to pile on Cornell, who broke down and confessed. But not to Britney's murder. He revealed the affair he'd been having with a married MSP, which was maliciously leaked to the papers. The MSP had the indignity of having to confirm these liaisons and destroy his career, in order to get the innocent man off the hook. Toal was shattered by this;

he agreed then to let you set up the bogus gravestone and the CCTV cameras at Stockbridge cemetery.

Britney's bogus funeral became an official one. Angela so skint, she'd pleaded, — Could youse no just, like, bury her for real? I'll never be able to gie her anything like that . . .

So the local-council taxpayer footed the bill from the police budget. And then, after Britney's remains were lowered into the earth, you waited in the van, watching on the screens every mortal soul who came close to her place of rest. It was a bleak and frustrating duty for everyone. It was impossible not to get backache or a stiff neck. November was on you and the world beyond the glass window was cold like curved marble.

On one occasion you'd gone for a piss. When you came back you found Notman standing outside, chatting to a woman. Enraged, you ran over to your colleague. — What the fuck are ye playin at?

Notman apologised as the bemused woman quickly walked away. — I just stepped out for five minutes to stretch my legs.

You went inside, played the tape back on one of the monitors. Nothing. Your heartbeat settled down. You thought about your team. It meant nothing to them, outside of their sneering pub and canteen bravado. It was just a fucking job: there were corners to be cut, time that needed stealing back. And you knew this because with anything else you were exactly the same. Notman, too, was now painfully aware of it. — This one's special to you, right, Ray?

— I want the cunt.

— I hope you don't think I'm talking out of turn, Notman said, — but you look fucking terrible. Are ye getting any kip?

— Naw. That wee lassie, she's getting plenty for both of us.

You took double shifts. Tired and psychotic, you popped Benzedrine and snorted lines of cocaine to stay awake in the unmarked surveillance van outside the graveyard. You knew you would only have one chance.

At the same time, another local drama was unfolding. Most of the officers were supporters of Hearts Football Club, and were shocked that popular manager George Burley's replacement was

Graham Rix, an Englishman who had served a prison sentence for having underage sex with a fifteen-year-old girl. It was the afternoon following this announcement in the office at HQ, and you were preparing the Stockbridge surveillance rota. Dougie Gillman came in with a new Scotland coffee mug, discarding his Hearts one into the metal waste-paper basket.

— What's up wi the Jambos' yin? Notman asked.

— I wouldnae put it near ma fuckin lips as long as there's a nonce in charge. Makes a mockery ay everything we stand for, Gillman barked.

Strung-out, you'd looked up and rounded on him. — What do we stand for, Dougie? What did you stand for in Thailand?

— We were on holiday. It's different.

— Different, my arse.

But Gillman wasn't at all defensive. — What about you, here? Wi Robbo? That wee lassie?

You fought the impulse to swallow hard. — That was nonsense . . . Robbo was a fuckin bam!

There had been a time when you and Robbo had been on an investigation and had barged in on a young couple having sex. The girl was underage, the boy not that much older. Robbo had gotten you to question the boy in the other room, while he spoke to the girl in the bedroom. He'd found pills, Ecstasy, in her bag. He'd briefly nipped out to ask you to confirm this. Then he'd gone back into the bedroom and cut a deal with the young girl. You often shuddered when you thought of what kind of deal it was, but no charges were pressed.

— Robbo was aw around the canteen wi that tale. Made the bird gam um, Gillman said. — Heard the wee lassie OD'd after. Stomach-pump job.

— If that did happen ah had nowt tae dae wi it!

— You kent what Robbo was like. Like you sais, a bam. You left him alaine wi an underage lassie. Think aboot that, Gillman sneered, sly and couthie. — Think aboot that when ye get on yir high horse and start telling tales oot ay school. Keep it oot, Lenny boy. Gillman provocatively tapped the side of his own nose. And you felt your eyes water, just as they had done in that Bangkok

199

bar when the forehead of your colleague had smashed into your face.

But there were other things to think about besides your escalating war with Gillman. At almost 4 p.m. on an afternoon already swimming in dreich, nebulous darkness, those lonely, tedious days and neck-cricking nights of sitting in the van finally paid off. You'd been at Greggs, and were enjoying the sharp brief pleasure of solitude en route to bringing back sandy-coloured pies and coffee for yourself and Notman. Out of the blue, you were mugged by hail. The cold white stones stung you like pellets from an air rifle. You dived into the van, where Notman was glued to the monitors. The cantankerous weather drummed on the vehicle's metal roof. It'll pass, you'd thought, and it did, but not before intensifying furiously. You gratefully sipped the coffee as you'd talked about Hearts and its new East European owner's penchant for controversy. The team under Rix was growing as quiescent as the overhanging trees in the graveyard, having their own winter shutdown.

Then you saw him on the screen. The man in the parka. Same parka. Same man. Standing above Britney's grave. The man who was at Nula's before being disturbed by Ellis. That snorkel hood of the parka, and the thrashing hail: would the mike pick up anything? It didn't matter, you were flying towards the front gates, yelling at Notman to get round to the side entrance and head him off.

You bombed down the wet path, at one point almost losing your footing. But the man didn't sense you advancing from behind him. Slowing down, you closed up on your quarry, creeping so near you could see the frosted breath coming from the side of the hood. — Sir! you shouted, pulling out your ID. — Police!

And Notman closing in from the other direction. You had him in a pincer movement. You anticipated a struggle, perhaps a desperate one. But the man didn't run. Instead he turned round slowly, as if he'd been expecting this moment.

You knew it was Confectioner. Eyes arresting, yet at the same time strangely dead. Thick brown hair, slightly grizzled at the temples. Ruddy complexion. Small, broad and powerfully built, like he was from farming stock, though he'd probably never seen a farm in his life.

Notman was with you now. The man gazed from one cop to the other. — Had a decent run, he half shrugged, half smiled, as if he'd been done for shoplifting.

That offhand arrogance. The abhorrent, horrendous world he inhabited, how he'd normalised it for himself. By extension, nurtured a contempt and loathing for broader human society that you would feel the unremitting brunt of. It scared you. Made you feel weak and small even though you had a righteous outrage and the whole British state and its citizens behind you. And now Mr Confectioner had a name. — I'm Gareth Horsburgh, he'd smiled cheerfully. — Call me Horsey.

You went to your father's office in Haymarket; you hadn't seen the old man in a while. You'd take him out for a pint. This would ensure that you'd just have one: you always screwed the nut in his company. You smiled at Jasmine, the admin assistant who worked with him, and who took you through to his small office, where your dad had just set down the phone. You could hear his ragged breathing. You couldn't see, through your own shit, just how messed up your father was. Emotionally, he gave little away. But there were physical signs. For a while, you'd been noticing a tightening and reddening of the skin on his face. Age was overcooking and reducing him; the scarlet marks where the cheekbones pressed from underneath had spread and flared.

But when your father spoke, your mind was on 'Horsey', the divorced civil servant who lived near Aylesbury with his invalid mother. A consensus through associates and work colleagues soon emerged: Gareth Horsburgh was depressingly ordinary. A pleasant enough man to say hello to, if a little pompous and pedantic in company. He could have been any suburban golf-club bore, the sort you felt comfortable about having one drink with before making your excuses.

You felt you were in the throes of some powerful auditory hallucination, a hangover from the grisly interviews with Horsburgh and the horror of the lugubrious beast's disclosures, as

201

the gravelly voice of your father informed you, — At least ten years it's been going on, Ray, he'd said in stunned outrage as he dumped a box file on to his desk, — her and Jock Allardyce. Fucking behind my back for ten years. My Avril – your mother – and Jock Allardyce.

It was the 'fucking' that got you. Not even because your dad never swore in front of any of his family, save for an injured 'bastard' you'd heard him gasp in grim disbelief when Albert Kidd's first strike hit the net for Dundee up at Dens Park back in '86. It was the image of your mother, sweaty and lusty, being humped by family friend and neighbour, old divorcee Jock Allardyce; the man you'd grown up calling 'Uncle Jocky'. Your skin prickled with the prudishness of offspring confronted with paternal sexuality. Staring into the goat-like eyes of your father, belligerent yet bemused, you had to fight down the desire to laugh out loud. — What will you do? You felt your finger rising nervously to the side of your nose. The cramped office had just got smaller.

— What can I dae? We'd stopped having sex, he said, matter-of-factly, — when I had the heart thing. It was the medication. It thins the blood. Ah cannae . . . He faltered and shrugged. — I tried Viagra, but they said it was dangerous for me. I even started looking at porn, to see if anything came back, but no use, just twinges. Your mother still wants sex, what right dae I have tae stand in her way?

— She's your wife, you said, now angry for the first time, both with the old man's lack of self-respect and your mother's betrayal.

— What sort of husband am I?

You cleared your throat. This was too much for you to take in. Horsburgh, violently stealing sex from children. Your father, unable to partake in it with his wife. Your mother, banging away with their friend and neighbour. You had no wish to be spoon-fed details. — Have you spoken to Stuart about this?

The old man looked surprised. — Why would I do that?

Try, cause I've heard a lot fucking more than I want to, you'd thought. — Stuart's good on that kind of thing. An actor. Understands people. Their motivations.

— I thought that as a cop –

— We lock people up, Dad.

Your father had nodded in disappointment as you took your leave, telling him you were too busy with this case for a pint, you'd just swung by to say hello as you happened to be passing. And that was to be the last time you'd see him. A few days later he dropped dead, discovered by Stuart on that same office floor. He'd been trying to tell you about a terrible secret that had haunted his life, and all you could think about was a despicable child killer.

Day Four

14

Sea Legs

The auction rooms are stuffy, crammed full of bodies. Lennox looks up at the sad, dropsical face of Bob Toal, who stands behind the lectern, hammer poised in his hand. The lot for sale is a life-sized female figure. It stands upright in a coffin, stiff and dead. It has the same blonde hair as Trudi, but the face of Jackie's doll.

— From the Victorian era, Toal says gravely, — and such a sad tale. A beautiful young girl kidnapped and murdered in foul circumstances. The corpse has been preserved in formaldehyde and the bones connected by lightweight aluminium rods . . . He moves over to the doll, taking its hand and shaking it. The wrist remains in the extended position. — As you can see, our tragic young miss has been rendered perfectly pliable. Will make an ideal companion for the sick and lonely, or anyone who values the time-old feminine qualities of passivity and obedience . . .

Lennox turns a stiff and heavy neck to catch Amanda Drummond in the crowd, brushing a tear from her eye. — . . . I would like to start the bidding at one thousand pounds, Toal continues, then looks to a raised hand at the back of the room. It belongs to Ronnie Hamil. — One thousand pounds. Do I hear fifteen hundred . . . ?

Another raised hand. It's Mr Confectioner.

— Stop this auction, Lennox shouts. — Ye cannae sell her tae them! Ye ken what they want her for!

Nobody seems to hear him. One more hand goes up. Lance Dearing, wearing a Stetson and cowboy suit, flanked by a grinning Johnnie. — Two thousand, Toal smiles, — and I'll take this opportunity to remind our friend Mr Dearing from the USA, that remuneration is in pounds sterling rather than US dollars, he jokes to polite laughter from the floor.

Lennox tries to move towards the stage but his shins suddenly have the density of metal bars.

— It's my fiancée . . . it's my . . .

Something sticks in his windpipe, rendering his cry a soft, frustrating gasp.

All he can do is look at the profile of Dearing, bathed in a green light, giving him a gator-like cast. — I am aware of the currency of transaction, Mr Toal, and he turns and winks at Lennox, — but I'm sure if I find myself somewhat short then my ol buddy Ray here will be pleased to help out for such a purty lil' prize.

— Let's up the stakes, a voice shouts in a thick Midlands accent from the back of the hall. — Two million quid.

Lennox looks round, but the man seems to be moving to correspond, always just out of his line of vision. There are others, but they remain in shadow. Exasperation and fear eat at him.

Toal is about to close the bidding when Lennox sees his old mate Les Brodie as a young boy, looking at him, tugging his sleeve, urging him to bid. — Say something, Raymie!

But his throat has seized up and Lennox can't speak. Toal's hammer comes down with a strong bang. It pulls Lennox into another, better place. Again.

A better place.

For a few brief seconds Ray Lennox thinks he can see flamingos, shrouded in soft white mist, dancing in the mangrove bushes. Blinking, it becomes evident that he's merely woken up into a gorgeous pink sunrise, the room bathed in a coral flush almost neon in its intensity.

That soft tap-tap-tapping on the door: cagey but insistent. He realises that the baseball cards are still in his hand. Quickly puts them back into the sheep bag on the bedside table. It's hot and he's drenched in sweat. His ravaged throat just about manages to squeeze out, — One minute, as he rises to the door, opening it up and peeking round.

It's Tianna. She has his *End of the Century* T-shirt on. — I borrowed this, she says, her mouth turned down in the self-loathing, apologetic manner of the morning-after drunk. — I gotta get my stuff.

— Right. Give me a second.

He shuts the door and pulls on his trousers, switching on the air-con unit before letting her in. — Okay, he says to the shame-faced girl, assailed by his own mendacious guilt as he steals a parting glimpse at the bag and considers the secrets it contains. Lennox goes outside, waits a spell, before furtively grabbing the T-shirt her extended arm passes out to him. Heading to his original room, he pauses in its doorway to marvel at the salmon-and-grenadine sky, and briefly enjoy the soft blare of truck horns from the distant freeway.

In his room he locks the door and discards the T-shirt and trousers in a heap at his feet. There is still a tiredness about him, behind his eyes, in his limbs, but he feels stronger and more together. He does a full range of boxer's stretches and, mindful to put the weight on the balls of his hands, one hundred press-ups on the worn carpet, feeling the satisfying burn in his muscles, before jumping under the shower jet, luxuriating there till the water gets tepid. Towelling quickly, he gets dressed, catching the dusky, honeyed scent of the girl on his Ramones tee as he pulls it on.

A short time later, Tianna returns to his room. Her hands clutch the sheep bag chastely in front of her. — I wanna say sorry for last night.

— You shouldn't behave like that, it isn't right. Because somebody's done bad stuff to you, you don't make up for it by doing something bad to somebody else, he says. — Do you know what I'm saying?

Tianna sits on the bed, still gripping her bag. — I'm sorry, Ray, she says wretchedly. — You been real good to me. Her eyes go watery before they rapidly fuse in panic. — You won't tell Momma?

Lennox looks at her. — You were wrong to do what you did, but I'm accepting your apology. I won't be saying anything to anybody.

— Like it's our secret?

Secrets between adults and children: nonce currency again. Lennox bristles. — Like I said, it's between the two of us. You did a bad thing, but you were big enough to apologise, so I'm being big enough to accept your apology, end of story.

Tianna sets the bag down on the bed. She forces a strained, kindly smile at him. — See, Ray . . . when he, when Vince, when he touched me and kissed me n stuff . . . it didn't feel right, y'know?

Lennox nods tightly.

— It felt all kinda dirty. But I thought that if I got to do it with somebody I liked, then it would feel right. Like it wouldn't be dirty, like things wouldn't be all weird.

— No. It's *meant* to feel all strange and nasty, because you're too young, Lennox states. — Good things'll happen to you, but they'll happen when you're ready for them. Don't let them take your childhood away. He thinks of himself at roughly her age, with Les Brodie, pushing his bike into that dark tunnel.

— There ain't nuthin wrong with bein a kid, she says, halfway between a declaration and a question.

— Of course not. Not if you are. That's the point of it, he says. — We start off as babies, we like certain things. You wouldn't expect a baby to like catfish or chocolate malt or *Beauty and the Geek*, would you?

Tianna's mouth forms a smile as she nods in agreement.

— But there's nothing wrong with being a baby if that's what you are. Then we grow into kids, we like different things. Then into adults, and it's different things again. He watches her nod in understanding. — This Uncle Chet, can you tell me a bit about him?

— He's my mum's . . . she begins, before conceding, — . . . friend. He's a friend. His granddaughter Amy is my friend. She's real nice. Chet ain't my real uncle. But he's been good to us. He ain't like Vince.

— Who's Vince?

— I don't like to talk about him to nobody, she says, then looks pointedly at him, adding, — only to Nooshka.

She knows that I've been going through her stuff. Or at least she thinks I might have and she's covering all bases. — Who's Nooshka? he asks coolly, in spite of the sinking feeling in his gut.

Tianna regards him cautiously before replying. — My best friend.

— She at school with you?

She shakes her head.

— A different school?

Tianna slumps back on to the bed, looking up at the ceiling fan. — I guess so. She's just always there when I need her most. I can write her bout things.

— Like a pen pal?

She seems not to hear him, as if mesmerised by the circling fan. When she finally speaks it's in a flat but sing-songy voice, as if she's going through the ritual of a game she's bored with. — You know, when I write her, things ain't so bad after. You know, when things don't go well and you ain't got nobody to talk to. I can talk to Momma sometimes, but only bout certain things.

— Did you ever tell your mum about Vince?

She twists round till she is prone on the bed, then props herself on her elbows. Her front teeth push down on her bottom lip. Then she looks at him and nods slowly.

— What happened? Lennox asks, fighting to keep his voice from slipping into cop-interrogation mode.

Tianna sits up and pulls her knees towards her, holding her shins tightly. She lets her hair tumble in front of her face. After falling silent for a spell, when she finds a voice, it's small and haunted, belonging to a younger child. — The first time I told Momma bout him, she just started to cry. Then she got real pissed at me. Said that I was wrong, and now there's anger in her voice, — that I was a bad girl. I was jus jealous and tryin to stop her bein happy. So I couldn't talk to Momma none. She loved those guys, I guess she needed them to love her, a bizarre, almost sanguine authority now seeping into her tones.

Them. Unease slithers under Lennox's skin.

— What was he like, this Vince? Lennox feels his voice assume that disembodied characteristic, like it's another self, separating from a common physical source.

That mechanism has served him well in distancing himself from unpleasantness on the job; she's deploying a version of it too. — Vince was real nice at first. He and Momma met on the computer. He used to treat her real good, and first he treat me good too. He told me that he loved my momma. Then he told me that I was a special girl and that he loved me too. Sometimes he would buy me things or take me out to a movie. It had to be our secret as Momma would yell and think that he was spoilin me. These were the best times, she says, actually glowing in the memory. — I used to call him Pappy. He liked that, but he told me never to say it in front of Momma. Then one day he said he had to confess that he loved me more than anyone, even Momma. Said he didn't like showin it too much in front of her in case it caused her hurt. Sometimes when we was out together, at a diner, if a waitress asked, 'Is that your little girl?' he would smile and look at me and say, 'It sure is.' It felt so good and I would have done anything for Pappy Vince. There are dark shadows under her eyes, though it's probably just the light.

Please stop . . .

Lennox can't bear to hear Tianna's words. Yet he can't protest; his own voice rendered silent in his starched trachea. Needs her to talk and wants her to stop. Sitting still in the green chair, paralysed, in a seemingly oxygen-free room, all he can do is wait for her to continue.

Holiday . . .

— Then he got us playin the secret games. Hide-and-seek, catch-and-chase. He started giving me kisses. Different to the ones he gave me before. Wet kisses that went on a long time, with his big tongue in my mouth. It didn't feel right and I didn't like the way he changed, her face creases in pain, — became all serious, like he was in a trance. Not like Pappy Vince at all. And the only way I could make him come back was to touch him; touch his boy parts until what he called the bad stuff came. Then he was fine again. But then he got to doin different things . . . like man and woman things.

Different things . . .

Wedding . . .

— Then I guess Momma got sad with Pappy Vince and wanted to move. That's when we went to Jacksonville and she met Clemson and then we came here and met Starry and Johnnie and Lance. Her eyes suddenly bulge in rage. — I hate them, Ray! I hate them all!

Lennox has listened impassively, his guts and mind churning. Clemson. He can't ask. He finds his voice. — You don't need to tell me any more just now.

— Ray?

— What is it?

— Can I get a hug? she asks, standing up and moving towards him.

— Course you can, princess. Lennox rises and takes the child in his arms. Wants to tell her that he'll make sure nothing can hurt her but then elects to remain silent. How many beasts had said that before?

Beasts like Mr Confectioner. They know all the weaknesses.

Even when I had him in custody. Interrogated him.

I interrogated him: that smirking, evil, arrogant, nonce cunt. I should have crushed him, hurt him, made him feel like he'd made them feel.

— Oww, you're kinda squashing me.

Lennox's mind shoots out from that interrogation room, crosses an ocean and thuds into his skull like an arrow. He lets go of the girl he has in his arms. — Sorry . . . He steps back.

She forces a grim smile as she rubs her shoulder.

He looks awkwardly at her. — Listen, Tianna, I'd really like you to be a bridesmaid, at my wedding back in Scotland. Would you do that for me? He gulps in horror at his own words. He's overstepped the mark with the kid, now he's bribing her. *Just like them. Just like the dirty nonces.*

— That would be awesome! she shouts, dancing ecstatically on the spot. — I get to wear a dress, right?

— Yeah . . . I mean . . . if it's okay with your mum.

— And go in a plane?

— Aye. He tries to calculate the cost of a plane fare in September.

She puts her hand up and they give each other the high-five. — Aye! she mimics. — You're the coolest, Ray Lennox.

I'm no the coolest but I'm no like them, Lennox thinks. *I'll never, ever be like them.* He hopes she's never had that perspective of him. But it's how the motel clerk views him that's pressing: he's disinclined to hang about and arouse suspicion. Each time his body threatens to relax, the enormity of the situation spears Lennox in the chest; he's a thirty-something man in a motel in a strange country with a young girl, who isn't his daughter. They check out at around nine forty.

Looking at his face in the car mirror, he notices a bit of grey coming in at the temples where the hair is growing back. Trudi had warned him about shaving it so closely. But he's oddly elated. There he was, depressed, lonely and hung-over in a strange place, without his medication and possibly more vulnerable than he'd ever been in his life. Well, almost. And with someone who trusted him, his sex drive returning as the pharmaceutical administrations ran down. He knew, though, that he would rather have cut off his dick than put it near Tianna or any other child. Ironically, her in-appropriate and sad behaviour has helped him. Helped to show him that no matter how far he'd fallen he had a line below which he'd never submerge. The bar wasn't raised very high. But it was there. Now he has to help her. He can raise it by helping her.

He finds himself contemplating some of the men he knows; men he calls friends, a few who had been abusive in relationships, others who'd went with prostitutes, who'd flown out to places like Prague and Kiev and Bangkok for sex holidays. What would they have done if they'd been in his shoes?

A sudden deluge of inky darkness smothers the light in seconds, followed by a crackling yellow vein in the sky ahead. Then an explosion of thunder rumbles in his ears, causing him to start and click on the headlights. Now the rain's thrashing down, beating a frantic, dread tattoo on the roof of the car. The wipers can't keep up; Lennox is about to pull over in desperation when it stops like a faucet being turned off, and the pinky-blue sky reappears.

There's no telling when Chet's boat will come in, but it might not be for a while. Breakfast is on the agenda, and the 107 Intersection delivers them to yet another suburban mall full of fast-food outlets. The International House of Pancakes is Tianna's breakfast choice, Lennox agreeing that it seems the least offensive of the franchise hell village they pull into.

The waitress approaches, a middle-aged, portly Latina woman, brisk and efficient. — Can I take your order?

— I'd like orange juice, two eggs over easy with hash browns, bacon and some coffee, Lennox says with a tight smile and a glaze in his eyes. The woman has given him the horn. He looks at her strong thighs and wonders what rubbish might spill from his lips if he were between them.

— You gat it, the waitress snaps sassily, scenting something in his aura. — What about you, Miss? She turns to Tianna.

— I'll have the same.

The waitress departs, soon to return with two big pint glasses of orange juice. — Enjoy, she threatens.

Lennox does. He has never tasted orange juice like it. The Florida sunshine explodes in his taste buds and a small glass would never have been enough. The food is a mass of congealed, saturated gunge; it's standard obesity fodder and he picks at it. — They don't do freshly ground pepper in the States, just this powdery stuff. There's no spicy food culture here.

— Stop complaining, Ray Lennox, Tianna says, the use of his full name reminding him of Trudi, — at least your Skarrish cold sounds better!

Lennox succumbs to a grin. It's good to see her happy, to find the kid back after the twisted nymphet of last night and the troubled old soul of earlier this morning. — The Florida sunshine is working its magic, he says, rising. — Now if you'll excuse me, I have to visit the boys' room.

As he departs, he wonders exactly how much she knows. How many 'Scottish colds' has Robyn suffered from over the years?

Inside the men's room: sink, toilet and urinal with plastic grate in it emblazoned with the slogan SAY NO TO DRUGS. Now people could line up and piss on the message. His urine is looking clearer; free from the drugs prescribed by self and others. The action of peeing, though, has made him realise he needs a more extensive toilet, so he sits down on the pan, finally relieved to be able to execute that business. He reads some graffiti above the toilet-paper dispenser:

HERE I SIT, CHEEKS A' FLEXIN,
GIVIN BIRTH TO ANOTHER TEXAN.

He feels satisfaction tighten his lips as they leave the diner and get back on to the road. They pass a pickup truck with a yellow ribbon and a 'Honk If You Support Our Troops' sticker.

— Ain'tcha gonna honk? Tianna asks, as sunlight showers like sulphur grains across her face.

— No. What business have American and British troops got being in Iraq? I haven't seen any Iraqi troops in our countries, dropping bombs on us, he says.

Tianna contemplates this for a few seconds. Then she looks evenly at Lennox and says, — I guess it's jus plain wrong to interfere with somebody smaller than you, jus cause you're bigger and stronger than them . . . and can try and trick em with words.

— Yes, he replies, feeling himself croaking up again. So he glances to the window at a banner fluttering outside a church: NO HIGH LIKE THE MOST HIGH.

His eyes are drawn upwards to more white fluffy clouds in the pale blue sky. Lennox's sinuses are clearing. His hangover is definitely receding. The long sleep has helped him. He doesn't crave cocaine any more, or even a drink. The sun is doing it all for him.

They listen to a country station as they pass a long strip of used-car dealerships on the way back to Bologna. Once more Brad Paisley's 'Alcohol' comes on the radio.

As they get back down by the marina, a large boat is sailing in. It has a black-and-white fibreglass hull and carries the name *Ocean Dawn*. It isn't the biggest vessel in the harbour, but it's substantial enough, about forty foot, Lennox estimates. Then a man waves from the bridge and Tianna starts fervently gesticulating back at him. — Uncle Chet!

— Why, hey there, Tianna Marie! the sailor booms. — What are you up to? He looks suspiciously at Lennox, then back at her. — Where's that crazy momma of yours?

— She's kinda sick, I guess.

— Now, that's too bad, Chet says, as he backs the boat in. Don Wynter, who has emerged from his office, helps him to tie it securely to the mooring posts. As the younger, and presumably fitter, man, Lennox feels it appropriate to offer a hand. Takes a step forward but then hesitates; they seem to know what they're doing. Don slaps Chet on the back and they exchange brief pleasantries before he heads back to the office, explaining that he has some calls to make.

Thank fuck for that, Lennox thinks, as Tianna and Chet embrace. He feels the genuine warmth in it; there is no stoat-the-baw sleaze coming from Chet Lewis. So he looks out across the harbour. A white-chested osprey swoops and soars off with a struggling fish in its claws. But there is no sense of human threat here. Chet is benign decency personified. It is over, and Tianna is now in safe hands.

Those hands belong to a man in his sixties, with a strong, fine face under a long-billed fishing cap, which he removes to reveal a salt-and-pepper crew cut. Some slight jowling is evident in his close-shaven face, but there is a youthful enigmatic spark in his blue-grey eyes. He has a casual, easy manner and a gentle strength that Lennox associates with the small-town America of the movies, though an undercurrent of dynamism seems to fuse his frame, packed around his strong shoulders. He's a contradiction; his accent and bearing suggest money, but his muscular build and flat stomach seem to indicate that he's no stranger to physical work. Wearing a tropical shirt, white flannels and sneakers, he sticks his hand out. — Chet Lewis.

As Lennox coughs out his title, another sabotaging frog jams in his throat.

— Pleased to know you, Lennox, Chet says, obviously failing to pick up on the given name.

Chet stares at Lennox. Normally he wouldn't take kindly to anybody evaluating him in such a blatant manner, but in the circumstances it seems entirely appropriate. He tells Chet the story, omitting once again his true occupational status. The old insurance tale does the trick.

The sailor listens patiently. He seems on the level and Tianna likes him, but Lennox needs to be one hundred per cent certain so he is happy to accept when Chet invites them aboard. As they climb on to the rear deck, the host says, — Thank you so much for looking after this young lady, as Tianna explores, going down into the cabins. His voice drops, to remove her from earshot.

— I'm not sure I know this Lance character, although I think I may have heard Robyn mention him. He and his cohorts seem very unsavoury. Robyn's a nice girl, but she does have . . . issues.

Lennox's expression accedes that irrefutable truth. — So how do you know her and Tianna?

— I have my granddaughter, Amy, to thank for that. Last summer she was staying with me for a week and we met Robyn and Tianna, who's the same age as Amy, at the Parrot World in Miami. The kids hit it off, but Robyn seemed a little distressed. So I invited them on to the boat the next day. We had a fine time and they were good company. The friendship just blossomed, Chet beams, before his jaw abruptly moves south. — But I have to say that she seems to attract a rather dubious sort of male companion. I've had a few tearful calls from her on that subject.

Lennox nods in agreement.

— So I'm sorry if I might appear a little suspicious.

— Perfectly understandable. I met those guys.

— Tianna will be safe here until I can find out what's happened to her mother. But now I have to check on some crab pots and lobster creels I put out a few days ago, which I stupidly forgot to pick up, so please, join us for a short trip out to sea.

— I'd love to, but I've got to get back to Miami Beach.

Tianna comes back up the steps and stands in the doorway. — Please stay a while, she begs. — You gotta come for a sail in Chet's boat, hasn't he, Chet?

— I think Lennox is busy, honey.

— How long will it take?

— Oh, about an hour, Chet says.

— Okay, he responds breezily, — I'd like to see a bit of the Gulf. He thinks of Trudi. Things seemed fine again. — I'm on holiday, right?

— Yes! That's so fucking awesome, Tianna says, then puts her hand to her mouth as Chet winces and moves up to the top deck.

— Aye, mind the language, Lennox says, — it shows lack of imagination and vocabulary.

— Sorry . . .

— I mean saying 'awesome' all the time.

— You don't mind me saying 'F'?

Lennox looks up towards Chet, then winks at her. — Next time maybe just say SFA. It's a term of endearment we use back in Scotland. After our much loved Scottish Football Association.

— SFA . . . she says before her eyes mercurially luminesce. — Did you really mean what you said about me being a bridesmaid?

— Aye. He grants with a wink. *Another thing to square with Trudi.*

Chet's distaste at the kid's expletive was real enough, but he recovers sufficiently to give Lennox a quick tour of the boat. — This is a 410 Express Cruiser. Good for both fishing trips, and cruising longer distances. I occasionally go to the Caribbean islands; and sometimes down to Key West.

— It's a fair old size.

— Forty-four foot.

Not a bad guess, Lennox considers as they move from the rear deck's open seating area. It leads to a door on one side, which takes you down to the cabins. Next to the door, a few steps ascend to the boat's helm. Lennox follows Chet up, and is shown the controls and the craft's satellite navigation systems. He's never been on a boat in his life, bar a police launch, which had been taken out to intercept *The Lassie of the Forth*, an old ferry ship booked for a private party that they'd busted for drugs. He hadn't enjoyed the experience much, being on a brutal cocaine comedown at the time.

Stretching out in front of them is the main deck area, bordered with a metal railing. It has three skylights cut in it to provide natural light to the quarters below. Two more skylights are dinted into the canopy above the helm. Lennox notices that on top of this roof there is a radio transmitter-receiver with an aerial, and a box and disc he assumes to be part of the navigation equipment.

Gripping the handrail in his good fist, he follows Chet on an arse-first descent down a small series of oak steps. The cabin smells of oiled wood and diesel, but it gleams in pristine opulence as they emerge into an oak-panelled kitchen and dining area, fitted with expensive-looking units, appliances and fixtures. The seating area opposite is decked out in white leather.

— Had the boat long? Lennox enquires.

— Just four months. A part trade-in on my last one. The broker's a personal friend, so I got a good deal.

— Bet it set you back, though.

— You do not want to know, my friend, Chet laughs.

Aye I do, Lennox thinks, I'm a nosy cunt of a bizzy. The kitchen is at least as big as the one in his flat back in Leith. It leads to what Chet a little pompously refers to as the formal stateroom, the main sleeping quarters under the front deck. It's dominated by a king-sized bed and plasma television, and there are more oak-panelled cupboards, done out in the same style as the rest of the boat.

There's a smaller bedroom at the other end of the vessel, with a lower ceiling as it lies directly below the decked seating area to the bow. It contains a bed and a long seat that runs the length of the cabin and which could be used as a bunk for a kid or a small adult.

— Sweet, Lennox says, as he peeks in the toilet with its handbasin, jacks and full shower. — It's bigger than my flat, eh, apartment, he corrects himself. — Do you live here full-time?

— Almost. Chet's aura expands. — I have a small place in a development close by, but it's a glorified storage place and mailbox. We're gonna cast off in about half an hour or so, and I gotta refuel and check on some things at the office. As I said, the trip should take about an hour, an hour and a half if we stop for lunch. You sure you can spare the time?

— Aye, Lennox says, checking a digital clock built into the units. It's still early, so he decides he'll call Trudi and let her know that everything is okay, before another thought gatecrashes. — Is there an Internet facility out here?

— Best bet's the café a few blocks back from the harbour road.

Lennox climbs out the boat and heads across the lot towards the car. Tianna comes running after him. — Where you goin, Ray?

— Just to find an Internet café. I'll be back in half an hour; then we go sailing and get some lunch. You stay here.

— Okay, she says, skipping away for a couple of steps, before turning round. — You will come back though, huh, Ray?

220

— Aye! I'm just going to make a phone call and then get the Scottish Cup draw, ya donut!

— Aye! She taps her eye with her index finger. — You're the goddamn donut! she shouts before bounding over to the boat.

— SFA! he laughs, watching her depart as he climbs back into the Volkswagen. He winces as the hot seat burns his bare arm. As he starts up the motor, maxing up the cold air, he can't help but think of the contrast with the freezing surveillance van parked outside the cemetery in Edinburgh, only a couple of months ago.

Lennox finds the Net café easy enough and checks out Jambos' Kickback. The discussion on one thread is ongoing, now eighteen pages long. It centres around whether it is desirable to have a man who has been convicted of unlawful sex with an underage girl as the coach of Heart of Midlothian FC.

The club's board appointed a nonce as team boss. He had a great coaching pedigree, they said.

Lennox can't decide. *The cunt made a mistake. If she's fifteen you're a nonce. If she's sixteen you're a lucky bastard. But no, you can say that when you're twenty but not when you're forty. He knew the score. He was a predator. But the boy was split from his wife and family. He was lonely. He made a human mistake. Fuck sake fuck sake fuck sake —*

He hits the next thread.

Did anyone feel, in all honesty, that there was a suspicion of offside at Skacel's winner against Kilmarnock on Saturday?

Then he saw that Maroon Mayhem was online. The Craig Gordon thread; a reply to his last point.

Who do you think you are to criticise my opinion? You should watch what you say, my friend. You're getting a bit personal. I'd watch that if I were you.

Who is this cunt?
Lennox signs in and batters the keys.

I'm not your friend. You are a ****ing muppet. Is that personal enough?

Then he switches over to the BBC Sports site. Hearts had drawn Aberdeen at home. Astonishingly, Celtic had lost to Clyde! Hibs had drawn Rangers at Ibrox, so their Scottish Cup nightmare would inevitably continue. It was shaping up nicely. He flicks back to Kickback.

This cretin had gotten back in touch.

You don't know who you are messing with here. I know a lot of the people. Watch yourself. You can be easily found.

Lennox feels a rage burning inside him; this loser has been known to make threats on the web before.

I'll save you the bother, and tell you exactly where I am. Miami. But I'll be back in Edinburgh on the 21st of January. On the 22nd I'll be at the Vodka Bar in Shandwick Place at 1 p.m. wearing a black leather jacket. I'll even tell you my name: Raymond Lennox. My season ticket number is O52 in the Wheatfield. Please make yourself known to me so that I can rip your head off. I'll be very surprised if you do. You and anybody else who gets their rocks off acting hard in this way are usually fourteen-year-old virgins or other antisocial retards who live at home with their mothers. But I'd be delighted if you were to prove me wrong. C'mon. Give me your name and where you want to meet up for a quiet little drink. Anywhere. Name it. I'll be there.

It takes time to check, send and post his message. Then, as he clicks refresh the board administrator comes on.

Okay, you two, it's time to call a halt to all this.

Lennox suddenly registers the clock in the corner of the screen. He is late. Panic rises in his chest. *What if —*

I shouldn't have left her. Not till I was totally sure. But Chet's . . . No, how plausible Confectioner had seemed too! They could be away now, her tied up downstairs, him taking the boat to a secret perverts' lair. And she'd wanted to come with me and I've fucking well left her!

Ray Lennox slams a twenty-dollar bill on the counter in front of a perplexed sales clerk as he tears out the café.

15

Fishing For Friends

Lennox scorches the tyres for the block's drive, ripping into the marina and parking the Volkswagen as close as he can to the moored vessels. Jumping out, he sprints round the corner to the brokers' shopfronts, his heart thrashing and the tint of metal in his mouth. *Britney . . . Tianna . . . I've fucked it again . . . the fucking boat . . .*

They all look the same, these iridescent symbols of wealth: that opaline glow against the black water of the harbour, the sleek sterility. Then his eyes register a familiar figure and a huge gasp explodes from him as he stops and bends, letting his hands rest on his knees. *Chet.*

It's still there. The boat. Chet is leaving the harbour master's office. *Tianna is . . .*

She is over on one of the gangways, watching a big pelican standing on a mooring post that protrudes from the water.

Chet sees the breathless Scot first. — Come on, Lennox, we've been waiting on you. Thought you'd run out on us!

Just as he savours the palpable relief on Tianna's face, Lennox realises that he hasn't called Trudi. The whole purpose of going was to call her, he ticks in self-flagellating remorse as his respiratory system regulates. *I sometimes think you care more about Hearts than me, Ray.* She knew not to say that again after the way he'd responded the last time: *I care more about Hibs than you.* It was a shabby old joke handed down through the generations, but the humour was lost on her. Perhaps Chet would have a phone on the boat or a cell he could borrow.

Climbing on to the craft, they cast off, Lennox this time assisting Chet, who informs him that the birds crushed on the road and which patrol overhead are black vultures. There is a funereal beauty to their languid circling and sudden, explosive swoops. Chet provides a band with crocodile clips on each end, for the purpose of attaching the Red Sox cap to the back collar of Lennox's T-shirt. — Old sailor's trick, he explains, — you lose a few of these at sea otherwise.

Lennox gratefully accepts the offering as they head on to the canal system, rather than traversing straight across the harbour to open sea. — It's a short cut, Chet, at the helm, says. They coast past glass-fronted homes with big orange-treed gardens backing on to the labyrinth of waterways. The water is a muscular greeny blue. The shade-splotched route is lined with palms of various shapes and sizes; cabbage, royal and coconut. Huge pelicans sit in mangrove trees, easily supported, Chet informs him, due to their slight mass. Again, Lennox thinks of the gulls he and Les Brodie had blown away in that spirit of adolescent cruelty that some are never quite able to shed.

A beam of white light falls under the Red Sox visor into his eyes, briefly obliterating the deific comedy. As his vision is restored, the birds' noises and colours make him think of romance and he wishes Trudi was here to share this with him, to see how good it all worked out. He thinks back to Edinburgh, the ornithological experience generally limited to scavenging seagulls, oily cooing pigeons and cheeping sparrows bouncing like shuttlecocks along slate pavements.

Chet Lewis is telling Ray Lennox how he and his wife Pamela, who died two years ago, retired to Florida from Long Island. They'd always loved to sail and had purchased a plot of land, building their own home on it. It was partially destroyed by Charlie, he explains. Lennox, thinking of cocaine, is about to say 'it happens' before realising that Chet is referring to the hurricane.

In spite of his superficial good cheer and health, Lennox can now discern that Chet's withering in the void left by his wife. There is a hollowed-out aspect to him, denuded by a terrible sadness that has settled in his eyes.

The banked homes and gardens are soon supplanted by the mangroves, which thicken to form a dense swamp. Chet explains that the bushes actually live on fresh water: rain, dew and the stuff

in the earth, their roots going down deep. Then Lennox is startled as, only a few feet from the boat, a diving duck suddenly
slams head first into the canal.

As they approach open water, a group of men are fishing from
a pier. Lennox envies their easy camaraderie, envisions them getting
older and fatter without bothering too much. Maybe age gives
you that grace, where, with mortality looming, you really do learn
not to give a fuck about anything other than the sun coming up
and you and yours being able to draw breath every morning. Or
perhaps they're miserable suffering bastards inside, and death
pounces when we finally see the futility of fronting it. He'll find
out soon enough, God willing. For the first time he wants to fast-
forward into old age, at least how he perceives the good version
of it; to drive out the vestiges of desire, ego, bullshit and insecur-
ity. To have found that well of contentment that you want to drink
from, and to just do that each day.

Tianna is sprawled on the front deck's lilo, reading *Perfect Bride*.
Ray's here and Chet's here, and they are on the boat and at sea,
away from Johnnie and Lance and the rest, but there is unease in
the sunken well of her guts. It's not Ray, it's not Chet, but it's the
boat itself. *Ocean Dawn* is making her sick, for the first time.

Chet yells for her to come down. — Gonna kick things up
now, he says, sly and knowing. Tianna shakily joins them at the
enclosed rear deck, while Lennox wedges himself in the seat next
to Chet as per the skipper's instructions. Chet pulls the throttle
forward and the motor roars into action as the boat tears over the
water.

They surge away under a white and hazy midday sky, while
Lennox looks back to the dwindling marina, baking and shim-
mering at the water's edge. White boats sit immobile in their
slips, like racks of training shoes in a sports store. An ibis flock
glides over the bay as if they are formation jets, combusting into
an ethereal magnesium glow as the sunlight hits their plumes.
Then it's suddenly dark, as the boat passes under thick, swirling
clouds. Chet explains that the light is often murky from late
morning to early afternoon. He cuts the engine, plunging them
into an eerie silence, and drops anchor. Lennox has been keeping

an eye on the navigation device and the sonic scanner, which reveals the distance between the hull of the boat and the seabed. In the strip of water between the Florida coast and the Ten Thousand Islands, he's noticed that the gap from the bottom of the boat to the briny floor could fall to just over one foot, and seldom exceeded thirty.

Chet hoists up his creel and seems pleasantly surprised that it contains only lobsters and his pot just a variety of crabs: spider, horseshoe, blue, calico. He turns to Tianna and Lennox, who are watching his activities, delighting in the satisfaction moulding his weather-beaten face. — Usually you get the whole darn lot gushing out; sea horses, pinfish, tunicates, parrotfish, jellies. I even had a ray in my creel once.

Tianna points at Lennox as laughter peals from her. A reciprocal chortle works its way out of him. Chet appears a bit nonplussed, but figures it's a private joke and sets about boxing his catch and throwing the smaller ones back. On completion, Tianna opts to go downstairs with the magazine as he restarts the engine, and the vessel rips across the sea. Soon, what appears to be an island comes into view.

As they draw closer, Lennox can just about make out the remnants of an old village, which lies on the right-hand side of the bay, next to yet another new marina and planned community. Chet moves the boat away from the lights, coming into an unmarked and barely posted inlet. It opens up to a concealed, antediluvian harbour and it's like sailing into a lost world. As they cruise past the old wooden homes and jetties, a decrepit boatyard with some grubby fishing vessels and an aluminium boat shelter lie to the fore, and some shacks behind rising to the higher ground. From the left, the big condos of the new community look ominously over a small hill, a giant ready to devour everything around it.

Tianna has emerged from down below, holding a solitary baseball card. She wears an intense frown of concentration. Her expression disturbs Lennox. He is going to say something, but Chet needs help to moor the boat. As he ties up his end, he watches her pull the rest of the cards from her woolly bag and stick the lone one in the pack.

The ibis birds hang around the boatyard. From an overhead tree, an osprey cheeps like a budgie.

In a pondering silence Tianna steps from the boat on to the wooden walkway. Her hand forms a fist as she bites on her knuckle. Lennox feels something swimming inside him. Thinks he's perhaps imagining things. He looks around, the air appreciably warmer after being out at sea.

The grizzled encampment gives off a sense that its days are numbered. The bar-restaurant, a tin-roofed, grey-painted wooden structure, and the hub of the creaking settlement, is propped defiantly on stilts, on a semicircle of mudflats that form the harbour. With its adjoining glitzy sister, the aged bay curves away towards the dark grey mist of the Ten Thousand Islands that buffer Florida's mangrove coast from the Gulf of Mexico.

The restaurant is an old school Florida cracker joint, the sort of place Lennox has heard much about but which are now almost as impossible to find, without a guide, as good fishing grounds. As they climb up the steep wooden steps, Tianna dragging behind, lost in thought, Chet says that, despite its island ambience, they have actually docked on a peninsula. — Although it might as well be. All the proper roads lead to planned communities and marinas full of swish boats. Apart from the sea, some of these old places can only be reached by dirt tracks. It's so easy to drive past those turn-offs on the highway.

Inside the restaurant, a large white woman greets and seats them at a table. Lennox takes the tendered garish, colour-clashing laminate and reads the welcome at its masthead.

FISHIN' FOR FRIENDS
SEAFOOD BAR AND RESTAURANT
'If seafood tasted any fresher we would be serving it on the ocean bed.'

The choices on the menu dance in front of their eyes. — What do you fancy, Tianna? Lennox asks her, wondering if he can manage some more catfish. Then the red snapper catches his attention.

— Reckon I'll have chicken, she says, without enthusiasm.

Chet scowls at Tianna and shakes his head at Lennox. — That is sacrilegious in a place like this, young lady. My God, you can take the girl out of Alabama . . .

Lennox feels like protesting on Tianna's behalf, but he's only joking; trying to impart some grown-up sophisticated ways. Chet catches his scrutiny and is gracious enough not to take offence and spare his embarrassment. — So what line of work were you in? Lennox quickly asks him.

— Not very popular work, Lennox, Chet confesses in glum cheeriness. — I was an investigator at the IRS. Corporate stuff. A much-hated man on Wall Street.

Lennox squints at the thick forearms and powerful biceps. — You don't look like a desk man.

— Ah, well, I was a powerlifter for many years. Competed all over. Chet's jovial reminiscence dissolves into a lament. — Missed out on the Munich '72 Olympic team by a whisker, which was probably a blessing. I got selected for Montreal the next time round, but I busted my shoulder and had to withdraw. He raises and massages it for effect. Perhaps it still bothered him. — Guess it wasn't to be. I still try to get to the gym at least twice a week, and usually manage it, the fates and the tides willing. You look in pretty good shape. Do you work out?

— Kick-boxing, Lennox replies in some guilt, thinking Chet is being generous in his assessment, — although I've let myself go a bit recently.

— I'm not saying I've lived like a monk, but I try to keep in shape. You realise in your later years that you get the pay-off, he smiles, putting down the menu and scanning the board for the specials. — I think I'm going to have the dolphin.

Lennox winces at him, disgusted at the idea of eating dolphin. *Those poor cunts have sonar power. They're not thickos like sheep or cows. It's worse than eating a dog. The Septics are crossing the line here.*

Chet senses his disquiet. — Don't worry, Lennox, not the *mammal* dolphin. It's an old name for a large green fish, commonly called mahi-mahi but we refer to it as dolphin here. That was the Spanish term before the English-speaking settlers came by and gave the intelligent mammal the same name. It causes no end of

229

confusion with British visitors. Not that we get that many on this side of the state. So tell me, how is the insurance game?

— It's a job.

Chet's baleful half-smile indicates acceptance of that gallows camaraderie that implicitly bonds those who work for bosses. — Is it as lucrative in the UK as it is here?

Before Lennox can answer, his host has, in an instant, launched into a spiel about hurricane damage, and the ineptitude, venality and avarice of the Federal and State governments. Both Bush brothers, particularly Jeb, are being slated. — . . . the corruption; the greed of their profiteering associates. Is it the same in Britain, Lennox? Is it?

Lennox gives a non-committal shrug. His job has made him averse to discussing politics with strangers as his own were generally out of sync with those expressed by everyone else. But then a single, simple motion from Chet ices his blood. He touches Tianna. Only smoothing out a tangle in her long brown hair, but it makes him sit in upright rigidity on his chair. Because he catches the sting of tension creasing her face and the brief glimpse of appeal towards him before the laminate rises to conceal her.

Both reactions have escaped Chet, a prisoner of his own concerns. — I fear for the children. I really do, he continues. — What a legacy we're leaving them, Lennox. People like you are still young enough to change the world for the better, but I'm an old fella now. I just want to sail my boat, do some fishing, and at the end of the day put my feet up with a good book and a nice glass of red wine. Not so wrong, is it?

Lennox concedes that it isn't, but this doesn't seem to satisfy Chet. — What can we do, Lennox? he asks sadly.

The food has arrived but Lennox, while ravenous, has taken heed that Tianna is barely touching hers. Her fork distractedly jostles a leg of chicken around her plate. — Wish I knew, he says, passing off the question with another shoulder feint, reassessing the situation by the second. Adjusting and fine-tuning; correcting, with the regularity of Chet's satellite navigation system. He can't figure it out. His Scottish polisman's reductive and misanthropic view of the world seems an inadequate lifebelt. The old certainties he's entertained: the morally bankrupt, malevolent rich; the ignorant, feckless poor; the fearful, petty, repressed bourgeoisie – even aggregated they don't appear impressive enough in their cretinism to fuck up the world to the extent it now seems to be. And he is too tired to even think about God. What was Robbo's world view? Fifty per cent of people are honest. You could forget all about them. They might commit minor misdemeanours, but they basically lived their lives toeing the line. The other 50 per cent were divided between the evil, around 10 per cent, and the weak and stupid, the other 40. Again, the evil weren't that important in the calculation; they were just there to be hunted down. The key group was the weak and stupid. They were the main perpetuators *and* victims of crime.

The older he gets, the more inclined he is to cling to such banal paradigms, as someone drowning might with a piece of soggy driftwood. It depresses him and he's aware that he wants a line of coke again. For a heartbeat or three it's *all* he wants.

— Can I get some more Coke? Tianna asks the waitress as 'Home Lovin Man' plays in ringtone, signalling a call coming up on Chet's mobile, reminding Lennox again that he needs to phone Trudi.

— Excuse me, Chet rises quickly, heading outside. His haste gives Lennox and Tianna the impression that the call is an important one; they track him through the windows of the restaurant as he wanders by the quay, past the aluminium boat shelters, phone talk underscored with feral gesticulation.

Lennox notes her face reflected alongside his in the glass. He becomes aware that she is mirroring him, copying his actions. He feels both troubled and honoured to be a mentor. Is he any better than Robbo had been to him? *Because it has to stop now: this suspicion of Chet. Like the guy in the car hire, or Four Rivers on the boat; they cannae all be nonces. Everybody in the world with a cock – or with a minge, cause there was Starry – they cannae all be beasts. The poor kids in the garage! Trudi was right.* He is tired. Jaded. Not himself. Scared even. Seeing things that aren't there. The ghost of Britney. His hands shake. He needs his antidepressants. He'd been a fool to discard them. He's ill, clinically depressed, and no amount of winter sun can fix that. *Chet is kosher. Surely.* He turns to Tianna. — He seems a nice guy. I just had to be certain, given the company we were in the other night. You understand?

— Thanks for looking after me, she says to him, but in a voice so small, her face a younger child's now – a surfeit of emotion over calculation – that he feels his essence vaporising. Something isn't right; hasn't been since she went below deck.

— Aye. Lennox swallows some saliva down. A terrible, poignant vision of taking her to Scotland floods his mind. She should be at a good school, with proper mates, having a laugh at Murrayfield Ice Rink or the Commie Pool, gearing up for Standard grades, doing family things. Not with him and Trudi. Not *his* Scotland; that would be out of the frying pan and into the fire for her. Lennox is realistic enough about his own circumstances, but he enjoys the Uncle Ray tag. Jackie and Angus have the two boys. He likes them, had taken them to Tynecastle, but they weren't that interested. Once she'd told him, before Angus got the snip, that she'd really wanted a girl. He doesn't have the stuff for the twenty-four/seven, but he could be a positive influence; the fun uncle, taking the kid on the odd outing. They could be pals.

He jerks himself out of his storybook fantasies. The best Tianna could hope for was a good set of foster-parents here in Florida. *Even then, she has a lot of work to do if she isn't going to turn out a miserable wreck like her mother.*

Chet returns, with a sombre nod to Lennox. He counts out some quarters and hands them to Tianna. — Put something good on the jukebox, honey, before the place fills up with crazy ol Crackers and their mad country songs. Maybe some Beatles or Stones.

Tianna silently takes the money and goes to the big Wurlitzer by the restrooms.

— That was Robyn, Chet now grim, but wild-eyed. — She got herself in a whole heap of trouble and ended up being detained. But I got my lawyer on the case, and she gets out tomorrow morning. So I'll take care of Tianna tonight and get her to Robyn tomorrow.

Lennox feels a trickle of unease from breastbone to belly. Cop instinct or drug-fiend paranoia, he doesn't know or care. He's just less than convinced by what Chet has said. — Robyn . . . I want to speak to her.

Chet's face adjusts to civil-servant archetype. — I'm afraid that's not possible.

— Why? Why can't she speak to me or Tianna?

Chet's expression is now etched with impatience. — Because she's in police custody back in Miami, Lennox. She got one phone call. But I got right on to my lawyer in Fort Myers; his buddy's on the case, a Coconut Grove smartie. She'll be out on bail tomorrow. He blows hard in exasperation. — Such a stupid woman. It was a damned cocaine bust. If the community care find out about this, she could lose that child.

Wasps crawl and buzz in the honeycomb of Lennox's brain. He knows next to nothing about the American criminal justice system. But common sense dictates that it isn't adding up. Detention would surely mean one night in the drunk tank, sleeping it off without being charged. It couldn't mean spending around thirty-six hours in a cell. And Lance Dearing had supposedly taken her there. What was his role in all of this? And if it had been a cocaine bust, she'd have been formally charged.

Then Chet's hand is on his shoulder, and in it, the submerged force of the powerlifter. That and the tone dropping an octave are enough to put jitters into Lennox's frame. — You done a good job, son. Not a lot of fellas would have gone and put themselves out of their way like that, not for a stranger. But I can take over now. Chet withdraws his grip, the breeziness back in his voice. — You have enough to do, with a fiancée to look after and a wedding to plan!

And it made sense. Lennox had intervened enough. You had to let go, to know when to let go. He'd kept Tianna away from Johnnie and Lance, which was his objective. He'd delivered her to the safety of Chet's boat, which had been her mother's wish. He'd saved Tianna, but only Robyn could rescue herself, by developing the sense to keep out of bad situations and the skills to look after her daughter. — I'll go over and say goodbye, he says, wandering across to the jukebox.

He pulls out Trudi's notebook, freeing the pen from its spine, scribbling two phone numbers and terrestrial and email addresses. Rips out the page and hands it to her. — This is where I am, if you ever need me. You got email, right?

— Momma has, Tianna says in doleful affirmation, taking the paper, looking at it and turning back to him, just as the sun comes in through the window and frames her in a golden stream of light. — I'm gonna miss you, Ray Lennox.

He can see the timeless humanity in her. She could be any age and is genderless. It feels like a religious experience. — Ah'm gonnae miss you.

She has the baseball cards. The one on the top he hasn't seen before. He looks at it. Hank Aaron. Tianna glances at the card, her finger slowly tracing round its edge. Her voice is small and lisping again, making his blood heat drop degrees. — I thought I wanted to go on the boat with Chet, she says in a whisper he can barely hear, — but I don't like that boat no more. I wish I could stay with you.

A voice tells Lennox: you can't leave her. But another says: let go. You're doing this for *you*, not the kid. The words of his fiancée resonate: *you're a self-indulgent prick.* She's *not* Britney Hamil. But then he's looking back at the smiling Chet who's heading over and he's saying to her, — You can come with me if you like. Stay at my friend Ginger's in Fort Lauderdale, meet his wife and Trudi, then we'll go and get your mum tomorrow morning.

Tianna nods in grim relief.

Chet is now standing by them, and he has heard the proposal. — I think she's fine here, he says forcibly. — You've been more than helpful, Lennox, and we really couldn't impose any further.

Ray Lennox looks him in the eye. — I can assure you, it's no imposition at all, he replies, his voice level, cop-like again.

— I guess I wanna go with Ray, Tianna says in appeasing tones, and now Lennox notices that she isn't making eye contact with Chet Lewis. Something happened on the boat. He couldn't have touched her; he was with him. She'd seen something downstairs. Found something. The other baseball card.

Then Lennox catches the abrupt change in Chet's expression;

he's seen it before, in countless other people. Features pushed outwards, a reflex smile; all mouth, the eyes remaining dulled and calculating. — Sure. If that's what you want.

— We seem to have a consensus, Lennox provocatively declares. He hasn't yet sniffed the beast in Chet, but if it's there, he'll flush it out. He breezily insists on picking up the tab, before they go back on to the boat. He helps Chet untie the vessel and cast off. They chug wearily out of the harbour, but on clearing its jaws, Chet hits the throttle to transform *Ocean Dawn* into the machine that rips across the bumpy green water.

Tianna is sitting back in the lower deck, staring out to space, her tense jaw vibrating in concert with the boat's chopping motion over the rippling surface of the Gulf. Hank's back, she thinks, then in the glare of the sun and with the engines roaring, her fingers skim the slick, moulded hull of the boat and her stomach feels six inches higher. She's sick, not seasick, but sick like Momma; stupid and feverish and not knowing where in hell's name she is.

On the bridge Chet has taken note of the doubtful furrow on Lennox's brow as he scrutinises the instruments. — We've gone a different way as I've another creel to check. It won't take a second, he explains as he cuts the motor and drops the anchor.

The creel has catch. Lennox feels for the lobster, operating innocently in its own environment, only to be kidnapped, boiled alive and devoured by aliens.

Tianna goes down into the cabin, pursued by Chet. Concerned, Lennox is about to follow, but notices Chet's cellphone sitting in an indent on the console. He picks it up and investigates the calls list. There it was; he hadn't even needed to check the digits against the ones he'd scribbled down in Trudi's notebook. The caller ID announced: LANCE D.

Lennox slips the phone back into the holder. There was no lawyer, probably no arrest. Robyn's cottoned on to something and Dearing and his cohorts are keeping her hostage until they've decided what to do with her. And he is probably on his way to the Grove Marina right now.

Outside the stateroom Tianna quivers as she looks in and gapes at the big bed. Closes the door and sits at the table, staring at the grinning bride on the magazine's cover, as Chet's flannelled ass comes down the steps. He turns to her with a tired smile. — I spoke to Amy on the phone last week. His croaky voice is heavy with loss. — She was asking after you. She's thinking of coming down soon. Don't you think you might be better here, on the boat? . . . I mean, Lennox seems nice, but your mother *did* say to bring you here so I really can't let you go with him.

— I wanna go with him!

— Put yourself in my position, darling, Chet begins, bushy white brows arching, — your mother –

— I don't wanna stay here!

— But you always liked –

— Can we get going, Chet? Like now? My fiancée, as you say, will be waiting, Lennox shouts as he half descends the steps.

— Yes, of course. Forgive me. Chet turns to him. — You *are* in a hurry, and he looks vainly back at Tianna before following Ray Lennox up the steps to the deck.

They reach the helm, and a supplicating Chet starts the boat. — But are you sure you don't want to leave Tianna here?

— I don't think she wants that. Do you? Lennox looks at the older man's stern profile. Sees that the knuckles of his big hands are white on the wheel.

— As you wish.

The outward journey had been a clear line across the bay from one harbour to the next. But now Chet is taking his time. — Can we go straight to the marina, instead of hugging the coastline?

— The tides have changed. We need to avoid the shallows or we could run aground, Chet points at the navigation system and the sonic depth meter. — It's only a foot deep in some places and this is a very heavy boat.

Lennox turns back to the screen. There was a route straight through where the water level was at its highest. — That way, he says, grabbing Chet's hand in his strong left and bending two fingers back. A searing pain lights up the skipper's face like the jukebox. Chet forces a smile at Tianna who is now on the deck at the back of the boat as the harsh, clipped tones of the Scottish polisman rasp in his ear. — Don't fuck me about, you cunt. You don't know what you're messing with here. Do I make myself clear?

— Crystal, Chet gasps, as Lennox relinquishes his grip. He resets the course and they are back within twenty-five minutes.

Ray Lennox knows that he hasn't broken Chet's fingers. But something in him has splintered as he sits miserably, painfully waving them off from the boat at Grove Marina.

Lennox and Tianna climb into the car and drive away. He'd spurned the temptation to use Chet's cellphone to call Trudi; it would mean the number of the hotel would come up, and he didn't want her anywhere near this. Now he isn't messing around with the Tamiami Trail. He has worked out exactly how to get on to Interstate 75: Everglades Parkway, or Alligator Alley.

16

Alligator Alley

The traffic is sparse and sinister as they drive down roads lined with narrow homes and green signs that herald street numbers and the names of distant cities. This, in turn, becomes another strip mall of bad-intention businesses. The Red Sox hat lies on the dashboard. He's given up on it, two depressions still visible on his temples. Lennox looks to Tianna, sitting silently beside him, the cards in her hand. — Did Chet ever mess around with you?

— No. She shakes her head, then frowns in tortuous bewilderment. — I don't reckon so, but I jus cain't figure it out, I felt all kinda weird bein on that boat.

— Well, you're okay now. Lennox paints a stretched smile over his angst. — It's good that you found that card, the one your dad left you.

Her gaze seems to cast him as just another collaborator against her, but her anger isn't for him, it's the precursor to another revelation. — My daddy didn't leave me no cards.

— Oh.

— I never knew him. He left Momma way before I was born. That's if they was ever really together in the first place. I found them cards in the roof space at this place we stayed at in Jacksonville. I used to go up there to get away from . . . she can barely say the word, — . . . Clemson.

Clemson. Who is this fucker –

Lennox feels his words freeze in the now infinite void between thought and speech. By the time he finds his voice Tianna's resumed talking, her tone now high and hopeful. — But I kind of felt that he would like baseball and they sorta make me feel part of him. I guess that's crazy, huh?

— No, says Lennox, — not at all. He remembers collecting

238

Esso World Cup coins as a boy, his dad helping him. Looking at the sad lower lip of the American girl, he experiences a moment drenched in such pathos that it might have choked him had he not snatched an insistent breath. — Who's Clemson?

— Tiger Clemson; his real name's Jimmy, Tianna says, her eyes charged with an electric ferocity. — He was Momma's boyfriend. He was always nice to her but real mean to me. I was real scared of him. He knew all about me . . . with Vince. Said that's just how I was like; that a man could smell it on me. She suddenly gasps in terrified panic. — When he did it to me, he used to say that this was what I was put on God's earth for. That he was doing me a favour, givin me a head start on all the other girls. But he was different to Vince; I know he didn't care nuthin for me. So it was easier to just think about other stuff, n let him do what he wanted. But he hurt me sometimes. Sometimes he made me bleed. He'd wait till Momma was asleep with her pills, then come for me. Told me if I said anything to Momma she would believe him n not me. Cause I know what you was up to before, he'd tell me. I used to run up to the roof space, hide away from him.

Lennox has slowed down and pulled off an asphalt exit that segues on to a concrete flatland, designed as a parking lot, but which has remained customless, plant life breaking through its cracked surface. He's stopped for his own sake as well as hers. His stinging hands still grip the wheel as the blood pounds in his ears. — How did he know? About what Vince did to you?

— I dunno . . . the girl shrugs. — Used to say that he knew girls like me, the type I was. That he could tell a mile away I was no virgin. That was what he said.

Bile scours his innards.

— Is it true, Ray? Can men jus tell what you're like? Is that what I am? Her eyes bulge in desperation.

Lennox grips her hands softly. — No. No, they can't. Listen to me, I think you've been really unlucky and you've met some very, very bad people. You've done nothing wrong. You're a nice girl. They're the ones who've done wrong and they'll pay for that. I promise you. Do you understand what I'm saying? He looks into her eyes.

— Yes.

— Okay, Lennox says, and starts up the motor.

Tianna.

She should be waking up on Christmas mornings in a house like Jackie's to presents and —

Lennox can't believe that he's having hopes for this girl's future, unlikely dreams. He plays comforting scenarios in his head, only to reprimand himself that they are foolish: miles away from how she'll probably end up. *The balance of probability. But that's the trouble with dreams: they willnae fucking shift. And the more vivid they get, the more action they compel.*

As he thinks of his own future and Trudi, an abrupt spasm flares in his chest: he realises that he's left the copy of *Perfect Bride* on Chet's boat. — You didn't pick up that bridal mag, did you?

— No, Tianna says in concern, — I guess I left it downstairs. Was it important?

— Nah, I can get another copy, he says evenly, but he's unable to stop his molars reflexively cracking together. Trudi had filled out some attached coupons. *The address. They have her address.*

It will mean nothing. But the thought taints him. *Let them try anything back in Edinburgh*, he grinds his teeth harder, galvanising himself with scenarios of violence until he genuinely relishes the prospect. Then his displaced, protective glance falls back on Tianna as they pull up outside a gas station with a phone box.

Lennox searches for the phone card in his pockets, can't find it and curses, then his fingers mine for some change, eyes set in peripheral sweep for the approaching calamity of Lance Dearing. Logic tells Lennox that it's unlikely to the point of impossible that their paths could cross by chance on the road, at a place like this. Paranoia, the stronger force, is simultaneously informing him of its inevitability.

The quarters tumble from his greasy hands, rattling into the machine. When Lennox estimates they've reached the requisite critical mass, his stiff finger punches the metal keys. A gruff voice scratches down the other end of the line: — Eddie Rogers.

— It's Ray. I need a favour. You and Dolores, he says, reasoning it would be easier to leave Tianna with a woman. He tries to steady the map his sweaty fingerprints have smudged up. — Can you meet me at the truck stop on Exit 49 on Interstate 75?

— That's right on the Everglades, Ginger's voice goes high, — at the Miccosukee Indian Reservation. But why do you–

— Reservations are for yuppies and Indians, remember? I need a favour, Lennox repeats.

Ginger purses a long breath of static into his ear. — Okay. I can be there in an hour and a half. Trudi called and told me you've gotten into bother. You need to get a fuckin grip, son. You think this is *CSF: Miami*?

Lennox exhales a small gasp at Ginger's joke, then tells him, — I hear ye. But just be there. Dinnae let me down, Ginger.

A silence grows in Lennox's head. Then its puncturing feels sharp enough to perforate his eardrums. — I won't, Ginger snarls, — and for the last fuckin time it's Eddie!

— Right, Eddie, Lennox says, the name like sour fruit in his mouth. — It's appreciated, mate.

— Okay, I'm leaving right now. Screw the fuckin nut, Raymie, he warns and hangs up.

On his return Tianna sits puffy-faced in the car, eye-whites pink with blood where she's been rubbing at them. Lennox thinks about saying something, but nothing comes to mind, so he elects to let it ride. He sparks up the engine and they leave the station.

They approach the toll at the start of Interstate 75. A sign indicates that Miami is 127 miles away, Fort Lauderdale 124. The rendezvous point at Exit 49 seems about halfway, so they should get there around the same time as Ginger. Lennox regards the toll clerk, a small, black man with a grey beard, who has his name on a badge above the title LABORER.

— Bastards, Lennox says as he pulls away, then he apologises to Tianna, — I mean, they know people get that they aren't the CEO of the toll company. Why do they have to rub their faces in it?

Tianna looks back at the man, then at Lennox. — You're a really nice guy, Ray, I mean, doing this for me, n all. She pauses, then asks, — *Why* are you helping me?

— We're mates, Lennox shrugs, — buddies, he qualifies.

— But you don't even know me really.

— I know enough to realise that you need a friend right now. He points to the radio. — And I need a tune.

Taking the hint, Tianna grabs the dial and twists it on to a disco station. A gutsy, pumping remix of Sister Sledge's 'Lost in Music' rocks the Volkswagen. The line *caught in a trap, no turnin back* causes them to look at each other in grim synchronicity.

It might have been an interstate with a 70 rather than a 55 mph speed limit, but otherwise Alligator Alley is much the same as Highway 41: a two-lane freeway with a big scrubbed verge in the middle. Fewer signs of hurricane damage are in evidence along the almost deserted road. Fences on both sides keep back dense vegetation, as desperate to engulf the concrete as a mob of teenage girls are a pop star. Lennox barely allows the Volkswagen to dip under 90 mph. Ginger wouldn't be hanging about and now he really needs to get back to Trudi.

The passing trees become a blur, her eyes blinking as they flash by. Then Tianna can see him, Tiger Clemson, standing in the doorway of her room. Looking down at her in bed. Your momma's fast asleep, he's saying, in his soft, gloating tones. She squirms in the hot leather seat of the car, feels the heat on the back of her neck, hears the sounds of the engine ticking over, so loud, like Chet's boat. But part of her is in the bed and Clemson is telling her that he's gonna do her real good this time, show her some ol tricks she'll never forget, but it isn't Clemson, it's somebody else and she screams . . .

Lennox is so shocked he almost loses control of the car. — Jesus, fuck! What's wrong? He slows down and pulls over on to the hard shoulder. Her screaming abates as she leans into him, forcing him to comfort her.

— I keep seein a face. A man's face. She looks up him, her features tight and crinkled.

— It's okay, he says, stiff and awkward as he pats her back, — it's just a flashback, like a bad dream when you're awake.

She buries her head in his chest. — Do they ever stop? her muffled voice asks.

— Course they do, he says, his hands now on her shoulders,

making her sit up and look at him. — Who did you see? Was it this Clemson guy?

— No . . . and she straightens and pulls away, wiping a snot-tered nose on her sheep bag, looking apologetically at him until he dismisses her concern. — I thought it was, but it ain't.

— Okay. Whoever it was, they won't hurt you.

— Promise?

— Aye, he smiles, and she tries to return it but fear has frozen her face muscles. He starts up the engine.

They maintain an edgy silence as they eat the miles, content to let sounds coming from afar fill the vehicle. Call-in voices blast out, citizens as proud to demonstrate their intellect in radio's anonymity as they are to display their stupidity in front of TV cameras. Then Lennox turns the dial and a throbbing hip-hop bass rattles through the Volkswagen, building so steadily that it seems to be propelling the accelerating vehicle. Soon a road sign announces the impending presence of Exit 49.

They step giddily from the car, taking a few seconds to adjust to the abrupt curtailment of velocity, and are walled by the hot, muggy air. The murky darkness is diluting the everyday miracle of the brown and green light that bounces off the great expanse of sawgrass and water. There's no sign of Ginger and Dolores. The old gas station, a rusted corrugated shack with three pumps, has a moribund neon Coca-Cola sign that pulses sickly in the window. It betrays no sign of life: most likely it kept irregular hours. The stillness is eerie; a pervasive silence, with no song-birds in the trees or cars on the highway. Tianna moves over towards a broken area of fencing that borders the mangrove swamp.

— Don't go too far from the car, Lennox warns. Four Rivers comes into his mind, probably because the turning for the reser-vation is nearby.

She moves over and leans on the bodywork of the car, fingering the solitary card. Catching him watching her, she looks up, brushing the hair from her face and says, — I found this card I figured I'd lost. It was on the boat. Hank Aaron. He was from Mobile too, y'know. But I cain't remember losin it there. I had it when I was last on the boat, and I *sorta* remember . . . it was like I was sick . . . I could see the water. It was like a dream.

The surrounding silence is crumpled by a rustling from the mangrove bushes, followed by the brief, snuffed-out shriek of some animal and a raucous bellow of triumph. Lennox looks nervously to the swamp, then back at her, as if to dismiss it. It heralds a brief cacophony of bird sounds from the dense growth, which settles back into silence. — What do you mean? Like you were on the boat and seasick? he asks, smelling the saltiness in the gathering breeze.

— Like it was on the boat, and it was a dream . . . but it kinda wasn't, she says in a dizzying moment of realisation.

Lennox's pulse quickens and he swallows down more nothingness in his throat. — It was probably just a bad dream.

Tianna is far too eager to agree. Sensing she needs mental space, Lennox falls silent, allowing her to ask him, — Do you ever get bad dreams, Ray? I mean dreams so really, really bad that you just cain't talk to anybody about em?

Now Lennox is stunned. He looks above. Expects to see dark stone instead of mottled blue. Seconds pass. — Yes, he finally says, his voice wavering and weak. — Yes, I do.

— Would you tell me them?

— Maybe later, pal.

She sweeps her hair from her face again. In the shaft of pale moonlight that filters through the trees behind the fence, she carries the gravity of a spectral prophet. — Y'all promise?

— Aye . . . Lennox hears his voice hover between a whisper and a gasp. Anxious for a diversion, he gestures to her to pass the baseball card and he reads:

HANK AARON
(b: February 5, 1934, Mobile, Alabama)

755 home runs in 23 seasons. A record in Major League baseball, he surpassed the legendary Babe Ruth.

Hank Aaron was Mobile's favorite son. His parents moved south from Selma to work in the shipyards. Originally play-

---

ing in the Negro Leagues, Aaron remembered how the
restaurant staff would break the plates that he and his
colleagues had eaten from. His Major League career spanned
over two glorious decades, split between the Milwaukee
Brewers and the Atlanta Braves.

Lennox recalls the name. Vaguely remembers reading about some
steroid juggernaut's joyless pursuit of Aaron's record. — He seems
some man. Sort of guy who'd never let anything hold him back.
The arseholes who smashed these plates, who told him he was
nothing, where are they now? Who cares what they think? He
pauses, hands back the card. — You know what I'm saying?

She meets his gaze with a fixed stare of her own. — I guess so.

— Remember that. Always remember that.

He leans into the car to start the engine and fire up the car
radio. They listen to Big 105.9 Miami's classic rock station; Duran
Duran's 'Is There Something I Should Know' plays. Then they go
on to the bouncy mayhem of a Spanish dance-music channel;
fast, intoxicating fun that makes him want a tequila or mojito.

They are both glad of the distraction, but then a sad ballad
commences and Tianna speaks again. — Nobody will ever marry
me, she says in a tentative sorrow, her brows rising. — Supposin,
just supposin, I was older and you was younger, would you marry
me, Ray?

Lennox smiles tightly. — You can't ask me that. You don't know
what I was like when I was younger, and for some reason he has
an image of himself in a pair of Falmer jeans, a hooded top, and
a long, floppy fringe. And that moustache. That daft, stupid thing
they'd all slagged him off for, *even* in the polis. It had grown in
correspondence with the cocaine habit. Trudi had loved it when
he'd shaved it off, but he'd instantly regretted it. He felt exposed
without it: naked and dirty. A lip dripping with spit.

He'd joined the force a few years after working as an apprentice joiner with a house-panel building firm at Livingston. The
vectors of educational opportunity and youthful excitement crossed
over on the Police Graduate programme, and he was sent to
Heriot-Watt University, sponsored for a BSc in Information

Technology. His boyhood mate Les Brodie, along with his plumbing apprenticeship, had taken up with the Hearts casuals as his outlet for the testosterone bubbling up inside him. But the police was a means rather than an end. Lennox had a mission; a buried, ill-defined quest that was pulled into sharper focus in the last few months than ever before.

The copper's life had been difficult for him. The antisocial loner tag he'd developed at school, then as a young carpenter, seemed intent on relentless pursuit. He was the first of the new breed, the educated cop who saw policework as a bundle of sciences – psychology, sociology, criminology, information technology, forensics and public relations – and incurred the wrath of the old school types, to whom it would always remain a street art. And then there was the isolating nature of police life. One of Ray Lennox's most excruciating moments came as a rookie on duty at Haymarket Police Station. Les Brodie got pulled in with some other guys after a minor footballing affray. Their eyes met briefly, then the estranged friends both turned away in shame, but not before they'd been witness to the other's humiliation. Lennox hid back in the office for the rest of shift, squirming with embarrassment, relieved that Brodie had been released when he came in to work the next day.

Now, by the side of the freeway that cuts through the moonlit swamp, Tianna is looking at him in an unsettling expression of coy indulgence. — I'll bet you was sweet when you was younger.

— A lot of people would disagree with that, he says gruffly. — Anyway, we don't know what you'll be like when you're older. Maybe you'll go to college and get a good job and a career, he hopefully speculates, then looks pointedly at her and asks, — What makes you think nobody is going to marry you?

— Vince . . . then Clemson. Said that if I told anyone what I'd done . . . what happened, then I'd be ruined for being married.

— *You* did nothing. It was those bastards who did wrong, not you. He slaps the car bonnet, livid with rage. — You never forget that, he says, — never.

Tianna's big eyes are contemplative in the silver light, but Lennox knows that his anger is scaring her as much as his words are affirming. Softening his tone, he adds, — When you do think about getting married, and you probably will, it'll be to a nice guy who loves and respects you.

— Like you love and respect Trudi, right?

— Aye, he gasps.

— Does Trudi have a good job and a career?

— Aye, I suppose she does, I mean, yes, Lennox concedes, weak in the face of his own selfish arrogance. He belittled Trudi's achievements. She'd done well at Scottish Power, got a couple of promotions, was regarded as successful. He'd got so up himself about his work, bleeding self-importance and radiating contempt for others. He feels regret's tender ache and if she had been there he would have said sorry, and meant it from the bottom of his heart.

The conversations with Tianna, though minimal, are like bursts of intense fire from an AK47. They leave him full of holes: far more disconcerting than when he talks to victims of sexual abuse as a cop. Here there's no role to play, no badge to hide behind. But as long as she's with him she isn't in the hands of monsters like Dearing, Johnnie and, for all he knows, Chet. He considers the Hank Aaron card.

— When your mum was sick and you went to stay with Starry, did she treat you okay? His head twists as a solitary car tears past on the freeway.

— I guess, says Tianna doubtfully. — But that Johnnie, her brother, he was always round. Always makin dirty talk. I hated it when he came round Momma's or Starry's.

— Johnnie is Starry's brother?

— Uh-huh. I guess I felt for Starry, her boy bein shot dead outside that 7–Eleven n all. But I didn't like Momma hanging out with her n Johnnie.

He'd detected no resemblance at all between Johnnie and Starry. — What about Lance?

— Lance is a policeman. You sorta think he gotta be a good person, right?

— Right, Lennox says weakly, looking up as the wind rustles in the trees. *Where the fuck is Ginger?*

And the magazine is back there. It is waiting. *Perfect Bride.* His calling card: his excuse to go back into that vipers' nest of nonces. He has all the reasons. It isn't just about Tianna now. Let them try to stop him. *Let them try.*

— Do you love Trudi?

That simple question kicks the wind out of him. His head spins. — I know that I used to, he says after a bit, — but sometimes I wonder if our time might be up. It's . . . well, we've got so much . . . history. Now, I don't know if it's love, or just a certain kind of life we've got used to. Sometimes I think . . .

— What?

— . . . that it might be time to walk away. It's not easy.

Then a vision of Trudi fills his head. When they took him to her place after his breakdown in the pub. Again, when she saw the state of him in the tunnel after the funeral: the tears in her eyes. *Oh my baby, my Ray,* she'd cried. Lennox feels something climb inside of him. — I do love her, he says with a certainty coated in sadness, because what he is really choking on is his own sense of unworthiness, — I always will.

— The worst one that Momma brought back was Vince, Tianna says, straining as she sucks in her breath, cause he told me that he loved me. It was all lies, but I believed it, and it ain't right to say that to somebody when it ain't true. She rolls her bottom lip south. — So if you love her, you got to treat her right.

— Yes, Lennox agrees, almost sick with melancholy, — I have to treat her right.

The dancing bushes with their shadows, and the strange sounds from the swamp, drifting in and out of earshot, gnaw at his nerves as they wait at the deserted stop. Before he realises it he's thinking of his pills again: the capsules, so smooth, sliding down the throat of a man who hates to swallow anything. He recalls his mother shouting at him when he couldn't eat his stew, the fat on the bits of meat reminding him of snot, the meat reminding him of meat. Keeping it in his mouth, excusing himself and going to the toilet to spit it out or retch it up. Jackie grassing him up, — It's disgusting, she would say, genuinely revolted. The tired compassion in his father's eyes, — Just eat *some,* son. You have to eat. Then his mother rounding on him, rendered witless by his behaviour, — It's best stewing steak!

Even then he wondered how steak only good enough for stewing could be described as 'best'.

Another infrequent car passes, and Lennox is at first elated, then paranoid. *It's getting late. Where is Ginger? Perhaps he won't show.* He should have explained, emphasised how crucial it was. *Dolores would have said no. She'd think it was a drunken rendezvous.*

Unless . . .

Unless the paedophile cops network ran right across Florida and Ginger was in on it too. The way he'd looked at that young lassie in the strip club.

Get a fucking grip.

Lennox feels his breath catching. He's snatching at gulps of air again. It's heavy like it's full of iron particles, pulverising his lungs. He wants to be away from Tianna. She can't see him this way. He's doing her more harm than good.

Then a vehicle slows down and pulls up. Lennox can't make it out in the soupy darkness of the swamp. It looks like a 4x4. He feels every muscle in his body tense up as it stops a bit away from them. It doesn't look like Ginger's motor: it's Dearing, he's certain. — Get back in the car, he shouts at Tianna. She complies and he quickly follows. Those windows in the darkness and the shadows cast by the trees; he can see nothing.

Then there's a rap on the windscreen. — Lennox! What the hell are ye playing at?!

Ginger's big round face pulls into focus. Tianna gasps in shock, Lennox in relief, as he climbs out. — Ginger! Thank fuck . . . He wraps his arms around the barrel frame. Ginger is with Dolores. The dog, Braveheart, has jumped out the car behind them and is barking frantically. He is answered in kind by a long, throaty groan coming from behind the dark screen of mangroves.

— Ginger? Dolores asks, smiling in intrigue, before shouting after Braveheart, who is sniffing around the side of the gas station.

— How many fuckin times – Eddie Rogers snaps in annoyance, turning to the retreating Dolores, who is in pursuit of the dog. — Just a joke, hen, he says, then looks back at Lennox. — Sorry we're late. We had to pick up –

Lennox looks over to see Trudi emerge from the back of the Dodge. She wears a long dark blue skirt and has her hair down.

Her vague air of reproach vanishes as he staggers towards her. —
Ray . . .

— I'm sorry, he groans, compelled to close the distance between
them and take her in his arms, feeling his own body shake as her
thin, sinewy, but python-strong limbs envelop him, her scent
seeping through his shut eyelids into his brain. — I had to try
and help. I had to get involved. I don't know why, he says, and
repeats, — I don't know why.

Trudi's soft voice in his ear, Lennox realising how much he
loves her tones, her middle-class Edinburgh habit of enunciating
every word. — It wasn't your fault with Britney Hamil, Ray. It
wasn't your fault.

— Whose fault was it then? And he thinks of the time when
he'd gotten suspended from school for flooding a corridor with
a fire hose, his distraught mother saying in response to his lame
protests, 'Whose fault was it then if it wasn't yours?'

— The beast who killed her, Trudi coos, like she is reading a
child a bedtime story, — it was his fault.

Now remembering Britney's mum, Angela Hamil, telling him,
— It's okay. You did your best . . .

Then Ray Lennox, in a terrible honesty, had admitted to that
destroyed woman, — I didnae . . . I made a mistake. I didnae cause
I made a wrong judgement about you. I thought . . . I could have
done better! He had her for over three fucking days . . . I could
have saved her.

And Angela's face was pinched and riddled with pain as she
turned away from him. — No, she quietly insisted, — you did
your best. Ah kent you really cared aboot Britney fae the start.

He can now hear a small, persistent voice. — What? Tianna
says. — What wasn't your fault?

Guilt leaks from him. He can't look at the young American
girl. If he does he knows he'll see a Scottish one in her stead. He
holds Trudi tighter. — He was scum, he hisses into her slim neck.
— He didnae, couldnae, know any better. Tae expect him to be
better is to expect him to be the human being he can never be.
I was the one who should have known . . .

— No. You did your job, Ray. You tried to help, Trudi says.

Then she feels a tug on her arm. It's Tianna. She looks tear-fully at Trudi. — Ray helped me, she says softly. Trudi smiles, and puts her arm around the young girl. — He said you were beau-tiful, Tianna observes, causing Lennox's face to pain further, as he can't recall saying anything of the kind.

— Hi, er, Tianna, isn't it? She looks at the sheep clinging to her back. — I really like your bag.

— Ray helped me, Tianna repeats, thin tears glistening in her eyes. — He helped *me*.

Lennox feels his throat constricting. Tianna's face seems to radiate with all the world's possibilities. She could grow into somebody strong, vivacious and beautiful, or shrink in on herself, pasty and haunted. And she has so little time to decode the cruel puzzle others have malignly made of her life. — It's okay, sweetheart, it's okay. This is Ginger and Dol—

— Eddie! Ginger spits, and he sees Dolores playing thought-fully with the name.

— Sorry . . . Eddie, Lennox forces a weak, defeated grin. Bad habits, they are so very hard to stop, so very, very hard. — Tianna, these are good friends of mine, Eddie and Dolores Rogers. I want you to stay with them and Trudi. I'll be back later.

— I wanna stay with you, she says, standing her ground.

Lennox's palms out-turn in appeal, mimicking a hundred Scottish con men he's put behind bars. — I'll be back before you know it.

Doubt and distrust colour Tianna's face: she could be his mother now. He's relieved that Trudi's here, and Dolores, who asks Tianna, — Do you like dolphins and marine life?

— I guess so, she says as Braveheart approaches, sniffing at her leg, tail wagging.

— Trudi and I were gonna take a trip to Ocean World tomorrow morning.

— And you can help me look at dresses, Trudi says, taking Tianna's hand as they lead her to the 4x4. But the girl looks back to Lennox. — Lance is a cop. He'll put you in jail! Be careful!

— Of course I will.

Trudi disengages and hastens back over to him. — It's time to let go, Ray. To get the local police involved, she urges, as Braveheart follows his nose over to the verge by the waterway.

— I cannae, I need tae −

— You need to sort out your own life. Trying to sort out other people's won't save you, Ray.

— But I −

They are distracted by a growling noise. The dog has gone sniffing over into a clump of mangrove bushes by the fence. An exasperated Dolores gets out of the car and follows after him. — Look, buster, I've had it with you!

Then something happens so quickly, they almost believe it to be a hoax. The emerging alligator looks like a plastic toy as its snout protrudes from the bushes, but it lunges out at speed and its jaws, in one terrible snap, seize the dog. — BRAVEHEAR-RTTT! Dolores screams, and runs towards the fence and swamp, only to be restrained by Ginger. — Don't, Dolly, for fuck sakes!

At first it seems as if the reptile is going to gorge the small mammal whole, then it bites down in bone-crushing repetition on the screeching dog. It semi-swallows, regurgitates and slaps the dog, now like a rag doll, against the ground twice, and then shoots over a large hurricane-flattened section of fence, the limp body in its jaws.

Lennox and Trudi head over in cagey pursuit. She halts at the edge of the swamp, Lennox takes a few steps into it, but stops as he can feel its leafy, boundless darkness multiplying around him. They draw back to where Dolores, straining against Ginger, screams in anguish. Lennox takes hold of her as Ginger runs to the back of his vehicle, telling Tianna not to move and swiftly returning with a flashlight, but both creatures have vanished into the night. Silence is restored to the swamp, though Lennox fancies he can hear a sweet, victorious groan coming from the glades. A shaken Dolores crumpled into the Dodge, where Trudi and Tianna try to comfort her.

— That's that then, Ginger observes, nervously looking back towards the gap in the fence.

— I'm so sorry, Eddie, Lennox says wretchedly. — I feel responsible. It was me who brought you out here.

Ginger drops his voice and sidles close to him, eliminating the others from earshot. — Don't be, he hisses in barely repressed glee. — Dinnae say anything tae Dolores, but that wee fucker was the bane ay ma life. I always wanted a bigger dug, like a German shepherd, a proper dug. Look, I'd better get the lassies hame. Ye comin?

— No. I'm going back. I'll be along later.

— Ray, Trudi has got out of the car again, — please come with us.

— Get back in the car! It's dangerous! Lennox snaps. But Trudi doesn't move.

— She's right, Ginger says. — You've done your bit. From here on in, all you can do is make a total cunt of yourself. And by that I mean an even bigger one than you already have.

— No way, Lennox says. He's thinking about Robyn. And Dearing, Johnnie, Starry and Chet. She knows something and they are keeping her quiet till they decide what to do with her. What will they do, given the resources they have? Now, out here in those swamps, it is so chillingly obvious to him. The sea. They'll lose her at sea. Lance and Johnnie are taking Robyn to Chet's boat and they'll dump her somewhere in the Gulf of Mexico. It's high risk, of course. Coastguards, terrorist alerts, illegal-immigration control teams, DEA helicopters. But they might now be desperate enough to try it.

But not as desperate as him. Because he wants them: Lance, Johnnie, Starry, that trinity of bad intent. Chet too, though the nature of his embroilment is harder to fathom. And the terrible possibility of Robyn's culpability won't dislodge itself from his overheated mind. The music in his head is winding down, because his part in Tianna's terrible ballad is over. Now there's a new song striking up, or a remix of an old forgotten one. And it isn't about Britney. It's about a frightened boy trapped in a dark tunnel. And despite Dolores's cries and Trudi's protests, it's all he can hear.

— C'mon, Ray, Ginger pleads.

Lennox thinks of *Perfect Bride* with Trudi's address in it. — I've left something, and he climbs back into the rented Volkswagen.

17

Edinburgh (4)

Y ou saw Police Headquarters at Fettes as a factory, one which measured and allotted the requisite units of humanity to everyone that came through its doors. The suspects. The members of your team: Gillman, Drummond, Notman, Harrower, McCaig. You.

Through his entire processing by the state's law enforcement and criminal justice systems, Horsburgh displayed only arrogance and disdain. The searches of property and assets. The intimate forensic tests. The interrogations. The psychiatrist's reports. The official charges. He enjoyed it as a game; savoured the embarrassment all round when he confessed to the Welwyn Garden City and Manchester crimes. It all meant so little to him. But it meant so much to you, and Mr Confectioner knew it.

It came to a head on a mid-November Wednesday, three weeks after Britney had been taken. You'd spent hours with this man, trying to find out what made him the way he was. Looked into his soul. Saw nothing. Exasperation got the better of you. — Why? Why did you do it?

— Because I could, Confectioner had replied in offhand candour, removing his reading specs, waving them gently to underscore a point. — It was the sport of it mainly. Oh, don't get me wrong, I got a lot of pleasure from the sexual side, but that wasn't the main motivation. Very fleeting, that sort of thing. Besides, this one was a little too young. I prefer them to have some sort of awareness of what's going to happen to them. His lips trembled in delight, knowing he'd got to you. — It was more the thrill of the chase, stalking them, building up the dossiers, evading you lot. We're thrill-seeking creatures, are we not?

You had fought to maintain silence and an even stare; to keep looking dispassionately for the clues. We studied our serial killers, nonces and murderers in the same way we did our scientists, intellectuals and artists, looking for answers to the mystery of our nature.

And Confectioner recognised that in you, this fatal curiosity; used it to toy with you. — You're different from the others, he'd pompously declared. — They just need to know how. How did I lure, overpower, fuck, kill and conceal. But you're really so desperate to know *why*. You want me to tell you that I was buggered by my father or the local parish priest or whoever. In your dwarf mind, there must always be cause and effect. But you're only protecting weaklings like yourself, Lennox. You can't accept that man is a hunter, a predator. Civil society's set up to protect the weak and the cowardly — be they rich or poor — from the strong and virtuous who have the courage to fulfil the destiny of their species. Who have the guts to take what they want.

The grimly cheerful smile. That rubbery mouth you wanted to tear from his face.

— You know, I had every police force in Britain looking for me for the best part of five years and you didn't have a fucking clue as to who I was. All this time I'd be lodging complaints at my local station about vandalism or noise coming from pubs, and you'd bend over backwards to help.

It was true. Mr Confectioner, 'Horsey', the pedantic Home Office civil servant nobody wanted to be stuck beside on the morning commuter train from Aylesbury to Marylebone, had conned them all. His whole persona was an act, concealing a warped but calculating mind. Photography was his supposed interest, but the darkroom upstairs in his home, out of reach from his crippled mother, was really a laboratory. All his weekend and holiday time was spent planning his abductions and murders. His true hobby was kidnapping, beasting and killing.

Horsburgh would hire a cottage within a couple of hours' driving distance from his intended target area. Nula Andrews was taken to a place in the Fenlands, Stacey Earnshaw the Lake District, and Britney Hamil to the Berwickshire coast. Horsburgh also told them where the body of a young French girl was buried in

Normandy. — A holiday romance, he'd chirped, meeting your seething rage with a television game-show host's smile. — They never last.

This disclosure resulted in the release of a farm labourer who had been in a French prison for seven years. Crucially, though, Confectioner refused to cooperate when you showed him pictures of other missing children. — Not quite ready to help you there, he'd said genially. But you knew there were more victims.

None of the missing kids was on Horsburgh's comprehensive database of young girls, or featured in his detailed notes. But also absent were records for Nula, Stacey and Britney; he'd obviously erased them on completion of each abominable mission. How many others were there?

You did find the white van. Horsburgh also had a black one, keeping both in a lock-up garage a mile from his home, using them solely for his crimes. He selected his victims at random, trying for a geographical spread. He also had the tapes he'd made.

If there was one thing more unsettling to you than talking to Confectioner, it had been watching the Britney tape earlier that morning with Dougie Gillman. — That's five times, his frozen, mordant observation, — he's fucked her, choked her unconscious, then brought her back for another shot. That's his thing.

Gillman's voice and those images snapped back into your head as you stared at Horsburgh's hands. You buckled under a sharp intake of breath, as you heard the soft, childlike plea escape from somewhere deep within you. — She was only a wee lassie.

The killer looked at you as if you were simple: with pity as well as contempt. Then you realised that Bob Toal had come into the interview room. He nodded for you to follow him outside, steering you into an empty office and closing the door. — You're losing it, Ray, he warned. — Go and get some lunch. I want to give Dougie a shot at him this affie.

You gripped his forearm. — Just one more session, you begged.

Toal looked over your shoulder into the middle distance. — Okay, Ray, he said finally, — you pulled him, you deserve the chance to see it through. Then he looked down at your hand, shaming you into withdrawing your grip. — But it's against my better judgement: you're a mess.

And you couldn't contradict him. Last night you'd turned up at Trudi's, a rambling drunk. There was an argument and you'd woken up on her couch, and gone straight into work. — I'm sorry, you told your boss, — I'll sort myself out.

Toal looked doubtful. — Leave the whys for the shrinks. Find out about those other kids.

— Thanks. I'll stick to the details, like you said, as you glanced at each other in impasse, both unsure of what to say next. You eventually managed to wheeze out your intention of getting some lunch, and you trooped down to Stockbridge.

Then, in Bert's Bar, as you watched Sky News, Robert Ellis appeared on the screen. Out of prison, self-educated, well read. Enjoying the new-found status of being the articulate good guy. — I feel sorry for the families of Stacey Earnshaw and Nula Andrews. They deserved genuine closure but instead they were forced to live a lie all those years. Most of all, though, I really feel for the family of Britney Hamil. While I was rotting in jail, this monster was out there, free to do these unspeakable things to that child. Heads will roll, he threatened. Ellis now a hero to those who forgot his vile rant at the grave of Nula Andrews. But you harboured the uneasy sensation that had he been as eloquent several years back, Ellis, instead of instigating bar-room brawls, might have been a man who led nations into war.

You couldn't stand it: you went to the toilet and snorted a line of cocaine.

When you returned to Fettes, you savoured the cold burn in your veins. Felt that you now had the measure of the beast. In the interview room you had distance back in your voice. — You'd have been pretend-tinkering in the back of the van, looking out for signs of life at the windows. Waiting till Britney had walked past and was blocked by the body of the van from any prying eyes on the other side of the road. You grabbed the kid, bundled her into the back, shut the door, secured her, probably with duct tape, maybe forced some Rohypnol or chloroform on to her, then climbed into the front, right?

— And tore off to my evil lair for the slow devouring. Horsburgh smiled. — You're a smart one, DI Lennox. Probably an IT background, I'm guessing. A 2:1 at some second-rate, but still decent uni. Perhaps even a master's –

— Shut the fuck up.

Horsburgh looked offended, then somewhat disappointed as he disdainfully raised his brows. — But you missed stuff. The CCTV footage of the grave. You've probably looked at loads of it. Kills the eyes, that sort of thing. How's your vision?

You sensed you were being played. Were suddenly very aware of your colleagues through the mirror. — What?

— Did you ever look at Parka Man's debut appearance?

— In Welwyn . . .

— Sorry, I meant my debut appearance in Edinburgh. He paused for effect. You felt the room grow bigger, Horsburgh receding from you. — The security footage from Burger Palace, at that dreadful shopping centre . . . you missed it, didn't you?

You battled to retain your composure. — Go on.

Mr Confectioner laughed like a waterfall, all shoulder-shaking shushes. — I suppose I overestimated you. Check it. The night before I took her, when she went with her mother and sister to that grotty fast-food place. Had you checked the footage, you'd have seen me there. Sporting the trusty parka. You were remiss, DI Lennox.

You could feel the eyes of the others – Toal, Gillman – through that mirror. Knew they wouldn't be on Horsburgh.

— I'd dumped my little device in the rubbish bin outside the window. A small bang to attract them all, then that blazing bucket. How children love a fire! So easy for me to swap Tessa's drink with my spiked concoction; I knew she'd go for Sprite, she always did. I hoped that Britney would walk alone to school the next day, and sure enough . . . He basked in self-approval. — The rest played out roughly as you described it. My discarding of the school books and bag was basically just to mess around with you. A little tease. It thrilled me to think of you earnestly pondering the deep significance of these completely playful actions. But . . . you didn't think to check the burger bar's CCTV from the night before? Shabby policework, Lenno –

You'd sprung across that cold distance between you and him and had your hands round Mr Confectioner's throat. But although his body went limp and he offered no resistance, fear was absent from his bulging eyes. Instead, a sick smile played upon his rubbery lips; he was like a terrifying ventriloquist's dummy. And you heard him rasp in a thin, ghostly voice, — Feels good, doesn't it?

Then, in a slow caressing movement, Gareth Horsburgh's hand went up to your genitals. You stopped, froze under the nonce's touch on your penis; that contact when you realised, with horror, that you were erect. You loosened your grip and backed away, just as Gillman and Notman burst through the door. — Now you're beginning to understand, Mr Confectioner said, rubbing at his throat.

Then you saw how it should be done. Saw Gillman move slowly behind Horsburgh. Watched apprehension replace the hauteur in the beast's eyes. Saw the unnerved nonce try to steel himself, and he was about to speak when Gillman said in an even, neutral voice, like he was talking about the weather: — You're mine now.

— No marks, Doug, Ally, you'd said softly, trying pathetically to maintain an authority you knew had left you as you closed the door, squeamished by the mutual information that hung adhesively between you and your brother officers, as cosy and wily as clandestine sex.

You went to the anteroom, slumped down in a chair next to Toal. Watched defeatedly through the screen. There are many ways you can hurt somebody without leaving marks. Every interrogator in every police force in the world gets taught them, either formally or informally, depending on the nature of the regime. You were sure that Gillman, standing behind the now disquieted Mr Confectioner, a white towel in his hands, knew every one of them. — All that stuff aboot being a hunter, he smirked as he snapped the ends of the towel tight, — made me laugh, that yin.

By his silence, Gareth Horsburgh recognised that true terror would now be visited upon him, by someone who really did understand punishment.

— Ye know, ah don't see that. Gillman shook his head. — Ah see a middle-aged guy who lives at hame with ehs ma.

You couldn't stay. You sprang to your feet, headed out and down the stairs, shamed again by the beast. A pursuing Toal caught up with you on the path outside. In the biting cold air, your boss gave you the spiel about being a good man, who'd done a good job. About not taking the Robertson route and going down. Then he'd whispered, — You were caught on camera, leaving a bar in Newcastle frequented by drug dealers.

— Boss, I —

— Don't say anything, Ray. Toal's head whipped back and forth. — It's been taken care of. Don't speak to anybody about this. I've made an appointment for you to go and see Melissa Collingwood in counselling. You are officially on leave till further notice. Go to Trudi's, Ray.

You nodded, walked down into Comely Bank Avenue and jumped in a taxi up to the Jeanie Deans pub. All you could think of was: I didn't consider the camera in the centre, at the burger bar. They had one there, to check who was going in and out of the toilets, and over the counters for robbery and staff assaults. I just didn't think about the night before. Why? Because all I thought about was Angela, what a dirty, lazy cow she was, who'd poisoned her own kid with her crap food.

So you went to the bar you used to frequent with Robbo and several other burned-out dissaffected cops. Met a few of the boys there and drank a lot of vodka, before being felled by a sick joke.

18

Decked

Lennox drives back towards the Gulf Coast at a steady eighty; air con off and windows down, taking in the scent of the night, as he vacates the freeway for the connecting fork to Highway 41, passing on to the curving slip road for Bologna.

At thirty-five he feels suddenly older, sensing the seasons quickly chasing him down. Twenty-eight to thirty-four seemed static, a welcome hiatus after two decades of almost overwhelming volatility, but then his thirty-fifth year had delivered a quantum leap into middle age. Smitten by angst, he wonders about his next cataclysmic anniversary, and the urge to savour almost overwhelms. Lennox feels he should be looking at the eminence of the flickering stars through the dark, naked treetops, but he's too intent on steering down this winding drive, treacherous after America's breezy highways and waiting to claim him for its own. His need to concentrate is a response to his fatigue, but also because he feels an uneasy seduction lurking in those heavens; the stars seem closer down here, frozen detonated fireworks clustering in the air with a judging, perilous aspect.

The air at ground level is still almost gossamer in its humidity, but the swishing palm trees overhead signal a building wind as the road snakes even more keenly. Then, to his right, lights of varying intensity shimmer through the trees as the town rises out from the mangrove swamp.

As he drives towards the harbour, the marina is on the left: moon-globe street lamps beam in ripples over the water, the stars now a pallid glimmer in the inky sky above, and he can see thunderhead clouds glowing ominously through the mottled darkness to the north. Passing over the swamplands, they draw winds from the mangrove bushes as they loom in menacing approach.

Pulling into the near empty lot, he sees Chet's boat moored under a burning lamp. As he exits the car, a solitary figure emerges from the office on the brokerage strip. — You're sure lucky to catch ol Chet. Don Wynter twirls a set of keys, glancing to the berthed boat. — Reckon he's plannin on takin a long trip. Down to the Keys, or maybe even the Bahamas. Plenty supplies; I know that cause I sell em to him, the old boy laughs. — Pretty tight-lipped about it all. Reckon he got some sweet thing tucked away.

— Anybody else on the boat? Lennox asks.

— Don't reckon so, the loquacious harbour master says, and begins to expand, but Lennox has turned abruptly and stolen off towards the vessel. Stepping on to the gangplank, he looks down at the oily water before hopping on to the pristine craft. It's dark, but light emanates from the cabin below. However, Chet is on the bridge, and both men are startled by the unexpected presence of the other. — Lennox. What . . . what are you doing here?

— I left something, he says gruffly and heads without invitation downstairs to the galley kitchen and dining area. The dog-eared *Perfect Bride* lies on the table where Tianna left it; apparently untouched. He picks it up, the beaming visage of the model bride strangely welcoming. Then he notes that the door of the larger bedroom is shut. He opens it and looks inside. Empty. So he heads up the four oak steps and back to the rear deck of the boat.

Chet stands trembling in front of him, but although a breeze is mounting, it hasn't yet shifted the humidity from the air and it isn't cold. He regards the magazine in Lennox's hand. — Must be valuable, for you to come back for it.

— Aye, Lennox acknowledges, — it is. Then he looks up at the sky. — Weather's turned a wee bit.

— Forecast isn't too bad though. The rain clouds should blow over us, Chet says, distractedly. — Tianna nice and safe?

Lennox's antenna tingles. Tianna's safety has become an after-thought. — Aye. She's with friends of mine.

— Good, Chet says uneasily.

Lennox feels something spike his arm. He lashes out with the magazine in his other hand, slapping sunburn, but crumpling the mosquito that has bloated on his blood. — Bastard, he snaps.

— You become immune and they don't carry malaria here.

— I don't intend to stick around long enough to become immune, Lennox says. — Just one question, although he knows, in cop tradition, that others will follow, — has Lance Dearing ever been on this boat?

As the words leave his lips, he becomes aware that Chet is actually looking over his shoulder. And then he hears a scrambling on the steps behind him. But Lennox can't react in time as he feels something collide with him at force and it's as if his teeth are being pushed out of his face from behind. He stumbles forward, fighting to stay conscious, but an explosion of orange in his head is fading to black. *Fight through this shite. Fight.* He feels no sensation but sees a mess of mashed-up red snapper and fries sloshing from him on to the deck. Then somebody is on him, forcing him down into his own vomit. He can't resist; he's a puppet with the strings cut. Immediately he thinks Dearing and Johnnie, as he feels his wrists being bound with something – he suspects fishing twine – followed by his ankles. Lennox slams his eyelids shut and grinds his teeth together. He's aware of a spasm in his gullet now, and counts silently, hoping for a lull that will enable him to either swallow or expel his partial regurgitations. Then he seems to be breathing cool air through a hole in his chest.

As his vision clears, he draws up his knees and examines his ankles, confirming his suspicion as to the nature of his bondage. Then a pole dancer in silhouette and a slogan I SUPPORT SINGLE MOMS comes into vision, and Johnnie is crouching over him. As well as the T-shirt he wears a pair of polyester slacks. Lennox's bleary eyes pan in jagged survey: no sign of Dearing. He sees the blue logo of *Perfect Bride* as the magazine lies face up in his vomit.

Johnnie holds a big, rusty shifting wrench, and he's barking something at Chet. Lennox can't make out the words. His skull throbs and the stink of his own vomit lodges in his nose and throat. His breaths have gathered the velocity of a steam loco-motive. Each one demands attention. Resting his head on the deck, he shuts his eyes and lies in a stupor for what might have been hours, but on opening them the distance from the harbour lights indicates the passage of only a few minutes.

263

He tries to swallow. Saliva won't come together in his arid mouth and throat. His head bangs, his eardrums pop, the acrid stench of his own puke rises from his shirt. The tendons in his neck are strained, as if his skull is lead. The tight binding on his wrists prevents him wiping the stinging sweat from his eyes. He considers his location, propped up against the deck seating at the rear of the craft. He can see Chet at the helm as the boat surges forward. The old taxman can't look at Lennox, as if witnessing his humiliation is too big a cross to bear.

A deep fear grips him. Dealing with people who had been murdered in suspicious circumstances has made him even less disposed to joining their ranks. Cops wanted to know what the dead person on the table ate, what they wore, drank, read, who they knew, who they fucked, and how they liked to do it. They'd poke around under your fingernails, in your mouth, up your arse, around your genitals and inside your stomach. Then they'd pore over your mail, diary, emails, bank accounts and investments, till they knew you better than you'd known yourself. Lennox has always been tormented by the mortifying sense that his spirit self would be compelled to bear witness to the ignominious abuse of his worldly remains.

The last thing he wants is to be touched but it's strangely comforting as a hand under his armpit yanks him upright. Then his skull hurts so bad, he envisions his head as physically split open, brains pouring from the back of it, slopping across the slick, white fibreglass of the boat into the sea. Sickness sinks through his body like a dropped anchor. He digs in his trainered soles, trying to get traction on a deck made slippery by his own puke. — It's okay, a voice says in his ear. His arse feels the moulded seat and he swivels his hips to assist the force guiding him on to it. — You okay? Johnnie asks, the genuine concern in his voice surprising Lennox.

— I think you fractured my skull. He stares at the thick stubble on Johnnie's chin. — I need to go to a hospital.

— If you're sharp enough to talk like that, then you don't need no hospital. Johnnie's manner is now contrary and childlike.

— So you're a doctor, then?

Johnnie has lost the wrench, but Lennox sees a sheathed diving knife attached to his belt, incongrous against the polyester leg. — I didn't wanna hurt you, he says, shaking his head, — but why you gotta go poking your big fucking nose into other people's business?

— It goes with the territory, he says, flexing against his bounds. The unyielding nature of the constraints induces a panic he struggles to fight. He's going to drown. To be cast overboard. To have his breath crushed from his lungs by the force of the sea. He can picture the last air he will expel, a bubble rendered tangible and measurable by the water around it. See it explode in liberation to the surface, while his lifeless body floats below.

— What territory is that? Johnnie asks.

Lennox can't think of what to say. Then Chet stalls the boat, cutting the engine to slow cruising speed. Thinking of the moth, Lennox shudders. As terror dances behind his eyes, he realises his notions of a dignified death were fanciful.

How did I get here?

Mr Confectioner, he was the one that fucked my heid. Every time Lennox encountered Horsburgh, he wanted the world to swallow one of them up. Afterwards, he'd repair to the pub; drinking to try and obliterate the stuff he'd heard spill from this man's mouth. A line of cocaine helped. Was it Horsey, Mr Confectioner, who'd led him here?

— What's the fucking hold-up? Johnnie roars at Chet. — We ain't here to look at no fuckin dolphins!

A seabird squawks, and Lennox feels the spray made by the boat cleaning his face. An astonishing calm descends on him, his thoughts seeming to become abstract. A strange but urgent consideration hits him: *the missing piece in the jigsaw has to be a twenty-plus-goals-a-season striker. At present there was far too big a goal-scoring burden on Skacel and Hartley in the midfield.* Then he sees that Chet is losing it, giving Johnnie the fear-of-running-aground routine. — We are in the goddamn shallows and this boat weighs twenty-three thousand pounds, and that was before your lardy ass stepped on to it. Unless you want me to run aground and have the coastguard out to us, I suggest we proceed with fucking caution!

Johnnie aims a sulky gape at Chet; he goes to say something then stops. Instead, holding the boat's peripheral rail, he turns to Lennox. — Right, asshole. Who the fuck are you?

Lennox still thinks of Mr Confectioner, Gareth Horsburgh. The arrogance of the taunting beast: like it was an act he'd run through on many private occasions. He recalls asking Stuart how he prepared for his acting roles; the corrupt young solicitor in *Taggart*, the intern vet in *Take the High Road*, the drug-addled ned in *The Vice*.

Find the character's essence. Become one with it, harness it.

What would Horsburgh do if he were the captive? He would be derisive, sneering his contempt at those insects. The supercilious civil servant, with his briefcase and sandwiches, would delight in being the biggest, brightest, most evil beast in this jungle.

— I never intended to get involved in all this, Johnnie. He hears his tones clipped and precise. — Now I'm going to ask you to do something for me.

— What . . . what the fuck do you want *me* to do for *you*?

— I'm going to ask you to get rid of me.

And Ray Lennox, Mr Confectioner, tries to rise. His arse gets an inch from the seat, before the boat's motion thumps him back, jarring his spine.

— Hold it right there or that is exactly what I will do, Johnnie says, — throw your miserable interfering ass overboard!

— But I want you to. I want to make it easy for you, Lennox the Confectioner urges, trying to thrust himself up again. — Just help me up and I'll jump.

— Not from my boat you won't, Chet blusters above the engine's growl. — I've never lost anybody at sea yet and I don't intend –

— Shut the fuck up! Johnnie bellows, then pushes Lennox back on to the seat with one hand, gripping the handrail with the other. — I'm warning you, asshole!

Lennox looks at Johnnie with his now deliciously half-shut eyes, feeling the throb of power in his constrained limbs. — You know what I want. Because you know that I'm like you and there's only room for one of us.

Chet's shoulders bristle and his back stiffens as he grips the wheel. When he turns, his eyes have the protrusion and burn of the death's head. — What in hell's name are you saying . . . ?

Johnnie gazes in stupefaction at Lennox, then there's a spark of interest.

— When I stumbled on your little nest of vipers I was so excited, Lennox expounds in a low lisp, his senses now merely a conduit to the voice of another: someone hated. — You see, I'd been emailing back home to my own organisation, trying to get in contact with like-minded souls in America. But no luck. I was prowling freelance when I met her, by accident. The mother. I could smell it off her; you always can. And the girl. You know what they called me back in Britain, Johnnie? Mr Confectioner. But I never tempted a child with candy. Their mothers though, oh, they could be bought off with a few drinks and some sweet talk.

He can see his own ugliness reflected back in Johnnie's eyes. Like he did looking at Horsburgh.

How he's marked me, how they always mark you.

— A dopey, negligent woman with low self-esteem, and a delightful little nymphet, taught how to give pleasure and say nothing. I was making my move when *you*, Johnnie, he tersely nods at him, — you almost ruined everything with your ham-fisted approach. But really I should thank you. It was your action that delivered her into my care. I had a wonderful night in that hotel room, Johnnie. That was a result, and much appreciated.

— You're full of bullshit, Johnnie says, both hands white on the rail, but his weak sneer can't conceal his entrancement.

— Shut up, Chet barks. — Shut up, you fucking perverts, and he disintegrates into an agonised howl. — I've had enough of this. All your fucking blackmail! IT ENDS NOW!

Johnnie looks from Lennox to Chet. — If I tell Dearing about this, you are fucking finished, old man!

— So to the victor the spoils, Lennox gasps, pulling Johnnie's attention back to him. — She's yours and I'll never know the beauty of a hairless minge again.

— We saw her first, you fuck: we staked that dumb-ass bitch of a mother out for months . . . you think I enjoyed balling that

267

stretch-marked hag? He points at the pole dancer on his chest. — I'm into young pussy, is all. I did the fucking dirty work and then Dearing breezes in . . . Johnnie stops, as if realising he's said too much.

— Fair enough, Lennox says as Chet moans something he can't make out. — So fuck it: throw me to the fishes. I like young pussy too; in fact, I can't live without it. It was a good run while it lasted!

Johnnie's head wobbles with vigour. — Nobody's goin to no freakin fishes —

— But Lance is calling the shots. He'll want rid of me, then he'll destroy you, long before you need to go down, Johnnie.

— You know nuthin about us —

— I know from what you're saying that you're doing the dirty work and he's getting the pay-off.

Johnnie stiffens, puts one hand on his hip. — Damn straight, he acknowledges.

— And I know that I could give you more options than this. Lennox looks out over the dark, still waters. — America's finished, Johnnie. It's crawling with Feds and DEA agents. Drugs, terrorism, illegals: all this crippling paranoia about borders. Over my way, we bring in some really beautiful girls: East European, Asian. The border controls are limited, the terror alerts almost zero. Most of them can't even speak English. Those Thai girls, Johnnie, he says as his adversary licks his lips, — they are something else. They come from nothing so they're happy to get anything. Not MTV-saturated brats who expect stuff; they're silent and obedient, just the way we like em, right?

A hatchet grin cleaves Johnnie's doughy face in two.

Lennox fights to return the complicit smirk. — I could get you sorted out, Johnnie.

— Sounds finger-fuckin good to me, Johnnie says. Then his face tightens again. — But Dearing —

— Forget Dearing. He's a cop. If you start getting rid of bodies, and it looks like this whole thing is going to shit, then who's going to carry the can? The cop or the stooges? He shouts over at Chet: — What about you, Lewis? You aren't a killer. Are you going to let Dearing lead you up the garden path?

268

— SHUT UP! SHUT UP, YOU FUCKING TWISTED PERVERTS!

Johnnie turns and looks at Chet. — Fuck you!

— Get onside with me, Johnnie! Lennox shouts, — and I won't let you down!

Johnnie nods in dim complicity, and Lennox can't believe it. *The fucking simpleton*. And now he's reaching behind Lennox and is cutting at his twine bounds with a serrated knife. *He's no right in the heid*. As his face is squashed into Johnnie's flabby breast, he almost feels sorry for Dearing, stuck with such a blundering side-kick.

— I could sure use a little help, Ray. Things have gotten a bit out of control. Dearing thinks he knows it all but –

Johnnie gasps as his eyes expand then roll in his head and he slumps forward, crushing Lennox, who vainly tries to slide out from under him. Standing above, holding a fire extinguisher, is Chet. Lennox is immobilised with Johnnie's stunned, heaving bulk on his lap, unable to free his wrists from the last of the twine. Disordered by fury, Chet keeps the extinguisher poised. — You fucking scumbags! I'VE HAD ENOUGH OF YOU ALL! He raises the metal cylinder above his head, as Johnnie slides off Lennox, rolling on to the deck with the slap of a landed fish.

— STOP! Lennox screams. — I'm NOT what you think!

Chet pauses, wobbles, but keeps his balance, as Lennox realises nobody is operating the boat.

— I made that shit up to buy time with that arsehole. He looks down at the groaning Johnnie.

— Nobody playing fucking fair, Johnnie wheezes deliriously, — only ol Johnnie here tryin to play fair . . .

Chet won't relinquish his hold on the extinguisher. — I've had enough bullshit and deceit –

— CHECK! For fuck's sake, check my ID in my wallet. I'm a cop! Lennox screams. — Tianna's safe, she's with my fiancée, Trudi. I've a number in my wallet with my ID, you can contact her there!

Chet finally lowers the canister. His powerlifter's mitt grabs Lennox's neck. — I should . . . he starts as Lennox feels his throat constricting, but the sailor's other hand is pulling the wallet from his pocket. He unleashes the grip and reads a card as Lennox rasps an intake of air. — Lothian and Borders Police? What the hell is that? That isn't even Alaska . . . or Utah . . . you have no jurisdiction here! What the hell has this got to do with you?

— Nothing, Lennox heaves, struggling to fill his lungs. — Absolutely fuck all. I'm a cop on holiday with my fiancée. We're planning our wedding. We had a big fight and I went off in the huff and met Robyn and her friend in a bar. Then, well, you know the rest. He nods at the moaning Johnnie, still spangled on the deck.

Chet looks at him for a few seconds. — I believe you, he says finally, — I'll cut you free and then −

But Johnnie suddenly springs up, the blood cascading down his back, grasping the blade from his belt. He swings it at Chet and misses, — YOU FUCKIN IDIOT! COULD'VE FUCKIN KILLED ME!

Chet shrieks and runs up on to the top deck, with Johnnie in pursuit. — Dinnae run away fae that fat cunt, you're a power-lifter: break ehs fuckin neck! Lennox roars. Then an irresistible, clattering halt, and he shoots off the seat under its impact, as he sees Chet and Johnnie vanish from the deck like magician's assistants. There's no time to work out what's happening; still trussed up, he's propelled across the lower deck, slamming back-first into the steps that lead up to the bridge.

Things slow down after that jarring loss of momentum; Lennox shakes his head to try and clear it. A wrenching racket from the engines, like a food mixer amplified through a sound system, tells him the boat has run aground. He tries to catch his breath. He can't determine Johnnie and Chet's fates as propulsion mechanisms continue to snarl and wheeze in impotence, but it seems likely that the impact has thrown them both overboard. He pulls himself along towards the steps that lead down into the cabin, letting his legs swing over. It's a steep fall and he's bound at the ankles, but he's no choice. Swallowing hard, he takes a deep breath to drain himself of everything superfluous to the jump. His body seems to leave his essence behind as it falls the distance, but they reunite as

Lennox hits the deck feet-first before crashing on to his side, a brutal signal of agony making him believe he's broken his arm. Forcing himself up against a kitchen worktop, he hops into position, sticking the fishing twine that binds his wrists into the teeth of the electronic can opener. Unable switch it on, he saws crudely. As it snaps free, the pain in his arm almost causes him to black out. Balancing himself with his pulped right hand, Lennox breathes in deeply, trying to force down his heart rate. Then he rummages through the opened drawers, finding another serrated knife and taking it to his ankles, wincing as he hacks himself free.

All around him the now twenty-degree-angled edifice emits wind-blown moans and whines, juddering and creaking as if its hull is being rent apart. Cupboard doors have sprung open on one side, sending provisions tumbling on to the craft's floor.

Lennox rubs at the back of his head with his throbbing right hand. There is an egg-shaped swelling, tender to the touch, but no blood. The left arm hurts unbearably; he can't lift it above chest level. Nonetheless, he feels adrenalin's charge and hoists himself up the steps, springing on to the bow. Johnnie is above him; top deck, starboard side, knife poised, threatening, but not striking at Chet, who is holding on to the railing, trying to climb back on to the tilted boat. — Let me on, or the engine will burn out, he warns.

Thank fuck they're amateurs who don't know what they're doing, Lennox consoles himself. Disgusting paedophiles, yes, but different from a deranged killer like Horsburgh. Noncing is their game, pure and simple; they have no contingency plans, no exit strategy. Things are going wrong for them, as he found eventually happened with all criminal activity. It was like the bookies or the casino: the occasional big win only hastening your next devastating loss.

But revulsion bubbles in him, and he craves violence's release. — C'moan then, fat boy, he shouts. — Let's fuckin have ye!

Johnnie turns and moves towards Lennox, the knife in his hand, struggling to negotiate the sloping deck. Despite his bulk, Lennox can see that the fear is ripping out of him. He'd miscast this masturbating stoner as bully of the barrio, but Johnnie's as out of his depth as the beached boat.

Lennox adopts the fighter's side-on stance and though his left arm still pains him, he is able to raise it into the blocking position. He gets in a couple of feeble jabs that hurt him more than his opponent, but the very shock of contact all but disables Johnnie. He manages a weak and wide swing of the blade but this puts him off balance, allowing Lennox to step inside, elbowing him with his right, to protect his damaged fist. He follows up by catching Johnnie with a roundhouse kick, sending him blindly flailing to the deck. After a few more blows, Johnnie has dropped the knife and is slowly being worked over. — I came on holiday with my fiancée to GET THE FUCK AWAY from scum like you. And this Dearing cunt is a fucking cop. His foot whacks into the fat man's face, extracting a doglike yelp. — Where is she, Johnnie? Lennox punctuates his questions with blows. — Where's Robyn? Where's Dearing? Where's fucking Starry?

Johnnie's groans can barely be heard above the noise of the engines. But when they abruptly cut out, he hears him howl, — I DUNNO!

Lennox looks to the top deck starboard. Chet had climbed back on the boat and got on to the bridge, shutting the power down.

Johnnie now snivels puplike as Lennox sits on top of him, injured fist round his throat, the other ready to hammer him more. Eventually he miserably concedes, — Robyn's at her place; Starry's with her. Lance is meeting some people . . . at the Embassy Hotel tonight . . . in Miami.

Assisted by Chet, Lennox reciprocates the treatment Johnnie meted out to him, binding his wrists and ankles in fishing twine.

— We wasn't gonna hurt nobody, Johnnie says meekly.

— Shut the fuck up, Lennox spits, striking him across the face with the back of his left hand. A yellow puddle spreading out from under the polyester trousers encourages him to stand up. Its slow path towards *Perfect Bride* makes him aware that the boat's angle has almost righted itself since Chet cut the engines.

Lennox kicks the magazine from the piss and gestures to Chet, and they head downstairs. They sit as he rubs at his arm, then massages his nipping eyeballs through closed lids. — I need to know the score.

Chet nods and looks at the mess on the floor, then he rises to a locked cabinet, producing a bottle of malt whisky and two cut glasses. Lennox grimaces at the volunteered liquor, nauseated by the smell. — I don't drink that stuff.

— A Scotsman and you don't drink whisky?

— That's the way it is, he says, but he certainly needs a drink. — Anything else?

— I've some Ukrainian vodka.

— That'll do.

— With soda?

— Fine, Lennox says, wondering why he is drinking with this man, even as he instantly imbibes the spirit, extending his glass for a refill.

As he replenishes it, Chet coughs out his understanding of events. — They're keeping Robyn at her place with Starry. They seem to believe she's cottoned on to what their game is, but I think they think she knows more than she does . . . if you follow me.

Lennox nods, pressing him to carry on.

— I need to get out of this, Lennox. These people are sick and evil. They are paedophiles and God knows what else. Dearing told me that you were one of them, an outsider trying to muscle into their sex club —

— No. I'm certainly not.

— Sorry. I couldn't be sure.

— But what about you? How did you —

— They were blackmailing me. I didn't know where to turn. Dearing is a cop, for chrissakes.

Lennox slowly blows out some air. As soon as he'd learned about Dearing, he knew he could never have gone to the police in Miami. It would be like some cop from the Fiji Islands wandering into Fettes HQ and saying to an officer on the desk, 'One of your polismen is running a paedophile ring.'

— Once they found my weakness —

— Aw aye? Lennox spits in threat. — And what weakness is that?

Chet looks sadly at him. — It's not what you think. I swear to

273

you I never touched Tianna or any other child, nor did I make them do anything. He says it so emphatically that Lennox can see he is disgusted at the thought. — I didn't make *anybody* do anything. I just liked to watch, not with the kids obviously, I knew nothing about that. Please believe me! he pleads.

— Go on.

— Pamela had gone, Lennox, and I was lonely. This was to be our retirement paradise; I'd worked and saved and invested carefully all my life so that we could have this dream together. We lived it for about eighteen months till she got sick and she was dead five months later. I was at a low when I met Robyn and Tianna.

Lennox raises his eyebrows.

— There was nothing between Robyn and me. She made it clear that she wasn't interested, and to be truthful, neither was I. But through her I met Johnnie and Lance. I knew they were lowlife, especially Johnnie, his head twists towards the bow, — and that they would do what they do. It was just women at first. All I ever did was let them use the boat, and watch the odd tape they made. But they're devious sons of bitches; they shot the stuff in a way that everybody would know it was being filmed on my boat. They knew this was my life and that I'd be finished here if it came out.

— So you got in so deep you felt you had to carry on, Lennox says. This was commonplace. People being blackmailed often capitulated, thinking they could buy time, but usually ended up compounding the problem by compromising themselves even more.

— Yes, Chet moans, — I would never *do* anything. I would never betray my Pamela's memory. I was just so lonely and fed up. I only watched a couple of times! He looks at Lennox in appeal.

That's the problem. Too many people like to watch. — When did you learn they were paedos, rather than just stag lads making gonzo porn?

Chet swallows a mouthful of malt. — I knew it was going to lead somewhere bad, but I had no conception that they'd involve children. Then, when I saw a tape they'd done with a young girl, that was the last straw for me. I started making copies of the ones they kept here, for evidence. I was going to bring the animals down before they got their hands on Tianna. She's my grand-daughter's friend, Lennox!

Lennox's index finger shoots up and caresses the knot of twisted bone at the side of his nose. — I think you were too late.

— What? Chet gasps, his face falling south.

— Where are the tapes?

— I have them here. Chet feverishly glances back to the state-room.

— Anything else?

— Oh yes, he says, — I've got a list of names. Of those monsters and their intended victims. I got on to their website. Johnnie was sloppy. He started coming here with six-packs of beer, lording it up. Demanding I took him out fishing. He'd sit downstairs and watch the tapes, or go on to the website. I encouraged him, waited till he was drunk and left the window open on his computer. It's all coded, of course. They have their own language; everything's couched in business jargon. It's all 'sales', 'marketing' and 'closing the deal'. But what they're really talking about is entrapment. He springs to his feet. — If that bastard has done anything to that child . . .

— Aye, Lennox agrees, but rises and grabs Chet by his wrist. — Later, he's going nowhere.

Lennox thinks back to the Club Deuce and Club Myopia and the guy he'd told to take a hike. Starry had obviously taken him for a nonce and tried to set him up with Robyn. — I get the picture. He taps the glass on the table. — I'll need a copy of these lists as evidence.

— I've plenty of that, Lennox, Chet says, heading through to the stateroom. Lennox follows, watching Chet produce some keys, open a locked cupboard and extract a box full of disks. There's a printout with a list of names; another has dates of events. Lennox looks them over. They are presented like sales conference docu-ments, denoting task forces of 'agents', 'potential customers' and 'leads'. One of the 'local sales managers' that stands out from a list is: VINCENT MARVIN WEBBER III, MOBILE, AL.

Then he sees a listing for: JAMES 'TIGER' CLEMSON, JACK-SONVILLE, FLA.

And: JUAN CASTILIANO, MIAMI, FLA.

— There's nothing for Lance Dearing. He'd be too smart to have his own name on record, Lennox says, noting a training session scheduled for tonight at the hotel where Johnnie had said Lance would be.

— Yes. With Dearing being a cop I knew I'd be crucified unless I had hard evidence. That's why I was building up a dossier, Chet says eagerly, the IRS investigator in him now to the fore. — With his police connections, who could I trust?

— Aye, Lennox admits, — sometimes it's hard to know who you can trust.

But there are urgent issues to consider. Chet explains that they're stuck on a sandbank, and that to get off, they must enlist Johnnie's assistance. They head up to the bow and retie his arms in front of him, then free his legs. He starts to kick out in panic when Lennox gestures at him to climb down into the water. — No way! he shrieks. — No way! You're gonna drown me!

— We *should* fucking drown you, Chet snarls.

— I don't wanna die!

— Fuck it, Lennox says, and he removes his socks, trainers and flannels and heads down the ladder into the waters of the Gulf. The shock of cold almost takes his breath away. He looks down to his underpants and braces himself, and is relieved to feel his feet touch the silty bottom a few inches before the water level reaches his groin. — Right, you, he shouts up to Johnnie, — get your fuckin arse down here!

Johnnie, with Chet's heavy-handed assistance, reluctantly follows. Chet climbs back up the boat as Lennox and Johnnie take hold of the ropes, pulling at the vessel on either side of the stern. As the cold fuses through him, Lennox feels his strength draining. His left arm throbs; his right hand is useless. Nothing is happening; the boat seems stuck fast. Johnnie's querulous, self-pitying Spanish soliloquies grate on his jagged nerves. — Shut the fuck up or we'll leave you right here, he threatens. Johnnie sees that he isn't joking, and redoubles his exertions.

276

With no previous indication that it was going to happen, the boat mischievously slips free of the sandbank and starts to drift past them. They drop the ropes and watch the vessel slide across the broken shards of moonlight blinking on the cold, mauve surface of the water. Then the engines roar into life and Lennox feels his heart sink as the vessel imperiously chugs away. He sees Johnnie standing waist-deep about twelve feet away, and both men instinctively look for the ropes, but they've gone into the dark water, out of sight and reach. Chet has left them on this bank, stranded until the tides changed and they drowned. He isn't a strong swimmer and he doubts he'll be able make the shore, especially with the condition of his arm. Johnnie has no chance unless he can be untied. Lennox's neck swivels, his gaze frantically seeking the lights of other boats, then helicopters above. But there's nothing through the murky darkness besides the tired moon and the dim and distant illuminations of Bologna.

He catches Johnnie's eye, just in time to be ridiculed by the kinship of fear that flashes between them. Then he sees the boat is circling back towards them. His heartbeat steadies as he ascertains that Chet's only manoeuvring the craft away from the sandbank into deeper water before dropping anchor. — Come on, he shouts, and they splash across the cold, tired yards through the thin sea and scramble aboard. Chet grudgingly hauls Johnnie on, and they secure him in the downstairs back bedroom. Lennox dries off and pulls on his trousers and shoes before they get under way.

He sits up at the helm with Chet. He's very cold, in spite of the cagoule Chet's given him. It's almost pitch dark at sea now, and he can hear nothing beyond the engine of the boat. But Lennox is distracted; there's something he needs to do.

Down in the stateroom he removes the box of tapes, fast-forwarding through them. Johnnie is among several men featured having sex with various women in standard home-made porn flicks, shot on two cameras and edited between mid-shot and close-up. The locations seem to vary but the boat features widely, the stateroom and the upper deck sharing prominence. In one he sees Robyn's face, spaced, yet intense as Johnnie fucks her from behind. But the next one features a Latina girl, who looks around twelve or thirteen years old. She performs fellatio on two men, one of whom is Johnnie.

Then Lennox sees a dirty black rucksack lying by the bed. He picks it up and looks inside. Some personal effects identify the owner as Juan Castiliano. Then he pulls out a drum holding several digital videodiscs. All have names and dates inscribed on them by Magic Marker. Flipping through them, Lennox's soul refrigerates as he sees: Tianna Hinton.

He inserts it and presses play, but switches off after just seconds of seeing Tianna, naked, in a heavy-eyed stupor, sweating on the bed where he now sits. Coming into shot and bearing down on her with lecherous menace is Police Officer Lance Dearing.

But the pictures clicking into blackness only spark up another set in his head. Horsburgh's dreadful show: he'd had to watch it in full. In the age of digital video, everything was recorded; sins more than triumphs, on phones and cameras, to be exhibited to the world online. Why would sex criminals, of all people, be immune to that narcissism? Murderers were the biggest divas: the Raskolnikov tendency heightened by accessible recording technology and the confessional culture. The criminal, the artist, the citizen, all driven by the compelling need to have their deeds recorded, to get a slice of digital immortality. And Horsburgh had his audience, when a frozen-faced Gillman had turned to Lennox, nodded and switched on that tape.

Horsburgh's video, in the rented Berwickshire cottage, had been poorly made. One mid-shot from a camera on tripod at two figures on a bed, the smaller one secured there, bound at the wrists and ankles to the iron bed frame. Mostly you just saw his body, thrusting on top of her, but then he'd turn his cold, cruel face and look into the camera, popping his eyes and licking his lips in a sickening theatrical caricature. At first only the horrendous mantra of terrorised disbelief informed you that the child was still alive. Her cries were less a plea for him to stop his relentless assault, and more an attempt to stoically deny what was happening to her. Then she'd started to whimper: — It's sair, you're hurting me, I want my ma, I want my ma . . .

It was unbearable to witness, but he had to stay put. Struggling to breathe, he stared at the brand plate of the monitor just below the bottom of the screen, trying to turn down the sound in his head, to concentrate on incidents beheld from the Wheatfield Stand at Tynecastle Stadium, to think of what the outcome of recent uninspiring results would have been had George Burley stayed in the manager's chair . . .

Then Confectioner had slapped Britney's face and forced her to focus, shouting, — Look at me! Fucking look at me, before twisting her head to the camera, compelling Lennox to gaze into the doomed child's terrorised eyes, — Look at the camera! Let them see who's doing this to you!

Gillman's finger jabbed the air. — That ring he's wearing. That's how he tore the bairn's vagina, right? It's aw been swabbed, right? Was it Eddie Atherton did that? He missed quite a bit in that Conningsburgh case, mind.

It was as if Gillman was seeing on-screen the highlights of the dull football game Lennox had been trying to picture in his mind's eye.

And now Britney is Tianna and he can't look. But he has to look. He can't *not* look. He presses play again.

It's different. Horsburgh is Dearing. It's well shot; there is even a soft elevator-music soundtrack. The pan pipes. He thinks about the car ride. *That music is kinda creepin me out.* Dearing's smiling face, his benign concentration. Like he was *making love.* The girl, the stunned, sleepy child, made vacant and toylike by drugs; it *was* Tianna he was doing this to. Gap-toothed wee Tianna with her sheep's bag and her baseball cards, and his hands grip the quilt on the bed and he feels the tears on his face he could never show when he'd watched the Confectioner video. But then a fingertip to his dry skin reveals them as phantom.

Lennox stops the machine. Rage grips his throat like a vice. He feels something in his chest going in and out of spasm. He rises unsteadily, removing the DVD, looking at the simple unmarked silver disc, seemingly so innocuous. Over the buzz of the engines, he can hear shouting coming from the other bedroom. This cuts out abruptly when its source sees Ray Lennox in the doorway.

— Carry on, please. I actually want you to keep shouting, he says to Juan Castiliano. — To just say one more fucking word. Cause that's all it would take for me to cut your fuckin heid off, and his cold, murderous black eyes hold the paedophile, who shrinks back in fear.

Bologna draws close as Lennox appears on the bridge behind Chet. The marina, as they pull ashore and tie up the boat, is almost deserted though the Lobster bar is still open. They go back to the stateroom, where Lennox shows Chet in fast-forward a selection of Johnnie's discs, though not the Tianna one, which he's kept. There are three other young girls: from their soon-to-be-removed clothes they look poor, mostly, he suspects, Central American immigrants.

Chet is dazed and zombie-like as he carries the box of tapes into the Volkswagen. They drive for two blocks, stopping at a building announced by a backlit white-and-blue sign as the Bologna Police Department.

— You made me drive to an Internet café when you had all those facilities on board, Lennox said.

— It's very expensive at sea. Johnnie was bleeding me dry.

— Any Scottish blood?

Chet bends his mouth a little as Lennox's fingers drum at the box on his lap. — Take all this into the station. Tell them the lot. How you got to know Robyn. How Lance and Johnnie were blackmailing you. Take them to the boat; they'll ID Johnnie from some of the videos. A good cop'll break him down in seconds.

A flexing of his shoulders shows Chet's relief that his terrible burden has been lifted, but the uncertainty in his eyes betrays the knowledge of a new ordeal, of uncertain outcome, yet to be faced. — You'll come in and vouch for me, Lennox? Tell them I was being blackmailed?

— I'll be happy to do that, Chet, but not right now. I have to go.

— What are you going to do?

— I have to get Robyn away from Starry and Dearing before the police get there. She needs a fighting chance to keep Tianna and get her life together. She deserves it, on that evidence you have here. He waves a copy of the lists. — I didn't think so before, but I do now. The courts and child welfare people, however, might take a different view. The paedophiles are meeting at the Embassy Hotel right now. You can direct the police there.

— Okay, Chet frets. — But you *will* back me up?

— You have my word.

Chet rubs his salt-and-pepper dome. — She had no chance, Lennox. They targeted her: right across the state line from Alabama.

— I know. Lennox pats his shoulder. — And Chet, he produces a strained smile, — my first name is Ray. Raymond Lennox.

— Is it? Oh . . . I beg your pardon . . . Ray . . . he stammers, as he climbs out the car with the box. Then he regards Lennox as if remembering something. — Your magazine; the bridal one. I think you left it on the boat.

— I'll pick up another copy. That one got a bit messed up.

— Right . . .

— Good luck, Lennox shouts as he watches the spectral-looking sailor making his way to the steps of the police station like he is walking the plank.

Lennox starts up the Volkswagen. Robyn can wait. He's going to bring them down first. His hands tingle on the wheel, as he recalls why he hates those bullies, and why he does what he does.

19

Edinburgh: Two Dark Summers

1981

Nobody likes bullies. Even other bullies – often especially – feel obliged to at least profess a hatred of them. Yet we've all been bullied and bullied others. It's in all of us; with nations we call it imperialism. You start to wonder about yourself.

Who are you? Your name is Raymond Lennox and you're eleven years old. It's summer, and you're excited because you've got your new birthday bike, and your football team, Hearts, have been promoted to the top division. You're looking forward to the new season, and you've been studying hard for a scholarship to a good secondary school.

Although it had rained a lot, the summer had, with customary Scottish reluctance, finally yielded to a heatwave. It was a bright July Sunday afternoon, two days after your birthday, 07.07.70, which Curtis Park, your Hibs-supporting pal, was prone to rubbing in the significance of, as Hibs had once beaten Hearts by seven–nil in a famous Edinburgh derby. The wooded Water of Leith walkway at Colinton Dell was lush with all shades of green as you and your best pal, Les Brodie, clad in T-shirts and khaki shorts, pushed your bikes along. You still couldn't take your eyes off the sleek beauty of the blue Raleigh as you grip its handlebars. Les had earlier picked up a flat tyre, hampering your progress, but you'd gone a greater distance than usual, seduced by tales of a spectacular new 'Tarzan' swing further up the river. Now the long, dark tunnel loomed ahead, not that far from the main road above you, but the submerged nature of the valley and the dense cover of trees hid the noise of the traffic, though you could hear the swoosh of the river below.

But you are Ray Lennox.

And who is he? Was he always scared? Always angry? No, but maybe Ray was just a wee bit fretful as a boy. Certainly, he was nervous of the big tunnel. He knew it from old Sunday walks with his father John and sister Jackie. That spot in the middle where it kinked, plunging him into total darkness; no light visible from either the exit ahead or the entrance behind him. He always panicked at that point, as if the omnipresent gloom could swallow him up. His dad and sister liked to stop there, enjoy the silence of it all, also sensing Ray's apprehension, and dallying to tease him. He soon realised that with just a few steps forward or back – depending on where the sun was – he could rejoin the light and break the tenebrous spell.

At the mouth of the tunnel, Ray and Les looked up at the tendrils of ivy that dangled above them. — The Tarzan on the other side's meant tae be barry, Les said with enthusiasm, although the sun had now sloped behind a manky cloud. Then they heard dirty voices and laughter coming from within. The boys looked at each other, first in apprehension, then ball-bearing resolve as they continued; neither willing to cede their fear. Ray wanted to say: let's just go back and check your pigeon loft. But Les would know he'd bottled it. He knew Ray didn't like the pigeons he and his dad kept. Then the growls from inside rose a little, obviously all male; he wondered how many there were, and their ages.

How quickly, how terribly he'd learn the answer. On registering their tentative approach, the voices dropped to ominous silence. Ray Lennox looked at the overhead lights, set about thirty feet apart, giving a weak, orangey-yellow glow which showed up the wet, gravelly ground under their feet. As they approached the dead black zone, they could make out the dark shapes in the shadows. Three men: early thirties, late and early twenties. At first Ray had been relieved that they were adults rather than older boys. He could hear the mechanical click of his bike's gears turning over on the wheel as he pushed it along. A quick, nervous glance revealed that the trio stood smoking cigarettes and drinking from a small bottle of whisky. Not that badly dressed, certainly not destitute. But then one of them, he had a hooked nose and wispy, thinning hair, gave the boys an abominable grin from his big, unshaven face. That smile would never be forgotten: it pulled them into another world. He stepped forward and stood in front of Ray in the dark tunnel. — Nice bike, he'd said in an accent the boy couldn't place.

Ray was silent. The man took the blue Raleigh by the handlebars, then pushed him aside and climbed on. He pedalled it a few yards, into the tunnel's black spot, Ray following him, hoping that he'd stop once he'd had his laugh. Then he heard a shout and looked behind him. One of the other men, thick dark crew cut, had gripped Les by the hair and backed him up against the wall, muttering dreadful threats. Then Les swung at him, tried to fight back but the man wrestled him to the ground. — Gie's a hand! he shouted, although he was easily overpowering Les. — Fuckin lively one here, his raucous laugh scalding the extremities of young Ray Lennox.

Still holding the whisky, the unshaven man quickly jumped from the bike and let it crash to the ground, then grabbed Ray by his hair, forcing him on to his knees. They ground painfully bare in the gravel and dirt, as the boy looked ahead into a wall of total blackness. — Grab his shoulders, he instructed the youngest man who sported a wedge of blond hair. He stepped in and complied as the unshaven man loosened his grip. Lennox looked one way, then the other. From where he was no light revealed itself at either end of the tunnel.

The unshaven man capped the whisky bottle and stuck it in his pocket. His eyes adjusting under the insipid overhead glow, Ray Lennox could see thick, black crescents of dirt packed under long nails sprouting from nicotine-yellow fingers. The man then unfastened his belt and unbuttoned his flies. — You fookin want this, he hissed as Les's screams and shouts echoed in the tunnel. — Naw . . . I have to get back for my tea . . . Ray pleaded, praying for somebody to come by. The man laughed. — You'll get your fookin tea awright, and he lowered his trousers and pulled his cock out of his underpants. It was large and floppy, but was stiffening before the boy's eyes. A beastlike, serpentine creature, with a will connected to, yet distinct from its host, like a devil's familiar. That was Ray's sense of what faced him.

— Open yawr fookin mooth, the man snarled.

Ray Lennox shut his eyes. Then felt the back of the man's big, heavy hand as it rapped across his jaw. Fireworks went off in his head, pursued by a brief but almost liberating numbing of the senses.

— Open yawr fookin mooth!

He shook his head, staring up at the man in the shadows, trying to locate his eyes with his own beseeching orbs. — Dinnae, mister, please dinnae . . . I need tae get back tae my ma's.

There was nothing in the man's gaze but a fearsome, burning indifference. He took the whisky bottle from his pocket, slugged back the last inch, then battered it against the wall of the tunnel, breaking off the base. He held the jagged bottle in front of Ray's face, then rested the smooth, cold glassy side against his cheek. — Open yawr mouth or I'll carve your fookin face up.

Ray Lennox opened his mouth. The man packed his stiff penis into the boy's face, making him gag first on the taste and smell of urine, then again as he drove it to the back of his throat. All Ray could think of was his nose, to keep breathing through his nose. His small teeth tried to threaten, but the man showed him the bottle again and he let his jaw fall slack as burning tears of salt stung his cheeks and the hands on his shoulders crushed his knees further into the dirt.

Gagging and struggling for air, he almost passed out. Too weak to understand the instructions the mocking voice conveyed, a torturous soundtrack to his ordeal, he could only try to comply as renewed hair-wrenching threatened to separate scalp from skull. The man's accent he would later think of as Birmingham. Play back every syllable in his head. Cast the net wider; West Midlands, Black Country.

Then the shouts from the other guy, the one fighting with Les, became more urgent. — Ah said gie us a fuckin hand! We've got a lively yin here! Help ays break him in, and he said a name that sounded like 'Bill' or 'Bim': a nickname of sorts, perhaps.

The unshaven man promptly withdrew, leaving Ray gasping and choking, struggling to fill air into his lungs. His shoulders ached, his knees were torn and his scalp throbbed. Looking around, he saw that the crew-cut man was on top of Les, struggling, trying to pin him down. Les was screaming and swearing, shouting, — FUCK OFF! FUCK OFF! RAYMIE!

His own adversary looked at Ray and punched him hard on the nose, causing his head to spin again and his eyes to gush. He let out a long squeal of a prayer as he saw his blood hit the ground in droplets. — Keep a hold of this bitch, Unshaven Man told the young blond guy. — He's getting done big time after this other little stallion gets broken in!

Then he sauntered over to his friend.

In a doe-eyed overture for mercy, Ray scanned the young man for traces of humanity. — Please let me go, mister. I'll no say nowt tae naebody. Please, he begged. He saw that the youth's eyes were soft, watery and hesitant, and he continued in desperation. — Ah just need tae get hame. Ah'll no say nowt. Ah promise!

They both looked over to where the two men were with Les. It was dark but Ray could see Les's bare leg kicking out. We're going to die, he thought. He looked back at the blond guy, who nodded, released his grip and Ray staggered to his feet. Suddenly, all he could think about was his bike and the consequences of its loss. He picked it up, climbed on it, pedalling manically as he heard the defiance ebb out of Les's screams, become pleads, — Stoap it, stoap it, then a disbelieving, — naw . . . naw . . . Raymie . . .

— You fookin idiot, get after him, one of the men, it sounded like Unshaven Man, who was holding Les's face down in the dirt, screamed at the blond. The young man gave chase, as Lennox pedalled for his survival, calf muscles exploding and lungs thrashing as he emerged from the dark tunnel into sunlight filtering through towering trees. He tore on frantically, not looking back until the tunnel and all its inhabitants were out of sight. When he stopped it was at a platform that overlooked the angled breakwater in the river below. Shouting for help along the deserted path, he searched for something that might serve as a weapon (although he knew he would be too scared to go back alone). Picked up and dropped a couple of weak pieces of wood, useless in his small boy's hands. After screaming in impotence, he headed on towards the road.

Then he saw them climbing up the green metal stairs that led from the wooden bridge over the river up to the walkway; two men, a woman and a dog. — MISTER! he screamed, as they ran up the steps towards him, out of breath as he frantically explained that some men were hurting his pal in the tunnel.

There followed a nervous discussion about whether they should proceed to rescue Les or find a phone and call the police. Eventually, they headed back down the walkway, Ray shaking with fear, his stomach flipping as he tried to work out what use this party of well-meaning people would be against the terrifying gang that had seized them. The tunnel was further than he thought. And just as he got to its mouth Les emerged, pushing his bike and hobbling. His face was cut and streaked with tears and dirt.

As he advanced towards them, Les seemed in shock, almost as if he couldn't see them. — Are you okay? one of the men asked.

— Aye, Les said.

There was no sign of the attackers. Ray was relieved that they'd retreated in the other direction. The adults wanted to get the police, but Les insisted he was okay. They escorted the boys back on to the main road, before leaving them to the short walk home.

— What did they dae? Ray asked fearfully, looking at his friend in profile, his tears smearing with the muck on his cheeks as Les phlegmatically stared ahead in silence. — Did they batter ye?

Les halted abruptly, and turned as if seeing Ray Lennox for the first time. — Aye, but ah didnae let them get the bike, Raymie.

— Is that aw they done? Cause ah thought –

Then Les's face contorted with rage. — They battered ays! They battered ays, right, he briefly sobbed, before fury burst through again. — N you'd better say nowt tae nae cunt aboot this, Raymie!

— Ah'm no gaunny say nowt, he protested.

— No tae Curtis, or yir ma or dad even, Les urged. — Promise?

— Aye . . . but we should get the polis ontae them.

— Fuck the polis! Les shouted in his face. — Promise, Raymie?

— I promise, young Ray Lennox had said.

That night he sat in his room staring out the window. His school books lay in front of him on a small table where he normally did his homework. There were also two pieces of paper: an application form for one of Edinburgh's more prestigious Merchant

Schools, and a reading list of the classic novels he was expected to have completed before sitting the entrance exam to this institution. He ripped the form up into tiny pieces, and crushed the list of books in his fist, putting it into the pockets of the shorts he then stuck in the bottom drawer of his wardrobe, never to wear again.

He didn't sense his dad entering the room as he gazed outside, just heard John Lennox's cough and saw him pointing at a pile of his school books and saying, — These are your windaes, son. Nothing out there but tatty hooses and snottery beaks.

1986

The promise to Les was kept; they never went back down Colinton Dell, or talked to anyone about the incident. Only once was it ever mentioned between them. It was 1986, a Friday, in early May.

Les's family had recently moved out to Clermiston, another scheme. The Lennoxes had bought their council home, sold it at a profit and moved to a modest private development at Colinton Mains. The boys were almost sixteen and had been drinking concealed vodka in their Coke with Shirley Feeney and Karen Witton, two girls from Oxgangs, whom they had met and got off with at a teen disco at Buster Brown's nightclub earlier. They went down by the canal to kiss and fondle. Dissatisfied with his rations, frustrated that there was nowhere else to go, Les started to pressure Karen, demanding that she perform fellatio. He became more insistent, working up to outright bullying and threats. The girl's obvious fear took Ray Lennox back to the tunnel. He'd realised he and Les were growing apart, held together only by the football. His behaviour scared and nauseated Lennox, while Les was angry with him for not colluding and subjecting Shirley to similar harassment. Manoeuvring him away from the increasingly distraught girls, Lennox said, — Mind that time down the Dell? Those three nutters?

— What aboot them? What the fuck's that goat tae dae wi anything?

But Lennox saw the shame that fuelled his aggression. He'd looked steadily at Les, till his friend's glare weakened.

— Cunts, Les Brodie said in a low growl. — Ah'd really like to meet those fuckers now.

It wasn't an empty boast. They had remained friends since that day at the Dell, but Les had changed. An unbridled aggression became part of his make-up, and the mark of the bully began to taint a previously playful soul. The seagulls. He loved to shoot the gulls. But Ray Lennox had also changed. They said he was anti-social at school. Not a burgeoning gang member, like Les. More of a loner. Withdrawn. Weird even.

Lennox felt intimidated by Les's new Clermiston pals; they seemed like the semi-feral bams of predatory cast that they'd studiously avoided back in Oxgangs. And the following day he was on the train to Dundee with some of them.

That morning he'd looked at the crushed booklist he'd kept secret all those years. He'd never read the books back then. He couldn't say why. Couldn't explain he wanted to so much but needed to find them for himself. Didn't want anybody giving them to him. He was currently enthralled by Melville's *Moby-Dick*, and wished that he could stay locked in the book instead of heading to Dens Park. When he put it down, he felt sick with nerves.

There were about two dozen loosely connected groups of friends who'd come up on the train. Like all mobs of fifteen-year-old apprentice hard men, it contained those just along for the laugh as well as others gripped, if fleetingly, by the excitement and the possibilities that such a scene might offer them. A few were already immersed in that life, evidenced by the dull, cold stillness in their eyes and the tightness around their mouths and jaws. Les had seemed to be avoiding Ray Lennox, surrounding himself with the more dangerous element. There was a hierarchy, which Lennox sensed he'd have to work his way up. But he did get to ask his old friend about his pigeon loft.

— Gittin rid ay it, Les had spat tightly, barely making eye contact. — Fuckin seek ay they things.

Ten thousand Hearts supporters had match tickets and packed on to the terracing behind one goal and the enclosure along the side of the pitch. All were looking to the tunnel under the stand, as their nervy team, clad in an away strip of silvery-grey shirts and maroon shorts, took the field to explosive applause. They believed that the League Championship flag was on its way to Tynecastle. After all, Hearts had now gone twenty-seven League games undefeated, thirty-one, if you counted the Scottish Cup.

Scotland's legendary commentator, Archie MacPherson, had perched on gantries even more rudimentary and less salubrious than the one he stood on at Dens Park, microphone in hand. No pundits to assist him, it was a lonely furrow to plough, but always the pro and enthusiast, he went for the big opening to do the occasion justice. — Well, who, way back in August, blessed with a second sight, the seventh son of a seventh son, could have fore-seen Hearts on the very last day of the season, playing for the championship, requiring only one point . . .

As ten thousand voices sang 'Hello, Hello, We are the Gorgie Boys', the club chairman, Wallace Mercer, took his seat in the direc-tors' box, giving the stage smirk of the man resigned to the fact that he'd never be as loved as he felt was his due. But something had evaporated inside Mercer. Almost before anyone else in the stadium, he believed that his team would not triumph. There had been a dressing-room virus precipitating the absence of Craig Levein, a key defender. Mercer had detected a lethargy about many of the players. When he had looked into their eyes before they went to change, they did not seem to him like men willing to take the prize. They looked as if they felt their work was done and now craved a long rest, resenting this further imposition.

Down on the terraces, the smell of Bovril, pies. Stale lager and whisky and tobacco. Of swaying men, intoxicated by alcohol and nerves. The referee's whistle blows and Dundee make the early running, as a shaky Hearts defence clear an effort over the bar. The first half flies by, then time slows down. Lennox can perceive it during the break. That sense of the speed of life fading like autumn light. Hearts have held their own against a lively Dundee, but no more than that. A feeling takes root that the day of celebration is turning into something else. If there is to be glory, there will be pain first. Disappointment, then a barely repressed anger are suddenly hanging in the air.

At half-time Mercer's gut is in such turmoil that he can't touch the food in the directors' hospitality or imbibe another drink. He's heard the news from Paisley, where St Mirren are tamely capitulating to Celtic, who are eating into the Hearts goal-difference advantage. Now one strike for Dundee will lose the Edinburgh side the flag. Like every other Hearts supporter in the ground, Mercer feels they need to score to be sure of the draw. He's heard from the dugout that Alex MacDonald has hooked midfielders Whittaker and Black, both of whom are spent. Feeling the sweat on his brow, Wallace Mercer heads to the washroom to wipe it off and move his thinning strands of hair back into place. He urinates, washes his hands and curses as boiling water from the red tap scalds him. He belatedly notes a sign that says WARNING VERY HOT WATER above the sink.

Shaking off the discomfort, he looks into the mirror, resets his face to its trademark grin. Mercer's spent enough time in front of cameras and in the business world to know that fear and anxiety are emotions best kept hidden. He straightens the tie he was unaware that he'd tugged out of place during the first forty-five minutes. An advocate of the power of positive thinking, he considers: we were ninety minutes away from the flag, and now we're only forty-five. So it's so far, so good. But other emotions intrude: he's seen enough games to be aware of how sport inflicts temporal distortions, how a goal conceded early gives you time to regroup and fight back. But a late strike . . . He knows the sense of entitlement success confers on those who have enjoyed it; doubts that Celtic, or Rangers, or even Aberdeen under Alex Ferguson, would falter at this point.

Worst of all, the businessman, a logical risk assessor, starts to whisper in his head: if you're unbeaten in thirty-one consecutive games, does that not make the probability of losing the thirty-second one even greater? He thinks of that fantastic undefeated run, comparing performances, trying to compile a balance sheet between the devastating victories where the opposition had been brushed aside, against the occasions where luck was ridden. It hits him that the team are short of class. They have Robertson's predatory strikes, Colquhoun's electric runs, the absent Levein's elegance and judgement at the back, but the rest are journeymen and old pros playing out of their skins in a well-organised side built on efficiency and work rate. And the virus has taken its toll on the team's engine. A silent prayer spilling from his lips as he leaves the toilets, Mercer heads back out to the box in the stand. Les Porteous, the club secretary, says something he doesn't catch, but registers its good intent with a nod and smile. The second half kicks off.

In a crowd of surly, youthful acquaintances, Raymond Lennox feels suddenly guilty that he's not here with his dad. The unspoken inference is that it would be fitting for father and son to watch the game together; the history-making match that wins Hearts the flag. He announces his intention of going to look for the old man. As he departs, he hears a derogatory remark passed. Turns to see some of the boys, including Les, laughing at him, but his momentum has carried him down the steps and he continues snaking through the crowd, not looking back. He touches the bumfluff under his nose. Mutters a curse on the treacherous Les, the hard man with his new hard-men mates. Continues his search for his father. In a sea of ten thousand, he knows he will easily find him behind the goal to the left. Somewhere.

Lennox looks at his watch. Sixty minutes now up. Two-thirds of the game gone. St Mirren folding like a broken deckchair in Paisley, but Hearts still in pole position. If we could only get to seventy minutes, he pleads to a higher power. Dundee are going for it. Hearts are starting to look sluggish, even downcast. Lennox fears that too many players don't want to be out there. They've come close a couple of times on counters, but Dundee are pressing. Hearts have won only two out of eleven against their bogey team. In the media build-up, Archie Knox, Dundee's combative manager, has taken great delight in making this point.

Knox sends on the mustachioed Albert Kidd, a dead ringer for comedian Bobby Ball from the Cannon and Ball duo, replacing Tosh McKinlay. Lennox breathes a little sigh of relief, as McKinlay is one of Dundee's best players. But still the home side swarm forward. Then Henry Smith makes a brilliant save for Hearts, pushing aside a drive from Mennie that came through a wall of players. Lennox yells in relief and delight as he and a stranger next to him embrace. He scents destiny in that stop. He's not the only one. The stadium lights up with the relishing chant of 'here we go', and the seventy-minute mark has been navigated. Then more nail-biting, and a terrible stillness descends on the crowd as we get to ten minutes between Hearts and the championship flag. Ray Lennox close to choking as he sees his cousin Billy first, then his uncle. His dad is to the left of them. He sidles up to John Lennox and touches his shoulder.

In the eighty-third minute, Robert Connor's corner kick from the right is flicked on by Brown. Albert Kidd is unmarked and clips a right-foot shot past Smith from close in. It's his first goal in the League championship this season. Lennox hears a series of gasps in the crowd and a curse coming from his father, the first time he's heard the old man use that particular word. — Seven minutes left, his cousin Billy moans. Lennox thinks of 07.07.70. Across Britain, the Videoprinter results service on the BBC will erroneously designate the goal to Hearts and their captain, Walter Kidd.

Latest . . . Dundee 0 . . . Hearts 1 (Kidd, W.)

Then:

Correction . . . Dundee 1 (Kidd, A.) . . . Hearts 0

Lennox feels the loss of the flag at that moment. The crowd bellow in defiant support, urging them on to get the equaliser, but the players look ready to succumb to exhaustion. Then John Lennox feels something tugging at his chest as his arm goes numb. He wants to tell the people around him, his son, brother and nephew, to stop jostling and give him room.

Ray Lennox sees his father easing himself down on to the terrace, as if he's going to sleep. A few guys shout— What the fuck – but they make space for him.

— THAT'S MA FAITHER! Lennox screams at nobody in particular, hunkering down by John's side. — Dad, ye okay? He looks to his Uncle Davie, to his cousin Billy and back to his father. John Lennox gives him a slow, enervated smile. — It's awright, he says in patently shallow tones, seeing the man he was, carefree and strong, able to enjoy, or at least bear hearty witness to afternoons like this, spilling indelibly into the past.

Albert Kidd scores a wonderful solo second goal four minutes from time. He storms down the wing, passes several Hearts players, plays a one–two and smashes a volley past Smith. He is not to know that he's reached his nadir as a professional sportsman; put on this Earth to torture Hearts and deny them this flag. These few minutes will be the longest in the lives of the players in the silver and maroon, who now just want to be anywhere but on the Park. Billy Lennox pushes through the crowd to summon trackside paramedics.

Some people head off. Many more stay, unsure of what to do. In tandem with the pain of defeat, a shared acknowledgement slowly ignites within the supporters. The sense of having lived through a significant event. The unarticulated but almost tangible realisation that this is far more crucial than the clichéd rituals of glory hunters in Paisley, celebrating another League win in front of the cameras. There is a sense that this drama they are all implicated in at Dens Park is an approximation of the life that so many people follow sport to actually escape from. Reality has bitten them hard and they have to share this moment, but there is no way to express it. All they can do is stay on to cheer Hearts, praise the team for a valiancy they know in their souls the side has not shown; they are bottle merchants who've blown it on the last day. But what the crowd is really trying to express is a much deeper communion with nothing less than the beauty and terror of life itself. But Ray Lennox misses this. He is in an ambulance with his stricken father, and his uncle and cousin, heading for Ninewells Hospital.

A consoling touch on his arm by Ian Gellatly, Dundee FC's chairman. Mercer nods in sober, dignified appreciation. With sadness, he thinks of team manager Alex MacDonald, whom he saw head dejectedly into the tunnel at the final whistle. Internally debates whether he should go down to the dressing room and be with the players, or give them a little space. Retreats somewhere briefly to reprogramme the smile. The businessman calculates the loss in economic terms, before re-emerging with a sparkling grace.

★   ★   ★

Ray Lennox rose on Sunday, having slept fitfully. His father had suffered a minor heart attack and was still in Dundee. He would be transferred tomorrow to the Royal Infirmary in Edinburgh. A new regime would be undertaken; diet change and medication, anticoagulants for the blood. There was a sense of revenge afflicting Ray Lennox. A need for justice. Emotions battled within him. He was determined to have it out with Les. To get clarification: friend or foe. He didn't care which any more, he just wanted to know.

He got on the bus to Clermiston and ducked down the side lane to Les's back door. But as he headed down the narrow paved passage that ran between the houses, Lennox was accosted by that stillness he now knew so well; the foreboding sense of something being not quite right. Then the calm was desecrated by urgent shrieks of terror filling the air. Ray Lennox could see a flash of fire, and it was hurtling towards him. Unable to avoid the burning projectile, he shut his eyes, giving thanks that it missed his face, though coming close enough for him to feel the sooted flesh in his throat, and the hair under his nose singe. He turned to watch it ricochet off the pebble-dashed wall of the house behind him, and fall on to the paving. The ball started dancing frantically and a terrorised eye in the flame begged for mercy as the stink of burning flesh and filthy feathers filled his nostrils.

Lennox backed away as the creature toppled, crumpling into silence. In the direction of the loft, Les Brodie's eyes seemed as small and reasonless as the burning pigeon's as he held another bemused bird at arm's length and was dousing it with petrol from the spout of a small can. Lennox felt his skin burn under the heat of his gaze. Turning quickly, he fled back up the side lane and into the front street, his boyhood friend's mocking laughter following him all the way.

Another squealing, flaming comet shot into the sky above him, clearing the rooftop of the house, before the ball of flame plummeted and bounced along the road. Lennox didn't look back; he headed swiftly towards the bus stop as a maroon-and-white double-decker drew near. Les had given him the answer he needed.

20

Sales Conference

The night heat swarms out of the mangrove swamps as Lennox takes the Interstate 75 east. He drives touching the 100 mph mark, the Volkswagen resonating dangerously as it bullets along the almost deserted Alligator Alley, heading for a hotel by Miami airport, and a training course.

He's read about groups of guys, usually nerds, who get together in seminar settings, sharing techniques on how to pick up women. They draw on a mixed bag of behavioural and situational approaches: transactional analysis, neurolinguistic programming and pop and pseudo psychology. Most are simply wanting to increase their drawing power in the sexual marketplace; bright, obsessive losers, they are trying to circumvent their social unease with females. For others, the women are practically incidental; it is more about inter-male bonding and competition, the schoolyard boasting of sexual conquests − real or imagined − taken into adulthood.

For some of the more extreme members of these groups, the thrill of picking up women and sharing in techniques and triumphs soon becomes passé. Many are openly dysfunctional; obvious victims of abuse, with an embittered and displaced vengeful aspect to their character. They are chickenhawks who've flocked together and their *raison d'être* is to seek and befriend vulnerable lone parents with prepubescent children.

The seminar is a house of paedophiles, at least one of whom is a copper. Lennox had become a policeman because he hated bullies. Then he'd been disillusioned to find out that, like everywhere else, the police force had its share. Right across the world, men like Dearing, attracted to wielding power over others, would hide behind the badge of service. He could do nothing to stop them, so, in his cynicism, had almost become one himself.

Without the righteous fire of his anti-nonce crusade, Lennox was too sensitive to cope with the savagery that surrounded him in Serious Crimes. Only through booze and cocaine could he talk its language, understand its dumb code on the requisite emotional level, even if the substances which gave him the zeal for the culture of violence curtailed his effectiveness at its practice. The martial arts, the kick-boxing, they only helped when he was physically capable of training three times a week. Then the gloved fists of other men in his face were reduced to annoyances, to be caught, blocked, sidestepped, countered.

Lennox freezes as a rhythmic slash of propeller blades overhead signals a helicopter closing in. Its searching light beam lasers the road behind him. *Surely Dearing couldn't . . .* But the sound is fading away over the Everglades, the biggest uninhabited roadless land mass in the United States. Of course choppers would scan its lush density; taking photographs, looking for drug smugglers, illegals, terrorists or just civilians behaving unconventionally.

Dedicated swampland becomes uncompromising city within the toss of a Frisbee, and Ray Lennox, the displaced Scottish cop who knows he can never do this job again, pulls into the Embassy Hotel car park, the seminar already an hour in. After the grimy functionalism of airport-zone Miami, to step into the hotel's ornate pink-marbled and gold-leafed courtyard of fountains and pillars is to enter corporate Eden. The diverse flora are so thoughtfully planted and meticulously maintained, through his glassy eyes they look like a shiny Photoshopped brochure. He studies the black felt-ribbed board, almost expecting to see NONCE CONFERENCE indicated by the white plastic lettering.

CONFERENCES AT EMBASSY AIRPORT HOTEL

Thursday, January 12
JONES BOATYARD INC.
Palm Beach Boardroom
8 a.m. − 5 p.m.

2005 HISPANIC JOB FAIR
Key Largo 3 & 4
10 a.m. – 8 p.m.

SONY ELECTRONICS DEALER TRAINING
Upper Atrium
11 a.m. – 1 p.m.

SUNDANCE MEDIA
Binini
3.30 p.m. – 9.30 p.m.

FEUER NURSING REVIEW
Key Biscayne
3.30 p.m. – 4.30 p.m.

SUICIDE SURVIVORS
Key Largo 2
7 p.m. – 9.30 p.m.

SALES FORCE 4 TRAINING SEMINAR
Key Largo 1
8 p.m. – 11.30 p.m.

Key Largo. Lennox thinks of the film. Bogart and Bacall. Asks a receptionist to point the way. She reminds him of Trudi in her body language and wary, slightly artful smile, to the extent of oblique but poignant arousal, as she indicates a flight of stairs. Climbing them quickly, he arrives at a mezzanine floor, clocks Key Largo. Head surreptitiously craned round the door, he looks inside from the back of the small room: five men seated round a table. Dearing isn't present, but the others look furtive and traumatised. He steps inside to confront them. — So this is the place, is it?

One bespectacled man in his thirties, sweating in spite of the air con, regards his approach. — I'm sorry, Mr . . . ?

— Lennox. Where's our friend Dearing then?

— I'm Mike Haskins, the man offers. — There's no Dearing

here. He puts his glasses on to his head and studies a folder. —
And I'm afraid I don't seem to have your name down here, Mr
Lennox . . .

— No. You won't have. I just want you to tell Dearing –

The man has put his specs back on his nose and is focusing
on Lennox. — I think you might have the wrong room. This is
the Suicide Survivors group.

— Eh . . . Key Largo . . . Sales . . . Lennox says timidly.

— This is Key Largo 2, the man patiently informs him, — Key
Largo 1 is across the way.

— Sorry . . . sorry. Lennox skulks out into the corridor. Guzzling
some deep breaths, he composes himself, elects to play it softly.
Let the police have the big showdown. He ducks his head round
the door of what is a bigger seminar room. A man standing at
the front makes a PowerPoint presentation. He can see the backs
of eight heads, in a semicircle. Only one turns, glancing at Lennox,
squinting, then looking back to the presenter. Lennox withdraws.
He's seen him before, in South Beach: the Deuce and Myopia.
Close to him, another recognisable figure. He hasn't turned round,
but there is no mistaking the denim back of Lance Dearing.

Lennox swiftly concealed himself behind some stacked chairs
in the hallway. He can hear the speaker clearly. — What do I do
when I get a lead? Nothing. I sit back and plan. I find out everything I can about the customer, before I present the product. The
initial product is *not* your own wants and desires. This is crucial:
the product is completely tailored to the customer, at first. Only
when the customer is completely hooked do we start to think
about modifying client behaviour.

Then familiar tones set him on edge: Lance Dearing. — An ol
dog knows you gotta hunt the fattest, juiciest lil' fleas with a wet
tongue rather than a sharp tooth.

— Amen, another voice endorses.

He has heard enough to know that confrontation will be useless,
and the lack of any obvious police presence makes him wonder
about Chet's alarm-raising capabilities. But he has the evidence,
and Chet and Johnnie. He decides to get Robyn and leave them
to it.

Then he hears the announcement of a coffee adjournment, and the gratified sounds of men stretching and rising eagerly, as chairs slide along the polished wooden floor. Instead of going downstairs, he quickly heads to the restroom, bolting the small cubicle shut, sitting and waiting. Two men enter: urine blasts against porcelain and the salts in the bottom of neighbouring latrines.

— How ya doin, Tiger?

— Ah'm good.

Tiger. Lennox sweats, feeling his blood pounding as if his heart is where his brain should be. He pulls the flush and moves out of the cubicle; stands alongside one of the men, who is washing his hands, while the other still pees. He looks at the delegate badge on the man's lapel: C.T. O'HARA. He's a big, full-faced guy with a benign smile. Wedding ring. Looks like a regular dad. Away from home a lot, working hard in sales to generate a college fund for his kids. Who married this monster, slept with him every night? Wouldn't they just *know*? *Why* would they?

The big guy gives his hands a cursory blast under the electric dryer and in departure teases his colleague who has advanced to the basin by Lennox. — You're gonna miss those chocolate-chip cookies, Tiger.

— Don't I know it. Them boys got appetites, Tiger grins, displaying a row of capped teeth, as his friend departs.

Lennox looks at his oily black hair, the snidey, reptilian cast of the features and the name tag confirming: J.D. CLEMSON. He could envisage him buying Robyn drinks in a bar. See him alone with Tianna . . .

He pulls his arm behind his back to scratch at his shoulder blade as he steps closer to Clemson. Sees the beast look up with a faint, vaguely uncomprehending smile on its lips, before he shoots the elbow forward at speed into Clemson's face. A satisfying crunch is followed by a screech and blood erupts, splattering across the white sink. Lennox pivots behind Clemson and forces his face down on to the edge of the unit, hammering it repeatedly, as teeth and bone crack and the man grows limp in his now painless hands, emitting nothing other than a low, gurgling groan. — Savour this moment, Lennox says to him, — cause this is as good as it gets for you from now on in. Your old life is over. *This* is what you were put here for.

Lennox releases his grip. As the bloodied Clemson falls slowly, sliding down, drunkenly trying to cling on to the unit, Lennox kicks him in the face, assisting his sprawl to the marble floor. He can't cease stomping Clemson, can't end the intimacy, yet he makes himself halt. But not before his senses have been assailed by that brief insight all men might be permitted before they become killers, that the achievement of that goal will produce an irreperable emotional downshift.

Phantom-like and serene as he opens the door and looks down the mezzanine's narrow hallway, he feels as if he's watching himself in a dream, where narrative perspective shifts from first to third person, usually when the nightmare becomes unbearable. He walks past the seminar rooms. Key Largo 2's door is closed. He glides by the half-open Key Largo 1 without looking in, the buzz of men chatting over coffee never changing in register as he passes. Then adrenalin shoots into him with the realisation that the police might just arrive to witness his brutal assault. He scoots down the stairs, across the hotel lobby, vaguely aware of KC and the Sunshine Band's 'Don't Go' playing in piped music, and runs across the lot to the green car.

As he drives past the airport, he thinks again about what Les endured, wondering how he would have coped with similar treatment. As a copper he was drawn to Serious Crimes, and he would often look through the sex offenders database, to see if he could recognise their three assailants. His mind played tricks; sometimes he was convinced he had identified one of them, only later to be certain it was someone else. But he knew that he hated all sex offenders: every one of those terrible, wretched specimens. Bringing them to book was the one and only thing he believed to be *true* policework. The system was played solely for the leverage to get to them, the *real* villains. This power was craved because he'd declared war on paedophiles. Never a policeman, Ray Lennox is a beast hunter and now that he has their scent he's compelled to take this as far as he can.

21

Showdowns

Lennox realises his fraught and hasty retreat from Dearing has confused his mental map of Miami. He finds himself heading east on the Calle Ocho strip of SW 8th Street at Little Havana, past the Cuban bakers and furniture shops, where groups of old men chat and smoke in the cooling air, as the central business district's skyscrapers glow in the distance.

The colour and word 'orange' burn in his head: the Orange Bowl Stadium and the exterior decoration of Robyn's apartment block. Pulling up outside the Latin American Art Museum, he asks a youthful couple for directions. They tell him to go left on 17th Avenue, and the faded grandeur of the college football arena contiguously comes into sight. But in the featureless rack of streets, locating Robyn's apartment reminds him of trying to find Notman's lost contact lens on an Edinburgh Parks Department football pitch. As he feels himself going in circles anger gnaws at him, unleashing a bilious frustration in his gut. *It would be easier to eat fresh sushi in Brigadoon.* He's ready to hammer his car horn in exasperated despair when the orange building seems to step out in front of him. — Thank fuck, he gasps in gratitude, parking across the street.

He hesitates in exiting the car; inspects his bloody fingers, throbbing like toothache. Driving through Little Havana, that sense of alienation and despondency has swept back over him. He is not a cop here. Thankfully, he can see no sign of police in the quiet street. But they would arrive soon, either Chet's testimony or his battering of Clemson would ensure that.

So Lennox steels himself, gets out and walks up the path, presses some buzzers that aren't Robyn's, shouting, — Pest control, and waits for the crackle before pushing the front door. He climbs the stair and bangs on the entrance of the apartment he visited two nights ago. Starry pulls it open in agitation. Her eyes widen in shock as she beholds Lennox. — What the fuck do you –

She never gets to finish the sentence as he rams his forehead into her face. The crack of bone splintering followed by a red spray tells him he's snapped the bridge of her nose. Starry screams, bending forward and teetering back, uttering curses in Spanish, as insistent bombs of thick blood fall through her fingers on to the hardwood floor. Lennox grabs her hair in his left fist and jumps into the apartment with a twist, smashing her head against the door frame. She collapses to the deck, where she lies stunned and moaning as he closes the door behind them.

Robyn runs in from the lounge, leaky-eyed and halting. — Ray! Where's Tia? Is she safe? She looks down at Starry in trembling bewilderment. — What have you done?

— Something you or some other cunt should have a long time ago. Anybody else in here?

— No . . . but what happened? Where's Tianna?

Lennox realises that he's never had violent contact with a woman before, if you discounted the obese lassie he'd had to sit on at the South Side station, after she'd freaked out and bitten off part of a uniformed spastic's ear. But this one didn't factor, because she was a beast, like the others. — Are there any firearms in the house?

— No . . . Robyn's eyes are like a Halloween mask. It's as if she's been caught in a cycle of crying and applying more eyeliner without thinking to wash her face. It nauseates him to consider that he could have had sex with her: more so, when he thinks about her daughter and his own fiancée. Robyn bunches her fists in front of her chest. — Where's Tianna?

— She's okay. She's with friends. What the fuck have they done to you? Where did they take ye?

— It was Lance . . . he said my drugs problem had gotten outta hand . . . an intervention, she rambles, then paralysis seizes her face as she's smitten by the ineptitude of her own words. — They were my friends . . . they knew what was best. I . . . she begs, halting as her flimsy conviction deserts her. She's a grotesque tear factory to him; afflicted by the strange notion that if she cried enough, she'd eventually excrete the source of her pain. Unlike Starry's face with

the Latin cheekbones and engorged lips, which grew more alluring in rage, Robyn's small, fine Anglo-Saxon features become pinched; petty and ungenerous. Stiff-upper-lipped stoicism is the way for our race, ostentatious anger always demeans us, Lennox considers. It is fear that diminishes Starry. He grabs her and hauls her to her feet, jostling her into the lounge and shoving her on to the chair.
— What have you done to her? Robyn asks again.

— You know what I've done and why I've done it, jabbing a finger at her, before turning back to his quarry in the chair. — You fuckin move a muscle and I'll throttle you to death with my bare hands. Got that?

She forces a defiant sneer, still holding her nose.

Lennox's face contorts as he takes a step closer to her. — HAVE YOU FUCKIN WELL GOT THAT?

And he thinks of when he lost it at his last interrogation, but now there's no Horsburgh, only Starry's abject shell, nodding in miserable deference. He charges through to the toilet, grabs a soiled towel and thinks of the uses it could be put to before he throws it at her. Then, remembering Robyn's cuffs, he goes to the bedroom and removes them from the nightstand. He experiences Robyn's presence as a background bleating sound as he snaps Starry's hand to a radiator pipe behind her. — It's fucking hot, she squawks through the towel.

— Good, Lennox says, as he looks back at Robyn.

— What's going on, Ray? Robyn asks, nervously picking burrs from her faded green top — Where's my baby? Did you take her to Chet's?

— I've told you, she's fine. Don't give me any performances, Robyn. I've seen one of your performances, and he pulls the disc from his pocket.

— You found the tapes . . . Her hand goes to her hair, and Lennox has to repress the urge to scream at her.

She thinks I'm fucking jealous! The daft cunt actually thinks that's what this is about! — Yes.

— Johnnie and I met through Starry. He liked to video when we . . . were together.

Lennox nods, thinking about guys who wanted to become porn

stars until they realised that they couldn't get wood on camera. In a couple of generations, he considers, we won't be able to get wood *unless* there's a camera.

Robyn whines, — Then he got Lance involved.

— Lance was my boyfriend, bitch, Lennox hears Starry's muffled hiss from behind the towel.

Robyn seems not to register, — . . . and it just got crazier and wilder. Then I found out that there were other women, other videos.

— Oh yeah, there were others, he caustically agrees.

Robyn looks to a broken-nosed Starry, holding her head up with the towel, groaning in agony, then back to Lennox. — Who . . . *who are* you, Ray? Who? Robyn's rasping sobs are punctuated only by the sound of mucus sliding down her gullet in heavy swallows.

— Later, he says, wondering if he'll ever be able to answer that question to his own satisfaction. — Did you see any of the other videos?

— No, of course I didn't –

— Chet's boat was where some of them were made.

— No, Robyn gasps. — No. No! I don't believe it . . . not Chet . . . where's Tianna?!

Lennox inserts the disc into the DVD player. — Here's one you missed.

—What?! We're going to watch one of these films? Now? What the hell –

— You need to see this. Need to see what the people you choose as friends are really about.

He didn't want to watch it again, and instead sits studying her reaction as the images appear on the screen. The voice of her drugged daughter: — I feel sick . . . I wanna go home . . . Dearing's kindly reply: — It's okay, honey, jus you relax . . .

— NO! Oh my God . . . No! Robyn's chest heaves. But her terror is real: he knows she wasn't part of Tianna's abuse.

— I'm sorry. He stops the disc with the remote. — I had to be sure that you weren't involved in this.

— What? What do you . . . who . . . Robyn's eyes bulge, her chest heaving as she struggles for breath.

Shame's mass aggregates in him and his eyes fall to the floor.
— They probably gave Tianna something, some kind of sedative.
Not on the boat, most likely in the car on the way out there,
on Alligator Alley. He looks back to her. — While you were in
rehab.

— But she was with Sta— Robyn starts, looks to the couch
and the face covered with the towel. — No . . . NO! WHAT DID
YOU DO TO MY BABY, YOU FUCKING EVIL BITCH?!

— Robyn, Lennox says, — do you remember Vince, back in
Alabama?

— Yes. Robyn is barely audible as her hate-filled eyes screw
into Starry, who holds the towel in front of her face like a mask.

He squeezes her hand to get her to focus on him. — You left
Mobile to get away from him. Took Tianna, cause you knew what
he was like? She told you, and you believed her, didn't you?

— I . . . yes . . . He told me he loved me!

— Vince was involved in an organised paedophile ring: the
same one as Lance and Johnnie. The same one that Jimmy Clemson
in Jacksonville was part of.

— No . . . how can that be . . . ? she cries, but a terrible understanding is starting to settle in her eyes.

— The deal is that they identify single women: marginal, lonely,
with young children. They exchange information mainly through
a website, but also on these sales training functions. I got the list
of members from the computer. They devise a control strategy,
pass the info around to other paedophiles, one or more of whom
then stalk the woman and attempt to manipulate her into entering
a sexual relationship with them. Once that goal's achieved, they
quickly move on to the child. If the mother develops any suspicion about what they're up to, they simply withdraw, passing the
woman's contact details on to the next member who steps in and
attempts to groom them again.

— Oh my God . . . Robyn whines through hands that cover her
eyes. — Tianna . . . what have I done . . . what have they done to
my Tia?

The ball in his throat burns again, but Lennox forces himself
to carry on.

— The code of the group is not to take risks. Gaining the mother's trust, they befriend the kid, taking an interest; becoming the surrogate father the child wants to have around, slowly building up the emotional intimacy and the physical contact. Take my hand. Give me a hug. A wee kiss. Then they declare love, but tell the child it must be a secret. All the time they praise the kid, singling them out, so they believe the love they share is special, thus rationalising the need to keep it secret and exclusive. That's how it ends up, Lennox nods to the screen.

Miserable, low, rhythmic sobs emanate from Robyn, her eyes still covered by her hands. Her pores seem to have opened up, as if in order to absorb everything out of the fetid air. Then she glares in seething rage at Starry, who sits silently, bizarrely, with the towel now over her head. — PUT IT BACK ON, I WANNA FUCKING SEE WHAT THEY'VE DONE!

— No, Lennox says. — If you want to watch more, it's on your own time. He looks to Starry, reminding him of a hooded falcon, a predator made passive by the cover. — This paedophile ring had a handover strategy. Once you worked out Vince's game in Mobile, he got in touch with Clemson in Jacksonville.

— I didn't know . . . how could I have known . . . ?

— You couldn't. When you sussed there was something dodgy about this Clemson guy, he got in touch with Johnnie and then Lance in Miami.

— He was a pig, Robyn spits. — Vince I would never have figured . . . but Clemson was a lousy fuckin pig!

— And some. So when they start getting more and more kinky, by this time, through the sheer process of erosion, you're thinking: 'That's what guys are like, maybe I'm just a little hung-up.' By now you've been isolated from all your girlfriends and family back home. And they have this fucker here, he points at Starry, — working for them, telling you it's all hunky-dory. You were starting to get suspicious, but they'd already gotten everything they wanted from you. He nods to the videodisc.

— They got me so fucked up, gave me all that free shit: the coke, the meth, the grass, the downers . . .

— Starry had you in that specific bar the other night, to meet someone, who, all being well, would have been your next beau. Remember that guy I had the run-in with?

A miserable nod, followed by a bloodcurdling, — WHY? at Starry. — Just tell me *why*!

Starry, sequestered by the bloody towel, is murmuring what sounds like a prayer in Spanish.

Lennox talks over them: — She mistook me for him. Then, when the real deal came along, she realised she'd fucked up. After trying to throw us together, she then started to vie with you for my attention, remember?

— I can't believe it. All of them . . . Vince, Jimmy, Johnnie, Lance . . . all in on it . . . Her eyes widen in stark horror. — Chet! Is Tianna with *him*!?

— No, she's safe. Anyway, Chet was different. He was a lonely old guy who missed his wife. They befriended him in order to get use of the boat. They used him like they used you. Employed similar tactics. Became his buddies. Dearing was a cop; like a lot of people, Chet trusted cops, he says, and she's so greedy for his words he feels like a parent bird feeding its fledgling. — They showed him some stag movies as buddies sometimes do. Lennox recoils at the thought: *sometimes buddies do more.* Then it was, 'We like to film our own shows. Can we use your boat?'

For a while Robyn can't speak. When she finally finds her voice she mutters, — My baby, my baby, my baby . . .

— She's safe now. She's a strong kid, he says briskly, — and she needs you, *we* need you to show some strength now. The cops'll be here soon.

She nods in assent, but her face is crumbling as Lennox continues. — Chet liked to watch the home-made stag videos. When he saw you appear in one, he drew the line and left them to it. But then Johnnie and Lance started getting more outlandish. The women became younger. Sometimes they weren't women. Chet was freaked out at those visitors to his boat, but by then it was plain blackmail. He's a proud, straight old guy. He didn't want the law or his respectable neighbours at Grove Marina thinking he moved in such circles. But they grew sloppy and careless, especially Johnnie. They started storing the videos on his boat.

Starry rattles the cuff against the pipes.

Lennox draws a deep breath. Clenches the fist that had pummelled itself into fragments. Never to be the same again. Shards floating around in cartilage and tendon. — Chet found their website. It wasn't incriminating, but it posted their membership list and a meetings timetable. There's eight of them, including Dearing, at the Embassy Hotel right now, or more likely by now on the run from the Miami–Dade PD. The subject of their conference was probably you and a few other single mothers in South Florida.

Robyn exhales in a long gasp, holding her shoulders and rocking. — Why did Chet . . . ?

— He was planning to go to the police. He was working up the bottle, the courage, he elaborates in response to her confusion, — gathering the evidence: Dearing's a cop, remember?

— So Chet's still my friend . . .

— In a sense, Lennox concedes, and recounts an old phrase his father often used, — but you're always better with a cunning enemy than a stupid friend, before permitting the cop in him to take over: — However, he was inadvertently assisting them and he'll have to live with those consequences.

Robyn's hands go back over her face. Then her voice wheezes through her fingers: — What have I done, Ray?

— You've been a victim of a particularly fucking evil scam, he says, as another holy recitation in Spanish comes out from under the stained towel.

— But why . . . why *me*?

— You've a young daughter. Your lifestyle makes you vulnerable. Exposes her, and you.

— I ain't a bad person, she pleads, — I jus –

Lennox waves her down. — I can't criticise your lifestyle, because it's pretty much the same as my own. The crucial difference is that I don't have a kid to look after. Get it together, while there's still something left.

— You . . . you're FBI?

— No. I'm from Edinburgh, on holiday. Planning a wedding, like I told you.

Robyn's baffled face again finds its focus by narrowing on Starry, now peering through her towel, like a burka. — You set the whole thing up. You! She looks at Lennox. — She hates me! Hates me cause I've got Tianna!

— My son was sixteen when he was shot dead, Starry groans.

— It was some gang thing! He deserved it! Angel was no good! Robyn screams, then tears across the room, her bunched fists flying at Starry. It's only when she goes to pick up a large tiger-striped glass vase that Lennox feels moved to restrain her. — LEMME GO, I WANNA KILL THAT FUCKIN EVIL BITCH!

It's not easy to hold on to her; fury has given Robyn a power supernatural to her slight frame. Eventually the fight leaves her and she dissolves in his arms, allowing herself to be led back across the room and on to the couch. — She'll get it, no worries. He crouches down and takes her hand in his. Guilt pours from him. *I let Britney down by misjudging Angela Hamil. Now I've let down Robyn by misjudging her — or judging her; it's the same thing.*

For some reason he recalls the time when, in twelve-year-old rage, he'd inexplicably barged into his sister Jackie's bedroom, un-intentionally interrupting her as she performed fellatio on a boyfriend. There had been a family row afterwards. Not about his intrusion or her indiscretion, but later when she'd found her old doll Marjorie in the attic, the one that was both their favourites. COCKSUCKING SLUT was scribbled on its plastic face in big biro letters.

He regards Robyn's pitted countenance, desecrated by mascara and tears. — Now we should go and get Tianna before the police come by.

Robyn is about to nod in agreement when she sees the door swing open behind Lennox. — They're right here already, a voice tells them.

Lennox turns to face Lance Dearing who dangles a spare key. — Lover's trust, he smiles. The second thing that Lennox registers is that there is something different about Dearing: bifocal lenses slice his eyes into an impenetrable dark section and a cloudy lower part. The third thing is that Dearing is pointing a handgun at him.

— Who the fuck are you, Ray? And don't gimme that wedding-planner shit. You sure got ol Tiger real good. Found him pretty bust up on that restroom floor: blood, shit and teeth everywhere. His head nods in wary admiration. — So who the fuck are you!

— Does it matter now? It's over, Lance.

— For you and me both.

— Lance baby, lemme go, honey, let's just take off, Starry begs.

For some reason Lennox looks Dearing up and down, suddenly contemptuous of his black, stonewashed denim shirt, tucked into off-white canvas trousers, with those showroom white sneakers. —You're no gaunny shoot me. You've never shot anybody, he says calmly, thinking of Bill Riordan, the retired New York cop. But this was the South. Was Florida the real South? Was it a hunting state? Fishing, surely.

Dearing scowls and something dulls in his eyes, behind the lower halves of the bifocals. — And how in hell's name would *you* know that?

In despair, Lennox realises that he has no way of knowing. He thinks about his father. About Britney. Wonders, in an instant, if he'll see them over the other side: if death really is like that.

— Lance, Starry implores.

— MY LITTLE GIRL, YOU FUCKIN MONSTER! Robyn roars, rising.

Dearing points the gun at her. — Sit on your dumb ass, you crazy bitch, or I'll make a fuckin orphan outta her!

Robyn shrivels up and falls back into the couch, her arms wrapped around herself, a trail of snot dripping from nose to chest.

— It's over, Lennox repeats, looking to the disc sticking out of the DVD player under the TV set. — Johnnie's in custody. Try calling him if you don't believe me. Or rather you might try Chet. He's turned himself in, and you too, obviously. I thought you'd have been busted at the hotel. Doesnae matter, the local cops will have circulated the list to the FBI. He points at the sheets of papers on the couch. Your name isn't on it, but they've got a copy of you starring in your own show. Johnnie was careless. Carried those DVDs everywhere: a veritable Blockbuster on legs. It's finished, Lance.

311

Dearing's jaw quivers a little.

Starry still wretchedly entreating: — Let me go, Lance, please! Let's get the fuck outta here!

Lance Dearing ignores her and looks down at the papers, then at the DVD. His eyes pop and a white incandescence seems to light him from within. — Never figured it would turn out this way. Jus wanted to do a good job, is all. Had some fun that got a lil' outta hand.

— It wasn't fun, Lennox says.

— Perhaps not, Dearing wearily concedes. — I guess we can all fall from grace.

— The best thing you can do now is —

Lennox is jolted into silence as Lance Dearing raises the gun and pulls the trigger.

22

Clean-Up

A thunderous boom, and for a second Lennox thinks he's been shot. Then he sees Dearing leap backwards, hurtling through the doorway and partially into the hall, blood pouring from his chin. Lennox advances quickly, grabbing the throw from the couch and dropping it over Lance Dearing's face, though not before he witnesses that the exit wound has come out of his cheekbone, shattering part of his top jaw. Teeth spill out across the floor like pearls from a broken necklace.

Robyn sees little, shielded by the door opening from the hall into the lounge. All that's visible to her are Lance Dearing's legs, writhing slowly on the floor. Lennox takes her by the hand, hauling her from the couch. She's in shock, almost as incapacitated as the spreadeagled Dearing; he knows his own shutdown is in the post. He pulls the disc from the DVD player and picks up the list.

He glances back at Starry. The bridge of her nose is swollen and her eyes are starting to blacken. Lennox can barely look at her; his own diminishment evidenced in her wreckage. In panic she thrashes at the fur shackle that fastens her to the radiator. — Don't leave me!

Lennox ignores her; she can stay till the police arrive and try to explain everything to them. He holds Robyn's head up, forcing her not to look at Dearing or the bloodstains on the wall or the stuff running down the door frame as he steps over the bespattered beast cop. — Now we'll go and see Tianna, right? he says as they cross the threshold. She's bewildered and feral, zoological-looking against cinder-block wall and cold metal banister. — Just wait here a wee minute, Lennox says, going back inside and closing the door behind him.

He crouches over Lance Dearing, astonished he still has the

gun in his hand, dragging it along the floor, manoeuvring it towards his own head. The throw partially spills off his bloody face. He fires again before Lennox is able to react. The bullet grazes the top of his skull and ricochets down the hall, sticking in the bottom of the bathroom door.

Dearing's next shot whistles into the skirting board. Lennox pulls back the remainder of the throw to expose the whole of the broken face. — Help me, Lance Dearing croaks softly, — finish it . . .

Lennox slowly shakes his head. — I already have, Dearing. But I'm fucked if I'm finishing *you*. No way, he says, stepping on Dearing's wrist, then, with his other foot, kicking the gun from his weak grip. — I'm no helping a fuckin nonce. With the blood you're losing, I just hope that the ambulance gets here in time and can patch you up. I don't want you to die, because you don't fuckin deserve it. You should be made to live with what you've done. Lennox feels gripped by a terrible energy. — Help a cunt like you? A stoat? A beast *polisman*? I look fuckin sweet, he spits, knowing that Miami's cons will be harder on Dearing than any bullet, and he wants this man to have the same fate as Confectioner: to live in fear of being stabbed, bummed, bullied, and he's shamed by this realisation. *They've won. Diminished us. Dragged us down to their level with our pathetic bloodlust. You could wipe them all off the face of the Earth, and you would still lose.*

Starry's screams and Dearing's throaty groans fill the apartment in a dread orchestration of misery. — SHUT THE FUCK UP, Lennox roars cathartically, and for a few seconds the noise abates. — Just shut the fuck up, ya nonce cunts, and think about how totally fucked youse are now, and he hears the burning growl of angry satisfaction come from deep within him.

He steps outside to see Robyn. Shivering, and self-cradling, she now looks about the same age as Tianna. *But the crucial thing is that she isn't.*

A young guy in a vest and tracksuit bottoms comes bounding up the stairs as Lennox shuts the door. — I thought I heard noises, he says. — It was like gunshots, I –

He sees the blood on Lennox. Looks at him in slack-jawed shock.

— It certainly was, Lennox agrees. — Somebody's just shot himself. Might be an idea to call the police, and an ambulance, he says, ushering Robyn down the stairs, his arm round her thin shoulders.

— Sure thing! The guy eagerly bounces back down the stairs ahead of them.

They get outside and into the Volkswagen and Lennox drives to the car hire. On the way he hears sirens, wonders if they might be for Dearing. Perhaps not. The shock is kicking in, and he feels a pervasive numbness swamping him. Then, as he sees the signs for a gas station, the mundane thought hits him: *fill up the tank.* — I need to bring back a full tank of gas, he astonishes himself by saying to a perplexed Robyn, as he pulls into the forecourt.

T.W. Pye is working the graveyard shift. He looks suspiciously at Lennox as he walks into the office. Then his eyes expand bulbously as he notices the blood and dried vomit down the foreigner's front. They go outside to the returning lot where the German car stands. Pye shuffles round it, lowers his great perspiring bulk inside, and pokes about for a bit. Lennox notes that a rash of oxide blight, like spots breaking out on someone's face after an alcoholic binge, has spored on the green body along the rim above the wheel. This has either escaped the clerk's attention or has no relevance to him. — Well, the car looks okay, he says, hoisting himself up and looking at a trembling Robyn. — And you got a full tank, he gripes at Lennox. — But you seem in a bit of a mess there, buddy.

— The other guy would kill to be in my shoes.

The sides of Pye's face burn. — Righty, I'll just . . . ehm . . . He waddles back to the office, followed by Lennox, and fumbles in the till, nervously counting out five hundred dollars.

— Great car, by the way, Lennox says as he takes the money and pockets it, starting to feel sorry for the fat man, who would head home to his one deadly friend, silent, white and immutable; the refrigerator that was killing him every time it greeted him with a big, brash light-bulb smile. He and Robyn head for the taxi rank. Thinking of Starry and Clemson, he can feel his adrenalin leaking, and the depression setting in, the penny-wise gain followed by the pound-foolish debit: the emotional mathematics of practising violence or abuse. They climb into a taxi. — Fort Lauderdale.

In the back of the cab he explains the situation to Robyn, leaving her in no doubt that he's calling the shots. — Here's the deal; you come and see Tianna in Fort Lauderdale with me. Then we go to the police station and tell them everything. Tianna'll stay with my friends for a week or so, until this shit's cleared up.

— But I need her with me —

— It's got fuck all, *sweet fuck all*, Lennox emphasises, thinking of Tianna and So Fucking Awesome, — to do with what *you* need right now. That wee lassie isnae gaunny be your sister any more. She's just a kid and you're a grown woman. If you don't start acting like it, I'll tell the authorities you're a slut and a cokehead, and believe you me they will listen. You'll do time for child endangerment if I show them that tape. Believe.

Her face buckles further under his onslaught. — But I thought you were our friend . . .

— I'm her friend, not yours. *You* have to start earning friendships and respect. Lennox's tone softens as self-reproach filters through him. — Get yourself together and you'll come out of this as a heroine in Tianna's eyes. Make her believe in you, Robyn.

She nods through her tears. And then he finds himself rambling; telling her that he's just a Scottish cop who wanted to be with his fiancée in Miami Beach and recover from a bad time. And plan a wedding. Maybe do a bit of sunbathing, with some fishing and sailing thrown in. Then Robyn tells him her tale, and it humanises her, as all stories do, and he sees a person of great misfortune, victimised and pulled apart like carrion by hyenas. And he remembers the trinity of bullies that made him a cop.

You can get better. He'd been as wretched as Robyn when they pulled him off that bar-room floor in Edinburgh, slain by the pub comic's sick joke. More so, when found lurking in the tunnel after his dad's funeral, hand pulped, ranting like a madman, protesting he had cocaine under control, as a wrap burned his jeans' pocket and his nose's cavities. Trudi, though, had taken charge; de facto moving him into Bruntsfield, going to his Leith flat to pick up his mail. She'd been in touch with Toal, agreeing sick leave, and signed him up with her doctor, not the police one, as he'd never bothered to register. He was prescribed the anti-depressants. She'd already booked the Florida sun, now the holiday would have the added agenda of executing the matrimonial plans. But first there had been his father's funeral.

The day before he'd gone round to his sister's place: a dull, wet and cold afternoon with progress down the leafless, grey avenue a turgid war of attrition against a vicious wind. Jackie had stayed strong during the period leading up to the funeral. She took charge of the arrangements, handled everything in her usual practical manner, displaying scant emotion. That morning when he called round at her home she flabbergasted Lennox by grabbing hold of him in the hallway, the one with the bottle-green Axminster that always smelt slightly of damp, though it had been lifted, aired and cleaned several times. — Ray . . . my wee brother. You know I've always loved you, she'd said.

This came as a shock to him, even more when he smelt the gin on her breath. — I hadnae suspected a thing, he told her, and she thought he was joking.

— You should go and see Mum, Ray. She needs us all.

— Has Jock been round looking after her? he asked quietly.

— Thank goodness for Jock, he's a star.

So she didn't know. Lennox fought his rage down. — Aye.

— You should go and see her, she repeated, this time with the assertion of a barrister.

— Aye, ah'll mibbe go n see her later oan, eh? he said in his cop voice, shot with the harsh vowels and scheme argot he habitually used around Jackie, to counterbalance her posh affectations. It killed the last of the intimacy between them. He then made his excuses and left, back to the order of Trudi's.

Sometimes a benign despot is more suitable than self-determination, he considers, particularly if you're a hopeless fuck-up. He looks at Robyn, sees her staring ahead, focused on something invisible. — It'll be okay, he says to her, and he hopes that he's right.

★   ★   ★

317

The reunion in Fort Lauderdale is emotional and tearful, as is the subsequent parting. Lennox informs Tianna that her mother is going to be helping the police put away bad guys like Vince, Clemson, Lance and Johnnie. Which is probably the biggest truth he's gotten to tell her.

Six Days Later

23

Holocaust

The full-length bathroom mirrors collapse, for his own critical eyes, a thousand naked Ray Lennoxes into infinity; each one carrying the maternal stain of infidelity. Avril Lennox was the surprise package; he'd been watching his father to see how he'd turn out and the old girl had sneaked up on the blind side, the one with the clandestine life and the lusty secrets. From adolescence through your twenties it had been about making your mark as an individual, concealing your hereditary legacy in the process. Then, suddenly, you were on the stage like a stripper under harsh lights; peeling off everything to reveal your DNA.

He clicks off the bathroom spots, watches them bruise to dark, swings the door open with a flourish. The oomph is back; that sexual urge, no, that sexual imperative. *Will I be able to do the right thing by Trudi?* he wonders, emerging into the pulsing light of the hotel bedroom.

He pulls a cord, twisting the blind closed as she clicks on a bedside light, like a chessmaster expertly countering an opponent's manoeuvre. She's as naked as he is, meeting his approach with a defiant thrust at him, her sunbed tan a new outfit. Her body, in his trembling hands, is even tighter than he remembers. In the light from the indented lamps above the headboard he can see a rash of milk-white hairs, finer than silk, across her light brown arms, broken up by the odd little patch of peeling pink that dismays her. She seems so fresh that to squeeze her would leave marks; a gingerbread girl from the oven. A wave of tenderness rushes over him and he has an irresistible urge to stroke her face. Misinterpreting this gesture, Trudi pushes him gently back on to the bed, swivelling round, her sharp, pointed tongue licking down his freshly scrubbed chest, heading south. It lodges for a few tantalising seconds in his navel. A cursory flick or two and it continues as her lips open around his prick.

Lennox gasps, feeling himself stiffen, his cock swelling up in her mouth. He looks at her adjusting to the newer, more formidable status quo, a gratified surprise in her eyes that accompanies the meeting of an old friend. He tucks her hair behind her ears to enjoy the feast of her face.

Both are determined the erection will last, and she's eagerly complicit when he groans, — I don't want to get there yet, and he pulls out and mounts her as they make love in a controlled, precarious way, almost delighted that they can, respecting the wondrous building power of each moment with something close to forensic intensity.

They climax together, wildly; Lennox's pulsing ejaculations so thick and heavy they almost hurt him. Trudi's eyes roll to the back of her head and a banshee-like howl he feared he'd never hear again fills the room. Spent, they quickly dissolve into a deep post-coital slumber. He feels himself careering across an ocean until he can see Toal behind the lectern at the auction rooms. The still and silent mannequin stands in the coffin. They are bidding, the others; all in shadow, but they seem weaker. Because Les Brodie is by his side, and they're not boys any more. The voice of a nonce behind him says, — Two million.

— Three million! Les screams.

— Four million, comes the cry, but there is now uncertainty in the voices of the men in the shadows. They seem to be coming from further away.

Lennox studies Brodie's face. Gets the signal. — FIVE MILLION! they cry out in unison, in that noise Scots make, through their inventions and their drunken carousings, their gift to Planet Earth of its anthem, 'Auld Lang Syne': the sound heard around the world.

— Sssiiixx milliiooonn . . . the nonce voices fade.

— I didn't get that bid. Could you repeat it? Toal asks. — No? The last bid was five million. Going . . . going . . . sold . . . to Ray Lennox!

The girl on the stage is now wearing a white bridal gown. She reaches up and removes her mask as Lennox flies to the surface from that mine of sleep, sweat and duvet. Opens his eyes. Trudi's face next to his on the pillow. Eyes shut, crooked smile. He takes a grateful, exhilarating gulp of air. After savouring a few moments of intense pathos and adoration, he wakes her with a kiss.

She's both delighted and irritated to be roused in this way. — Oh Ray . . . what's up, baby? You've not been having those horrible dreams again?

— No, beautiful dreams of white brides, he says, reaching out for her.

Trudi snuggles into him, then after a pause, where she's so still and silent he thinks she's fallen back asleep, says, — At least give Stuart a bell, Ray.

— Later, he forces a smile, pulling one arm behind his head on the pillow, feeling the wastage and shrinkage of his biceps muscle and thinking gym, gym, gym, — we're on holiday.

— Okay, she says, and gets out of the bed and heads to the bathroom. He watches her move with lithe, coltish grace, admiring the slender tautness of her buttocks, the blades of her shoulders and the smooth indentation her spine leaves in her back. Then she's gone and he hears the water jets hiss.

Stuart.

What had happened to the elfin-eyed kid with the clear skin and golden-brown curling hair?

Their father's funeral. Stuart's face reddening after every whisky; that vile, sickening concoction. The pastry from the sausage roll he was eating flaking off into his glass without him noticing. Pulling Lennox into the corner at the funeral reception and whispering in a nervy excitement. Beetroot countenance and flaring nostrils in such proximity. How Stuart had no notion of personal space at the best of times and just how smotheringly close he got when he was drunk. — It was embarrassing having to go and tidy out his office. I found a porn stash in the desk.

Lennox had raised a tired eyebrow, wanting him to stop, but too weary to insist. His skin crawling from being up all night freebasing coke in his Leith flat, where he'd gone after he'd walked out on Melissa Collingwood and the counselling.

Stuart misread this sign as intrigue. — Everything in it, Raymie, I shiteth thee not. Couldnae believe it. Dad! I took Jasmine for a drink. She admitted she felt terrible because when she'd looked through his office window and saw him all tensed up, she thought he was having a wank. He must have been known for it! So she turns away sharpish, then she hears stuff crashing around. She opens the door and sees Dad lying on the deck. He hadnae been jerking off. He was huvin a fucking heart attack.

The poor old bastard. Trying so hard to find his sexuality, that cardinal component of the self, but buried by the pills that were keeping him alive.

Lennox looking at his young brother, seeing blemishes on the skin he'd never noticed before. They might have been new. Beholding a slack-jawed muppet; an actor, a performer, always onstage. *The more fucking drama, the more spoiled wee Stu would absorb it, would thrive.*

— Are you going to talk to Mum?

— Just keep her the fuck away fae me, he'd said, watching his teary mother. Trudi standing beside her, consoling her. Trying to explain the inexplicable. *Why isn't Ray talking to me, Trudi?* He'd told Trudi, of course, but he wasn't sure if she'd believed him or had put it down to a deranged fantasy to be placed in the 'stress' dustbin.

Then Jock Allardyce had moved across to him, and he was followed by Avril Lennox, her trembling hand unwittingly teasing a glass of red wine. Big Jock's shock of white hair, lustrously gelled back, his sad, blue eyes. — Look, Raymond, I just want to say –

— You get the fuck out ay my face, Mr Confectioner, and take her wi ye. He turned to his mother. — Ma faither's still fucking warm, ya sick bastards!

He recalls Jock's horror and bemusement, and his tearful, oval-eyed mother trying to cough out some words, but breaking down instead, to be comforted by Trudi and Jackie. Even at the time he knew it was petty and inappropriate to call Jock by the nickname they'd given to the murdering paedophile Horsburgh. 'Uncle Jocky' had never been employed in this way, nor did he have a sweet tooth. Even Horsburgh hadn't used candy to lure his prey, just fire and Sprite.

Then Stuart was over, chameleon face and gait trying to assume the shape of nightclub bouncer. — What's the story?

— You love this, he'd sniped at his young brother. — Well, you can bond with stepdaddy here, I'm offski.

Stuart had rounded on him. He recalls his brother balling his fists up, standing on his toes, his whisky breath an inch from him. — You think that because ye work with shite in yir fascist job that ye ken everything about human nature? You're a fuckin novice, Raymie. You dinnae have a clue what Mum needs or wants oot ay life!

And Avril Lennox repeating a closed-eyed prayer, — It's ma fault, it's ma fault, it's ma fault . . .

Lennox had calmly planted his hand on Stuart's chest, pushed him back a couple of feet. — I'm sure *you* do. Go and swap fucking make-up tips. He'd turned away and headed outside into the car park, his mood blackening like the dark clouds that swirled above. Walking for a bit, without knowing where he was going, he ended up back at the graveyard, sitting on a bench. Thinking how he couldn't ever tell his dad, or any of them, what happened to him in the tunnel. Wondering what it must have taken John Lennox to let go of his own big secret.

After a while there was the sound of gravel crunching underfoot, and a thin shadow passed over Lennox, making him aware that somebody had joined him on the bench, parked a respectable distance away. Les Brodie, cigarette in hand, was staring ahead, squinting in the weak sun that was trying to reassert itself. Lennox was going to ask to be left alone, but Les was saying nothing, just looking up into the murky sky.

Lennox could feel the cold air on his neck now, which throbbed with his pulse.

Les eventually spoke. — Cauld yin, El Mondo.

His childhood nickname. Used only by the immediate family and Les. That's how close we were, he'd thought. — Things are as fucked up as they can be, Lennox moaned, looking round.

— They can always be fucked up mair. Les Brodie shook his head. Then a smile played across his lips and he turned to Lennox, meeting his gaze. — But they can be made better as well.

— That cunt, and my old lady, shagging him, bringing him there while my old man's still warm in his grave.

— Jock was his mate, Raymie.

— Aye, some fucking mate, eh, shagging his wife. And that wee cunt Stuart —

— Aye, folk can be a bit strange. Les Brodie nodded in the way people do on such occasions; banal and vacuous in the face of the insolvable riddle of mortality.

— Tell me about it.

— But you've got to let go, Raymie.

— How? How the fuck, Lennox began, and his mind shot back to the tunnel and a broken Les emerging into the light with his bike, — how can *you* let go?

Les cleared his throat. — You know what those cunts did to me, Raymie? They raped me. Two of them, one after the other. Never told you that, did I? Never came right out and said it. Two of them, he said again, his eyes creasing around the laughter lines. — Just when I thought it was over, the other started. I was waiting on the third, the young guy, but he bottled out.

— Fuck sake, Les, I — He couldn't say any more. He'd gotten away. Should he have stayed, fought, screamed and taken his punishment — as they might say, like a man — by Les's side? That question had tormented him all his adult life.

— I could go into more detail, but I won't. Les fished out some smokes and offered one to Lennox, who declined. — I'll tell ye about how angry I was though, how I was looking for people tae hurt for what happened to me, and lookin tae hurt myself. I went way, way off the rails, he smiled in bitter reminiscence. — All that hate, naewhere to go. I even hated you, for getting the fuck out ay there.

— I hated myself for that, Les. I tried tae get help, tae raise the alarm. I got those people tae come, but it was too late.

Les took a deep drag on his fag. — Have to pack these in, he said. — Naw, mate, you did right. If you hadnae got away they'd have taken their time, and the other boy might have, he raised his brows, — you know.

Lennox dipped his head a few degrees. He realised that his

326

closeness with Les had never been compromised, that the years apart had only incubated it. Les hadn't rejected him, they were just at different ends of that long, black tunnel that stretched between them. — Did ye ken that was the reason I became a cop? I wanted those bastards, Les. I still fuckin well do. If you knew how many mugshots I've looked at in my spare time since I joined the force. Every sex offender on our files, UK-wide. Nothing. That was why I got into Serious Crimes, to get that kind of access to those cunts. Tae hunt the bastards doon. But zilch. He shook his head. — Maybe they just vanished into thin air.

Les Brodie's smile grew wider. — Yeah, maybe they did.

Lennox stared at him, agog. The cop in him rose to the surface, before he could stop it. — What! You're saying that you –

His old friend let out a long, hollow laugh, dropped his cigarette butt and crushed it into the gravel under his heel. — Nope, I fuckin wish. For a long time I'd have given anything to have found them. But they're no in ma life now. Dinnae get ays wrong, I hope they're in a place where they cannae harm any other kids, but I made the decision tae wash my hands of it all.

— But how could ye?

— Because I have tae, Les said, reaching into his jacket, pulling out a wallet and a family photograph of his wife and children. — I've other people to worry about. I don't want ma wife's husband and ma children's faither tae be a fucked-up bam. I need tae be there for them, no obsessed wi auld vendettas. Your girl, Ray, she's a cracker. Dinnae lose her. No tae a bunch ay fuckin nonces, that would be the *real* tragedy.

You could hear words like those a million times and understand the sense of them, but until you were emotionally ready to embrace them, it was trying to sow seeds on a motorway. After another silence Lennox rose from the bench like a football substitute in injury time, no role but to run down the clock, and shook his old friend's hand. Les stood up and pulled him close, but Lennox was stiff in his embrace, managing only a cursory pat on the back. — I need tae get a wee walk, Les, clear the heid, he'd said, breaking the hold.

— Want company?

— Naw, I'm awright.

— Ray? Les Brodie paused. — Let it go, mate.

— See ye, Les.

Lennox walked without realising where he was going; mud and gravel under his feet, the water roaring below him, the river visible through the threadbare winter trees. The tunnel ahead, now so small and benign to his adult stature. He walked into it, headed to the dead zone in the middle, wanted it to work its magic and transform him again. Change him back. Then he craved their re-appearance, the three very human monsters who had changed the boy, to come back and face the man. Willing something to happen. Voices to start up. Anybody. Anything. — C'MOAN THEN! he roared. — COME OAN THEN, YA CUNTS! His right hand jabbed out, pummelling the big, unforgiving stone bricks of the wall. There was a halting charge of pain but he smashed through it, then could feel nothing but a sick throb in his chest, his hiccup-convulsive breathing, and watch the blood from his pulped fist drip on to the harsh ground.

He had no idea how long he sat in that tunnel, head resting on his knees, lost in psychotic ramblings, but Trudi and Ally Notman found him there. — Ray . . . oh my Ray, my baby . . . Les said you'd be here . . . Trudi began, before seeing the state of his hand, her gaping mouth freezing in the egg of horror.

But Les had known he'd be there.

See ye, Les.

And he resolves that he will try. When he gets back to Edinburgh he'll look Les up. Take the friendship outside that glass storage tank while they still had time to enjoy it. He stretches out the fingers on his damaged hand. Picks up and clicks on the remote.

He is seized by the programme. The local Miami-Dade County channel: a show called *Sexual Offender Watch*. Mugshots of wild-eyed and stone-faced men designated either 'sexual offenders' or 'sexual predators' – Lennox doesn't know the difference – are paraded on a loop with name, race, eye colour, hair colour, d.o.b. and accompanied with a cheesy supermarket instrumental version of 'Caravan of Love'.

The revolution will not be televised, but the register will be, he thinks as he watches for a bit, but recognises none of the men from the nonce conference. They were all white, while almost everyone here is black or Hispanic. He laughs bitterly and clicks on the real-estate programme. A breathless female voice coos: — People who live in glass houses, then breaks into a forced frivolous laugh, — have more fun!

It seems that a luxury condo overlooking South Beach, Biscayne Bay and downtown Miami is twenty thousand dollars cheaper than it was last week. Then a new advert starts up, as a hunky, young Christopher Reeve-type sits at a table by a pool with a laptop and cellphone, finishing a staged call. He faces the camera. — At Bonaventure, the emphasis is on *ad*venture, and he rises and looks across to a pier where a boat moors, waving at the family who disembark and tie up the craft. The camera pans to the tower block. Then we cut to the luxury apartment and the man takes us around.

Trudi emerges from the bathroom, naked save for the towel round her head, looking at the screen as the chiselled-featured salesman says, — I'm Aaron Resinger and I'm not just selling the dream, I'm living it. That's right. When I say this complex has the highest quality design specifications and is the ultimate in luxury, stylised living, its more than just fancy sales talk. When I built this place, I decided that I simply couldn't find anywhere better to live. So come take a look, Aaron urges, then produces a full, toothy smile and with a minor self-deprecating shrug, adds, — and the neighbours are pretty darn nice too.

Trudi freezes and turns away from the screen.

— I'll bet you'd fancy some ay that! Lennox says.

— What . . . ? she gasps.

— Marble-top kitchen tables, hardwood floors, built-in mod cons, sun balcony, breathtaking views, boat moorings and car parking, I saw your eyes widen . . . Lennox teases, and his hand rests around the small of her back. The other grazes between her legs. — Hey . . . you think we might have time . . . ?

She pulls away from him. — We have to get ready. We're going to Fort Lauderdale to have lunch with Ginger and Dolores, and pick up Tianna remember, she says and switches off the television.

— Right . . . Lennox says reluctantly and heads to the bathroom to confer with other selves, who will all sing the same song.

Robyn had come through, making a full statement. Johnnie and Starry had been taken into police custody, no bail set. He'd be informed of the trial date, and would need to come back to Miami. There had been a number of charges made in three states. They had questioned him about the condition of one of the men they'd arrested, a James Clemson, who was found in a city hospital having been brutally assaulted. — I should imagine that bunch would turn on each other pretty viciously when it went tits-up, Lennox had observed, deadpan, to the interviewing officer, who had looked pointedly at him, but it was obvious that it was going no further.

Lance Dearing had made it as far as the ambulance before the lights had gone out. Technically he'd hung on another three days in limbo, his body eventually succumbing to the septic poisoning caused by the wounds. Lennox hoped he could feel every second and that they'd spared the morphine. For those who satiated their drives by handing out life sentences to children, he was short on mercy.

He sits in a restaurant, awaiting Tianna's arrival as he talks to Dolores's granddaughter, Nadia, a teacher. She is spending time with her grandmother, who has not taken well to Braveheart's demise. Dolores hadn't been the same at the ballroom-dancing tournament the previous night, where Bill and Jessica Riordan had easily defeated her and Ginger, who is still rankled by this. — Have you ever heard of a Paddy who could dance? he asks the assembled company of Lennox, Nadia, Dolores, Bill and Jessica over pre-lunch drinks in his favourite Mexican Cantina.

— Michael Flatley? Jessica retorts.

— Poofs, faggots; they can always dance, Ginger scoffs, — I'm talking about normal heterosexual Paddies like Bill here.

— Flatley's not gay. He's married, Jessica says, lifting a margarita to her lips.

— He dances like that and he's straight? Ginger laughs in derision.

El Hombre de el Cantina de Fettes, Lennox considers. Then, thinking of Tianna, who is on her way following an impromptu shopping detour with Trudi, he asks Nadia about the way the girls at her school dress.

— It's my biggest headache, she says, crunching a dipped salsa chip. — I gotta send kids home all the time. Ten, eleven, they wear short skirts; you can see their panties. I tell em, 'You gotta go cover yourself up, girl.' In most cases they don't think anything of it, it's just the fashion. They look at me like I'm some evil old spinster hag, she says, sweeping her long, curly hair out of her face. — But what happens if you let it go? Young guys and not so young guys start giving them attention. And they like it, so they start all the sexy prancing around, without really knowin what it is they're doin.

Lennox has found himself paying attention to young girls' consumer habits over the last week: how they dressed, what they read, the records they bought, how they spoke to each other. He'd read that they were hitting puberty and getting their periods earlier. It seemed that growing up was more stressful than ever. He considers his own childhood. It had seemed fine until the dark curtain abruptly came down on it that summer's day in the tunnel. But perhaps even the happy memories were rose-tinted.

Les Brodie. He could tell him what it had been like before then. Because Les hadn't been fucked up by what happened. Yes, he'd gone off the rails in his teens, been a bit of a tearaway, but now he's the family man, with a successful plumbing business. Ray Lennox is the disturbed one. Les has just absorbed it, and got on with things. What would have happened if it had been him those nonce jailbird guys had buggered? All he did was suck some cock. He finds his shoulders shaking in nasty mirth, the idea now briefly seeming as slapstick and benign as pantomime at the King's Theatre; certainly not worth a crusade over. How would he have reacted, have turned out, had the roles been reversed? Probably even worse, he grimly considers, as he sips on his orange juice, while craving the margarita he can't trust himself with. He was the real nutter, so consumed with his own fear, he hadn't realised how badly he'd spooked Dearing and the nonce gang from the off.

One thing he is sure of; America is a far more complicated place than he's allowed on his previous visits. It is more than a country of big cars and strange sports. Or a place where even feted novelists can't write a book without mentioning Jell-O and where animals excel athletically in the movies. He's learned a little about himself as well. He'd often hid behind the curtain of Calvinistic gloom his tribe could wear like plaid, knowing that the heart would be taught bitter lessons in spite of all our conceits. But he's seen how behaviour shapes outcomes. He would now find it hard to shrug the years away as a passive stoic.

— Thank God for that, I'm famished, says Ginger, picking up a menu, as Trudi and Tianna skip excitedly into the restaurant together, clutching bags containing the sort of stories Lennox loathes. They'd spent a lot of time together in the last week, enough for them to assume the corporate appellation, 'the girls'. Tianna has her hair tied back, with big shades resting on her head. She wears a knee-length claret dress with white polka dots, white silky scarf tied round her neck, cream pop socks and black shoes. She looks like somebody's cool ten-year-old. — These shades are SFA, Lennox tells her.

— Skarrish Football Association, she smiles, giving him a niece's peck, then Trudi follows up with a smack on the lips, a slice of tongue slyly left in. She pulls out some moisturiser she's gotten him, applying some to his dried, baked face. — You need to take care of your skin, Ray, she says. The contention makes sense to his playfully speculative mind: it has been trying to run away from him for so long, maybe he should be treating it a little better. He is being babied, even minorly humiliated, but he dosen't care. Sex has come back into their lives so emphatically, it's already impossible to conceive of it as ever having gone. Another wall has tumbled down; they'd soon be fucking with a grateful lack of inhibition. And like any drug, it numbs concern over other issues. Life was slowly returning to what he thought might be normality. — So how are the landlords? Still treating

you well? Ray Lennox asks Tianna Hinton, as he winks at Eddie
and Dolores Rogers.

— They're pretty cool, she giggles.

— Good stuff. So where would you like to go this affie?

— Skatlin.

A cloak of sadness falls over Lennox's shoulders. They are heading
home tomorrow and he'll miss the kid. Trudi has gotten attached
to her too. He's begun to enjoy their playful collusion against him,
usually regarding the forthcoming wedding plans. But there's something he wants to do with her before leaving. And for that they
need to be alone.

The food comes and Trudi regards her fiancé, how he looks
sweetly dumb when he eats something, as if lost in it. He's finally
wearing shorts, which she approves of, his legs losing their milk-
bottle whiteness. Tianna delves into a bag to show off something
to the table.

Lennox turns to Ginger. — How's it worked out, Eddie?

— An awfay sweet wee lassie, and she's been nae bother at aw,
Ginger says. — In fact, her being here's really helped Dolores,
cause she doted on that fuckin dug.

After a spell Trudi raises a downy wrist to check her watch.
Lennox takes the hint, and he, Trudi and Tianna say their goodbyes and head outside, getting into Trudi's rented car and driving
down to Miami Beach. As they leave the Julia Tuttle Causeway
and drive down palm-lined streets with handsome stucco homes and
lush tropical gardens cutting into the bay, Lennox thinks this is
a spot a newcomer could take his Colombian, Haitian, Cuban
or Scots family and they'd proudly say: this cunt's done awright.
And how the American dream is never the property of
Americans, but belongs to aspirational citizens of the globe, and
how it will fade and die when the US seals its borders up, as
it will inevitably do.

Trudi parks at a garage on Alton, then they head down to
Lincoln, the upmarket strip of restaurants, bars, galleries and designer
stores that is Miami Beach's glitzy beating heart. Lennox, an orange-
and-black backpack hanging from one shoulder, wants to stop and
look at the Britto Central Gallery as an appeasement to Trudi,

just to go through it quickly, believing that if you see something that moves you, it's best not to linger too long and dwell on it, and ruin some of your capacity for wonderment. But Trudi isn't keen, instead taking Tianna into a nearby fashion store. Afterwards, they call in at an Internet café on Washington, where they have a coffee and do some Netsurfing. Tianna and Trudi check out Scottish Wedding websites, while Lennox goes on to Jambos' Kickback. He sees Maroon Mayhem's last entry into the Craig Gordon thread, which had little to do with the Scotland goal-keeper.

I deeply regret the things I said to Ray of Light. It's no excuse, but I was drunk at the time. Anybody who knows me will tell you that I'm not in the habit of behaving that way.

Lennox types a reply into the thread.

No worries. These things happen. My head wasn't in the best of places, so I apologise for my overreaction. I also know what drink can do. If we ever meet I'll buy you a beer – or maybe we'll both stick to tomato juice!

Yours in Hearts

Ray

As they move from their terminals to settle down in the dedicated café section of the premises, Tianna says to Lennox, — So where is it you're taking us? Not here?
— No, it's close by. But there's something I've got to explain first, he says. — Those dreams we were talking about, mind I promised to tell you about them?
— Yes.
— Ray, Trudi intervenes, — Tianna doesn't want to hear –
— Please, give me a moment, Lennox is insistent, — and I want you to hear about this too. I've never told anybody before.

334

Not my mum, dad, anybody. It's something I dream about a lot, something that happened. He looks over his shoulder. The place is almost deserted as they sit in a cramped corner, sipping at the coffee or milk and eating chocolate-chip cookies.

Lennox speaks softly, but authoritatively. There is no cop in his voice, at least to his own ears. — I had a very good friend. His name was Les, he tells Tianna. — When we were round about your age, we were out on our bikes, going through a long, dark tunnel, like a disused train tunnel. Some really bad, disturbed people were waiting in there and they caught us. At first we thought they wanted to steal our bikes, he says, looking at her for understanding.

Tianna dunks the cookie into her milk. She looks up warily. Trudi's bottom jaw tightens and slides out towards him. — This is Les Brodie and you?

— Aye, he says, then turns back to Tianna. — I managed to get away, but not before they did something bad. I've never told anybody this before, but one of the men made me suck his penis.

— Ray, Trudi gasps, — that's terrible, could you not tell the pol— She stops and looks at Tianna.

The young American girl has hung her head shamefully. But a small, defiant voice rises from her. — I know . . . Vince . . . he used to . . .

Lennox lifts her head up. — It's not your fault. You're a kid. I was just a kid. It wasn't my fault. I never told anybody because I was ashamed and embarrassed. But it's not me who should've felt that way. I did nothing wrong. It wasn't my fault. He takes his hand away.

Her head stays up. Her eyes locked on his. — No. It wasn't your fault. It wasn't our fault, Ray.

— They got a hold of Les. He didn't manage to get away. I tried to find help, but it took so long. They did bad things, terrible things, to him.

— Did they do . . . she whispers, casting a privacy-checking gaze over the café, — like, sex things with a man's penis inside him?

— Yes, Lennox says. — Yes, they did. After this, Les was very

335

angry for a while. He was angry because it wasn't fair what they did to him. But he was so raging that he caused himself and other people a lot of hurt. Then he realised that by doing this, they were winning. They were controlling him still. All that anger, not going to the people that caused it, but back at himself and everybody he loved, right?

— Yes, she nods. — Yes, that's right.

— I've tried to find those people who did that to Les. And me. I haven't done so yet. But I will. I'll never stop.

— You won't stop because you're good, Ray. You're a good person, she tells him.

— No, I won't stop because I don't like what they do. My friend Les is the good person, because he was big enough to get over it. Do you understand?

Yes, it was true. Trudi shares a simultaneous notion with him: Ray Lennox is stunted in his emotional growth. Part of him will always be that fearful little boy in the tunnel. The rest, the kick-boxing, the policework, the hunting of nonces, it's all a futile attempt to negate that. As long as he has to do the job, he's stuck in that mode. *He has to let it all go.*

I have to let it all go.

She can feel the frightening honesty bursting from him, compelling her to mirror his behaviour, to confess, to start their married life with a clean slate. *The real-estate guy; I need to say . . .*

They leave the café in silence. Lennox wants to stop off at a Walgreens for some unspecified reason, and Trudi is disconcerted when he emerges with a small can of gasoline. They go back down Lincoln but he swings left at Meridian Avenue and they walk up a few featureless blocks. — Where are we going, Ray? Trudi asks in mounting concern.

— It's not too far, Lennox says, as the art deco district starts to thin out, building slowly into north Miami Beach's high-rise condo land. Passing the Convention Centre, the girls struggle in the heat to match Lennox's driven stride.

But Tianna Marie Hinton suddenly remembers how she likes to walk, loved to walk in Mobile, and she's in keen pursuit of him, feeling her feet hit the ground and arms swing, her essence

336

rising up through her body. Not buried so deep inside her that the conquerors of her flesh would never be able to dig it out, but rippling and crackling around her in the heat and light. She thinks of what Ray said about Hank Aaron and the plate smashers in the restaurant. *Fuck those assholes!* Trudi Lowe, inspired by the girl's reanimation, quickens to keep pace.

Then, when they cross 19th Street, a startling sight greets them; to their right, a huge green hand rises into the air. At first it seems as if it belongs to a drowning body, but its reach into the azure sky is as defiant as it is pained. What initially appears to be a tangle of weeds wrapped round its wrist, is, on closer examination, a confused knot of life-sized human bodies, all undernourished and writhing in agony. Drawing closer, an impending sense of something tumultuous crackles in their bones and the air around them. The hand sprouts out of an island in the centre of a pond cut into a flagstoned plaza. As they walk on to the paved area, a statue of a weeping mother and two children ambushes them, with the slogan on the wall behind the petrified family reading: 'Then in spite of everything I still believe that people are good at heart.' The quote is attributed to Anne Frank.

A guard in uniform, with the uncompromised skin tone and features of the African rather than African American, sits outside a booth in the sun. Traffic seems to rumble up Meridian Avenue in a hushed reverence. Palm trees, still and solemn, tower over the pond, which is semicircled by foreground pillars interspersed with white-blossom plants, forming a canopy over a marble wall, stark and candid as bone. On this edifice, vandal-proof words and images are engraved, conveying the story of the Holocaust. A blackboard nothing can whiten, deface or erase; a library of last resort. Then there are the names: hundreds, thousands, millions of them: the adults and the children who perished in the death camps.

An enclosed bridge splits the crescent, and leads to the island and the green hand. Inside the tunnel, the names of the camps, household ones like Auschwitz and Buchenwald, sit mounted in blocks in the wall alongside ones Lennox hasn't heard of before: Belzec, Ponary, Westerbork.

Unlike the other tunnel branded in his memory, slats of sunlight

337

cut through this one like lasers, pouring in from the spaces above. At the other end they are greeted on the island by more withered green figures and yet more names, etched into another, inner marble circle. Lennox looks at the family names, so many young lives wiped out. He wonders if it ever occurred to the Nazis and those who served them that they were working for a giant child-abuse ring.

— I need to talk to Tianna, Lennox says to Trudi. — You understand? he asks both of them.

— Okay . . . Tianna says, — . . . but Trudi can come too.

— We all make mistakes, Ray. Trudi looks warily at him. — We all . . . She falters and thinks of that stupid night, looks down on the grassy knoll by the path, hands bunching into fists, ready to say *something*, but when she lifts her head she sees he's moved away and is walking sombrely out of the memorial, through a gate, with Tianna alongside him. Trudi's first impulse is to follow but something overrides, freezing in her synapses, rooting her to the spot. Dangerous thoughts stampede within her. Ray and Tianna had spent all that time alone. People did strange things alone. He'd been abused and never, ever told her this dark secret. What other secrets did he have?

Trudi Lowe is suddenly frightened. She sets off in pursuit of her fiancé. Wonders if she knows him any more than the facade, any more than she knew that smiling, toothsome real-estate man in that night of tortured fantasy. How well can we truly know others when we only see them through the lens of the self? She turns into the gate. The sun stinging her face like a peeling cosmetic mask left on too long. In the gardens she squints but can't see Lennox or Tianna. The air is still and dense with heat.

Then she stumbles into a clearing, and to her relief, they come into view and have stalled by a bench. She hears Lennox say to Tianna, — Remember when those scumbags gave you stuff to make you sleepy, and then mucked about with you, on the boat. You remember, don't you?

Listening intently, but keeping her distance, she hears Tianna's faltering words: — Yes. I thought it was a dream, but it wasn't no dream, she says. — Starry gone and drove me there. They gave

338

me roofies, or something. I keep dreaming about him, that Lance Dearing, touching me . . . I thought they was dreams and that I was dirty for having them . . . Dearing said he was a cop and that he'd know if I'd been a bad girl, and that he could put away bad people . . . he'd know if I was dirty . . .

— No, not you. *You're* not dirty. It's *them*. These people are paedophiles. They're nonces. What do you do when somebody tries to touch you, or says dirty things to you?

— You walk away, or you run away, she says, chewing on her bottom lip.

— Aye. And you tell them to fuck off, he says, and now Lennox trembles as he can see that sweaty prick in his face, feel the taste of it in his mouth. Touches the bristle under his nose. Grown to cover his lip. To put turf on the pitch. Scare away the beasts. The moustache that said, a little too desperately: I'm a man. — You say: fuck off, ya dirty fuckin stoat!

— Fuck off, Tianna shouts. — Fuck off, you dirty fucking stoat!

Trudi approaches them, touches his arm. It's as stiff and unyielding as a bus stop. — Ray . . . Lennox turns and looks at her in pain and what she thinks is accusation. *He knows. That guy I went with. He knows. He can tell.*

Then he sharply turns back to Tianna. Trudi's aware that he's formed a terrible bond with this young girl, one that she can never share. — That's right. Fuck off, you tell them, her policeman fiancé says. — Fuck off, ya dirty fuckin beast. And you shout and scream, he urges, — from the bottom of your lungs. You make people listen, you make them hear, right around the world, and Ray Lennox closes his eyes and he can see the men in the tunnel, the men that pulled him into this strange and terrifying world, who made him a cop, and Gareth Horsburgh and Lance Dearing, Johnnie and Starry, as he bellows a primal roar from the pit of his stomach and the depth of his soul in denouncement of all the tricksters and bullies and pervert beasts he or anyone else would ever encounter: — FUCK OFF, YA DIRTY NONCE!

His roar echoes and shakes around the still and peaceful garden. An elderly man and woman walking along a path jump back in alarm, and quickly retrace their steps.

339

— Ray, we need to go, Trudi says, but now Tianna is screaming manically along with him: — FUCK OFF, YOU DIRTY FUCKING NONCE, AND LEAVE ME ALONE!

Lennox seizes at the air, his gulps like punches. It's time to get rid of it; to start expunging the black leaves and dead water that fill his heart. To stick with that process, no matter how long it takes. They shout together until they are breathless. Then Trudi puts her arm round the sobbing girl's shoulders. — Ray, we have to go now!

— Wait. A panting Lennox raises his palm, looks at Tianna, then takes her smaller hands in his. — They had a list, these nonces. It's a list of the kids they were planning to hurt. To get at through their mothers, like they tricked Robyn. The police have a copy of it, he says, as he tugs a sheaf of white papers from the backpack. The sun blasts off them in dazzling reflection. He takes out the can of gasoline and pours its contents over them. He sets the soggy papers down in an empty steel-framed garbage basket. — Now this isn't the right thing tae do, not in a park, but on this occasion it's justified.

Tianna nods as Lennox clicks open a lighter. Trudi looks nervously around. He catches her objection. — We have to do this one thing.

Anger surges through her. — There's always one thing, Ray! Trudi grabs his shoulders and shakes them in exasperation. What does he want? To tell him that he caught one of Britain's most notorious child killers or broke up a paedophile ring spanning three American states would be offensive to his ears. He will only ever see the Britneys, Tiannas, Leses and his own younger self he's been unable to protect. He is a man who will always define himself by his failures. — Then what? Then what do *we* do? What do *you* do?

— Then we . . . Lennox breaks into a slow smile, — then we go back to the hotel and I give my mother a phone, he says, — and I tell her I'm sorry. He rubs his face, his breath catching. — Then I get a shave.

Trudi swallows stiffly, filling herself with Ray's brown eyes, misty with self-reproach, nodding her head slowly in acknowledgement.

— This is all that's left of them, Lennox tells Tianna, looking

340

at the papers in the trash basket. — Your mum's put them all away where they'll never get at you; Vince, Clemson, Dearing, Johnnie and loads of others like them. It's rubbish, cause that's what they are, and he hands her the lighter. — Burn it. Go on. Burn the bastards.

Trudi, jaw clenched, sucks some air in through her teeth.

Tianna looks at him, then the papers; her eyes now in iron focus. She takes the lighter and crouches, smoothing out her dress over her knees. At first it's hard to see the flame in the bright sunlight, it's only when she feels the heat on her hand and pulls it away that she realises she's achieved ignition. They watch the papers warp and blacken for a bit, then in a silent procession, leave the gardens together.

Exiting the park, they head through an adjoining floral-wrapped iron gate, back to the Holocaust memorial. They return to the crescents of marble and the concourse of paving stone in front of the green hand. On Meridian Avenue, the traffic is now busier. Yet Lennox still has to look up at the blue sky and the apartments across the street with their verandas, in order to realise that he isn't standing in a field in Poland. In fact, across the road is the Miami Beach Chamber of Commerce, which has its own visitors centre.

Tianna's crying has intensified; her slow, halting sobs are breaking into loud wails. Then it dawns on him, from Trudi's concerned reaction, that tears are streaming down his own face. He looks at Tianna and sees Britney Hamil, in that striking photograph, the one that found its way on to the cover of every newspaper in Britain. — I'm sorry I wasn't there for you, he says miserably.

Trudi is about to speak, but Tianna beats her to it.

— You were, Ray. You were the only one who ever was, she cries, embracing him, and he sees that this is a different child, from the other side of the world. And this one was alive as all children should be. He's thinking of why we have stories, songs and poems; why we'll always have aspirations for something we call love. And now he sobs in unison with her, in pain, but also infused with a simple gratitude for being free, clear and present, underneath a big green hand in the Florida sun.

Acknowledgements

M uch love to Elizabeth, as always, for the emotional and practical assistance (research, driving me all over the Sunshine State and telling me my first draft was crap). Big thanks again to Robin, Katherine, Sue, Laura and everybody else at my publishers for their (apparently endless, but I won't push it) indulgence of me.

A shout of appreciation to my fellow Scottish pensmiths, Andy O'Hagan and Alan Warner, for unintentionally inspiring this title during a relaxed drink in one of my favourite hostelries in Wicker Park, Chicago. To Mike and Dawn Quinn of Punta Gorda, Florida, for their kind hospitality as well as their willingness to share their local knowledge of south-west Florida. To John Gee, John Hood and Janet Jorgulesco, three native South Floridians who helped this Edinburgh chap feel at home in Miami.

I chose, for obvious reasons, not to research this subject on the Internet. Instead, I limited my sources to published papers in academic, social work and clinical psychology texts, as well as self-help material. I spoke to survivors of childhood sexual abuse; their tales were as harrowing as their courage and strength were inspiring. One UK book that I found particularly invaluable as a starting point and continual reference was *Breaking Free: Help for Survivors of Sexual Abuse* by Carolyn Ainscough and Kay Toon. While I respect their obvious need for anonymity, I have to record the generosity of some police officers and social workers in the states of Illinois and Florida who gave time and information on the modus operandi of organised sexual abuse rings, and their help was greatly appreciated.

Eternal gratitude to the usual mobs in Edinburgh, London, Dublin, Chicago, San Francisco and elsewhere. Everybody who has either praised or slagged me: thanks for taking the time to care. For those who are indifferent: much gratitude for leaving me in peace.

Bologna, FLA, is a construct of my imagination. I drew heavily on the south-west Florida towns of Naples, Punta Gorda and Fort Myers as physical inspiration for this composition.

Sadly, in real life, the greatest of ills tend to happen closest to home. Most abuse of young persons – sexual or otherwise – takes place within the family or the community. Organised underground sex-abuse groups and cults, while disturbing and headline-grabbing, are not a widespread problem in modern society. This book, as a work of fiction, does not mean to imply that they are.

Irvine Welsh, Miami Beach, Florida

.